A fireball shot down the stairwell...

...and along the tunnel toward the big house, bowling over its occupants. Stress in the tunnel increased as space narrowed. Finally, supporting beams reached and surpassed their level of tolerance and gave way with a deep, sickening crack. When the roar of the explosion finally sounded, it muffled another *whumpf*—the tunnel falling in on itself, like a collapsing star. Clods of earth shot into the air, then settled back into a newly formed crater.

For the next four or five seconds, echoes of the blast bounced and ricocheted off neighboring high-rises and turnpike walls. At last all sound faded away, and for a time an eerie silence reigned over the rubble. Under a twinkling night sky, smoke and dust motes swirled and pirouetted in a mute, macabre dance of death.

Then the screams began.

THE
BEST OF
ENEMIES

TAYLOR SMITH

MIRA BOOKS

ISBN 1-55166-476-3

THE BEST OF ENEMIES

Copyright © 1997 by M. G. Smith.

MIRA and the Star Colophon are trademarks used under license and registered in Australia, New Zealand, Philippines, United States Patent and Trademark Office and in other countries.

Printed in U.S.A.

For Paul and Rita,
with love and thanks for the greatest gift.

Acknowledgments

Several people lent their expertise and friendly advice in the preparation of this story. If I got it wrong, it's not because they didn't try. Deepest thanks to: Gary Bale, Orange County Sheriff's Investigator and fellow novelist; journalist Sheila Whyte, who brought insights on the Middle East to bear, along with her fine editorial skills; Paul and Barbara Couturier, my stellar hosts and guides in Newton, Massachusetts; former CIA case officer Sandi Lucas; Special Agent Jack Trimarco of the FBI Los Angeles Field Office; and Joe Lauderdale, Youth Theater Director for the Laguna Playhouse. The memoirs of Terry Anderson, Thomas Sutherland and others are a deeply moving testament to the courage of the Beirut hostages. Their power to survive, forgive and move on with their lives leaves me breathless. I tapped many written sources during my research, but none finer than Robert Fisk's stunning *Pity the Nation: Lebanon at War*. My editors, Amy Moore and Dianne Moggy, are a constant reminder of what comes when you combine intelligence, professionalism and charm. And finally, to Anna, Kate and Richard: without you, my sweets, none of it means a darn thing.

Great hatred, little room,
Maimed us at the start
I carry from my mother's womb
A fanatic heart.

—W. B. Yeats,
Remorse for Intemperate Speech

Please to remember the fifth of November,
Gunpowder, treason, and plot.
I see no reason
Why gunpowder treason
Should ever be forgot.

—Old English nursery rhyme

Something Rotten

1

The clock was ticking—thirty-four minutes to quitting time, six days till Angie Pirelli's due date. But babies are notorious disrespecters of clocks, calendars and ultrasound predictions. They arrive when they're ready, not when they're supposed to.

This baby would never arrive at all.

Angie leaned back in her chair at the Data-Trax reception desk, stretching her spine, swiveling her neck from side to side to work out kinks. Like everything else in the high-tech research facility, her chair was the latest in ergonomic design. But given Angie's condition, it was probably inevitable that she would be uncomfortable by the end of a long day, no matter how user-friendly the work environment.

The atrium lobby in which she sat was open and airy, with interior greenery that seemed to sprout right through transparent walls into the parklike grounds. The exterior glass had been coated with a thin layer of Mylar to defeat covert electronic eavesdropping on the company's top-secret activities, but the security feature was subtle. Located off the Massachusetts Turnpike in the Boston suburb of Newton, the building could have passed for a huge greenhouse, if you missed the strategically mounted surveillance cameras.

Exhaling a weary sigh, Angie closed her eyes and ran small hands over her enormous, round belly, stroking rhythmically to soothe the restless little guy inside. At her last ultrasound exam, the technician had asked Angie and her husband, Alec, if they wanted to know the gender, but they'd hesitated. That was like opening your Christmas presents early. Then, curiosity got the better of them. They wanted to see what the tech saw when she looked at that grainy image on the monitor. So they'd said, "Sure," and the woman had pointed out the baby's cute little weenie—pretty obvious, once you knew where to look. Now, after thirty-nine weeks, Baby Matt-or-Scott—Alec and Angie were still arguing about the name—seemed as anxious as his parents for the big day to come.

"Little guy jumping around?"

Angie opened her eyes and smiled at the gray-haired security guard sitting to her right at the reception desk. Phil Hudak had just hung up the phone. "Is he ever! Must be bored—feels like he's shooting baskets in there."

"Won't be long now," Hudak said kindly. His gaze shifted to the big front doors. Outside, a car was pulling in under the buttressed glass canopy that covered the circular drive outside the main entrance. An old-model Mercedes, full of dings and dents, took the handicapped visitors parking spot nearest the building, bumping unceremoniously to a stop when its front tires hit the curb.

Angie sighed. "Friday's my last day, thank God. I can hardly wait—for the baby *and* to be able to sleep on my stomach again!"

Hudak nodded sympathetically as his eyes dropped to the bank of monitors before him. He toggled a switch, and one of the exterior cameras zeroed in on the car outside.

"Been a long time since Flo had Linda, but I still remember how she could never sleep toward the end."

Angie felt a stab of annoyance at the comparison between her pregnancy and Flo Hudak's, then immediately regretted the instinct. She was fond of the old ex-cop and his wife, and there was no way their misfortune could rub off on her—she *knew* that. But until she could see her own baby and count fingers and toes, maybe it was normal to worry.

The Hudaks' only child had been born with Down's syndrome. Phil had taken this security job after retiring from the Boston PD to build up the trust fund that would see to Linda's care after he and his wife were gone. Linda was twenty now, and she and her mother often dropped by to visit him at work. If Linda had a new sweater or picture book, she would burble the news to everyone in sight. Hudak's weathered old face would light up with affection and pride, as if his daughter had just announced her graduation from Harvard.

Angie stroked her belly again, for luck and reassurance. Her baby would be fine, she told herself sternly. She and Alec would be bouncing grandchildren on their knees at Phil and Flo's age, not wondering how their child would manage without them. Wouldn't they?

"Must be the people the front gate just called about," Hudak said, frowning at the security monitor. "I don't see a handicapped plate, though. They should have parked in one of the regular visitor spaces."

"Who are they here to see?"

"Guy has a four-thirty with Ron Rosenberg in Personnel. You might want to phone up, see if he's ready."

Angie made the call while they watched the screen. The driver's door opened, and a girl stepped out. Petite but long-legged, booted and blue-jeaned, with a thick mass of blond curls that tumbled over her shoulders, she looked young to be driving a car like that. In the fading light of late afternoon, her billowing tan jacket glimmered with the soft patina of good-quality lamb or deerskin. That was no ninety-nine-dollar Leather Barn special, Angie decided, admiring its buttery texture. Straightening, the girl reached up a hand, sweeping back her tangled frizz of hair to reveal a pretty, heart-shaped face.

The shadow in the passenger seat, meanwhile, had made no move to get out.

Withdrawing a leather knapsack and hiking it over one shoulder, the girl shut her door, walked to the back of the car, opened the trunk, reached in, then closed it again. Before Phil and Angie had a chance to see what it was she'd withdrawn, the passenger door opened, blocking their view of her as she came up the far side of the car.

"Personnel's sending down an escort," the receptionist told the guard as she hung up the phone. He nodded, but kept his attention focused on the monitor.

The passenger finally emerged. Older than the girl, but not by much, he was slight of frame, with black hair and thick eyebrows over deep-set dark eyes. He wore no overcoat, but it had been a warm early-spring day, with the smell of winter's end in the air, making people itch to lose heavy outerwear and clunky boots, misshapen after repeated soakings. A dark suit hung loosely on the young man's thin frame. The Data-Trax dress code—if such a thing even existed, Angie thought—was casual, like at most high-tech outfits. But job applicants, she'd noticed, always tried for a good impression.

She glanced again at the security guard. Phil's attention was locked on the monitor, his wrinkled face creased deeper by a frown. She sensed his tension—found herself infected by it, without understanding the reason for it. But

Phil always said that old cop instincts never die, and something about these people was obviously bothering him.

The couple finally stepped away from the car, slamming the passenger door. As they began to move forward, Angie heaved a sigh of relief. "Crutches! He's on crutches, Phil. That's what she was getting out of the trunk."

The guard nodded, but his focus never wavered from the screen. The girl aimed her key fob at the car, and its headlights flashed twice as it chirruped a response. The couple started up the short walkway to the door, the young man hobbling on the aluminum crutches, handling them with an awkwardness that suggested he hadn't had much practice. The girl kept her pace matched to his, leaning toward him, eager and anxious. Like she would be willing to carry him if he asked, Angie thought. When they came through the doors, she noticed that the girl was wearing a Sesame Street T-shirt, a big red Elmo figure peeking through the opening of her jacket.

She held back while the guy hobbled up to the reception desk. He stopped to catch his breath, giving a nervous nod in the direction of the security guard. Fully upright, without the crutches, he might have been five-nine or -ten, Angie guessed. Not six feet. She knew, because Alec was an exact six-footer, and her head tucked cozily under his chin when they danced slow numbers. This guy's chin would probably hit her in the nose. When he turned toward her, Angie took the full brunt of huge brown doe eyes, ringed with dark lashes. Eyes to die for, she thought. A woman would spend a fortune on mascara and eyeliner to get killer eyes like that. His lips were full and wine-colored, but the pewter cast on his cheeks saved him from looking feminine. It was the kind of shadow a man with an especially heavy beard always had, no matter how often he shaved, its hollowing effect emphasizing his thinness.

When he spoke, the young man's voice was soft, his words punched with the studied care of someone who had come late to the English language. "Good afternoon," he said. "My name is Khoury—Karim Khoury. I am expected."

Winslow, Massachusetts: 4:47 p.m.

Ambassador Stroud was phoning from halfway around the world, but thanks to the twin miracles of digital technology and satellite communications, Leya Nash heard him as clearly as if he were in the next office. His voice was imperious, fitting her memory of the man, but she also heard an undertone of stress and anger in it, natural by-products of a father's worry.

She'd met Arthur Stroud the previous fall, when he and his wife had accompanied their eighteen-year-old daughter, Holly, for her first freshman day of the fall term at Mount Abbey. Small but prestigious, the unisex college had a reputation for close faculty involvement with students, and for graduating strong-minded women who went on to become community leaders. Through the foreign-service net, the ambassador had learned that Carter Nash's daughter was teaching at Mount Abbey, so he'd made a point of looking Leya up and asking her to keep an eye on Holly while he and his wife were abroad.

"I knew your father back when he was running the Middle East division at Langley," Stroud had said. "Good man, enormously well-respected. How's he doing since he retired? Stroke, wasn't it?"

"Yes. He made a nearly full recovery. He moved up here last year," Leya added. "If you'd like to see him, I know he'd—"

"Definitely, definitely," Stroud said heartily. "We've

got an early flight out today, but next time we're in town, I'll be sure to look him up.''

Leya had nodded and smiled, knowing he never would. Arthur Stroud was not the kind of man who wasted his time on people who had nothing to offer him. When Leya's father had been a senior CIA official, his confidential briefings had been in demand by presidents, ambassadors, congressmen and corporate heads, all of whom had hung on his every pronouncement concerning the latest global hot spot. Men who'd worked field operations under Carter Nash had been impassioned in their loyalty and admiration. More than once, at private parties in Virginia or abroad, Leya had been on the receiving end of quiet, boozy tributes from one or another of his colleagues. ''A great, *great* man. Saved my life, you know,'' they would whisper hoarsely, one arm slung around her shoulders, free hand clutching the glass in which they found refuge from the dark world of secrets. But when ill health had forced his retirement, her father's friends and admirers had drifted or been pushed away, one by one. Carter Nash's dynamic, globe-trotting life had been reduced to solitary shuffles around the little town of Winslow, Massachusetts, and the world had gone on turning without his help.

Arthur Stroud was calling Leya now from his embassy office in Tel Aviv to report that his daughter was missing. ''We've been calling her residence all weekend. I just spoke to the house mother at Escott Hall, but Holly's not there, and Mrs. Garibaldi says she hasn't seen her in several days. Have you?''

''I'm afraid I haven't, Ambassador. She wasn't in class this morning. We're supposed to be at drama rehearsal right now, but I canceled it because two cast members called in sick, and then Holly didn't show up, either. I thought she might be down with something, too. We're doing *Hamlet,*" Leya added. "Holly's playing Ophelia."

"So she wrote. Her mother's getting worried about not being able to reach her."

"Is it possible she went away for the weekend? Spring skiing, maybe? And decided to stay over an extra day?"

"It could be. But what has us concerned, Professor Nash, is that Holly was talking to her mother last week and said something about a fellow she's been seeing. She wouldn't say much over the phone, but today we got a letter from her. She sounds serious, but we don't know anything about this boy—not even a name. Do you?"

Leya hesitated, caught between an anxious parent and the discretion she owed a student. She knew Holly had been seeing Tyler Newman, a local entrepreneur. Leaving campus late one evening several weeks earlier, Leya had spotted them as Tyler dropped Holly off at the residence. The intensity of their clinch had convinced her that, if Holly wasn't already sleeping with him, the pressure was probably on. Faculty adviser or not, Leya had been reluctant to poke her nose into the private business of a bright student whose grades and extracurricular participation had been good—at least, until recently. On the other hand, Holly was young, on her own and vulnerable. Tyler was older, intensely attractive and undoubtedly more experienced. Knowing firsthand how incendiary a combination that could be, Leya had gingerly broached the subject of relationships a couple of days later, when she and Holly were walking across campus on their way to drama rehearsal. Their discussion had been interrupted by the arrival of other students, and since then, she hadn't caught Holly alone. Now, Leya wondered whether she should have tried harder.

"I'm sure I don't have to tell you," the ambassador

added, "that there are security concerns to be considered, given my position."

"I know she's been seeing a local fellow," Leya said cautiously. "He and his mother run a small bistro here in town. They seem like good people, Ambassador. I'm sure there's nothing to worry about, but I will try to track Holly down and have her call you."

"I'd be grateful. Would you tell her that her mother and I are very anxious to talk to her?"

"Yes, of course."

Hanging up the phone, Leya did the rounds of her small office, closing file cabinets and packing her briefcase. As the most recent addition to the English and theater-arts department at Mount Abbey, she'd been given a tiny office, barely larger than a closet, when she'd taken up her job three years earlier. It was opposite the second-floor landing of the broad, circular granite staircase that ran up the middle of the Arts Building. Hordes of students and faculty trudged past her open door every day, but with six baby-boomer colleagues ahead of her in the departmental seniority queue, all in disgustingly good health, Leya knew it could be years before she inherited one of the coveted, wood-paneled offices overlooking the leafy quadrangle at the heart of the campus. She also knew she was lucky even to have a teaching position, when so many fellow English grads were stuck in low-paying, dead-end McJobs.

"Hey, there! Something's rotten in the state of Denmark. I thought you had rehearsal this afternoon." Kerry Nyland's lanky frame draped itself around her door.

The history department was one floor up, and after a couple of weeks of eyeing her as he passed by on the way to and from his office, Nyland had been one of the first faculty members outside her own department to introduce himself. As they'd chatted, Leya had seen his eyes drop to her left hand. Her ringlessness had sparked a ten-point leap in Nyland's charm quotient.

"I did, and it is," she said. "Rotten, I mean. Turned out my melancholy Dane has laryngitis, Polonius has the flu, and Ophelia's flown the coop. I canceled."

"Good. Now we can go for coffee, after all."

Leya smiled. He was nothing if not persistent. In his mid-forties, divorced, with two kids and a gray ponytail that extended halfway down his back, Nyland was amiable and perpetually restless. Surrounded by the forbidden temptations of three thousand healthy young women who were strictly off-limits to faculty, he'd apparently decided that a toffee-eyed young colleague was a good antidote to what ailed him. Holding him at bay had quickly become part of Leya's daily routine. By now, it was almost a game between them.

She shook her head, mahogany hair skimming the shoulders of her creamy silk blouse. "No can do. I just got off the phone with Arthur Stroud, calling from Israel. He's misplaced his daughter, and I have to see if I can track her down before he calls out the Secret Service."

"Holly, right?" Nyland came in and settled on a corner of Leya's desk. With his legs sprawled in the crowded space, Leya had to hike her skirt a little to step over them and reach the credenza. "Pretty blond thing? Writes articles for the student paper, full of righteous indignation over the poor and downtrodden?"

Leya glanced at him as she gathered the stack of essays her freshman AmLit class had submitted that day and slipped them into her briefcase. "What a cynic you are! I thought your generation was into peace, love and good vibes."

Nyland clutched his chest and leaned back, his expression pained. "My generation? Ooh! Cut to the quick." He did a rapid recovery and shrugged. "Naw. Threw all that out with my love beads. So how about dinner?"

Leya shook her head again. He never gave up. The day before, he'd called her at home to try to convince her to go for a Sunday-afternoon cruise on his new Harley. Fire-engine red, with enough gleaming chrome to supply an entire Detroit production line, it had inspired Nyland's recent wardrobe additions—black helmet, black leather jacket, crisscrossed with silver zippers, and heavy, multi-strapped black boots that he wore over, not under, the cuffs of his houndstooth-check pants. It was a sort of Henry-Higgins-Meets-Hell's-Angels look, and it was driving his ultraconservative departmental chairman up the wall. Nyland was having a classic midlife crisis, Leya had concluded, mourning his lost youth. Aiding and abetting his rejuvenation scheme were low on her priority list.

"I have a date."

"Not with the stockbroker, please! Anyone but him."

"Investment counselor," she corrected. She'd brought John Merriman to the arts-faculty Christmas party, mostly to discourage Kerry Nyland's amorous ambitions. "We've got season tickets at the Lyric."

Nyland groaned. "So you're going to drive thirty-seven miles into Boston for this guy, when I'm right here, day after day?"

"Yep." Leya pulled on her suit jacket and shrugged into her camel coat, knotting the belt loosely. Grabbing her briefcase, she shooed him out of her office so she could lock up. "See you around, big guy. Gotta go find my Ophelia."

She left him on the landing, looking over the carved granite banister, head shaking as he watched her descent.

Newton, Massachusetts: 5:01 p.m.

The sky had gone a dark gray beyond the transparent walls of the Data-Trax lobby. The atrium's interior was now reflected back from the glass, obscuring the outdoor view. But during the day, from their vantage point at the reception desk, Angie Pirelli and Phil Hudak could look out across the parklike compound to a large, Colonial-style mansion, once the home of a New England textile magnate. When Data-Trax had bought the site a decade earlier for its Boston headquarters, there had been no way to retrofit the big house to meet the company's technical and security needs, but instead of tearing it down, management had turned it into an employee-services complex, with an auditorium, party rooms, a gym and a day-care center. A few weeks earlier, Angie's colleagues had held a baby shower for her there. After she returned from maternity leave, her baby would spend his days in the complex, comfortingly close to Angie and her husband, a computer analyst who worked upstairs.

Angie struggled into her red woolen coat. The lower buttons no longer met over her middle, so she draped a long, knitted scarf around her neck and let one end drop over the opening. Flipping the other over her shoulder, she examined her reflection in the large glass windows. Like hanging bunting on a boat, she thought ruefully. Who would have thought she could get so big? Alec said she was beautiful, but he was so excited about the baby and punchy from interrupted sleep as she tossed restlessly in bed, trying to get comfortable, that his judgment was probably clouded.

He'd called down a few minutes earlier to say he was turning off his computer and would meet her in the lobby. Angie had tidied her work space at the reception desk, handing over the switchboard to the night security guard who had arrived to replace Phil Hudak.

Hudak was at the big front window, hands cupped around his eyes to block out the interior light as he kept watch for his wife and daughter. They were coming to take him to dinner and then an early movie at the cineplex down the road—a revival of Walt Disney's *101 Dalmatians,* Linda's favorite. "Except she closes her eyes whenever Cruella deVil comes on," Phil had told Angie, grinning.

Elevator doors opened and closed in a waltzing rhythm as employees flowed out of the building or down the wide staircase off the lobby. The stairs accessed an underground tunnel leading to the mansion across the compound and its day-care center. Angie turned each time the elevators swooshed, but Alec was slow to appear. Must have had a last-minute phone call, she decided.

She saw Ron Rosenberg from Personnel emerge from one of the elevators, accompanied by the young man on crutches. The pretty blond girl who'd driven him had been sitting in the lobby, waiting while the man had his interview upstairs. Under the circumstances—given the fellow's crutches and the fact that it was late in the day—Hudak had decided not to give her any grief about parking in the handicapped spot without a sticker. She'd taken a seat in the waiting area near the window, smiling shyly at them once or twice, but saying nothing. Mostly she'd been flipping through magazines for the past half hour, although she hadn't seemed to take much interest in them. The big red Elmo figure on her T-shirt had grinned at Angie over the pages of *Byte* and *National Geographic.*

The girl jumped to her feet when Rosenberg and the other fellow appeared, watching as they shook hands. Rosenberg's expression, Angie noted, was polite but no more, and the interview hadn't lasted long. From the look of things, she would say this Khoury fellow wasn't getting whatever job he'd been applying for.

As Rosenberg turned and headed back to the elevators, Khoury hiked the crutches under his arms and shot the girl a grim look. "Let's get out of here."

She studied him for a moment, as if trying to read his expression, then nodded and turned toward the big front doors, which swung open. When she aimed her key fob at the old Mercedes, it chirruped a welcome. Khoury tossed his crutches in the back seat before getting into the car. A moment later, it careened out of its parking place and sped away.

Angie shifted her weight uncomfortably from one swollen foot to the other, wondering what was keeping Alec. Catching her reflection in the glass, Phil Hudak turned and gave her a sympathetic smile.

"I don't know what's keeping Alec," she said. "He's—"

Her remaining words were stillborn, as a flash lit the air, turning night to day. The brilliant light cast the security chief into stark, silhouetted relief, but before Angie's brain had time to register a reaction to this strange phenomenon, every last molecule of air was sucked from her lungs. A microsecond later, a tornado lifted her, propelling her across the lobby like some rag doll flung by an angry child. Her flight was brought to an abrupt halt by the marble slab sheathing the elevator bank, and the violent slamming of bone against stone shattered Angie's skull, seven ribs, her pelvis, and both femurs. Those injuries, however, were superfluous. Even before her body hit the wall, the shock wave had already ruptured all of her internal organs—and those of the baby she carried.

Phil Hudak, who had turned his back to the window only a second before, suffered similar, so-called acoustic injuries, expanding gases filling his blood vessels so rapidly that they exploded under the pressure. Like Angie's, his heart, lungs, liver and intestines all burst from the pressure wave that pitched them both across the atrium. A hundred-pound shard of glass nailed Hudak face-first to the marble wall, just inches from where his erstwhile partner at the reception desk had landed, his body nearly severed in two. Intense heat melted the back of his polyester uniform, but not before its weave pattern had seared itself into the skin of his neck, back and calves.

In the same split second that the old ex-cop and his pregnant young co-worker suffered these violent indignities, shattered glass was whipping through the lobby at such velocity—nearly ten thousand feet per second—that not one of the departing Data-Trax employees caught in the hailstorm managed the instinctive but futile reaction of a blink. Those razorlike fragments that missed soft tissue drove deep into the marble facing of the interior walls, just before the heavy slabs themselves cracked and toppled.

From the first moment of the flash, gases had been expanding to thousands of times their normal volume. Starting from ground zero, air pressure had exploded in all directions, walloping everything it encountered. Hard architecture provided some protection to employees on upper floors of the building, but those in less resistant locations, including the wide stairwell off the lobby, were nearly as vulnerable as those in the lobby itself.

A fireball shot down the stairwell and along the tunnel toward the big house, bowling over its occupants. Stress in the tunnel increased as space narrowed. Finally, supporting beams reached and surpassed their level of tolerance and gave way with a deep, sickening crack. When the roar of the explosion finally sounded, it muffled another *whumpf*—the tunnel falling in on itself, like a collapsing star. Clods of earth shot into the air, then settled back into a newly formed crater.

For the next four or five seconds, echoes of the blast bounced and ricocheted off neighboring high-rises and turnpike walls. At last, all sound faded away, and for a time, an eerie silence reigned over the rubble. Under a twinkling night-sky, smoke and dust motes swirled and pirouetted in a mute, macabre dance of death.

Then the screams began.

2

Leya walked from the Arts Building to Escott Hall, the red brick, Colonial-style student residence near the center of campus where Holly Stroud boarded, and where Leya, too, had lived during her own undergraduate days at Mount Abbey. The black asphalt walkways were damp and gleaming after the day's thaw. How long, she wondered, until she could chuck her winter boots, once and for all? Thick stands of evergreen dotted the campus, interspersed with willow, oak and shagbark hickory, and she studied their branches for buds. A little longer yet, she concluded.

When she reached the portico of the residence, Leya scanned the intercom board, then pressed the button next to Holly Stroud's name. Waiting for a response, she turned to watch knots of young women strolling by. Their pace lethargic, they seemed as starved as Leya herself for new life and vibrant color. Fed up with wet, gray and cold. The air was redolent of rotted-leaf mulch and wet, squishy earth—the scent seductive, like a musky harbinger of new beginnings, with the perennial power to stir something deep in the human spirit. Wafting in on a breeze, its vague promises could seduce even the most pessimistic of souls, kindling restlessness and hope.

It was a nasty trick of nature, Leya thought, to keep reigniting this fire of expectation. She'd spent far too many springtimes under its quivering spell, aching for something fleetingly experienced, then lost, a long time ago. A shudder ran the length of her body, as if it were fighting off a pernicious infection. Not this year, she resolved. This year, she would resist that insanity. Some things were best forgotten.

She leaned on Holly's buzzer once more. When there was still no response, she tried the house don. A few seconds later, a voice crackled through the speaker. "Hello? Who is it?"

"It's Leya Nash, Mrs. Garibaldi."

"Oh, hello, dear! Come in! You remember where my door is?"

"How could I forget?"

The lock release sounded, and Leya pushed her way through, heading right down a blue-speckled carpet. Mrs. Garibaldi was such a fixture at Escott Hall that it seemed she must have been there since Mount Abbey's founding, a hundred and ten years earlier. But her husband had been the field-house caretaker for thirty years, and Mrs. G. had moved into the housemother's job and the tiny Escott Hall apartment only later, after he'd passed away. She looked as if she would go on forever.

Her door opened before Leya had a chance to knock. "It's about time you dropped by for a visit!" Mrs. Garibaldi exclaimed happily. Small and round, with pin-curled hair that she covered with a scarf, she looked like Mrs. Tiggy-Winkle, the little hedgehog washerwoman of Beatrix Potter fame. "I haven't seen you since—what? Christmas? No. Valentine's Day, that's right! You brought me that lovely box of chocolates. Well, don't just stand there, Professor,'' Mrs. Garibaldi bubbled. ''Come in, come in!''

''It's great to see you, too, Mrs. G. But don't call me 'Professor.' Seems a little silly, don't you think?''

''You earned that title.''

''That may be, but you've known me nearly half my life, since I was an obnoxious seventeen-year-old.''

''You were never obnoxious. You were one of my favorite girls.''

Leya gave her a hug. ''We're *all* your favorite girls.''

''You're all special. You just happen to be more special than most. Come into the kitchen. I'll make tea.''

Before Leya could reply, the older woman was already on the way to her kitchenette, fleshy elbow wattles flapping beneath the sleeveless cotton shift she wore year-round, even if it was twenty below and blowing a nor'easter. Her thermostat had gotten stuck on ''high'' when her body went through ''the change,'' she'd once told Leya. Students sometimes gave her sweaters for Christmas. Mrs. G. would flush with delight, exclaiming, ''Just what I needed!'' and for the rest of the year, the sweater would be draped over the back of her favorite rocker, as if she'd just slipped it off. Then, after everyone left in May, the Maryknoll Sisters at the nearby Holy Cross convent would inherit a brand-new sweater. Leya often saw them in the streets of Winslow, Mrs. G.'s vividly-colored cardigans brightening sober skirts and blouses.

''I can't stay,'' Leya called after her. ''I have to check on my house, then run into Boston. I've got a theater date.''

Mrs. G. made a U-turn back to the sitting room. ''Are you sure you don't have time for a quick cup? It won't take but a minute.''

''Not this time, but thanks, anyway.''

"I went by your house on the way to the Shop 'N Save this morning. They were delivering lumber."

"I'm having some renovation work done. My father's convinced I'm going to bankrupt myself on the place. He could be right."

"Nonsense."

"I don't know," Leya said, shaking her head ruefully. "Meantime, I'm trying to track down Holly Stroud. Her father just called. I gather he called you, too?"

"Yes, but I didn't know what to tell him, Leya."

"Why? What's she up to?"

Mrs. Garibaldi wrung her pudgy hands. "Oh…well…"

"I'm not asking you to betray any confidences, Mrs. G. But I'm a little worried about Holly, myself. She's been cutting classes and drama rehearsals. I told her father she'd missed today, but she skipped rehearsal last Friday, too. That's not like her. She's one of my best students."

The older woman sank onto the sofa looking anxious.

Leya settled beside her. "Do you know what's going on?"

"It could be boyfriend business."

"That's what the ambassador said. Holly's been seeing Tyler Newman, hasn't she?"

"She was, but there was some trouble a couple of weeks ago. They had an argument on the sidewalk outside my window. I couldn't hear what they were saying—not that I would eavesdrop."

"No, of course not," Leya said. The old girl was most likely lying through her teeth. She kept herself so well plugged in that Leya used to get the eerie impression she was psychic.

She'd lost track of the number of times Mrs. G. just happened to show up at her door, right after Leya had gotten off the phone to her father, calling from overseas.

Her mother had died when she was born, and Carter Nash had raised Leya alone. He and Bhu Kedar, her Indian *ayah*, were the only family she'd ever known. She'd missed them when she'd gone away to school, but Mrs. G. had always seemed to know when to put in an appearance with a cheery smile and a cup of Earl Grey tea. The spring of her senior year, if it hadn't been for Mrs. G.'s well-padded shoulder to cry on after the business with Peter, Leya doubted she would have pulled through. The perfumed scent of Earl Grey tea still had the throat-catching tendency to remind her of that black period, and although she hadn't the heart to tell Mrs. G., Leya had despised the old girl's favorite brew ever since.

Leya shook off the memory. It was the smell of spring that always raised those old ghosts, she thought, as well as seeing Mrs. Garibaldi.

"I invited Holly in not long after," the older woman was saying. "She looked like she needed some tea and sympathy."

"Did she tell you what was going on?"

"At first, she wasn't saying much of anything. But then, it was the strangest thing. She asked if I knew about marriage laws in this state. How old you had to be, where you got a license, blood tests, that sort of thing. I thought maybe she and Tyler had made up and were thinking about eloping. I tried to find out if she was...you know...." Mrs. Garibaldi blushed.

Leya felt her own face go hot and her chest constrict at the sudden sense of déjà vu. "Pregnant?" she asked, her voice firmer than she would have thought possible. "Oh, dear. And?"

"She wouldn't say, just got more upset, and left soon after. I still don't know what it was all about. I've run into her a few times since, but she just says hello and hurries off to class.''

Leya sighed. "Not mine, I'm afraid. Damn! I wish I knew what was going on with that girl.''

Newton, Massachusetts: 5:09 p.m.

The first 911 call, from an office complex across the street from Data-Trax, came in two minutes after the blast, but the emergency dispatcher had received several duplicate reports by the time the rescue trucks began screaming into the compound.

As a matter of routine, all 911 calls were tape-recorded, and in the days that followed, investigators would replay them over and over as they struggled to nail down the exact sequence of events surrounding the incident. Although telephone lines into and out of the building had been disrupted by the explosion, one of the survivors had a cellular phone. Somehow, the tape of his 911 call leaked to the media, and it was a heartbreaker, given what rescue workers found in the devastated lobby. One man's agony soon became a symbol of the wider horror.

On the recording, broadcast around the world, the dispatcher's voice was heard first.

"Nine-one-one. Is this an emergency?"

"We need help here! There's been an explosion. We've got smoke everywhere. People are screaming."

"Where are you, sir?"

"The Data-Trax Corporation."

"In Newton, right? Just off the Mass Turnpike?"

"Yes."

"Okay, we're already on that. What's your name?"

"Pirelli. Alec Pirelli. It's awful! Part of the building's gone—blown away."

"Try to keep calm, sir. The fire department's on the way. Is anyone with you?"

"Yeah. Fifteen, maybe twenty people."

"Anyone injured?"

"Most of us are cut up some. One guy's unconscious. There must be people on the other floors, too." The caller gasped. *"Oh, my God! Angie..."*

"Where are you right now, sir?"

"Angie's down there!"

"Sir? Where are you?"

"In the Data-Trax building!"

"I know, but where, exactly? What floor?"

"On four. We tried to go down the stairs, but the stairwells were full of smoke. We had to go back. There's smoke coming under the door now."

"From the stairwell?"

"Yes."

"But the air's still breathable where you are?"

"Yeah. The windows are blown out."

"Okay, listen to me, sir."

"Angie!"

"Sir? Alec? Listen to me," the dispatcher repeated. *"Can you put something against the bottom of the stairwell door? To block the smoke?"*

"Something? Like what?"

"Rolled-up clothing, maybe? Can you get some of the people with you to help do that? To keep out the smoke?"

"Yeah, I guess."

"That's what I want you to do, then wait where you are. I'll relay your location to the firemen."

"I need to get downstairs. My wife's having a baby."

"She's in labor?"

"No...I don't know. The baby's due any day. She was in the lobby."

"Ambulances are on the way, Alec. The best thing you can do right now is get that stairwell door blocked and keep everyone calm. Can you do that?"

Strangled sobs, then, *"Oh, please, God, not Angie—!"*

"Alec? Could you block the door and keep those people together so the firefighters can find you? I need you to organize that. All right?"

"Yeah, I guess…"

"Help is coming. Just hold on."

A deep intake of breath. *"Okay. I'm okay."*

"Good. I need to hang up now, Alec, but will you do what we talked about? Get that smoke blocked?"

His voice was lifeless. *"Yeah, I'll do it."*

"All right. Seal the door, and then sit tight. Help will be there soon. Just take it easy, okay?"

"Okay. Bye."

"Good luck, Alec."

3

Dry rot. It moved in stealth. Treacherous and silent, the fungus attacked foundation and support structures, turning solid wood to pulp. Then, one day, something would shift and crack, and a noble old home that had endured a century's worth of New England gales would suddenly seem a fragile refuge.

Walking in her front door, Leya shrugged out of her coat and headed for the stairs, anxious to check out her second floor. After striking out at the student residence, her hunt for Holly Stroud was on hold, for the moment. With luck, the girl would show up for class the next morning, and Leya could take her aside and pass on the ambassador's message. In the meantime, Leya had an hour or so to kill before she had to be on the road for her date in Boston, and she was curious to see what changes had been wrought in her old house.

When she'd left for work that morning, the carpenters had been lugging up crowbars and sledgehammers, their faces twitching with the half-crazed grins little boys get when they have a fresh pile of snowballs at hand and a hapless victim in their sights. Outside a moment earlier, her contractor had given her a weary but cheerful thumbs-up. Victory in the demolition challenge, it seemed.

On the staircase, Leya encountered Duncan, her contractor's assistant. Alternately sullen and cocky, the muscled youth hadn't said three words to her since starting the job. But that morning, as she was getting ready for work in the downstairs dining room, which was serving as her bedroom for the duration of construction, Leya had caught his reflection in her mirror, smirking through an open door—one she knew she'd closed. She'd spent an uncomfortable few minutes, trying to guess how long he'd been there and what he'd hoped to see.

Rather than move aside now, Duncan glanced around, then halted one step above her. His boss was out in the yard, Leya registered, checking over building materials the lumberyard had delivered that afternoon. Duncan's brackish green eyes lost their usual furtiveness and settled on her with a look that inspired the urge to shower.

"Hi there, Pro-fes-sor," he said, dragging out the syllables. "Didn't know you were back." His skin had a wan cast, like that of something whose usual habitat was the underside of a rock, she thought.

"I just got home. I thought I'd take a look upstairs."

Duncan stretched out a hand and gripped the banister, blocking her path. One boot clumped down to her level, but still he towered over Leya's five-five. His white T-shirt was soiled and gamy-smelling, she noted now that she was in sniffing range—closer than she had any desire to be. "We're just finishin' up for the day here," he said.

She backed down. "I didn't mean to get in the way. I can look later."

Duncan turned his burly frame sideways and made a sweeping motion with his free hand. "You're the boss lady. You can look at anything, any time you want." The inside of his arm bulged with the snaky veins and tendons of someone who lifted weights on a regular basis. Leya had nothing against physical fitness, but she had the feeling that his training regimen had more to do with intimidation than good health.

After a brief hesitation, she slipped by him and felt a strand of her hair lift as his warm breath blew across her head. Ignoring the juvenile taunt, she continued on her way, but felt his gaze on her backside until she rounded the curve at the top of the staircase. Only then did he resume his downward saunter.

Leya listened to the receding clump of his black combat boots, teeth gritted. How the hell had she gotten herself in the position of being the object of some obnoxious teenager's perverse curiosity? In her own home, for crying out loud. She was thirty years old, a tenure-tracked college teacher, and the proud owner—along with the bank holding her sizable mortgage—of a pretty Victorian that had been referenced in *The Guide to New England's Architectural Heritage*. Just a footnote, admittedly, but it was there, nonetheless.

Exhaling irritably, Leya surveyed her upper floor and wondered if it qualified for Red Cross disaster relief. While she'd been at work, the carpenters had demolished all the non-load-bearing walls and ripped out every square inch of horsehair plaster on those that remained. Along the outside walls, newly exposed studs resembled the rotting rib cage of some long-beached whale. Cracked and curled linoleum floors were split along lines that defined where five poky little rooms and a cramped bathroom had stood just a few hours earlier. Enamel plumbing fixtures, chipped and rust-stained, lay detached from their foundations, waiting to be carted away.

It was field-house showers for the foreseeable future, she thought ruefully.

Her house was two blocks from the common that marked Winslow's town center. It had been built in 1889 as the manse for the Presbyterian church that had once stood next door. Three ministers and their families had occupied the house before the church burned to the ground in 1923 and the congregation decided to rebuild both the church and a new manse on a larger property. For the next thirty-nine years, the house had been occupied by the Harmer family—first Dr. Sam, his wife and four children, then his eldest daughter Margaret, who was widowed, childless, in the opening days of World War II and who stayed on alone in the old house until she died in 1962. Leya had discovered, tracing the title records, that after Margaret Harmer's death, the house had been converted into a boardinghouse—hence the chopped-up little rooms that had been made out of the three big upstairs bedrooms— after that a law office, then an insurance office.

By the time the previous owner had purchased it in the mid-eighties, few traces remained of the house's once genteel and unique interior except for a pressed-tin ceiling on the upper floor, which had been painted over so many times that its fleur-de-lis pattern was barely discernible anymore. Restoring the ceiling was only one of the daunting tasks faced by Leya's renovation budget and the contractor she'd hired.

She studied the cracked and curled linoleum, laid over pegged oak floors sometime in the 1920s, when natural wood had been deemed hopelessly antiquated. An ancient, cloth-wrapped electrical conduit snaked across its faded-flower pattern. As Leya reviewed her budget, trying to recall how much rewiring was going to set her back, swirling plaster dust sent her into a fit of uncontrolled sneezing.

Seven in a row, a new personal best. She rummaged in her skirt pocket for a Kleenex.

"Bless you, Professor!" Ernie Latouche rounded the banister at the top of the stairs, his thumping work boots underscoring the clank of tools in the belt slung under his ample belly.

"Thanks," she mumbled through the tissue. "I can see why you need the mask."

The contractor's breathing filter dangled around his neck, snagged in the grizzled bush at the collar of his shrunken T-shirt. Dewey's Lobster Shack, the shirt advertised. Best Seafood in the Bay State! His navy baseball cap bore a Gothic red *B* for Latouche's beloved Boston Red Sox, now in spring training down in Florida.

"Gets pretty dusty," Latouche agreed. "'Specially at this stage, when we're into the *de*struction part of the project."

Again, Leya noted, the corners of his mouth twinged with the mad glee of a rambunctious kid. Despite all her careful reference-checking, she had the sudden uneasy feeling she'd put her hopes and her stretched finances into the hands of a deranged lunatic.

"Just the linoleum left to rip up. This time tomorrow, this junk'll all be out and we can get to work on them rotted studs."

"So what do you think, now that you've had a chance to get a closer look? How many need to be replaced?"

Latouche shrugged, and his hairy navel winked in and out of sight over dusty Levi's, their waistband dangerously weighted down by the tool belt. "Ten or a dozen, maybe. C'mon back here, lemme show you something." He led her to the rear of the house, lifted a screwdriver from his tool belt, then squatted. Averting her gaze from the sudden view of his bristly butt, Leya examined the base of the wall, where the wood he was prodding crumbled like sponge candy. "Found more rot in this soleplate here. *"And what's that going to cost her?"*

The familiar, booming voice torpedoed what little was left of Leya's already sinking optimism. She turned in time to see her father mount the last step of the oak staircase, gripping the newel post with one hand, ivory-and-ebony cane clenched in the other. A crimson storm had broken out over the craggy terrain of his face. His navy overcoat was flung open, and under the black turtleneck sweater he wore, his chest heaved with the effort of recapturing his breath after the climb. Nevertheless, she noted, his approach had been silent. Age hadn't dulled the old spy's tradecraft. Or his hearing.

"Dad! What brings you here?"

"Taxi," he snapped. Nearly five years after losing his driver's license because of the peripheral-vision deficit caused by his stroke, he was still pissed off about it.

"But—why?"

He pushed back the snowy hair that flopped over his forehead and glowered at the other man. "Came to keep an eye on things. I thought you'd still be at work."

"My last class was at three. We were supposed to be rehearsing *Hamlet* now, but I cut it short. Ernie," she added to the carpenter, who'd gotten to his feet, "this is my father, Carter Nash. He lives in the Revere Complex over on Jefferson. This is Ernie Latouche, Dad. He's renovated several heritage homes around town and comes *very* highly recommended."

Nash probably heard the plea in her voice, but he ignored it. "And now he's finding problems that will end up costing an arm and a leg. What did I tell you?"

Latouche, to his eternal credit, remained unflapped. Way

to go, Ernie, Leya thought admiringly. At sixty-eight, her
father was still an imposing figure, and he'd lost none of
the single-minded intensity that had seen him through a
long and dangerous career—one he rarely discussed, although Leya suspected his old secrets couldn't be worth
much to anyone these days. Tall and broad-shouldered,
with fierce eyebrows and an even fiercer temper, he cowed
most people into nervous submission. Always had. In recent years, it had gotten worse, because he'd acquired the
habit of leaning forward in an aggressive, head-butting
stance when he spoke—a result, perhaps, of his peripheral-
vision problems.

"So?" he demanded, toe-to-toe with the carpenter.
"How is it you didn't anticipate this dry-rot problem?"

Latouche shrugged. "Never know what you're gonna
get when you open up an old place like this. Gotta be
prepared for a few surprises. I seen worse, actually. Most
of the structure's pretty sound."

"'Most of it,'" Nash repeated scathingly. "But fixing
the rest won't come cheap, I suppose?"

"I think we can stay within budget. Might be able to
reuse some of them studs, save a little there."

The two old crocks were talking right around her, Leya
noted. As if it weren't her house and she weren't the one
paying the bills. "Is that wise, reusing old wood?"

The carpenter finally seemed to remember she was there.
"Old stuff's not bad, long as it's solid and can be set back
nice and plumb. It's fully cured and dry, so it ain't gonna
do no more settlin'. If we have to waste too much time
jury-riggin' it in, though, ain't worth the bother. Better to
go with new."

Nash harrumphed, then stomped around the gutted area,
pausing here and there to smack at the wood framing with
the hard ebony shaft of his cane. Leya turned her back to

him, determined to maintain some shred of authority in her own home. "Use your best judgment on the studs, Ernie. I suppose we'll have to get the electrician to deal with this wiring?"

"Got him lined up for Thursday. Should have the inside framin' mostly up by then. Need to get those electrical boxes roughed in before we do any plasterin'."

Leya gave him what she hoped was a decisive nod. Her father, she noted from the corner of her eye, had stopped banging walls long enough to peer out the windows of the small turret at the front. Looking past him, she saw a black sedan parked at the curb outside. Not a car she recognized, but with the Winslow Public Library just around the corner and its tiny parking lot usually filled to capacity, that was nothing new.

The clump of another pair of boots on the stairs announced Duncan's return, a load of two-by-fours balanced on his shoulder. Nash shifted his disapproving glare as the youth's shorn head bobbed to a half-heard beat from his Walkman. Duncan crossed the open floor and deposited the wood noisily at the far end. Like Latouche's, his baggy jeans hung precariously low on his hips, but from the boxer shorts pillowed above his waistband, Leya concluded that, in this case, the look was carefully calculated.

Latouche frowned. "Duncan?" No response. He said it louder the second time, but the kid was oblivious. The carpenter let out a bellow. *"Duncan!"*

He lifted a pad off one ear. "What?"

"What did I tell you? No headphones on the job. It ain't safe."

"Oh, man! I thought we were done for the day."

"Not till the rest of this trash is downstairs. Now, lose 'em!"

Duncan slipped the headset around his neck as he made

his way, fully loaded and still grumbling, back down the stairs.

Latouche turned to Leya's father and grimaced. "My sister's kid, eighteen," he said. "Been hangin' out with a useless bunch. Got picked up for DWI last month. Figure he'll shape up if he's gotta earn a livin'. I keep tellin' him, construction site's a dangerous place and you gotta stay on your toes, but what are you gonna do? He don't want to listen to the voice of experience."

Nash glanced at his daughter. "They never do."

Newton, Massachusetts: 5:24 p.m.

Neither rescuers and reporters, nor survivors of the disaster would ever forget the devastation they witnessed that day at the Data-Trax compound. In seventeen years with the local fire department, Lieutenant Ken Ealy had never seen anything like it. How could this have happened, he wondered, in cozy, suburban, upper-middle-class Newton?

Eerily lit by emergency floods, the scene resembled something from old newsreels of the London blitz. The building's glass facade had been ripped away at ground-floor level, and all the windows of the upper stories were gone. Steel girders and concrete pillars extruded at weird angles, dripping rebars, cables and conduits that no longer connected to anything. Between the fireproof materials used in the building's construction and the oxygen-sucking effects of the explosion itself, there had been little by way of actual flames for the firefighters to deal with, but thin pillars of black smoke rose from the ruin, evidence of smoldering plastic and short-circuited electrical wires. Cars that had been parked near ground zero sent up a smudged cloud from scorched paint and burning rubber. The stench mingled with the odors of pulverized cement, decayed leaves and wet earth, all of it subtly underscored by the musky perfume of death.

Stunned Data-Trax employees roamed aimlessly through the compound, their soot-blackened faces etched by streaming tears. Some were calling out names—of people still missing, Ealy presumed, and possibly buried in the rubble. A young man brought down from an upper floor had taken one look at what remained of the lobby and charged forward, a torrent of screams rising from his throat. He'd been caught and held by a burly firefighter, and after a moment of struggle, had crumpled, dropping to his knees and sobbing the name, "Angie," over and over. If she'd been one of the unlucky ones caught in there, Ealy thought grimly, it could be hours or days before they found her body.

So far, rescuers had taken out about three dozen casualties, including four dead and three or four more who probably wouldn't make it. No one knew for certain how many employees and their children were still in the building rubble or the collapsed tunnel, and how many had, by a stroke of enormous good fortune, left for the day just minutes before the blast occurred. Without personnel records, still somewhere in that shell, there was no way to get an accurate head count. What—who—could have done something like this? the firefighter asked himself for the hundredth time.

The media were already massed at the front gate, held back by police but demanding instant answers. Experts from the FBI and ATF—the Bureau of Alcohol, Tobacco and Firearms—would be called in on this one, Ealy knew, and they would go over the site with a fine-tooth comb to determine the cause of the explosion. In the meantime, police spokesmen would issue vague statements to the press, leaving open the possibility that it was all just some horrible accident. But Ealy knew that no transformer or gas-line mishap was responsible for what they were seeing here.

Turning away from the devastation, he lifted his heavy yellow helmet to wipe away the sweat streaming down his forehead. Replacing it, he glanced down the long driveway and spotted a policewoman squatting next to a girl sitting on the curb. Arms wrapped around her knees, the girl was rocking and seemed to be muttering to herself, eyes fixed on the roadway in front of her, avoiding both the policewoman and the sheet-draped body lying on the ground a few feet away.

When the rescue trucks had first arrived, they'd found the drive blocked by the Pontiac sedan in which the girl had been a passenger. Ealy, riding in the cab of the lead engine, had jumped down and approached the car. Its motor was running, but the white-haired woman at the wheel sat motionless, her head flung back against the headrest. The car's front windshield was gone. Crouching for a better look, Ealy saw the driver's unblinking eyes staring at the ceiling, a lump of concrete the size of a golf ball embedded deep in her forehead. He reached out automatically, checking the woman's carotid for a pulse, knowing it was a waste of time.

Withdrawing his hand, he glanced over to the passenger seat. A pair of almond-shape blue eyes behind thick glasses peered back at him, wide with terror. Down's syndrome, Ealy's brain registered, taking in the rounded cheeks and slack jaw. He gave the girl a halfhearted smile. "Hi. Are you okay?"

Her eyes darted, landing for a split second on the driver, then leaping away, as if stung. "I c-can't talk to strangers," she whimpered.

"I'm a fireman. I'm here to help."

"We gotta pick up my dad. We're goin' to the movies. Goin' to see *101 Dalmatians*."

"That's fine, but right now, I need to move this car."

The girl's head gave a vigorous shake. "Uh-uh. My dad's waitin' for us."

Straightening, Ealy motioned to the rescue truck for help, then walked around to the passenger door, glancing over the car's roof as two of his buddies approached. "We have to get it off the road," he said to them quietly. "I'll take the girl out, then you remove the body and pull the car over." He started to open the passenger door, but the girl grabbed the armrest and yanked it back.

"No!" she cried. "We gotta go!"

"It's okay. We're just going to move your car so we can get the fire trucks around it." Still, she resisted. "What's your name?" Ealy asked.

"Linda Florence Hudak."

"Linda, you need to get out of the car while we move it."

"My dad's waiting."

"He won't mind, I promise. We have to get our fire trucks by. It's an emergency. You can wait over here while we look for your dad."

"We're goin' to see *101 Dalmatians*," she repeated.

"Come on, Linda. Out of the car, please."

The girl glanced over to where firemen were lifting out the driver. "Mommy?"

Ealy took her hand reassuringly in his. "We'll take care of your mom, honey. She can't help us right now. One of the firemen will move the car. Come on, that's a good girl." He eased the door open and Linda climbed out reluctantly. Ealy had led her to the side of the road, then motioned for a cop to come and take her in hand so he could get on with his job.

The policewoman who was with the girl now got to her feet and wandered over.

"How's she doing?" Ealy asked.

"Hard to tell. She's not too communicative, but I'm not sure how much is grief over her mother, and how much is the retardation. She just keeps talking about going to the movies and singing that Disney song about Cruella deVil."

"They've got a makeshift morgue set up in the house across the park. Someone should move the body."

"We tried a few minutes ago, but the girl got hysterical. We let her be for a minute—figured if her father came out, it might make things easier." The policewoman shook her head. "Doesn't look now like that's going to happen, so we're trying to locate a friend or relative who can take charge of her."

"You found out who her father is?"

"Yeah. Name's Phil Hudak. He's an ex-cop. My lieutenant knew him when he was on the Boston PD. Says Hudak started working security here after he retired from the force. One of the employees told us his station was in the main lobby."

The firefighter stared at the cop for a moment, then they both looked over at the black, tangled pit at the base of the ravaged facility. "Shit," he muttered.

4

The carpenters were leaving for the day. Leya had gone down to see them out, determined to put distance between them and her father before the situation deteriorated any further. As Latouche backed his pickup down the drive, she caught Duncan's smirk through the passenger window. She had an urge to pick up a rock and chuck it at his stupid, bald head.

When she and the old contractor had come downstairs a few minutes earlier, they'd found Duncan in the kitchen, getting himself a glass of water. It suddenly occurred to Leya that he had free access all day to her personal belongings, temporarily crammed into the ground floor. Closing the front door, she went from room to room, checking for sawdust, mud or rearranged objects, or any other telltale sign that Duncan had been snooping. Nothing obvious, as far as she could see, but the place was in such chaos it was hard to tell. Maybe her father was right, after all, and she was an idiot to have let strangers into her house.

He was still stalking around upstairs, poking, prodding, banging walls. Grumbling to himself. Leya debated going up, but knew she was in for one of his diatribes. She could wait for it, she decided.

While he continued his tour of inspection, she moved to the large kitchen at the back of the house. Standing at the center island, she sifted through her mail and listened to her phone messages. The mail was nothing but junk flyers and bills, but there were three messages on the answering machine. One from John Merriman, confirming their date for that evening and telling her to be at the Copley Plaza no later than seven. One from her half sister Susan, inviting Leya and their father to spend Easter with her family in upstate New York. And a nervous one from Holly Stroud, her missing Ophelia.

"Professor Nash? I dropped by your office, but you weren't there, so by the time you get this, it'll be too late, I guess. I mean, rehearsal will already be over? Sorry, but something real important came up. I know this is, like, the second rehearsal I've missed, but I couldn't help it, honest. I promise I'll be there tomorrow. And, oh—I need an extension on my Hemingway essay? I know they were due today, but I had this real big problem? Not with Hemingway—something else. Maybe I could talk to you about it? I'll try to, like, call you later, or tomorrow, or something...?" Her voice drifted off uncertainly, then the machine beeped and went dead.

Leya frowned. What was *that* all about? Holly Stroud was one of her favorite students, and, remembering her own lonely days as a boarder when her father was posted abroad, Leya was prepared to cut the girl a little slack from time to time. Holly was beginning to push the limits of benevolence, however.

Leya was reasonably certain the girl had never been anywhere near her office that day. The departmental secretary sat near her office door. Dot Rankin, a long-suffering fussbudget, kept close tabs on comings and goings, making the students leave notes in the professors' pigeonholes so she couldn't be accused of garbling a message. Dot also knew Ambassador Stroud's daughter by sight—knew Leya felt a sense of responsibility toward the girl—and would certainly have reported if Holly was looking for her. Now, Holly's creative mind had another day to come up with some explanation for her goofing off that Leya might actually buy.

She sighed, then considered returning her half sister's call. Susan and her sister Grace were the offspring of their father's first marriage. Their mother had died the previous summer, still bitter about Carter Nash, thirty years after he'd divorced her to marry Leya's mother. A clinical therapist and family counselor, Susan had apparently decided she needed to heal the rift in her own clan if she were going to have any credibility in her chosen profession. Her sister Grace, however, wanted nothing to do with Leya or their father.

Before Leya could pick up the phone, the thump of his cane on the tile floor announced her father's return. She had no idea how long he'd been hovering behind the door, eavesdropping on her phone messages. "Susan called," she said, glancing up, "inviting us for Easter."

"Why does she bother?"

"What do you mean, 'Why'?"

"Is she a glutton for punishment? After the last happy reunion she organized, I'd have thought she'd learned her lesson."

Leya grimaced. The previous fall, the two of them had visited Susan and her family at Thanksgiving. When Grace had arrived and found them there, she'd fumed through drinks and appetizers, and the situation had eventually turned ugly, with Nash storming out of the house mid-meal. Leya and Susan had spoken by phone since then, but up to now, neither had had the courage to suggest another family get-together.

"Grace and her husband are going to be in Florida," Leya said.

"Aha! So the coast is clear, is it? Well, I don't know...."

"Oh, Dad. Give her a break, would you? Susan can't help how Grace feels, but she wants her kids to know their grandfather. She wants to spend time with you, too, before—"

"Before I kick the bucket?"

"Before any more time is wasted." He looked unconvinced. This was going to take some work, Leya thought, but eventually, he'd come around. She'd *make* him come around. Susan didn't deserve this grief from him.

"Would you like a cup of coffee?" she asked.

"I don't want to hold you up."

"There's no rush. I'm not meeting John till seven."

"The turnpike into the city will be slow."

"I'll be going against rush-hour traffic. It'll only take half an hour. Tell you what—I'll give you a ride home, and on the way, we can stop for a bite to eat."

"I thought you and John were having dinner before the play."

"Drinks before, then a late dinner after. But I wouldn't mind a cup of coffee while you eat."

"I don't want to be a bother. I'll just call a cab and go back to my apartment."

Leya sighed. "It's not a bother, Dad." She came around the island and looped her arm through his, dredging up a smile. "It's a pleasure."

For the first time since his arrival, his face softened. "All right, if you're sure. Where would you like to go?"

She thought about that for a moment. "How about Tyler's? I need to check on one of my students."

"She work there?"

"Hardly. Holly Stroud's never waited a table in her life, I'm sure. But Tyler Newman's a friend of hers. I've been trying to catch up with her."

"She having problems?"

"I'm not sure. Holly's a good kid, very bright, but lately, her work's been slipping. I'm worried she's going to blow it if she doesn't pull up her socks. Also," Leya added, "her father called me this afternoon—Arthur Stroud?"

"The ambassador to Israel?"

She nodded and reached for her coat. "Remember I told you I met him and his wife at Mount Abbey's open house last fall, and how he spoke so highly of you? Holly's their youngest. They worry about her, being so far away."

"He asked you to keep an eye on her?"

Leya nodded again. "But I don't think I'm doing a very good job of it. I have no idea what she's up to these days. Holly's supposed to be Ophelia in this production of *Hamlet* I'm directing. She missed rehearsal today for the second time in a row—no warning, no good excuse that I know of. She needs to know she can be replaced if she doesn't shape up."

Nash's brows knit together. "How the hell do you do *Hamlet* at an all-girl college? There aren't but two roles for girls in the whole play."

"Women, Dad, not girls. Get with the program, will you?"

He waved a hand dismissively.

"It's done a lot," Leya said. "In Shakespeare's time, all the women's roles were played by men, so turnabout is fair play. And it's not like Shakespeare wrote many noble parts for women. All his female characters are victims or conniving witches. I wanted to give my students something meaty to sink their teeth into. They're having a ball. We've even got a fencing master to choreograph the sword-fighting scenes.''

"Hmph! Seems silly to me.''

She punched him lightly in the shoulder. "That's because you're a big old Neanderthal. Ready to go?'' He rubbed his arm, suppressing a grin, and nodded.

Out in the car, Leya draped her right arm across the back of the passenger seat and began backing her little blue Civic down the drive. Her father was frowning at the house.

Shingled and hip-roofed, with an eccentric, stenciled turret on one corner, it was referenced in the *Guide to New England's Architectural Heritage* as "a classic 'Painted Lady' Victorian-style residence.'' With a broad, inviting veranda and stained-glass windows in its front door and turret, the old place had seen glory days and ruin. It had been a prestigious address when the pretty little town was a thriving textile center, but after World War II, when the mills had moved south in search of cheaper labor, Winslow had fallen into decline, the town center crumbling along with its tax base. Now, Winslow was enjoying a period of renewal and renovation, as urban professionals starting families sought refuge from the crowded neighborhoods of nearby Boston.

The Yuppie who'd bought the house in the eighties, when it was run-down office space, had refurbished the exterior and restored the first floor to its original residential configuration, doing some halfhearted fixing up. Then he'd run out of money, or enthusiasm, or both. The New England real-estate market had crashed in the interim, and when he couldn't flip the place for a profit, he'd simply walked away from the mortgage. Anxious to cut its losses and get the house off its books, the bank had put it up for sale the previous fall at a bargain price. Leya had jumped on it.

"I know what you're thinking," she warned her father. "Don't say it."

He said it anyway. "It's a sinkhole."

"Maybe. But it's *my* sinkhole, and I love it."

They'd had this conversation a dozen times before. No doubt they'd have it again, but for now, Leya was grateful that he let it drop. She was weary of the debate. There was no way to make him understand her attachment to the house. It existed. Period.

As a teenager, she'd often spent weekends and holidays at the home of Beth Durgin, her best friend at their Virginia boarding school. Beth had been a day student at Saint Michael's Academy, and her large family had lived in and around Williamsburg for nearly two hundred years, their roots spread out like some fast-propagating rhizome, until it seemed there was scarcely a street in town on which some Durgin home or business hadn't sprouted. Thanksgiving, always celebrated at the home of Beth's grandmother, was a crowded, raucous affair, with groaning trestle tables extending from the dining room across the front hall to the living room, as Durgin relatives squeezed in, elbow-to-elbow, for meals that had to be eaten in shifts to accommodate everyone. Beth would roll her eyes, mortified, as old family stories and scandals were told and retold, but never having had much of a family of her own, Leya had been fascinated—and envious.

She glanced again at her father, knowing there was no way to explain her need to stay put and sink roots without it sounding like resentment of her childhood.

She backed her car toward the street. Straining to see

around the Dumpster perched on her lawn like some rusted, postmodern sculpture, she only spotted the car parked next to her drive at the last second. Yanking the steering wheel to avoid clipping its fender, she veered the Civic around it. Her father lurched and grabbed the armrest, then shot her a dark scowl. Leya felt sixteen all over again, getting driving lessons on rutted roads in East Africa, where he'd been working at the time. "Sorry," she said sheepishly.

He shook his head and turned away. Leya shifted out of Reverse, preparing to take off down the road, but hesitated when she saw him peering at the parked sedan—a black Ford Taurus, the same car he'd been studying from the upstairs window. The glare of passing headlights bounced off its darkly tinted windows.

"What's wrong, Dad?"

He turned slowly, his face a mask except for a single muscle that twitched under his left eye. Leya felt her chest constricting. When he'd had his stroke, she'd learned about it only hours later, when someone had contacted her at her grad school in New York and advised her to get down to D.C., fast. She'd lived every day since in fear of another, possibly fatal, stroke. For all she knew, there might be early warning symptoms, and this stony look might be one of them.

"Dad? Are you all right?"

He stared at her, then finally returned from wherever it was that his mind had been wandering. "I'm fine. Let's go."

Boston, Massachusetts: 5:28 p.m.

"Explosion of unknown origins. That's the press line, for now."

Newton PD had alerted the FBI's Boston field office within minutes of the first emergency vehicles screaming into the Data-Trax compound. As soon as his phone had pealed, Curtis Pullen, the acting SAC—special agent in charge—had sensed trouble. His adrenaline had been pumping even before the first tense words came across the line.

"Between you and me," the police liaison added, "it sure sounds like a bomb. They say it left a twelve-foot crater at ground zero. Collapsed most of the first floor, blew out all the windows."

Until the phone's ring had broken his reverie, Pullen had been gazing down from his newly acquired office on the ninth floor of the JFK Federal Building in downtown Boston, watching headlights twinkle on damp pavement as bureaucrats streamed out of Government Center. He'd been made acting SAC just ten days earlier, when the regular guy, Arch McCreary, had gone in for his routine annual physical, only to be sidelined on medical disability when a cancerous polyp was found on his throat. Between laser surgery and chemotherapy, no one knew for certain when or if Arch McCreary was coming back to the field office. Pullen's appointment as acting SAC had been an interim measure by headquarters. He intended to do everything in his power to make sure it became permanent, if McCreary didn't return.

After the call from Newton PD, Pullen waited just long enough for a dial tone, then placed two calls in quick succession—to his wife, and to the J. Edgar Hoover Building in Washington, D.C., in that order. After thirteen years, Janice had long since given up complaining about the overtime he was obliged to put in, but Pullen had learned he could avoid a scene if he let her know when an emergency had arisen, so another dinner wouldn't turn to leather while she waited for him. In this case, he was also eager to tell her about the opportunity the crisis in Newton presented.

"If it's terrorists," he said, after sketching the details, "we'll probably end up asserting jurisdiction. I'll be the local agent in charge of the investigation. It's a real lucky break."

"It's a bomb, Curtis. People are dead."

"Yeah, I know, it's awful. But think of the visibility. They're sure to confirm me as SAC after this."

"Oh, sure. More likely they'll send in somebody else to take over, if this ends up being a real big deal."

Pullen's stomach cramped. "You think? No. Damn! They can't do that."

"Of course, they can."

"But I've waited so long for a chance like this!"

"Well? Are you going to let it slip through your fingers?"

"No," he said uncertainly. "I guess not." But he'd never handled a bomb case before. What if headquarters didn't think he was up to it? What if he fumbled the evidence? What if—

"Curtis? Are you going to take control?"

"Right," he said. "I'm taking charge." *Visualize it,* he told himself, remembering the motivational tape he'd been listening to on his way into work that morning. *You're a take-charge guy. Headquarters is lucky to have you on the job here.* "I'd better go, Jan. I want Washington to know I'm on top of the situation."

"All right, then. Good luck. Call me."

Pullen took a deep breath and smoothed back his receding hairline. Then he punched in the number of the Bureau's criminal investigative division, reciting his mantra each time his finger poked the keypad. *A take-charge guy, a take-charge guy...* Thirty seconds later, Leonard Rick-hauser was on the line. He was the assistant director-in-charge, or ADIC, of the FBI criminal division, whose area of responsibility also included antiterrorism. Pullen related details of the bombing to him as reported by the Newton PD.

"Information's still sketchy," he added, shifting forward in his chair, "but Newton PD figures explosives of some kind. They're a little department, but they've already called Boston PD's explosives-ordnance unit for assistance. They've asked that ATF be brought in as well—under FBI jurisdiction, of course. I'll be calling their local field office next."

"I'll do it from this end," Rickhauser said. "What about casualties?"

"At least four confirmed dead, but the count's sure to rise. Place was just starting to shut down for the day. People got caught in the lobby, which took the full force of the blast. And that's not even the worst of it."

"How much worse can it get?"

"Try little kids."

"Kids? Christ! How?"

"Apparently there's an underground tunnel connecting the building to an annex that houses a company day care. Tunnel's partially collapsed. Fire department can hear kids crying under the rubble."

The ADIC's sigh whistled across the long-distance line. "Okay. Get over there, see what's what, but keep in touch. I'll have a team mobilized and on a plane out of here within two hours. And Curtis?"

"Sir?"

"VanAken's still up there, isn't he?"

Pullen's shoulders slumped. "Yeah, far as I know."

"Bring him in on this."

"Maybe we should wait, sir, see if we really need the extra manpower?"

"Better not. No telling what we're dealing with. By this time tomorrow, we'll have a dozen callers claiming responsibility. Mostly your basic kooks du jour, but you can bet at least some of them will be quoting from the Koran. I want vanAken on the trail while it's still hot."

"All right," Pullen conceded, making a face he wouldn't have dared if Rickhauser had been in the same room. "I'll give him his marching orders."

"Someone will let you know when the team's in the air so you can meet 'em at Logan."

"Roger that. I'll be in touch, sir."

Pullen hung up, slammed the desk and uttered a curse. So what am I? he fumed. Some local flunky who's supposed to go running to meet the out-of-town team and carry their bags? His nervous stomach roiled again. Maybe Janice was right, and Rickhauser would send a special investigator who'd shove him aside and take charge. It wasn't clear. And then, to make things worse, the ADIC had ordered him to bring in bloody vanAken, of all people. Cursing again, Pullen rose from Arch McCreary's chair and headed for the door.

In the overcrowded outer office, where agents manned scuffed wooden desks—government issue, circa 1960—phones had already begun ringing off their hooks, rendering the bull pen more chaotic than usual, despite the late hour. Even with a complement of two hundred and sixty agents, Boston field office was always stretched thin. It was the tenth-largest of over four hundred bureau facilities scattered from one end of the union to the other. With a territory that covered Massachusetts, New Hampshire, Rhode Island, and Maine, most of Boston's caseload dealt in racketeering, organized crime and police corruption.

But there were plenty of crazies out there, too, fanatics with a political agenda who preferred action over debate, and who'd bomb you as soon as look at you. The regular SAC, Arch McCreary, had spent much of his FBI career tracking IRA terrorists, some of them financed through Irish-American friendship societies based in New England, which was why he'd been named to head up this field office last time the job had opened up. Now, Pullen decided, it was *his* turn to shine.

He cast his eye around the office, knowing even as he did that vanAken wouldn't be there. Guy was an out-of-towner—a lone wolf who seemed to show up at odd times, lurk in the shadows for a few days, then disappear again. One of the newer agents had told Pullen he'd seen vanAken at the FBI Academy at Quantico, where he was apparently on staff. But what he was doing popping in and out of Boston seemed to be a closely held bit of business.

The regular SAC, Arch McCreary, had called vanAken in when his sick leave was announced to introduce him to his number two. Pullen had taken an immediate dislike to the guy. Somewhere in his mid-thirties, vanAken came across as sullen and insolent—couldn't so much as be bothered to shake hands. Although Pullen was presented to him as the replacement SAC, it wasn't apparent this vanAken character had ever heard the term "chain of command."

For that matter, he didn't even appear to be a career agent. Didn't walk the walk, or talk the talk. In an organization where J. Edgar's ghost still held sway, and where military-style haircuts, beardless faces, white shirts, and spit-shone shoes were the standard, vanAken stood out. He strode around like some college don, in scuffed boots, jeans and tweedy jackets, dark hair curling over the open collars of his denim shirts. And then, there was the matter of those scars.

When vanAken had shown up in McCreary's office that time to be introduced, he'd wasted little time on social niceties, abruptly handing Pullen a copy of a memo from FBI headquarters, then walking off before McCreary had even dismissed him. The two-year-old memo ordered the field office to furnish any assistance vanAken required, but failed to say what, precisely, he was doing there. McCreary wasn't much more help. "He's Rickhauser's man, Curtis. I'd advise you to give him whatever he needs and leave it at that."

"But what's he doing running around unsupervised in our territory?"

The old SAC had shrugged, uninterested in bureau politics, his mind obviously on the medical ordeal ahead. "I've got my suspicions, but apparently we have no 'need to know.' Let it lie."

That might be good enough for Arch McCreary, Pullen thought, but it wasn't good enough for him. The day after McCreary's sick leave began, he'd called vanAken back in and tried to corner him on his mandate. VanAken had made some reluctant, grunted reference to an undercover investigation, but when pressed for details, he'd stormed off. Except for one return to requisition a different car, he hadn't been seen in the field office since. Pullen didn't regret the absence. His assessment of the man: a loose cannon and potentially twice as explosive.

But if this loose cannon was going to be rolling around *his* territory, he still wanted to know what the hell the guy's agenda was. He'd contacted Rickhauser at headquarters, but the ADIC had told him, basically, to mind his own business. Pullen had then put in a quiet call or two to his own sources—bureau agents who owed him favors—and was able to confirm what he'd already come to suspect—that vanAken was CIA. Or at least, used to be.

Turned out the guy had been stationed in Beirut in the early eighties, but had been kidnapped by Islamic fundamentalists and held hostage for four years, along with a couple of dozen other Americans and foreigners. That explained the scars, Pullen thought. Finally, it seemed, vanAken had escaped, only to find himself targeted back home by some sort of top-secret internal investigation and forced out of the agency under a cloud. Len Rickhauser had been doing a stint in the CIA during the vanAken inquiry, and it was he who'd subsequently hired the ex-spook as a bureau consultant and to teach courses at Quantico on militant Islamic groups.

None of Pullen's sources knew what other mandate vanAken might have that would bring him to Boston, but it turned out he'd been on the interagency team working the World Trade Center bombing and had apparently been key in nailing the ring of Muslim zealots responsible. Which might explain, Pullen thought, why a hard-ass, by-the-books chief like Len Rickhauser would be so determined to have him brought in on the Data-Trax bombing, in case a similar group was responsible.

But no matter how shrewd the former spook might be, Pullen hated the thought of working with the arrogant son of a bitch. Ever since vanAken's arrival, the acting SAC had been hoping each morning to come into the field office and discover that he'd folded his tent like an Arab and silently slipped away, back to Quantico or whatever hole it was he'd crawled out of. Now, it looked like he'd be underfoot a while longer.

"Why me, Lord?" Pullen grumbled under his breath. Then, he let out a bellow: *"Anybody know where the hell vanAken's at?"*

5

Tyler's was nearly empty when Leya and her father arrived in search of food and Holly Stroud. Fragrant odors of cinnamon, fresh bread and coffee greeted them at the door.

The place had opened three years earlier, about the time of Leya's own arrival in Winslow to take up her teaching post. The bistro fronted on the town common, and was housed in the old railway station, which was no longer used for trains. The freights had stopped running to Winslow when the textile mills shut down, and the MBTA commuter line from Boston had located its terminus on the edge of town, where parking was better.

Tyler's managed to be both spacious and cozy, with rough quarry-stone walls, gleaming hardwood floors, soft lighting and golden oak fixtures. Serving gourmet coffee and food that was neither too plain for gourmet tastes nor too strange for the local meat-and-mashed crowd, the place had attracted a loyal clientele. Joanna Newman kept it humming during the breakfast-through-supper trade, while her son, for whom the place was named, was king of the evening crowd—young singles who appreciated the bistro's laid-back ambience and country-pop music, live on weekends.

Carter Nash stood aside at the threshold to let his daughter pass, his walking stick tucked under the arm that held open the door, his free hand cupping Leya's elbow as if to steady and guide her, and catch her if she stumbled. As if this were yet another hurdle she couldn't manage without his assistance, Leya thought. As if it weren't he himself who was far more likely these days to trip over a doorsill.

Frustration shot across her emotional radar, accompanied by its usual shadow of guilt. Both emotions, the frustration and the guilt, emanated from somewhere deep in her psyche, a subterranean cave of old fears and resentments that Leya had long since decided was best left unexplored. It suddenly occurred to her, however, that John Merriman had the same habit of coddling her elbow.

She shrugged off the uneasy realization and glanced around the bistro. She recognized a couple of Mount Abbey students, but most of them would still be in the library, researching spring term papers whose deadlines loomed. Working people would start drifting in for dinner soon, but at the moment the other customers seemed to be mostly retirees like her father, who liked to eat and head home early in case the warm spring temperatures should plummet, turning melted snow puddles to treacherous, hip-breaking ice.

Holly Stroud was nowhere to be seen. Well, Leya thought, it was worth a try. With luck, the girl would show up for next day's rehearsal and Leya could try to get to the bottom of whatever was going on with her. In the meantime, before she took off for the city, Leya could make sure her father had eaten a decent meal.

Tyler Newman was behind the bar, cleaning the cappuccino machine. In his twenties, big-boned and tall, he filled out his white T-shirt like a guy who broke horses for a living, not one who tucked a striped towel into the waistband of his faded jeans and served up rounds of double-skinny *lattés*. As he rubbed the stainless steel to a high polish, his biceps strained against the short sleeves of his shirt. Tyler himself, not the music or food, Leya suspected, was a large part of the bistro's appeal for her students. She'd seen their eyes follow his movements behind the polished oak counter, and heard them exchange the smothered giggles with which young women have always signaled to one another the presence of an agreed-upon hunk.

He glanced up and broke into a smile when he spotted her. "Hi, there, Professor Nash!" With short-cropped rusty hair, blond lashes over blue eyes, and a splattering of freckles on his cheeks and forearms, he had the coloring of a man who'd sire redheaded kids, Leya thought.

"How's it going, Tyler?"

"No complaints. Grabbing an early dinner?"

"Just coffee for me, but my father will have something. Have you met my dad? Carter Nash—Tyler Newman."

Her father nodded curtly. "We've met. How's your mother?"

"She's fine."

"Tyler, I'm looking for Holly," Leya said. "Have you seen her today, by any chance?"

The young man's smile faded, and his gaze dropped to the cloth in his hand. "Not today, no."

"Or in the last couple of days?"

He looked up again, his broad smile firmly in place once more. "Nope. But she's been busy, you know—papers and exams." He gave the cappuccino maker's stainless-steel case another vigorous rub. "You two grab any place you'd like," he added over his shoulder. "I'll be over in a minute to take your order." Leya hesitated, but Tyler's body language spoke volumes.

For as long as Mount Abbey College had been in Winslow, there had always been an invisible gulf between "Abbies" and "Townies." Although they might share common ground like Tyler's, young people from the two groups rarely mixed, as if both sides recognized that the Abbies were just passing through, on their way to busy lives elsewhere, and couldn't be bothered to make an investment in friendship. Holly was one of the few Mount Abbey girls Leya had ever known, now or during her own undergraduate days, to wade across that social Rubicon. But whatever Holly and Tyler had argued about outside Mrs. Garibaldi's window, it looked as if the town-gown divide was back in full force.

"Shall we sit?" her father asked.

Leya nodded. Out of long habit, she headed to a corner table and let him claim the chair facing the room and the door. It was like being related to some old Mafia don, she thought, dealing with these ingrained security fixations of his.

He took her coat and shrugged off his own, hung them on pegs on the wall, then settled into a chair and propped his walking stick against the table. One of his African finds, it had an ivory head carved in the shape of a Bantu demon, smooth and polished from years of handling, the ivory aged to a warm shade of tan, like old piano keys. The walking stick was one of a dozen or more in his collection. Even before his stroke, he'd often carried one. In any other man, the affectation might have seemed foppish, but he'd cultivated the habit of twirling it over his fingers, or stabbing it into the ground as he spoke, or laying it down ominously before him on the table, like Excalibur— in short, wielding it in a vaguely menacing style designed to both mesmerize and intimidate. Now, the cane also served the more prosaic function of steadying him.

From a pine holder on the table, Nash withdrew one of the menus hand-lettered and decorated by Joanna Newman, Tyler's mother. Her domestic wares were displayed for sale on pine shelving near the cash register—row on row of colorful preserves, hand-thrown pottery jars, aromatic potpourri she'd gathered and dried herself, and note cards featuring pressed blooms from her garden. An old flower child who'd progressed from crunchy-granola hippie to New Age domestic environmentalist, Mrs. Newman was Winslow's own Martha Stewart. It would be easy to despise the woman, Leya thought. No one should be *that* clever or energetic.

She caught her father frowning at the bill of fare. Or was he squinting? He was overdue for a checkup, but resisted her efforts to get him into a doctor's office. Despite being legally blind for driving purposes, because of his peripheral-vision deficit, he prided himself on not needing reading glasses, his battered ego taking gratification wherever it could, refusing to concede defeat to anyone or anything, least of all his own traitorous body. His color was flushed, Leya noted, his breathing faintly audible. Constantly trying to read him for clues as to how he was feeling, she'd resigned herself to enduring a crotchety tirade whenever he caught her at it.

"What do you feel like eating, Dad?"

"I don't know. Nothing with sprouts, that's for sure. I don't know why she can't serve normal things, like a BLT and fries."

"Do you know how much cholesterol there is in a BLT and fries?"

"Plenty. That's why they taste good. A body needs that."

"Right. Fat, salt and sugar—the essential food groups."

"You forgot alcohol."

"Silly me. Come on, Dad, buck up! There are other things you'd enjoy that won't gum up your arteries. The Southwestern chicken's good. Why don't you try that?"

He heaved a martyred sigh and tossed aside the menu. "Whatever. As long as it's quick so you can get on the road. Weather can change from one minute to the next, this time of year. I don't know why you have to be the one to drive into the city. Why doesn't John come here?"

"We've got tickets for the revival of *Saint Joan* at the Lyric Theater."

"Seems like a lot of bother, just for a play. Tell me, what does he say about this building project of yours?"

Leya grimaced. The house, again. "What does it matter what he thinks?"

"He's an investment counselor. You know he'd have advised against buying that place, if you'd bothered to discuss it with anyone before jumping in."

"I didn't think anyone's permission was required."

"Has he told you you're throwing good money after bad with these renovations? It'll never end, you know. You should get rid of it now, cut your losses."

"In case you hadn't noticed, Dad, I passed the big three-oh last month. Theoretically, that makes me old enough to make my own decisions, wouldn't you say?"

He fiddled with the cutlery. Temporarily silenced, but with no intention, Leya knew, of abandoning the campaign. Sure enough, he found another angle of attack. "John won't want to commute from Winslow into Boston every day."

"No one's asking him to."

"Not yet, maybe, but what happens when you get married? You'll never get back what you're dumping into the place.''

''I'm not looking to take my money out. And who said anything about getting married? We're just good friends.''

Nash's skeptical expression told her he knew different. Not surprising, Leya thought. She'd never been able to con him, and while marriage might not be on *her* agenda, he obviously knew what was on John Merriman's. John was, in fact, the only man she'd ever brought around who'd met with Carter Nash's approval, and the two of them had become allies in the effort to wear down what they saw as her unreasoning resistance.

Time to change the subject. ''So what about Susan's invitation? Will you go?''

''Why can't she come here?''

''She's got a family and a career.''

''Now, maybe. But where's she been for the last thirty years? Neither she nor Grace has ever shown any great desire to be with me before. Now, all of a sudden—''

''It wasn't easy when their mother was alive.''

''She was spiteful. They took her side.''

''They were caught, Dad.''

''That wasn't my fault. Rose was the one who forced the issue.''

''You didn't make things any easier.''

''You don't know what you're talking about, Leya, so I'd suggest you drop it.''

''I just—''

''I *said*, drop it.'' He turned his attention to withdrawing and rearranging packets of raw cane sugar from a box on the table, shuffling them between the pink-and-blue sweetener packs—closing conversational doors, as always, whenever they led to the past.

After all these years, Leya thought wearily, he was still

drawing lines in the sand, forcing his children to take sides in old family battles that should have ended in cease-fires long ago. It wasn't just Susan and Grace's mother. Relations had been equally fractious with the family of his second wife. Leya hadn't seen her maternal relatives since she was five years old. Frustrated, she sat back in her chair, but when Tyler approached their table, she forced herself to smile.

"Sorry to keep you guys waiting."

"No problem. Are you on your own here today, Tyler?"

"For now. One of my girls is on break."

"How about your mother?" Nash asked. Leya's ears perked up. It was the second time he'd asked after Mrs. Newman.

"She takes Mondays off, but she'll drop back for the dinner rush. She usually does."

Her father nodded, his expression neutral. His apartment complex was just around the corner from Tyler's, and despite his grumbling about the annoyingly healthy menu, it occurred to Leya that he'd been awfully quick to agree to coming here.

"Were you going to go with that Southwestern chicken, Dad?" When he said yes, Leya turned back to Tyler. "I'll just have coffee."

"One of the daily specials?"

"What's brewing?"

"Costa Rican Mocha, French almond, Kenya gold, Guyana decaf—"

"Just a regular *latté*, I think. Nonfat."

"Gotcha. How about you, Mr. Nash?"

"Depends. Do you have any coffee-flavored coffee? American? With *cream*," he added. For her benefit, Leya knew.

Tyler grinned and nodded. "I think we could manage that."

The black Ford Taurus sedan pulled up outside Tyler's and idled at the curb. The driver peered through the big front window, studying the crowd. Elderly couples mostly, eating slowly, saying little. Talked out, apparently; every conceivable subject exhausted after decades spent together. Still, vanAken thought, that was a lot of talking. He had to exert superhuman effort for the infrequent conversations he had with anyone.

He watched a gaggle of teenage girls at a table near the bar. They seemed to have no problem finding things to say or reasons to say them. Their mouths moved nonstop, as they fidgeted and played self-consciously with their hair, alternately giggling and feigning sophistication of the eye-rolling variety. Little girls poised uncertainly on the brink of womanhood. Stay young, vanAken telegraphed. Keep your innocence.

His gaze continued its circuit of the room until it landed on the corner, where a waiter was taking an order from a dark-haired woman and the snowy-haired man across the table. Her father, vanAken happened to know.

Reluctantly, he found himself studying the woman. Her bearing was more mature and self-confident than he remembered. When she spoke to the waiter, he saw lines at the corners of her mouth. "Smile lines," they were called euphemistically. Accurately, in her case. Her smile—shy, tender, eager, maddening—was the first thing vanAken always remembered when he thought of Leya. But a woman's smile—the comfort of a woman's smile—was an illusion. A trick to bewitch and lull a man, rendering him oblivious to danger.

Once, vanAken had been so hexed by that smile that

he'd been utterly blindsided by an act of treachery that had nearly cost him his life. No, not nearly. It *had* destroyed his life. Even if his body had survived, everything he'd ever valued had been ripped away. Ideals, hopes, dreams, a career, not to mention peace of mind and the people he'd most loved in this world. What he had now couldn't be called a life.

He examined Leya more closely, dissecting the elements of her, coolly, analytically. Petite frame—average height, but small-boned. Nothing special about her body, objectively speaking. Dark brown hair that shone under overhead spots. Well, why not? She was healthy, wasn't she? Eyes the color of her hair, and large, relative to her facial proportions. Some might call them warm, but that would be subjective. Coloration was just a matter of genes, after all. Inherited, in her case, from a Latina mother she'd never known. VanAken's gaze moved down her face. Sensuous mouth, naturally deep in color, the upper lip nearly as full as the lower. "Bee-stung," he'd heard lips like that described. Stupid. As if there could be anything attractive about an allergic reaction to insect venom.

She's not beautiful, vanAken told himself. Striking, perhaps, but definitely not beautiful. She smiled at the waiter again. Same old smile, he thought grimly. It hadn't changed, but it didn't have the power to captivate that it once had.

VanAken took a deep breath. *Calm*, he intoned. *Think calm.*

He went back to cataloging her deficits. She was no girl anymore, as evidenced by those lines in her face. Her hair was too short—sliced to shoulder length, tucked conservatively behind pearl-studded ears. Once, vanAken recalled, it had tumbled in loose waves halfway down her back, getting tangled in those bangly earrings she'd liked to wear. Gone, too, were the Indian cotton skirts and peasant blouses that had floated around her like angel wings. This tan suit she had on now was—what? Professorial, he decided. Admittedly, if she'd been teaching when *he* was a student, dumb and naive, he might have spent entire lectures imagining what lay under that creamy silk blouse, just as he'd once itched to get under those peasant tops of hers. Of course, the students she taught were all female, but who knew what lusty thoughts stirred young women at a single-sex college?

As a bleak smile tugged at the corners of his mouth, vanAken realized he was daydreaming even now. He snapped back to reality quickly enough when her gaze led him to the man seated across the table from her.

Nash had aged, no question about it. VanAken contemplated the white hair and fallen jowls, the gnarled fingers fussing with sugar packets, the ivory-topped cane propped against the table. The man looked grandfatherly and positively benign.

An ache rose in his jaw, and vanAken realized his teeth were tightly clamped. Carter Nash may have turned into a senior citizen, but he was today what he had always been. Whatever ailments he suffered, they were nothing compared to the agonies he'd inflicted.

VanAken's hands reached up to clench the steering wheel. His outsize cuffs slipped back, revealing hairless wrists, each one encircled by a wide, disfiguring band of rippled scar tissue, extending down to misshapen knuckles. Under the streetlights, the ragged flesh and knotted bones shimmered whitely and unevenly. He glanced at his ugly hands, then dropped them self-consciously into his lap. With the movement, his left biceps brushed against the butt of the Glock automatic holstered under his arm.

The scars were only an external reminder of his hatred,

a rage that would never die as long as Carter Nash lived. And if the man were obliterated from the face of the earth? vanAken wondered. Would that bring him peace, at last?

For a long time now, he'd been incapable of any emotion except deep, caustic anger. Day after day, it ate at him, like a vulture picking at his entrails. Dying would have been easier than living like this. His only comfort came from the grim satisfaction of knowing that each tedious day he survived denied Carter Nash an easy victory. Every breath he drew was an act of defiance.

But it wasn't enough anymore. He was tired, of how he lived and of what he had become. Thoughts of revenge flickered through his mind. Get it over and done with, he told himself, and then finally—maybe—he would find rest.

A scarred hand withdrew the Glock from under his jacket, and another ran its fingers over the gun's hard curves and angles. The steel was warm, always kept next to his body. The gun held seventeen rounds in its magazine, but he wouldn't need seventeen, of course. For Nash, it would take one shot to drop him, one for the coup de grâce. To be sure the bastard was dead. For himself—only one.

VanAken watched the old man, doubt gnawing at the edges of the plan formulating in his mind. It wasn't that he was afraid to pull the trigger, against Nash or himself. But the issue here was retribution. Appropriate retribution. Was execution sufficient? For a man like Carter Nash, reduced now to a shell of what he once was—a shuffling has-been, his power stripped away—death might actually be a favor. A kind of release. Release was the last thing vanAken was prepared to grant him.

His gaze traveled to Leya once more. Maybe justice

demanded that Carter Nash pay a greater forfeit, he thought. Maybe it required that the man lose something he held even dearer than his own contemptible life.

6

A television murmured above the bar at Tyler's, its volume turned low. Leya sat with her back to it, but her father's gaze kept drifting over her head, his attention trapped by the box's flickering images. She watched the screen's light reflected in his eyes. Once molten blue, they'd long since cooled to a pale memory of that shade, like a physical gauge of his fading strength. It was just one more of the indicators that she studied and tracked anxiously.

"Did you take your blood-pressure pills today, Dad?"

His watery eyes shifted, and he frowned, thinking. "This morning. Not this afternoon."

"Why not?"

"I'm out."

"You're *out?* Dad, I asked you just yesterday whether you had enough!"

He shrugged. "I did then. Now, I don't."

"The doctor said you're not supposed to stop taking them abruptly. It's dangerous."

Nash turned back to the television. Gritting her teeth, Leya glanced at her watch, but it was too late to do anything about it now. The local pharmacy that had his prescription closed early on Mondays. She'd have been all right if she'd taken it to the Wal-Mart, recently opened outside town, but she'd made a personal decision to patronize Winslow's small businesses—do her part to help keep the town center alive. Idealism, however, required a certain amount of advance planning.

"Okay," she said. "Haddad's opens at eight in the morning. I'll stop by for your refill, and drop it off on my way to work tomorrow."

"I can run over and pick it up myself."

"No, the sidewalks are too icy in the morning. Anyway, I want to make sure you've taken your medication before you go traipsing all over town."

"Oh, for chrissake, Leya, stop fussing!"

She leaned her head in her hands and sighed, trying to pinpoint exactly when this role reversal had kicked in— adult child assuming responsibility for the aging parent. She might say it had been after his stroke, but that wasn't really the case. She'd rushed to his Virginia hospital bedside, but after a few days, he'd ordered her to return to her studies at Columbia. The doctors had told her she was doing him more harm than good, given how agitated he became about her "wasting time" with him when she should be working on her thesis. In any event, he'd made a quick and almost full recovery, except for his wonky peripheral vision.

But a year or so later, when the CIA had decided it had no place for an aging, half-blind covert operative and urged him to retire, Nash had been so furious that Leya had feared he'd work himself into another stroke. "Thirty-five years! And this is how they repay me!" he'd bellowed, over and over.

Leya was back living with him in Virginia by then, finishing her thesis and job-hunting. It was a grim period.

Her father grew sullen and withdrawn, sitting alone for hours in their darkened apartment, staring at the walls, refusing all efforts by Leya and old colleagues to draw him out. At the same time, he was suspicious and paranoid, demanding each time she walked in the door to know whom she'd seen while she was out, accusing her of consorting with enemies, spreading lies about him. Leya knew it was depression talking, but the situation grew intolerable. He either wanted her under his watchful eye every minute of the day, or he wanted her as far away as possible, preferably in another state or country altogether. There was no happy medium.

Then, when her undergraduate alma mater offered her a probationary position in its English and theater-arts program, he practically threw her out. "I can manage just fine without you. Go! I don't need you watching over me like a mother hen!"

Leya had found him a part-time housekeeper and breathed a guilty sigh of relief at the chance to get away for a while. But when her position at Mount Abbey had been confirmed on the tenure track after a probationary year, she'd hesitated to stay on. She and her father were back on good terms, but he was adamant she not give up the job. College-level openings were few and far between, he noted, especially for new teachers with little experience. His arguments fell on receptive ears. For the first time in her life, Leya had begun to think she could make a home for herself here in this little college town, with Boston and all its attractions close at hand.

But her father was isolated. His old Langley stomping grounds were nearby, but he saw fewer of his former colleagues with each passing year. He couldn't drive and felt exposed and vulnerable on public transport, so it fell on Leya to make the eight-hundred-mile round trip to visit him—difficult to manage very often. Nor could she count on her half sisters to help watch over him, given lingering resentments on that side of the family.

Finally, she'd suggested to her father that he move in with her. He'd refused outright, but she knew how lonely he must have become by the previous spring, when he'd telephoned, hinting about looking for a place in Massachusetts. She'd taken his oblique cue, although when she told him about the apartment in the Revere elders' complex, he'd acted as if he were doing her a favor by relocating.

Leya studied his face, bathed in Tyler's soft lights. Probably most seniors found it difficult to accept their declining capabilities and resented becoming dependent on their children. In Carter Nash's case, however, there was no question of going gentle into that good night.

She felt a movement of air and caught a whiff of Ivory Snow, which seemed to float in on a breeze. Tyler's mother had appeared at her elbow. Joanna Newman set down Leya's coffee and her father's dinner, flashing a warm smile at him. "Hello, Carter."

As his attention shifted from the television set, his face underwent a subtle transformation. "Joanna—good to see you."

She turned her crinkly eyes on Leya. "And how are you, Professor Nash?"

"I'm fine, Mrs. Newman, thanks. But it's Leya, please."

"That's so pretty. Is it a family name?"

"No, it's Hindi. It means 'lion.' My parents were living in India when I was born, and my *ayah*—my nanny—chose my name. She said it would make me strong."

"Actually, it was because you roared so much," Nash said. Leya made a face at him.

The older woman laughed. "And I'm Joanna, please."

"Joanna," Leya said, smiling.

Small, with a dense, compact, matronly figure, Joanna had a crop of silver blond hair which had a tendency to flop into her eyes. They were a vivid shade of periwinkle blue. Strong cheekbones dominated her still-handsome face, and Leya guessed she'd been quite beautiful as a young woman. By the deep lines on her skin and the age spots on the back of her blunt, scrubbed hands, Joanna looked to be in her fifties, but her energy level was enough to leave Leya gasping for breath whenever she saw the older woman bustling around the restaurant.

Joanna withdrew two gleaming glass jars from the pockets of her crisp bib apron and set them on the table in front of Leya's father. "I was hoping you'd be in today, Carter. I made some of those gooseberry preserves we were talking about the other day. I can't promise they're as good as the ones you remember your mother making, but I hope you like them."

Leya was astonished to see him blush. "You shouldn't have gone to all that bother," he protested.

"It was no bother at all. But I want you to be honest with me. I'm always trying to improve my recipes, so let me know if it's missing something."

He turned one of the jars around in his hands. It bore a hand-decorated label—Made Especially For You By Joanna Newman. "I'm sure they'll be very good," he said.

Leya propped an elbow on the table, resting her chin in her hand as her eyes moved from one to the other. "Joanna"? "Carter"? His mother's gooseberry preserves? My, my! she thought. What is going on here?

"Do you have time to join us?" Nash asked.

"Why not? For a few minutes, anyway. Tyler can manage while things are quiet."

Nash jumped up to pull out a chair, moving with a speed

Leya hadn't seen in him for quite some time. He waited until Joanna was settled before reseating himself. Despite a lifetime spent in the gritty world of covert ops, he'd always had a courtly manner where women were concerned. Leya knew there was a measure of pure chauvinism in that charm, but it amused her to see how effective it was, even now at his advancing age.

Joanna responded with a girlish blush, then swept her bangs out of her eyes and leaned toward him. "Did you read that article I gave you on vitamins?"

He nodded. "I did."

"It's the antioxidant group that's really important. Keeps those free radicals under control."

"Where radicals are concerned, firm control's the best policy," he agreed, a smile playing at the corners of his mouth.

Joanna did a double take, then slapped his arm lightly. "Now, that's the old spy talking. You go ahead and make fun, but you'll see, it makes a world of difference."

Leya's amusement was growing in tandem with her curiosity. Her father had obviously told Joanna about his background—something he almost never did. And they were flirting with one another! When had she last seen *that?*

Examined objectively, she supposed, her father was still an attractive man, with his mane of white hair and proud bearing. But as far as Leya knew, it had been ages since he'd had a lady friend. She felt an old, sad twinge at the isolation to which he'd condemned himself after her mother's death.

Carter Nash had been in his late thirties, the father of two preteen daughters, when he was assigned to the CIA station in Caracas, Venezuela, working under diplomatic cover at the American embassy. His wife, disenchanted with the roving life-style demanded of military, diplomatic and spy families, had decided to force the issue by taking the girls home for a vacation after a few months, then refusing to return. Nash had been obliged to finish out his posting alone.

Whether he and his wife might have eventually resolved their problems became academic when, a few months after her revolt, Carter Nash met and fell in love with another woman. Elena Macario was the daughter of a Venezuelan government minister and was already engaged to the son of a prominent judge. When the two furious local families found out about her involvement with the embassy official, they persuaded the country's president to declare the American persona non grata. Too late. Nash had already asked Elena to marry him when the expulsion order came through.

He was cross-posted to the CIA station in New Delhi, India, again under diplomatic cover. Elena accompanied him, and they married as soon as his divorce became final. Leya was born ten months later, but Elena never saw her infant daughter, nor held her in her arms. In Delhi's heat and humidity, she'd suffered a massive cerebral infection after coming down with malaria. The doctors had barely managed to keep her alive long enough to perform a cesarean section and save her baby. Left with a motherless child, Nash had set out to raise Leya alone, accepting help only from old Bhu Kedar, the *ayah* Elena had hired before falling ill.

Leya watched Joanna Newman coaxing her father out of his crusty shell. Growing up, she'd always sensed that women were drawn to him. Whether it was his taciturn surface, underscored with flashes of stunning generosity and loyalty, that drew them, or his archaic mannerisms around the ladies, Leya couldn't recall a single posting where some woman hadn't tried to be her surrogate mother/big sister/best friend, hoping to engage a coconspirator in her effort to snag Carter Nash. In one or two cases, Leya had been happy to cooperate. Persistence, she'd soon learned, only hastened her father's inevitable rebuff. He would permit himself short reprieves from his self-imposed condemnation to a life of solitude, it seemed, but never a full pardon.

Leya's old *ayah* was in her eighties now, but Bhu had followed the little family of two through six postings in fourteen years. She'd retired back to Delhi only when Nash, determined that Leya's education not suffer because of his nomadic calling, had enrolled her in a girls' boarding school in Virginia, and later, at Mount Abbey College. Or maybe, Leya suspected, it was to shield her from the young marine guards at the embassy, whose military readiness was exceeded only by their readiness to party.

Leya still corresponded with Bhu, although her written English was as idiosyncratic as her speech, with a tendency to twist the language in mystifying ways. When Leya had confided her worry over her father's bouts of depression and anger after his stroke, Bhu had written back: *"Some things you are not changing, little one. Your father is always living with anger, because he can never be turning back the cheek."*

"Turning back the cheek?" Leya had puzzled over that one. Did Bhu mean turning back the clock? Maybe. No doubt there were things Carter Nash would have done differently if he could have reversed the hands of time— including, she suspected, not stealing his beloved Elena from her home and another man, only to lead her into a premature death.

Or did Bhu mean that his problems stemmed from his fierce, inflexible nature that could never turn the other cheek, lashing out instead at every perceived slight, whether from man or God? That, too, Leya thought, was an accurate description of her father. If it made him prickly and difficult, the fact was, he'd always been harder on himself than on anyone else.

Taking a sip from her coffee cup, Leya stole a glance at her wristwatch. Her father caught her at it. "It's getting late," he said. "What time did you say you're meeting John?"

"Seven."

"You'd better be off. You don't want to be rushing on the turnpike."

"You aren't planning to go into the city, are you?" Joanna asked.

Leya nodded as she reached for her coat. "I'm meeting a friend at the Copley Plaza for a drink, and then a play at the Lyric."

"You won't make it tonight. They say there's gridlock on the Mass Turnpike and all the surrounding roads. The turnpike's closed down at Newton."

"Closed down? Why?"

"Didn't you hear?" The older woman nodded toward the television. "There was a bombing there about an hour ago."

Leya glanced at the TV, but the weather report was on. "A bombing?"

"Yes. A big one. The FBI's been called in. All the networks and CNN have been reporting it."

Nash frowned. "What was the target?"

"A big, high-tech company called Data-Trax."

"I've seen the place," Leya said. "It's right alongside the turnpike. Why would anyone want to bomb them? They make medical scanners, don't they?"

"Among other things," her father said quietly. His gaze

shifted back to the television. "There's a news report coming on now. Could we get that turned up, Joanna?"

"Certainly. Tyler," she called, "turn up the TV, would you?"

Her son found the remote under the bar and aimed it at the box just as the news anchor ceded the screen to an on-the-spot reporter, who was standing in front of a brick wall featuring the Data-Trax logo. Behind him, through a gate, fire and police officers moved about, illuminated by flashing lights.

"Four people are confirmed dead, and dozens more have been injured in a blast that shook this research facility and the Boston suburb of Newton less than an hour ago. Police say the death toll is likely to rise, with employees still trapped in the rubble of the building's main lobby and in an underground tunnel that connected to a company day-care center. There's fear the victims may include children, caught in the tunnel at the moment the blast occurred.

"Forensics experts from the FBI and the Bureau of Alcohol, Tobacco and Firearms are rushing to the scene even now. In the meantime, police are refusing to confirm that a bomb was involved, or to speculate who might have wanted to target this particular facility, and why.

"Reporting live from Newton, Massachusetts, this is Larry Flynn, ABC News."

As the anchor reappeared on the screen, a map of west Boston was mounted over his right shoulder, with a large red-and-yellow explosion symbol plastered over the town of Newton and the Massachusetts Turnpike. It was the only route to Leya's Back Bay rendezvous with John Merriman that would have gotten her there on time.

She sighed and turned to Joanna Newman. "Could I use

your phone? It looks like I'm going to have to take a rain check on that date of mine.''

Winslow Municipal Airfield: 6:13 p.m.

VanAken stood on the flood-lit tarmac, squinting against scouring eddies of dust kicked up by the descending Bell Jet Ranger with FBI stenciled in bold, reflective white letters on its side. The helicopter's skids touched down, but the rotors continued to turn as the rear door slid open.

Curtis Pullen, acting SAC of the Boston field office, had reached him by cell phone a short while earlier as vanAken had sat in his car, glowering at the front window of Tyler's. Pullen didn't appear to be in the helicopter now. VanAken spotted a pilot and copilot, and a third figure standing beside the open door. This one looked all of eighteen, although his somber suit, crisp white shirt, boring tie and dark overcoat marked him as a freshly hatched federal agent—either that or a door-to-door missionary. Despite the swirl of wind around the aircraft, not one hair rippled on the kid's close-cropped head.

VanAken crouched low and ran forward. As soon as he was inside the helicopter, the other agent followed and pulled the door shut, and the bird began to rise. The two passengers strapped themselves into facing seats, then the younger man thrust out his hand. ''Agent vanAken? I'm Special Agent Wilf Berger, from the Boston field office.''

Eyes bright, the kid looked ready to pee with excitement. A rookie for sure, vanAken decided. Probably his first case. Raking his unruly hair out of his eyes, he ignored the young agent's proffered hand, but caught the shocked expression when Berger spotted his scars. VanAken shoved his fists into the pockets of his battered overcoat. ''Where's Pullen?''

"We dropped him on the way over. He sent me to pick you up. I was working late when the call came, and I got pulled in, too, so I guess we'll be working the case together, hey?"

"What's this all about?"

"The SAC didn't brief you?"

"We spoke on the cell phone. It wasn't secure. He just said there was an emergency."

"Newton PD called us in about an hour ago. Apparently, a bomb went off at a company there called Data-Trax. They're a high-tech outfit that—"

"I know who they are. They develop remote-imaging technology for spy satellites."

"They do? No kidding. I knew they made medical equipment, and I just got told they did defense research, but I didn't know—"

"They're sure it was a bomb?"

"Local boys seem to think so. A joint FBI-ATF squad's on the way from Washington now."

"Anyone claim responsibility?"

"I—I'm not sure. Maybe—"

"What does Pullen want with me?"

"Well…" Berger seemed deflated, disappointed that his junior, know-nothing status had become apparent so quickly. "I'm not at liberty to say," he ventured—one last-ditch effort, vanAken thought, to give the impression he was more than Pullen's gofer.

He leaned back and closed his eyes, but he felt the young agent eyeing him curiously.

"SAC says you're down here on TD from Quantico?" When vanAken nodded, Berger asked, "Doing what?"

VanAken considered a moment. "Research," he said, opening his eyes but avoiding Berger's gaze, fixing instead on the kid's shoes. An old man's style of black wing-tip, they squeaked every time Berger fidgeted and looked as if they'd been coated with high-gloss polyurethane. Must have sat up half the night buffing them, vanAken thought. A real keener.

Had he himself ever been this young and enthusiastic? He couldn't remember a time when he hadn't felt hollow and used up, driven only by anger and a dull, gnawing ache. He'd tried to put it behind him, thinking eventually the desire for revenge would recede. Tonight, he'd been forced into the realization that it never would.

Berger's shoes squeaked again. The bushy-tailed, junior G-man was obviously itching for small talk, vanAken thought wearily. In an effort to discourage him, he peered out into the night.

No such luck. "So," Berger said heartily, "you teach at the academy?"

"Sometimes." Below them, the Mass Turnpike was at a standstill.

"What subject?"

VanAken studied the landscape passing under the belly of the bird, pretending he hadn't heard. He felt rather than saw Berger lean forward. Felt the incursion into his personal zone of untouchability. He loathed any breach of that zone. VanAken's eyes closed, and the balled fists in his pockets pressed into his thighs while he fought against the urge to throttle this fool, who crowded him at his own peril.

Berger, however, seemed to think the problem was that he couldn't be heard over the rotors' thunder, so he raised his voice to a bellow. *"What's your specialty, Agent vanAken?"*

VanAken willed himself to take a long, slow, deep breath. And then, to be safe, one more. Finally, he opened his eyes, fixed the earnest young face with a frigid glare. "Silent assassination," he hissed.

Berger recoiled, averting his gaze. They finished the short journey in blessed silence.

7

John Merriman's voice was baritone deep, with a soothing resonance that inspired confidence and seemed to offer shelter from life's storms. It was the kind of voice that could induce corporations to hand over control of their pension funds, and widows to consign their life savings to his fiduciary care. It had even convinced the ever-suspicious Carter Nash that Merriman could be entrusted with his daughter's well-being.

His melodious voice also set off a thrumming deep inside Leya that was both seductive and irritating. For a year and a half now, after meeting him through mutual friends, she'd been struggling with its genial assault, at first drawn to, then resisting the embrace of its owner. Lately, she'd felt her reflexes growing more defensive, despite any easily explained reason to reject a pleasant, attractive man whose only defect seemed to be blind devotion to her and to making money.

When Leya reached him by phone at his Milk Street brokerage firm, in the heart of Boston's financial district, Merriman sounded both disappointed and relieved. ''I was worried you'd gotten hung up in that snarl on the turnpike.

I'm glad you're not, but dammit, Leya! I was looking forward to this evening.''

''I was, too. This production's been getting great reviews, and I know the director.''

''Oh, the play…sure. But I want to see *you*. With the tax deadline looming, I've been swamped. It's been almost two weeks. Now a bomb, for chrissake, just when we finally had a chance to be together.''

''If there were any way—''

''I know, but I don't even want you to try, sweetheart. It could be hours before the roads clear. They say police are crawling all over the area to make sure no other bombs are waiting to go off.''

''It's appalling. This is the kind of thing you'd expect in Beirut, not Boston. There were little kids there, for crying out loud. Who could be so sick?''

''God only knows, but they deserve swift justice and a slow, agonizing death. Not that it'll happen. Our system coddles criminals. That's what these people count on. We deserve what we get, letting in these damn foreigners with their fanatic causes.''

Leya felt a stab of irritation at his knee-jerk xenophobia, but her curiosity was also sparked. ''Did you hear something new? Did they find out who it was?''

''CNN's comparing it to the World Trade Center bombing.''

''Muslim extremists?''

''Probably. In any event, it's really messed up our evening.'' Merriman's voice was regretful, but in the background, Leya could hear the clack and beep of his computer terminal. Obviously, he wasn't so upset that he couldn't see clearly to work.

''What are you doing? I hear your keyboard tapping.''

''I'm on the Net. I want to get my Data-Trax 'Sell'

orders in the queue early, so I can dump them as soon as the market opens in the morning.''

"John!"

"The share price is going to plummet. I've got a responsibility to my clients to make sure they don't take a bath."

"It still seems like kicking a guy when he's down."

"Oh, Data-Trax will rebound in the long run," he said blandly. "This is a short-term blip, but the company's pretty solid. I'll start buying again when they bottom out. How about you? You want me to pick up some personal security stocks for you—armored-vehicle manufacturers, insurance companies, gun manufacturers, something like that? Their prices always rise after an incident like this."

"Honestly, John! No, thank you."

"Whatever. Listen, honey," he said, changing the subject, "how about taking the train? You could still make it in time."

Leya glanced at her watch. "Barely," she said, "especially with transfers."

"No transfers. I'll pick you up at the Back Bay Station."

"I don't think so. The last train returning to Winslow leaves at eleven. We'd barely be out of the theater, and forget about dinner."

"I was hoping you'd stay over."

Leya felt a guilty pang. She'd known the pressure would be on to spend the night in the city. Subconsciously, she'd breathed a sigh of relief when her father had given her an excuse not to. "I can't," she said. "My father's blood-pressure medication ran out. He's already missed one dose, and it's dangerous for him to do that. I have to get his refill taken care of first thing in the morning."

Merriman sighed. "All right. How about if I run out there?"

"But the turnpike—"

"I'll swing through the north end, come around the back way."

"That could take a couple of hours."

"Doesn't matter. I can stay over, no problem. My first meeting isn't till ten."

"My place is a disaster," Leya said. "Talk about bombs—it looked like one went off there today, after the workmen got through with it. And they're going to be back with their sledgehammers at 7:00 a.m."

"I want to see you. I've been thinking about you all day."

"I'm sorry, John. It just isn't working out."

The line crackled through a long silence. "You're playing hard-to-get again."

"I'm not playing anything. You're stretched to the limit right now, and frankly, so am I. I've got tests and papers to mark, and lectures to prepare. And this production of *Hamlet* I'm directing—I'm having trouble with one of my cast members. Then there's the renovation and that mess. Not to mention," she added, after a glance at the table where Carter Nash and Joanna Newman were still deep in conversation, "the fact that my father's on my case again."

"About what?"

"What else? The house. He came over this afternoon to supervise my work crew, thinking I wouldn't be there."

"He's worried about them taking advantage of you."

"You sound just like him. I'm not a child, John. I'm fully capable of managing my own affairs."

"Of course, you can. I wish you'd give a little more thought to *our* affair."

I have, Leya mused, and I'm so muddled about it, I'm beginning to wish it had never happened. But she wasn't going to get into that conversation on the phone from Tyler's bar. "Look," she said, "I really am sorry, but it's not my fault some wacko decided to bomb Newton."

Merriman exhaled a long sigh. "I know it's not, honey, but I've had a lousy day, and I was looking forward to tonight. I was hoping you were, too. But," he added, sighing once more, "I guess I'm a boring guy who just doesn't do it for you."

He was holding out his fragile male ego, trembling and palpitating, Leya thought. How could she stomp on it? "That's not true," she said—cowardly lion that she was.

"You mean that?"

"Sure."

"How about tomorrow night, then?"

"I've got *Hamlet* rehearsal till six tomorrow."

"No problem. I'll drive out and take you to dinner. We can invite your dad to join us, if you want."

"Now, why would I want to do that?"

"I'll calm him down for you. We'll have a couple of beers, some guy talk. He's probably feeling cooped up. I'll see if he wants to take in a hockey game or something on the weekend."

A stone seemed to roll off her chest, and Leya felt a warm rush of gratitude. "Oh, John, that's sweet of you. He enjoys your company. He's been a bear lately, but you're one of the few people who seem to cheer him up."

"Good. I like the old coot, too. And listen, while I'm at it, I'll tell him you've made a brilliant investment in your house."

"Do you really think I have?"

"Well…" he hedged.

"Never mind."

"Look, honey, in this market, nobody gets into real estate for the financial return—not in the short run. But if you like the house, that's great. You go ahead and have fun with it."

Leya grimaced. "Why do I feel like I've just been patted on the head?"

"I didn't mean to. I think it's great you'd take on a big project like that. It's just a starter house, after all. I really think we should be checking out the Back Bay area, though. I know we could find something there we both like. But," he added, frustration creeping into his voice again, "we've discussed this before, haven't we?"

Leya felt another stab of guilt. What was wrong with her, that she kept him dangling like this? If she had any guts at all, she'd have done the right thing long ago— moved forward or walked away, once and for all. Wasn't he a good man—intelligent, steady, reliable? And wasn't he terrific at handling her father? That alone earned him points for heaven.

"Sounds like a SNAG," Susan had said, when Leya described her dilemma over what to do about Merriman.

"A snag?"

"A sensitive, New Age guy—and successful and good-looking to boot? Pretty lethal combination, theoretically. But only you can decide if this is someone you can spend a lifetime with."

A lifetime—that was the objective, Leya recalled. People spent lifetimes together. Except in her family. It wasn't like she had many role models, after all.

"So," Merriman said, "I'll come out tomorrow and work on weakening that resistance, shall I?"

Leya leaned against the bar, smiling now. He did have some distracting aptitudes, when she thought about it. "Going to wear me down, are you?"

His voice dropped to a low rumble. "Only in the most gratifying of ways."

"How can I refuse?" She laughed. "Okay, my place, around six? You've still got a key, right? In case I'm running late?"

"Yep. Are you going to invite your father?"

"Depends how crazy he makes me. As a matter of fact," Leya added, casting another puzzled glance at the whisperers in the corner, "he may have plans of his own."

"Plans? Like—*date* plans, you mean? With a woman?"

"Could be. I'll tell you tomorrow."

Newton, Massachusetts: 6:33 p.m.

VanAken and young Agent Berger were standing before the wreckage of the Data-Trax building, being brought up-to-date by the acting SAC, Curtis Pullen, when they spotted a very tall man approaching in the company of a police officer. Bloodstains smeared the man's suit, and his face was scratched and soot-marked. Otherwise, he appeared to be uninjured.

"You guys FBI?" the cop asked. They nodded. "I'm Sergeant Greer, Newton PD. This here is Mr. Sennett, vice president of Data-Trax. He was just brought out of the building. Mr. Sennett, why don't you tell the agents what you told me?"

The big man reached out a hand to Pullen and then Berger, but vanAken's attention was fixed on the damaged building when the hand came toward him. After a second's hesitation, the VP withdrew it and addressed the others. "Mike Sennett, VP for administration," he said. Despite his shaken appearance, his voice was firm. "You people are in charge of this investigation?"

"I am," Curtis Pullen said, throwing his shoulders back

and his chest out. He looked like a penguin working on his command presence, vanAken thought, turning to the other men. "Newton PD called us in. I understand you people are doing federal defense work?"

Sennett nodded. "Data-Trax has been in the forefront of medical scanning technology for several years—CT scanners, magnetic resonance imaging, that sort of thing. That's what we're best known for. But a few years back, we branched out into long-range imaging. A while ago, we won a major federal contract to work on the next generation of overhead surveillance satellites. Most of the research work is being done here in the Newton facility."

"Was that made public?"

"It's certainly well-known within the industry. Anybody who reads *Aviation Week* could have picked it up."

"Do you know anyone in particular who might have wanted to target the company?"

Sennett shrugged. "We get occasional letters of protest from the lunatic fringe, like most defense contractors, but I know of no specific threats."

"Well, it seems pretty likely this was an act of terrorism, all the same," Pullen said. "Which means we're probably talking federal jurisdiction, here."

"There could be an international connection," the VP said, nodding.

"What makes you say that?"

"I was just telling the officer here, we had a suspicious character come in late this afternoon. The explosion happened right after he left."

"Suspicious? How?"

"He was an Arab—Palestinian, I think. He came in for a job interview."

Suddenly, vanAken was interested. "Name?" he asked, stepping forward.

The Data-Trax VP turned to him. "I can't remember, unfortunately."

"Can you give me a description?"

"'Fraid I can't help you there, either. My director of personnel did the interview, but he got hurt. Ambulance left with him a little while ago. Rosenberg had just dropped by my office and started telling me about this guy, when all hell broke loose. When the windows shattered, he got glass in his eyes," Sennett added, head shaking. "He may lose his sight."

"And what did he say about this Arab?" Pullen demanded, edging vanAken aside, as if to clear up any confusion over who was in charge.

The VP seemed momentarily irritated by the decibel level, but he turned his attention back to the SAC. "Apparently the fellow was an engineering student from MIT. Applied for an opening we had, looked good on paper. Said his citizenship was American, naturalized, but Rosenberg said he had an accent. The guy also mentioned that he'd spent time in a Palestinian refugee camp."

"As a federal contractor," Pullen said, "you'd need security clearances on all your employees. Wouldn't happen if the guy was suspected of having even a remote connection to the PLO or some other group like that."

Sennett nodded. "That's what Rosenberg figured, too. We're barred from asking questions about ethnic background on our applications, just citizenship, so it's hard to know in advance whether there's going to be a problem. Mind you, we've got a real mix of people here. Lots of foreign-born—Vietnamese, Chinese, Indians. Takes a while to get a security clearance in some cases, but if they're good, we're willing to wait. Some of these people are top-notch, and damned hard workers to boot."

"But your personnel chief ruled out this guy, even before requesting a security clearance?"

"Yes, once he'd met him and sensed what his background was. Guy had an fairly common Muslim name, so Rosenberg had figured from the application that the guy could be Pakistani or Malaysian or something."

"A common name?" vanAken pressed. "Like 'Muhammad' or 'Ali'?"

"No, I don't think so, but I can't remember what it was. Maybe it'll come to me. Anyway, when the guy mentioned spending time in a PLO camp, Rosenberg figured the security clearance was a nonstarter, given the kind of work we do, so he cut the interview short."

The VP's gaze shifted to the mayhem around them. A backhoe had been brought in to attempt to excavate the collapsed tunnel, rescuing parents and children still trapped. Two toddlers, one critically injured, had already been pulled out, but a few minutes earlier, the backhoe had to be abandoned when its vibrations threatened to set off another underground avalanche. Rescuers were on their hands and knees now, frantically removing debris, piece by piece.

Sennett's hand went to his forehead, and his voice, when he spoke again, was shaky. "I don't know—maybe this guy realized he was getting the bum's rush, and got angry enough to do this."

"He'd have had to come prepared," Pullen said. "More likely, the employment application was a ruse to get into the compound. Can we get the paperwork on him?"

The VP inclined his head toward the devastated building. "It'll be up there somewhere, along with a couple of tons of soaked files and scattered computer printouts."

"What about security?" vanAken asked. "I noticed cameras over the main gate. He would have been photographed coming in, wouldn't he? At the very least, we could get a make on his car.''

"Yep. We've got cameras at the building's front door, too—or used to have," Sennett amended, giving the tangled pile of steel and concrete another rueful glance. "Input from those cameras is recorded on videotape. I'm sure we'll have the guy's face on them, except..."

"Except what?"

"The cameras are wired to a recording system located in the security office."

"Which is where?"

"In the basement, directly under the lobby."

All the men stared again at the ruin. "Buried," young Agent Berger said glumly, pointing out the obvious.

"What about a visitors log?" vanAken asked. "Did the guard at the main gate keep one?"

"Yes, that's right, he would have!" Sennett said, brightening. Then, his shoulders slumped again. "But the security shift changed over at four-thirty. If the day man had already gone off duty, he would have submitted his log before leaving the compound. That means it would be in—"

"Don't tell me," vanAken said. "The security office, right? Which means the log's buried, too."

"And maybe the guard as well, if he didn't get away quick enough. I don't know if he's accounted for yet."

VanAken turned to Pullen. "We need to task an excavation crew to get down there, right away."

Sergeant Greer had been standing quietly off to one side, but he stepped forward, shaking his head. "Not a good idea. Engineers say what's left of the structure's fragile as hell. We're still trying to locate and haul out victims. The sniffer dogs just arrived. We get too many people crawling around over there, the whole thing could collapse before we have a chance to get everyone out.''

"If this is our guy," vanAken argued, "chances are he's already heading for an airport and a flight out of the country. We need to ID him on the double. If we wait, we'll miss our chance.''

"I can't allow any more of our employees' lives to be placed in jeopardy," the vice president countered.

"You want a bomber to walk away scot-free?"

"Of course, I don't! But you're not—"

"Hold on, Mr. Sennett," Pullen intervened. "We aren't going to do anything to hinder the rescue effort. Getting the victims out is priority number one. *Then* we'll locate those logs," he added, fixing vanAken with a glare intended to stifle him.

It didn't work. "There's no time to wait. We need those security logs and recordings.''

"Those are my orders, agent! I suggest you try to find other witnesses who might be able to tell us more about this Arab, or anything else out of the ordinary they might have noticed today. Then you'll—"

"I want that name, and I want it now." VanAken wheeled away from the other men and headed down the drive toward the main gate.

8

Leya pushed aside her plate and leaned toward her father. After the phone call to cancel her date, she'd opted for a quick bite before heading home to tackle the pile of work she could no longer avoid, now that John—the whole question of John—was postponed for another day. Her father's blue eyes flitted around the room, following Joanna Newman, who'd gone to handle the dinner crowd. His expression reminded Leya of her students whenever Tyler was on duty behind the bar.

"What's with you and Mrs. Newman?" she asked.

His attention snapped back, and he frowned at the grin she was having trouble suppressing. "Nothing. Why?"

"I didn't even know you and she were on a first-name basis, let alone exchanging family histories."

"We haven't."

Leya arched one eyebrow. "Grandma's gooseberry preserves? First I ever heard of them."

"Subject happened to come up. Joanna researches traditional American cookery."

"Watches your vitamin levels, too, it seems. What other tonic interests do we share, hmm? Therapeutic massage? Herbal aphrodisiacs?"

"You watch your mouth, young lady."

"Oh, relax, Dad, it's nothing to be embarrassed about. You're allowed."

"Allowed what?"

"To have a girlfriend."

"Don't be ridiculous."

"Why is it ridiculous?"

"I'm too old for that nonsense." He crumpled his napkin and slapped it down on the table. "And even if I weren't, what would she see in an old goat like me?"

"Are you kidding? You're a handsome devil."

"Hmph!"

"And she's a lonely widow."

Nash frowned. "She's been widowed a long time. She told me her husband died before their son was born. A woman like that, seems strange she never remarried."

"She's certainly taken a shine to you."

Her father said nothing, turning his attention to his coffee cup, swirling the last of the brew. But then, his gaze rose again, following a path toward Joanna's cheery voice, and something melancholy flickered across his features. Given his usual orneriness, Leya found the vulnerability of that look disconcerting. To a mother hen like Joanna Newman, she guessed, it'd be a killer.

The Newmans lived at Bethany Hill, a small farm just outside Winslow, bordering the Mount Abbey campus. Reportedly, Joanna—ancient flower child that she was—cultivated huge gardens of the fruits, vegetables and blooms that she used in her cooking and crafts. The farm also had the reputation as the hangout of choice for Tyler's friends and assorted young people when he was off duty—her "strays," Joanna called them indulgently. It was no real stretch, therefore, to imagine the softhearted Joanna Newman taking on the hard-nosed Carter Nash. They were such polar opposites, Leya thought, that it was probably inevitable they'd be drawn to one another.

She reached out and covered her father's hand with hers. He let it rest there a second, then drew back. "Dad?"

"What?"

"Do you ever wish…"

"What?"

"That you'd married again? After my mother died?"

He seemed startled by the question and took a sudden interest in the red-checked tablecloth as if a microphone might be hidden in the warp and woof of its fabric. Finally, he sat back and murmured, "For your sake, maybe."

"My sake?"

"You needed a mother."

"I was fine. I had you—and Bhu, the old sweetie."

"It's not the same."

Leya shrugged. "You don't miss what you've never known." That wasn't entirely true. She liked to think she'd come to terms with her motherless state, but still remembered the envious ache of the child she'd once been, watching friends wriggle away from their mothers' schoolyard kisses. She wouldn't have wriggled away, she'd always thought. "What about you? You must have been lonely, and there was more than one lady over the years who'd have been happy to be the next Mrs. Carter Nash."

"No, they wouldn't, not really. The way I lived wasn't what most women wanted in a marriage. And anyway," he added quietly, "after Elena…" His broad chest rose and fell.

"Nobody else measured up, did they?"

"Not by a long shot."

Leya watched him twist his napkin into a tight coil. This was the closest this reticent man had ever come to admitting the depth of his feelings for her mother. And yet, she thought, what a passion it must have been, when even now, thirty years after her death, he could barely bring himself to utter her name.

This was also one of the few conversations they'd ever had on the subject of Leya's lost parent that didn't involve strictly factual details, like the color of her hair or her eyes, or the music she played, or the way some aspect of Leya— her walk, for example—reminded Nash of Elena. Even those conversations had been few and far between. As a little girl, Leya had learned that, if she persisted in her childish quest to build a picture of her mother, he would suddenly remember he was late for some meeting. Rather than drive him away, too, she'd learned to avoid the subject.

Her father looked up. "John must have been disappointed you couldn't make it into town."

"I'll see him tomorrow. It's just as well. We both have a lot on our plates right now."

"You're taking on too much."

"I don't think I am."

"John says he has trouble getting hold of you."

"It's not like he's sitting on his thumbs, waiting for me to show up, you know. He's busy, too."

"I know. He's a hard worker. It wouldn't kill you to be a little more supportive."

"*I* work hard, too, Dad!"

His thick white brows knit together. "You need to get your priorities straight. He's not going to wait around forever."

She shook her head, incredulous. "I can't believe I'm hearing this. Whose father are you, anyway?"

"Yours, but I won't always be here to watch over you. I don't want you ending up all alone."

She could almost hear his subtext—alone like me.
"There are worse things than being single."

"It's my fault, I suppose. I haven't set much of an example for you."

"It's not that. In principle, I'm not opposed to marriage.
I'm just not sure I've met the right person yet."

"I don't know what you're expecting. Merriman's
steady and solid—"

"A real brick."

"He's loyal—"

"So's a golden retriever."

"What do you want? Prince Charming? A bolt of lightning? That's fairy-tale stuff. In real life, you meet a person,
you tally up the credits and debits, and if the pluses outweigh the minuses—"

"Is that how you chose my mother?"

Nash was taken aback. "I—no."

"Bolt of lightning, wasn't it?" He said nothing, but
Leya knew she'd scored. "What about Susan and Grace's
mother? Was that another bolt?"

"No, it wasn't the same with Rose."

"Why did you marry her, then?"

He shrugged. "We'd known each other a long time."

"So?"

"Everyone expected us to get married."

"Expected?"

"That's what you did in those days," he snapped. "You
didn't just flit from relationship to relationship! You made
a commitment."

"Even if you didn't really love the person?"

"We cared for one another. People were more practical."

"I care for John, but that's not enough, however many

tick marks he gets in that 'plus' column of yours. And being 'practical' didn't make you happy, did it?''

"I didn't worry about being happy."

"It obviously didn't make Rose happy, either, in the long run."

"It wasn't the marriage. It was the way I lived she objected to."

"The way you lived was part of who you were. You don't pick and choose pieces of a person, keep those you like and trash the rest. Your needs just weren't compatible. It seems to me that neither are John's and mine," Leya said, "fond as I am of him."

"Compatible needs! Touchy-feely psychobabble. You sound just like Susan."

"You couldn't make Rose happy, nor she you," Leya insisted. "You weren't meant for one another. You understood that when you met Elena, didn't you?" He said nothing. She folded her arms. "I rest my case."

Nash fell silent. For a very rare change, Leya thought, she'd gotten the last word. She'd also managed to wrestle a few scraps of meaningful conversation out of him on matters of the heart, a topic he'd always run from. She watched him back into his corner like some great white tiger, temporarily subdued. It was a hollow victory, she decided. He was old and tired. Why did she still feel the need to try to best him in this war of wills they'd been fighting for as long as she could remember?

Joanna Newman breezed up to the table, as if she sensed the need to cut the knot of their tension. "More coffee, anyone?"

"Not for me, thanks," Leya said. "I should be off. I've got a ton of work to do."

"How about you, Carter? Are you in a hurry, too?"

"Not especially."

"Stick around, then. I'll bring the paper and join you in a while. Things are quiet tonight."

The deep line between his eyebrows softened perceptibly, and Leya felt another stab of guilt. "I'll be off, then," she said, rising from her chair. Remembering her original reason for coming, she turned to the other woman. "I was hoping to run into Holly Stroud, Joanna. You haven't seen her today, have you?"

"Holly? No, I haven't. Not for quite a while, I'm afraid."

Leya tried to read her expression. "Is something wrong?"

Joanna sighed. "Holly and Tyler were seeing each other, but they broke up."

Leya glanced over at the bar. No wonder he'd looked so uncomfortable when Leya had asked about Holly's whereabouts. "I see. Well, Holly's been acting a little odd lately, but I guess that would explain it. She seemed very fond of your son."

"Not fond enough, it seems."

"How so?"

"Oh, I don't know," Joanna said, pulling back. "Maybe Tyler's mistaken. I'd hate to spread stories if they weren't true."

"I'm her faculty counselor, Joanna. If Holly's got a problem, I'd like to help. I feel a special responsibility toward her. Her parents are out of the country, you know." Joanna nodded, and Leya added, "I promised I'd keep an eye on her. Until recently, she seemed fine, but lately, she's been kind of edgy." Leya bit her lip worriedly. "It's not drugs, is it?"

Joanna sighed. "I don't know. The worst of it is, I feel responsible."

"You? How?"

"I introduced them."

"Who?"

"Holly and Karim."

"Who's Karim?"

"Karim Khoury. One of my strays."

Newton, Massachusetts: 6:41 p.m.

The minute vanAken walked out the main gate of the Data-Trax compound, a horde of reporters lunged forward like a pack of dogs picking up a quarry scent. Up to then, they'd been corralled behind wooden barricades and yellow crime-scene tape, but the cops on guard were taken by surprise at the surge, and the barrier toppled. Half-a-dozen cameras swung in vanAken's direction, blinding him with their lights.

"Excuse me! Channel 4 News—"

"*Boston Globe,* here! And you are—?"

"What's the word? Was it a bomb?"

The police moved quickly to re-exert control, but not before one reporter had squeezed past them and thrust a microphone under vanAken's nose. VanAken reacted instantly, smacking the mike aside and grabbing the man's arms. Spinning him around, vanAken frog-marched him, tippy-toed and double time, back to the line.

"Get that thing out of my face and clear the hell out of here!" he snarled, shoving the reporter away. He spun toward the cops. "Keep these vultures behind the damn barricade!"

As they scrambled, vanAken strode over to the small brick structure that served as the main guard hut. Inside, a skinny kid with bad skin was cowering on a stool in one corner. The word Security was embroidered in fluorescent-yellow thread on oval patches stitched to his cap and windbreaker. As always, vanAken marveled at the stupidity of so-called security experts. The patch on the kid's jacket, directly over his heart, would make an ideal target for a high-powered rifle. The one on his hat would draw the perfect head-shot.

"FBI," he said, flashing his shield.

"Yes, sir."

"You're the night guard?"

"Yes, sir. Chris Hearn."

"What time did you come on duty?"

"My...my shift starts at four-thirty," the kid stuttered.

"Did you sign in a guy who had an appointment with a Mr. Rosenberg in Personnel?"

"No, sir. I—"

"Or sign him out?"

"Visitors are signed out at the main desk inside, sir. We don't log departures here, just arrivals."

"The guy on the shift before yours—had he already left when the explosion happened?"

"Yes, sir, only just. Actually, I was a bit late getting to work. I didn't mean to be, except—"

"I don't care about that. The day guard—what happened to his arrivals log?"

"The logs are usually turned in at the end of each shift—"

"Shit!" vanAken muttered.

"—but he didn't."

"What?"

"It wasn't his fault. It was mine, because I was late, so I said I'd do it for him. We called up and cleared it with the chief, and he said it was okay 'cause Larry—he's the day man, Larry Krebs—he had a dentist appointment. Had a toothache and needed a root canal, only now he was running late on account of me, and—"

"Where's the bloody log?"

The kid held out a clipboard. "Right here."

VanAken snatched it away and ran his finger up the page, looking for an Arab-sounding name. None of the entries sounded right.

"Underneath, sir," the young guard ventured nervously.

VanAken looked up. "What?"

"That's my log on top. Nobody there but family members coming in to pick up employees. Krebs's log is next sheet down."

"Why the hell didn't you say so?" vanAken grumbled. He flipped the page to find a crowded table of scrawled entries, each one noting a time, a name, a Data-Trax contact for the visitor, and a car license-plate number. He scanned down the page, then froze. In an entry logged in at 4:24 p.m., he found the name of the man who had come to see Rosenberg in Personnel. It was a name vanAken recognized, one that had even flashed through his mind when the company vice-president was describing the young Palestinian job applicant. But until he saw the name actually written down, he wouldn't have believed it possible. "Khoury," he breathed. "What the hell are *you* doing here?"

"Sir?"

VanAken ripped the sheet from the clipboard. "I'm confiscating this."

"I'm not sure—" But vanAken was already on his way out the door. "Sir?" the young guard called after him. "What about the log? I'm responsible for it."

"Not anymore. It's evidence." VanAken strode over to a police car parked across the driveway, and flashed his badge at the cop standing next to it. "FBI. I want you to trace a license plate for me."

The cop peered at the badge, then at the scarred hand

clutching the crumpled sheet. "All right," he agreed dubiously. Slipping into the driver's seat, he swiveled the computer terminal mounted on the center console. "What's the number?"

VanAken gave it to him.

Within minutes, DMV records had provided the information he was looking for. A moment later, the police radio crackled, and the officer lifted the handset. "Three-twelve."

"Greer, here," the voice on the other end said. "You seen an FBI guy out there, name of vanAken? His people are looking for him. Last we knew, he was heading your way."

"He was here, but he's gone now."

"Gone? Where?"

"Don't know. He had me trace a license plate, then disappeared down a back alley, away from the press. Last I saw, he was headed toward Washington Street. You sure that guy was FBI? Sure as hell didn't look like any bureau agent I ever saw."

"Got me. His CO here's fit to be tied, wants him to report in, pronto. Let me know if you spot him again."

"Ten-four."

9

Leya pulled into the driveway of her house. At this point, she didn't know what else to do, except return home and hope Holly Stroud called again. After speaking to Joanna Newman, and earlier, to Mrs. Garibaldi, then remembering the garbled message Holly had left on her machine, Leya was more anxious than ever to speak to the girl. Maybe the situation would turn out to be harmless, but she didn't need her father's arched eyebrow across the table to tell her that the sudden involvement of Ambassador Stroud's daughter with a young Palestinian merited concern.

It was Holly's youthful empathy that had drawn her to this Karim character, Joanna had said. "He came out to Bethany Hill a few weeks ago with one of Tyler's friends. Brian Eglund grew up here in Winslow, and he's studying at MIT now. He and this Khoury fellow were teamed up on some class project, and they were out this way, collecting materials from Brian's parents' house, when they dropped by the farm. Brian was having some problem with his car that he wanted Tyler to take a look at. Tyler's very handy," she added proudly.

"And Holly was there?"

"She came by, yes. She's been spending a lot of her

free time over at Bethany Hill the past couple of months. She seemed to like it out there. Mind you, there's nothing elegant about it, compared to what she's used to, but it's a pretty spot."

"I think she misses her parents. I can understand that, having been a foreign-service brat myself."

"Everyone's welcome at Bethany Hill. In fact," Joanna said, "I was thinking perhaps you and your father might like to come out to dinner. Maybe tomorrow night?"

"I'm afraid I'm tied up tomorrow, but as for Dad…"

"Carter?" Joanna asked, turning to him.

"I'd like that," he said with more enthusiasm than Leya had seen him muster for anything in a long while. Once again, watching the two of them watch each other, she felt like the chaperon at a high-school dance.

"Great. Anyway," Leya prodded, anxious to be on her way and leave them to their own devices, "Holly met this Karim, and…?"

"And they seemed to hit it off," Joanna said, "which was nice. Until Holly showed up, Karim had been hanging in the background while Tyler and Brian talked. Brian mentioned to me later that Karim seemed to have no friends or social life."

"But you made him feel welcome, didn't you?" Leya said, smiling.

"I tried to. And after I introduced him to Holly, and Karim found out her parents were posted in the Middle East, the two of them spent the better part of that evening off in a corner by themselves. I was glad that she'd been able to draw him out a little."

"Was Tyler upset?"

Joanna glanced over at her son, then lowered her voice. "Not really. He and Holly had been drifting apart, you see. Tyler's a working fellow, after all. He hasn't had the advantages some other young people have," she added defensively. "As a single parent, it was all I could do to keep a roof over our heads while he was growing up."

"You did a fine job, Joanna," Nash said. She gave him a grateful smile.

Leya nodded. "Yes, you did. Tyler's a nice guy—and very popular with the girls, isn't he?" she added, smiling.

Joanna rolled her eyes and laughed. "The girls! The calls we get at home, you wouldn't believe!"

"I'm sure. So, he and Holly were drifting apart?"

"Yes. You see, Holly—well, she's idealistic, I suppose. Not very practical, sometimes, but then, she's young, isn't she? Still, Tyler was getting a little exasperated. He'd already decided to break up with her. When Holly started seeing Karim after that night, that seemed to clinch it. Tyler wasn't too impressed with the fellow. To be honest, I found him a little—uh—different, too."

"But are you sure she has, Joanna? Become involved with this Karim, I mean?"

"Tyler seems to think so."

"Could he have been overreacting?"

"Maybe. Not that it matters to him, you understand. He's just not sure it's best for Holly. But what can you do? She has a mind of her own, doesn't she?"

"That's very true."

"Anyway, Tyler's seeing another girl now. And, of course, he's busy here." Joanna waved a hand. "You know how it is with youngsters. They're always falling in and out of relationships."

"I guess you're right. But frankly, I'm worried about Holly. I hope she's all right."

"Oh, she's a bright girl, Leya. She'll be fine, I'm sure."

Newton, Massachusetts: 7:12 p.m.

Gridlock had seized the area's roads, but vanAken gambled that the MBTA commuter line would still be running. Jogging toward Washington Street and the West Newton Station, he arrived in time to leap aboard a westbound train with a scheduled stop at Winslow.

As the train started to pull out, he stood on a platform between two rail cars and glanced into one, then the other. Caught between the devil and the deep blue sea. Both were packed with late rush-hour commuters. VanAken debated remaining where he was for the duration of the trip, but aside from the freezing wind, the wheels were kicking up mud and debris as they accelerated.

Then he noticed the folding seat next to the Rail-Link phone at the end of the car to his right was unoccupied. He slid open the door and squeezed into the space without lowering the seat. Turning his back to the crowd, vanAken pulled out his cell phone and punched in the number of the Boston field office. At his request, the night-duty agent patched him through to the Data-Trax site and Curtis Pullen.

"Where the hell are you?" Pullen shouted.

"En route to Winslow. I traced the registration on that car."

"What car?"

VanAken moved in close to the wall, keeping his voice low. "The one driven by the man that Sennett, the VP, mentioned."

"What?" Pullen snapped across the staticky connection. "What man?"

"The one who came in for an interview just before the incident. The one his personnel chief told him about."

"Well, who told you to do that? I don't recall giving anyone in my command clearance to go running off on wild-goose chases."

"I'm not a member of your command."

"You are as long as you're assigned to this case!"

"Whatever. The point is, I got the name and pulled the DMV records on the car he drove. I want to track down those leads."

"What *you* want, vanAken, is of no interest to me. We're shorthanded until the team from Washington arrives. You're tasked to work the crime scene until I tell you different."

"The car's registered to an address in Winslow," vanAken went on, pretending he hadn't heard. "That's where I was when you called me in on this. My ride's still there."

"What the hell were you doing in Winslow?"

"Working another case," vanAken said—a case that had taken a precipitous downturn of late, he thought, not to mention the fact that an old personal obsession had suddenly reared its ugly head, further undermining what little enthusiasm he had for this work he found himself doing. But Pullen had no need to know any of this.

"You're working this case now," the acting SAC said, "although I'm damned if I know why. Hopefully, I'll be able to release you back to that other investigation in short order. In the meantime—"

"I know this guy."

"*What?*"

"The one who came in for the interview. I know him."

"How do you know him?"

"He—" VanAken hesitated again, but his reluctance had little to do with the crowded rail car. How much did he want to tell this idiot? Not much, he decided. "I've had him under surveillance in the past, that's all."

"Well, you did a piss-poor job of it," Pullen said archly. "And now, he turns out to be our prime suspect. I'd say your ass is on the line, mister."

VanAken ignored the note of triumph. "I can be of most use to the investigation by tracking him down. I know his movements and his contacts. I'm the only one who can piece together where he fits into this business."

"Where he fits? What is this, rocket science? He's smack in the middle, obviously."

"It's not that simple. If he did this, he wasn't acting alone."

"If he—" Pullen spluttered. "You don't find it coincidental that this Arab shows up minutes before a blast takes out a federal defense contractor? How dumb do I seem to you, vanAken? You think you're going to run off and cover up the tracks of your own incompetence? The Bureau is going to have some serious explaining to do when it gets out that your lack of diligence resulted in the deaths of innocent people. I intend to demonstrate that I reined you in, pronto, the minute I found out you screwed up."

"Now just hold on one minute—"

"So you turn around and get your ass back here, you hear me? After I put in a call to Rickhauser, we'll see what further role—if any—there is for you in this case. In the meantime, give me what you've got on that Arab and the car. I'll get the local police to put out an APB. As a matter of fact," the SAC added, "I'm going to release that information. The press is out there, clamoring for something. If I announce we've already got our suspect, the public's gonna know we're really on the ball, here. Might bring in some more leads."

"Bad idea. All you'll accomplish is to set off a wave of hysteria, and send this guy and his accomplices to ground."

"Leave investigation strategy to people who know what

they're doing. You just get the hell back and debrief me on the suspect. Others will take it from here.''

"No, I'm going to bring him in myself. You gather your crime-scene evidence, Pullen, but this character is mine.''

"Don't you—" Pullen's bellow set vanAken's hypersensitive ears to ringing, so he hung up the phone. When he turned, he found the conductor standing beside him, waiting patiently for him to finish his call.

"Ticket?'' the man asked.

VanAken pulled the leather folder out of his breast pocket and flashed his shield. "FBI,'' he said quietly. "Official business.''

The conductor pushed back his pillbox hat and peered at the brass badge. "Is that so? Whaddya know?'' He glanced around, then lowered his voice. "You expecting trouble here? Anything you want me to do?''

"No, nothing.''

"'Cause if you describe who you're lookin' for, I could tell you—''

"I don't expect any trouble on the train. Thanks,'' vanAken added as an afterthought, hoping that would shut the man up.

The conductor looked disappointed. He touched his forefinger to the stiff brim of his hat. "Well, okay then, carry on, officer. Or is it 'agent'?''

"Agent.''

"Right. Well, carry on, agent.'' He nodded again and lumbered on down the aisle, love handles rolling over his belt as he bent to collect tickets from other passengers.

Exhaling deeply, vanAken lowered the seat next to the phone and settled in for the short ride, staring at the spotted vinyl floor, trying to pretend he was alone. But his flesh had begun to crawl, and he sensed he was being watched. He glanced up. Passengers were sitting, standing, rocking to the rhythm of the train. The conversations around him, which had seemed to die down when he flashed his badge, started up once more. Someone laughed. At what? van-Aken wondered anxiously.

He noticed a woman across the aisle, staring openly at him. When their gazes locked, she smiled almost imperceptibly, and her head gave a subtle nod of greeting. Attractive, well-groomed, about his own age, she had an open laptop computer on her knees, but seemed to be finding him more interesting than her work. Casting covert glances at his hands from time to time, her face was a shifting mask of frank curiosity and barely concealed shock. VanAken was reminded of squeamish tourists in Third World countries, simultaneously fascinated and repelled by the sight of leprous beggars.

Tugging down his cuffs and tucking his hands under his armpits, he looked out the door at the space between the cars, trying to focus on the task ahead. The click of the train's wheels counted out pieces of the puzzle. Khoury, Data-Trax, girl, bomb, Winslow, car—

Clammy sweat broke out in beads along his hairline. VanAken felt panic rising in his chest, beginning to claw at him. He tried to fight it. No good. It had been a mistake to get on the busy commuter train, he realized. There were too many people. Bodies seemed to be edging closer, crowding him, filling every last inch of space. Sucking up all the air. He felt as if he'd been sealed alive in a closed, swaying coffin on wheels. He was suffocating.

Backing himself tightly into the corner, vanAken pulled at his shirt collar, gasping for air as the claustrophobic dread washed over him. He inhaled deeply, resisting the sensation of drowning. Stale odors assaulted his nostrils— damp wool, dusty vinyl, the acrid smells of rubber and hot steel. Normal, everyday things, he tried desperately to reassure himself. Boring conversations were going on all around him, about some TV show and somebody's mother's recipe for something.

He forced himself to focus on the *kerchunk-kerchunk* of wheels on rail. It was just a train, he told himself. Just a train. But even as he struggled to find reassurance in the banality of sounds around him, the murmuring voices and thudding wheels grew louder and louder, echoing and reverberating in his ears, combining finally into a single, deafening whine that threatened to split his skull down the middle.

A profound sense of vertigo swept over him, and van-Aken clamped his eyes shut, resisting its dizzying pull. No use. The spinning din spread, filling the corners of his mind. He felt himself turning. Falling. Down, down, down. The rail car and its occupants faded and disappeared, as vanAken spun away, deeper and deeper, lost in dark, woolly silence.

And then, the visions exploded in his head—ominous memories that haunted him day and night. Images of terror, tedium and dread.

He was trapped and helpless once more.

A malignant face hovered above him, shrieking spit-laden obscenities. Howling. Screaming that they knew who he was and what he was. Demanding his secrets. Demanding confession.

The one who called himself Ali was the undisputed leader of the tiny, militant Shiite band that had ambushed him in the street and dragged him off to a basement, deep in the southern suburbs of war-torn Beirut. VanAken knew he was only one of a dozen or more Western hostages, but he soon realized that the bearded young man holding him was more than just another fundamentalist fanatic. Ali was a certifiable sociopath, pure and simple, who delighted in his power and in the infliction of pain. He would work himself into a fury every time he hauled vanAken from his cell to harangue him for imagined crimes. The sessions would begin without warning, day or night, coming to an abrupt end only when Ali grew bored or weary and decided to plunge him back into solitude. His rages were accompanied by vicious beatings, so many of them that vanAken lost count. All he knew was that his body was continually stiff and bruised, encrusted with blood and festering sores. His own stench filled his nostrils.

It went on that way for weeks. Eventually, the beatings grew less frequent, but the situation was no less desperate. His keepers left him in a basement hole, virtually forgotten, for long periods on end. The damp, windowless room, lined with concrete, was lit by a single bulb in the ceiling. A mildewed mattress and two buckets—one for fresh water, one for slops—comprised its only furnishings.

The room was so small that the smelly mattress refused to lie flat. VanAken's head and feet touched opposite walls when he lay himself down to try to lose himself in sleep. His arms, if he could have reached out, would likewise have defined the narrow space. But he couldn't reach out, because his hands were manacled, joined by a length of chain that looped through a heavy iron ring bolted to the wall over his head. Every movement was a struggle against it. Every extension of one hand yanked the other back toward the ring.

He was left alone—day after day, week after week, month after month. His only human contact occurred twice a day when one of Ali's silent underlings clanged open the heavy iron door of the cell, bringing him a fresh water bucket and a plate of stale pita bread, rice and lentils, changing the slop bucket that was his only toilet. Once a week, he was led, handcuffed, to a shower stall down the hall, handed a sliver of soap, and given ten minutes to wash himself and his rank clothes as best he could. The guards stood by, AK-47s trained on him while they watched. Then, dripping wet, clutching his clothes to his chest, he was led naked back to his cell. He had to put his shirt back on before they reattached his chains, or go without it until the next time the guards returned. In hot summer months, when the cell grew stuffy, that was no hardship. But in the frigid cold of winter, a damp shirt drying on his body only increased his misery. Sometimes, he went weeks without washing it.

In those long periods of solitude, the routine never varied, and vanAken thought he would die of the tedium, if nothing else. Despite limited mobility, he devised exercises to keep his muscles toned, most of them involving some variation of resistance against the chains that restricted his movement. And he played mental games, as well, reciting memorized verses of poems in English, Farsi and Arabic, translating them from one language to another. Recalling, in sequence, the names and dates of Egyptian pharaohs and Persian shahs, learned at the knees of his father, a prominent archaeologist who had traveled and worked the length and breadth of the Middle East as vanAken was growing up.

He worked hard to keep his spirits up, too, tapping every resource of faith and inner strength he possessed, stubbornly determined to survive until he was released, rescued or managed to escape. But the loneliness grew so intolerable for him, once the most gregarious of young men, that the return of Ali's obscenity-screaming face could almost provoke him to tears of gratitude. Almost, but not quite.

Day after day, week after week, month after month, year

after year, it went on. Time ceased to have any meaning. He knew only a flat, hellish eternity of blinding light, that screaming voice, harsh blows and red-hot prods, then endless silence in the narrow, damp hole.

Only once in all that time did the routine change. It was during a period of heavy fighting, he guessed from the sounds of bombs exploding all around the building in which they were entrenched. And for a few days, vanAken found himself imprisoned with other foreign hostages, a dozen in all. They had been taken, one by one, over a long period, by young militants promised eternal glory by their fanatic Iranian masters, determined to bring the West, and especially The Great Satan, America, to its knees. Salted away, like emergency currency, to be bartered at the appropriate time for arms and political concessions.

On this occasion, when safe havens must have been at a premium, vanAken found himself blindfolded and crowded with twelve others in a different fetid, dreary space, which echoed with moans, curses and weeping— theirs or his?—and prayers to be free, or to be dead. It amounted to the same thing, really. They were the living dead, who stubbornly refused to die.

If they tried to speak to one another, they were beaten, but they whispered their names in the dark, anyway. And even if they hadn't, vanAken knew from their nightmares that there was a German, two Frenchmen, three Brits, and six Americans. Two of the Americans died in captivity, he later discovered, and he mourned the passing of those brothers in chains with whom he'd spent a few days of the hundreds that he was a prisoner.

But for the rest of the time, he was bound and alone, as day after day, his captors subjected him to their abusive tirades, or to the hole—damp, cold, solitary, with only skittling spiders and cockroaches for company. It went on and on, long after he gave up all hope of rescue or release. Long after the world and anyone he cared for, he concluded, would have written him off as dead. Long after he should have been dead.

Four years. Fifteen hundred and eighty-six days. Thirty-eight thousand hours. Two million, three hundred thousand minutes...

And then, suddenly, everything changed. One day, Ali's screaming face ventured too close, and scarred, bloodied hands—vanAken didn't know whose—grabbed it. Thumbs ground into eye sockets, until the orbs collapsed with a nauseating pop, and the blood-streamed face fell away, mouth twisted in a shriek of agony. Another horrified, murderous face appeared a moment later, but not before those same disembodied hands had produced a length of wire, painfully and painstakingly scratched, over a period of weeks, out of the mesh reinforcement discovered inside the cell's concrete walls—the hole hidden behind the mattress whenever footsteps approached.

And that day, the wire found a throat, the scarred hands found a key and a gun, and the obscenity-screaming faces retreated at last, returning only in the nightmares that had haunted vanAken ever since.

The rail car rocked rhythmically. Somewhere, out on the far edge of awareness, vanAken sensed its motion. His mind reached out and grabbed on to that sanity-preserving scrap of reality, holding it tight. He forced himself to inhale deeply, clearing his air passages of the remembered, hateful reek of his own filth and fear.

Finally, he gratefully discovered that he could smell wool and vinyl once more. He turned his thoughts to other, more soothing memories—of sunlight and warm sand, of the glassine surface of the Mediterranean on a midsummer afternoon. Floating on that comforting image, he felt the tension slowly drain from his exhausted body.

Then, brake pads squealed, metal against metal, and inertial forces pressed him gently into the vinyl padded seat, announcing the train's slowing. Somewhere, a door opened, and a cold gust of air passed over his sweat-dampened face. Shivering, vanAken opened his eyes and looked around. Commuters were buttoning coats and gathering up briefcases. The woman across the aisle was gone, and no one else seemed to be paying him any attention.

Outside, Winslow Station was pulling into view.

10

A short cab ride from the Winslow commuter rail station to the municipal airfield where he'd met the FBI helicopter, and vanAken had his car once more, as well as unfettered freedom to track the enigmatic Karim Khoury.

Although loathe to tell Curtis Pullen more than he needed to know, vanAken had, in fact, been running the young Palestinian for nearly two years, part of some closely held business known to no more than three or four officials in Washington. And most of them had only sketchy details of the undercover counterterrorism operation, code-named Operation Menelaus—MENELOP, in FBI nomenclature. Chosen by vanAken, the name appealed to his inbred love of the classics. In Greek mythology, Menelaus was the Spartan king whose wife, Helen, was kidnapped and held hostage in Troy. After years of warfare, Menelaus managed to spirit a wooden horse and hidden operatives inside the Trojan camp, finally defeating his enemies and retaking what was his.

Within the Palestinian-American community, where a tiny minority was susceptible to the violent dictates of a few power-hungry demagogues, Karim Khoury was a Trojan horse and vanAken was his Menelaus, operating under direct authority of the FBI assistant director, to whom he'd first proposed the operation. No one else, Len Rickhauser had recognized, was as uniquely suited as vanAken to run it.

A decade earlier, as a CIA operative in Beirut, vanAken had arranged a U.S. immigrant visa for a then-thirteen-year-old Karim Khoury, whose parents had died in an Israeli bombing of a refugee camp in southern Lebanon. Karim's grandfather, the former mayor of a West Bank village before the Israeli occupation had driven out his family, had been one of vanAken's regular intelligence sources among the Palestinian exiles. Desperate to save his grandson from the violence that had taken his daughter and son-in-law, the old man had begged vanAken to expedite Karim's departure to live with sponsors in the U.S.

Years later, in the aftermath of the Gulf War and the World Trade Center bombing, vanAken had been stunned to find Karim's name on an FBI watch list of U.S.-based terrorism suspects. The list was unreliable, he knew—the result of a vacuum-cleaner investigative approach that sucked in anyone with an Arab-sounding name or the vaguest connection to the Middle East. Most Arab-Americans deplored fanaticism and violence. Like earlier generations of immigrants who'd fled poverty and strife, they came determined to build peaceful lives and avoided those with other agendas.

Nevertheless, vanAken had decided to take a closer look at the now adult Karim Khoury. The boy's grandfather had since died, confident he'd saved Karim from a probable early death. But the FBI had received intelligence that Karim was being courted by the Izzidin al-Qassam military arm of Hamas, the Palestinian charitable organization that sponsored schools, orphanages and hospitals in the Middle East—and terrorism. The engineering student was a potential "sleeper," bureau analysts calculated—an ideal candidate to carry out an internal attack on Israel's mentor state, should the organization decide to expand its military theater of operations. If he could be motivated by guilty reminders of the debt he owed his martyred parents and his vanquished people, Karim would be Hamas's Trojan horse in America.

To vanAken, Karim had seemed an unlikely soldier for anyone's army. Thin and shy, he claimed to deplore violence as much as his grandfather had. He also wore his Islamic faith lightly. Like back-pew, Christmas Eve Christians, Karim's religion was part of the cultural heritage that defined him, but vanAken had seen no evidence that he found in it a pretext for hatred. Karim had admitted to having been approached by people he thought were Hamas activists, but had said he'd refused to get involved, wanting no part of politics. His ambition, he'd said, was to work in medical or environmental science when he graduated from MIT.

VanAken had spent months checking into his claims and his actions, probing his loyalties. Finally, judging him to be a safe recruit, he'd set out to convince Karim to play along with the local Hamas cell and help the FBI build its case if the group decided to expand its operations to terrorism on U.S. soil. Karim had agreed, reluctantly, to play the infiltrator's role. He'd started attending fund-raisers, political meetings and strategy sessions in mosques, halls and private homes, reporting back to vanAken on what he saw and heard, helping a sometimes-befuddled Bureau distinguish between legitimate charitable activities and potentially violent ones. As with the old Irish-American friendship societies, the trick was always to know whether a dollar raised went for guns or butter—and if it was guns, where those weapons were intended to be used. Slowly,

Karim had seemed to be working his way toward the center of the cell, although nothing he'd told vanAken suggested he was privy to plans for a terrorist operation—on U.S. soil or elsewhere.

Until a few days before the Data-Trax explosion, vanAken had been confident that he had his young informant and MENELOP well under control. Then Karim missed a scheduled meeting. When he failed to show at the prearranged backup rendezvous the next day, vanAken experienced a familiar, sick feeling of having been had.

He told himself it wasn't possible. There was nothing about Karim he didn't know—no detail of the young man's life, before or after his immigration, that he hadn't subjected to intense scrutiny. No claim he hadn't verified through at least three independent sources. As his handler, vanAken had come to know the person inside the life story, as well, spending hours cultivating Karim, earning his trust, bringing him on board. He had tapped the youth's beliefs, his fears and his hopes, remolding them to his own agenda until, for all intents and purposes, Karim had become his creature. Now, his creature had gone missing.

There could be a simple explanation, vanAken told himself. No matter how well planned an operation, glitches were bound to arise. Murphy's Law. Agents got sick or were waylaid by people or commitments they couldn't escape without arousing suspicion. They had accidents. They got drunk. They forgot contact locations or dates. They saw shadows and panicked.

But not Karim, he realized. Karim was intelligent and focused. In all the time vanAken had been running him, forcing him to memorize complex and ever-changing arrangements for dead drops, contacts and emergency backups, he'd never fumbled. Not once. Until now. Why now?

Given the danger of the operation, particularly to Karim

himself, communication between the two had, from the start, been subject to strict security arrangements. But in a worst-case scenario—if Karim feared his cover was compromised, or that he had picked up an unshakable tail, or that his life was in danger—he had an emergency telephone number and a single code-word committed to memory. One call, thirty seconds, tops, and he would have been whisked off the streets and hidden so effectively, his own shadow would have had difficulty finding him.

But Karim had never made the call. Which meant he was dead, or captured, or had been turned by the competition. Or, vanAken now feared, Karim had been committed to the other side from the very start, and he himself had been suckered. Once again.

The previous morning, still brooding over the scrubbed backup rendezvous, vanAken had decided to pay a visit to Cambridge, Massachusetts, and to the run-down boarding-house near MIT where Karim lived. But sauntering up to the front door violated every rule of intelligence gathering and common sense. Until that point, he had never approached Karim on open ground, unless they'd taken elaborate security precautions. If the FBI had an interest in the young Palestinian-American, so had others. Showing his hand now, risked destroying two years of careful work.

Hovering down the block from the rooming house, located in a seedy area of Cambridge beyond the ivy enclaves of Harvard, Radcliffe and MIT, vanAken kept an irritable watch for his man, or for some other emissary who might have inspired Karim to abandon his mission and follow another path. Nothing. After eight hours of unfruitful surveillance, he decided the situation called for a gamble.

Pulling into a blind alley behind an Italian grocery, van-

Aken popped the trunk of the car and flipped open a suitcase. Tossing his sport coat aside, he withdrew a tie and knotted it around the neck of his denim shirt. It was a godawful piece of work, with vibrant red-and-yellow golfers swinging and putting down a field of polyester green, but its garishness possessed the virtue of drawing eyes away from the wearer's face. A Kevlar vest went on next, as much to fill out and camouflage vanAken's lean frame as for protection against possible ambush. Then, a nondescript navy windbreaker.

Rummaging through the suitcase's side pockets, stuffed with badges and fake ID cards, vanAken selected a plastic name tag with the words B. Williams, Customer Relations engraved under the logo for NYNEX, the New England telephone company. Large corporations were a spy's best friend, their vast operations and bureaucratic anonymity providing ideal cover. After pinning the name plate to his chest, vanAken clapped a ball cap with matching NYNEX logo onto his head and wound a rubber band around the ends of his shaggy hair. He tucked the short ponytail into the collar of his shirt, giving himself a close-cropped look, then pulled on a pair of tinted, thick-lensed glasses, which distorted the size, shape and color of his gray eyes.

Finally, a paper-laden clipboard clutched to his chest, vanAken glanced at his reflection in the car's side window. Satisfied that he looked like the kind of generic service rep who attracted no notice, he slammed the trunk of the Taurus and headed back to the street. Mounting the rickety stoop of the boardinghouse, he took a deep breath and rang the bell. Just as the handle of the inside door began to turn, he remembered to give the cuffs of the loose-fitting windbreaker a tug, pulling them down well over his mangled hands. Then he flipped through the dummy computer printout sheets on the clipboard, feigning a busy schedule.

"Yes?" a querulous voice asked.

VanAken peered through the window of the aluminum storm door. Nothing. He hesitated, confused.

"*Yes?*" the voice repeated, louder. Irritated now.

His gaze dropped, and he located its source—a squat, elderly woman in a flowered housedress and bulky-knit cardigan. Four-six or -eight, she seemed wider than she was tall, an aged and miniature sumo wrestler in drag. She peered up at him suspiciously.

"Hello, Mrs.—ah—" VanAken paused, flipping papers for a moment, as if searching for a name. It was in his head, of course, not on the meaningless printouts. The first thing he'd done two years earlier, even before approaching Karim, was to run a background check on every occupant of the house, including the owner. "Mrs. Debycky. My name is Bill Williams. I'm with the phone company, ma'am, customer relations. I have some questions—"

Suddenly, Mrs. Debycky was transformed into a four-and-a-half-foot pit bull. "I'm not paying that bill! I explained it to you people already. I didn't make those calls."

"You didn't?" vanAken asked, mystified.

"No! So don't you think you're going to stick me with them. You people and your computers—think you can't make a mistake. Think old people are stupid, won't notice if you pad our bills. Well, you think again! I'm on a fixed income, but does anybody care? Oh, no! They just go ahead and bill you for anything, or call at all hours, try to sell you something and won't take no for an answer, or give you a bunch of malarkey about being a grand prize winner, like you was born yesterday and didn't know all they want is your money. And then, you people! Like I told that young girl when I called about the phone bill—"

She finally paused to inhale. VanAken plunged into the

opening, grateful for her oxygen requirement and for the tactical advantage she'd unwittingly given him. "Well, that's just why I'm here, Mrs. Debycky. To see if I can straighten out this problem with your bill."

"You are?"

"Yes, ma'am. Could I come in?"

Her suspicious expression hardened, and she made no move to open the door. "Not much point. You're not going to change my mind. Don't think you are, because I'm a person, when I'm in the right, I don't back down. My late husband, Walter, used to warn people. He'd say, 'Don't cross Bella, 'cause she gets mad, she's a dog with a bone, and she don't give up for nothing.'"

Bella Debycky spread and planted her stumpy legs, and folded her wrists across her chest—arms too short and bosom too ample to quite manage the defiant gesture she'd intended. She had hair the color of rusted plumbing and drawn-on eyebrows to match. Except her eyesight must be failing, vanAken thought, because the brows were scratched unevenly, one higher than the other, giving her a permanent expression of irritated surprise. Karim had mentioned that the woman could be difficult, but having come this far, vanAken intended to get into the house, one way or another, even if it meant bowling over the old battle-ax.

He made one last attempt at appeasement. "I'm sure you're right, Mrs. Debycky. The computers often make billing mistakes. If you could just get me your copy of that bill, I'll bet I can straighten this out in no time and be on my way."

She seemed to waver. Her arms dropped, and she looked deflated—as if a nice little tussle would have been just the thing to brighten her dull day. "All right, then, that's more like it," she grumbled. "Might as well come in while I fetch it. You're lettin' all the heat out.'' She unlatched the storm door and shuffled back.

Stepping into the vestibule, vanAken ran smack into a lurking cat. ''Oops! Sorry, puss.'' The tabby skittled behind the old woman, then peeked around her chunky legs, meowing pathetically. Both of his ears were chewed and tattered, and one eye was sewn shut.

''Oh, it's not your fault. He's always getting underfoot. Go on now, Rufus, git!'' But the cat stayed where he was, insinuating himself around the woman's wrinkled stockings, letting out another pitiful cry. She bent down with a grunt. ''You stupid, mangy thing!'' Her gentle scratching behind the mangled ears belied the harshness of her words.

''Rufus looks like he's been through the wars.''

''Seems like. He's an old stray one of my boarders found in the alley a coupla winters back. They all know my policy—no pets. But there old Rufus was, half froze, all chewed up, one eye gone. What could I do? Had to let him stay for the night, anyway, didn't I? 'Course, once he got cleaned up and warm and fed, no way was he puttin' foot outside again. Just settled right in, didn't you, Rufus, like you was king of the castle? Lotta damn gall, you ask me.'' All this time, she'd gone on stroking him, and vanAken could have sworn the cat was smirking. The woman finally straightened with another grunt. ''I'll go find that bill. Wait here,'' she ordered, shuffling off down a long hall toward the back of the house.

As her footsteps receded, vanAken moved away from the door. Rufus followed, slithering between his legs, clamoring for attention. ''Shh, damn cat,'' he whispered. The animal only meowed louder. VanAken set aside his clipboard and picked him up. Cradling the cat in his arms and scratching his tattered ears, he conducted a quick visual search of the entryway. Two pairs of winter boots,

one a woman's style, the other a man's, were lined up in
a boot tray. The men's pair looked to be about a size
eleven, too large for the slightly built Karim. He opened
the hall closet. It was jammed with coats, but the green
down parka Karim usually wore didn't seem to be there.
Kid was always cold.

VanAken wiped his feet hurriedly, then walked out of
the vestibule and into the long central hall. It was a gloomy
space, smelling faintly of must and old lemon oil. Brown
wallpaper covered the wall. Its pattern might once have
been floral. A couple of long strips, like iodine-soaked ban-
dages, peeled down one corner, as if the old house were a
casualty of Revolutionary War battles.

Still stroking the cat, vanAken stuck his head into a
room off the hall to the left. A sagging sofa and chair and
an old console television squatted on a Persian carpet that
had seen better days. No, his brain registered, not Persian—Turkish. An old Ushak pattern, pre-Islamic, as evidenced by the bird motif on the carpet's border. Islamic
law, or *Sharia,* forbade the representation of human or animal figures. VanAken bent closer, curious to see if the
carpet really was an Ushak or, more likely, a reproduction.
Then, he pulled up sharp. *Get on with it! You didn't come
to examine artifacts.*

Turning back to the hall, he peered up a scuffed, paint-
chipped staircase running along the right wall. He knew
Karim's room was on the second floor of the three-story
house, but there was no way he could get up and down
again before the old woman came back. He racked his
brain for some pretext to go up and look around. Checking
additional phones, maybe? Malfunctioning telephone
jacks? He spotted a phone on a table in an alcove under
the stairs. Did the old woman even *have* an extension?

As he pondered his options, the landlady returned.

"Here," she said. "I've marked the ones I'm not paying for."

VanAken put down the cat, who protested loudly, and took the slip of paper she held out. She had circled six items, all of them calls within the 617 area code, amounting to a grand total of about four dollars in toll charges. Clearly, no fraud was too insignificant to escape the eagle-eye notice of Bella Debycky. He did a double take when he panned across the page and realized all the calls had been made to numbers in Winslow, Massachusetts.

"You don't know anyone in Winslow?"

"Not a living soul." Her jaw jutted defiantly, two bristled hairs sprouting from the point of it.

"What about your boarders?"

"I've only got one at the moment, and he swears these aren't his. He's from Indiana, and he does make long-distance calls to his folks back there, but he's never tried to cheat on the phone bill, so I believe him when he says he didn't make these."

"You only have one boarder?" That wasn't right, van-Aken thought. He knew for a fact that she usually had two or three.

"Right now. One of them moved out at Christmas, and I can't rent his room, 'cause it's on the top floor, and the roof's sprung a leak. Made a big mess on the ceiling. Been too icy to get anyone up to fix it. Anyway, that one left before those calls were made."

"No one else in the house could have made them?"

"No. There was Karim, but he's gone now—"

VanAken felt his blood freeze. "Gone?"

"Yeah. He was an engineering student. An Arab, actually, but he was all right, even so. Polite. Clean and sober. They don't drink, you know. Always paid his rent on time, too, cash. All those Arabs are loaded, you know."

If Karim were loaded, vanAken thought, he wouldn't have been living here. "Maybe that fellow made these calls?"

She shook her head. "Not likely. Didn't have any friends that I ever saw. He was a real hard worker, though, I have to give him that. Studied in his room till all hours. You hardly knew he was around, most of the time."

"But you say he's gone? Where? When?"

VanAken worried that the landlady might find it odd that a telephone man was so nosy about her former lodger, except from her look of consternation, it seemed Mrs. Debycky was wrestling with an even bigger puzzle. "Well, now, that's the funny thing. I'm not sure."

"How's that?"

"He just vanished three days ago. It was the day I got this phone bill. I shouted up the stairs to ask Karim if he knew anything about those calls, but he didn't answer, so I figured he must have left for class while I was out shopping. But he never came home that night—which was strange. He usually kept pretty regular hours."

"You're sure he wasn't up there?" *Isn't* up there? van-Aken thought, his mind swirling with visions of a dead body in Mrs. Debycky's second-floor room. With the door closed, a couple of days could pass before a body became sufficiently pungent to cut through the musty brume of the old house.

"Real sure. I went up. That's when I knew he was gone for good."

"How?"

"His room was empty. All his books and clothes and things, gone. I can't complain, mind. Place was wiped down, clean and shiny as a new whistle."

No fingerprints, vanAken registered.

"My other boarder never saw him leave, neither. What

we can't figure is how Karim managed to carry all his stuff down the stairs, what with the crutches and all. But maybe he took a cab and the driver helped him.''

"Crutches? He was on crutches?"

"Yep. Broke his foot last weekend. So it seems like a fool time to up and move, now, don't it? Not that it's any of my business. I don't poke into my boarders' private affairs, mind. Long as they follow rules, they pretty much come and go like they want. And Karim left an envelope with three months' rent in it—paid up past the end of term, so it's no skin off my nose. Still, it seems strange.'' She shrugged. "Maybe that's how they do it over there where he comes from. Kind of rude, though, dontcha think?''

"In that envelope—did he leave a note? Or a forwarding address? So we can ask him about those calls,'' vanAken added hastily, for fear the landlady might finally twig to the fact that he was asking too many questions about her missing tenant.

"Just a line. Said he'd had a job offer all of a sudden, had to relocate. And there was a phone number.''

VanAken's hopes soared. "Have you got it?''

"Nope. I threw it out. It was a wrong number.''

His hopes plummeted again. "How do you know that?''

"I called, but it was the Burger King over on Concord. He musta gotten the number mixed up.'' Mrs. Debycky waved her forefinger at the bill in vanAken's hand. "Anyway, I'm pretty sure he never made these calls, and I'm not paying—''

"No problem, Mrs. Debycky.'' VanAken fastened the invoice to his clipboard. "I'll make sure your bill is settled up.''

"Because I—'' The old woman paused, openmouthed. She had to know her position was weak, but that had only seemed to make her feistier—at least, until she realized what he was saying. "Settled up? The whole thing, you mean? I don't have to pay any of it?"

VanAken touched the peak of his cap. "We pride ourselves on service, ma'am, especially for our most reliable customers. I don't know whether this fellow stuck you for his calls, or whether, like you say, it was a glitch in our computer. Either way, don't you worry. We'll take care of everything. It's the least we can do."

Mrs. Debycky stepped forward, smiling broadly, and vanAken had a horrifying premonition she was going to hug him. He beat a hasty retreat before she had the chance.

Now, back at the Winslow airfield parking lot, unlocking the car, vanAken plotted his second foray that day into the small town. The first time had been to scope out the addresses on the receiving end of those calls to Winslow from the boardinghouse—and they *had* come from her line. Phone-company computers, despite what he'd told the old woman, were highly reliable when it came to tracking calls. If they hadn't been made by the landlady or her other boarder, then they had to have been made by Karim. Until he'd gotten hold of the Data-Trax arrivals log, those numbers had been the only lead vanAken had as to the whereabouts of his missing agent, so he'd had no choice but to follow where they led.

The irony was not lost on him that his search for Karim had led him to the Nashes, father and daughter. He'd tried not to think about that. He'd always known where they were, but resisted the impulse to do anything about it. Maybe he should have given in long before now, he thought. Dealt with it, then erased them from his mind, once and for all. Self-restraint, after all, hadn't done a damn thing to lay old ghosts to rest.

But personal business would have to stay on the back

burner until he'd resolved the mystery of Karim Khoury. The waters became thoroughly muddied, however, when phone-company records revealed that one of Karim's calls was to a number belonging to none other than Leya Nash. It was that bizarre discovery that had led to vanAken's first tense surveillance of her house and the restaurant to which he'd tailed her and her father—and to his realization that time had done nothing to dull his hatred of Carter Nash. Now, with the Data-Trax bombing and Karim's probable involvement, the stakes had risen dramatically.

Before pulling out of the airfield parking lot, vanAken paused to reread the DMV record on the mysterious car Karim had apparently taken to the Data-Trax facility that afternoon. A glance at a local street map gave him another moment of pause. Curiouser and curiouser.

Slapping a spinning red light onto the Taurus's roof, vanAken careened out of the parking lot and raced toward the town, traffic parting before him like a vehicular Red Sea.

11

Leya's CD player juggled discs, shifting between Mozart, Coltrane and Bonnie Raitt—music to think and be energized by. Except it wasn't working.

She slid her wire-rimmed reading glasses off her nose and tipped back wearily in her oak desk-chair. Swivel-based, it was a newspaper-office cast-off she'd found the previous spring amid items auctioned off when the *Winslow Weekly* had computerized its presses and sprung for some complementary high-tech furniture for its two low-paid staff members.

Leya squeezed the bridge of her nose, trying to pinch off a budding tension headache that was wrapping its tendrils around her skull. No time for this, she told herself, not with papers to grade, a midterm to set, stage positions for *Hamlet* to block, and the minutes of a faculty committee meeting to draft.

Sighing, she pushed up the sleeves of the baggy Boston Marathon sweatshirt she'd changed into before settling down to work, stretched out her jeans-clad legs, and propped her bare feet on the computer table next to her desk. The desk itself was a rolltop, pigeonholed, flea-market beauty that she'd stripped, oiled and polished until the golden oak gleamed. Not that her hard work was displayed to best advantage, at the moment. The desk was jammed up against the bed in a corner of her crowded dining room, and except for the small work space she'd cleared in the center, its surface was buried under teetering piles of books and papers.

But when Ernie Latouche was finished his work and she could spread herself and her belongings out again, the desk would move upstairs, to nestle in the turret room that gave her old house its eccentric air. That sunny front room was going to be her private haven, where she could read, work and think in peace, and make a start on the novel she'd been plotting in her head for years.

When she'd first landed her job, she'd thought she could write between classes at Mount Abbey, but the location of her office had guaranteed a steady stream of visitors, encouraged by the door she felt obliged to leave open—at first, for fear of seeming unfriendly, and later, to underline her personal commitment to accessibility. Good intentions, except she'd soon discovered she was at the mercy of students looking for advice, extensions and sympathy, a departmental head with a mania for committees that needed staffing, and colleagues like Kerry Nyland with firm opinions and loose gossip they were convinced she needed to know. Chronically incapable of saying no, Leya found herself continually squeezed by other people's demands on her time.

Her mortgage papers had been a kind of hopeful declaration of independence from all that, her house the refuge she'd dreamed of since childhood—a place of familiar, comfortable permanence, where she could define herself and be herself. All her life, she'd lived in a series of foreign-service homes that bore the smells of other people's cooking and the scuff marks of other families, whose passage there had been as temporary as Leya and her father's. This old house had its ghosts, too, but they were happy, long-term residents—specters of people who'd been born, lived full lives, and died under the house's eccentric roof-line.

In reflective moments, Leya would imagine the hands that had gripped the old banister in the front hall. Tentative toddler hands, reaching up for support. Grimy, childish hands, rolling toys down its incline. Sweaty teenage hands, leaving on first dates. Callused, work-worn hands, pulling weary bodies upstairs to bed at the end of a long day. Gnarled and feeble hands, tightly gripping the rail, as fearful of falling as the tiny toddler.

Leya swiveled her chair to peer through the leaded-glass doors that separated the dining room from the parlor, whose walls were a deep slate blue, a color she'd settled on only after covering one entire wall with stripes of different, custom-mixed shades, then studying them for several days under various lighting conditions. John Merriman had told her she was making a mistake.

"Paint the whole place out in white," he'd advised. "More practical. Improves your resale chances."

She'd also stripped, sanded, stained and Varathaned the wide-planked, pegged oak floors and the deep Victorian baseboards and moldings, liberating them from decades of paint-crusted imprisonment, returning them to a rich golden glow.

"Colossal waste of time," her father had snorted dismissively. "Next owner will just cover them up again. You'll see."

Not in this lifetime, Leya thought as she slipped on her glasses again and swung back to the essays waiting for her attention. On returning from Tyler's, she'd decided to tackle the Hemingway papers her introductory American lit class had handed in that day. Her youngest students, she found, learned best when she gave their papers quick turn-around, while an assignment was still fresh in their minds. It conditioned them, as well, to respect deadlines, knowing she held herself to the same standard of effort she demanded from them. Also, when it came to freshman papers, work delayed was just pain delayed. Marking them was a grind, until the kids caught on that she could smell a Cliff Notes rewrite at fifty paces and started thinking for themselves.

Picking up her red pencil, she glanced at her watch, dismayed to realize she'd been at it less than an hour. It seemed like longer. Then, she smiled, as something bubbled to the surface of her memory—herself as a child, asking her *ayah* for the umpteenth time when her daddy would be coming home. *"A watched clock never boils, little one,"* Bhu would always reply in her singsong voice.

Leya had hidden in a pantry once, spying on the kitchen clock to see if it would bubble and boil if it weren't *aware* of being watched. Eventually, when she'd repeated Bhu's adage to one of her International School teachers and the teacher had burst out laughing, she'd realized the mistake. But when she'd first seen Salvador Dali's paintings of melting timepieces, Leya couldn't help wondering if old Bhu hadn't been his *ayah*, too.

When she opened the next essay, her smile faded to a grimace as she read. Compared to the garbled prose some of her students handed in, Bhu's malapropisms were a model of clarity.

Leya had worked her way through four more agonized efforts when, mercifully, the doorbell rang. She lowered the volume on the stereo and walked to the front hall. Opening the door, she found Holly Stroud on her front veranda, looking nervous, as if she expected expulsion for skipping rehearsal and missing an assignment deadline.

"Holly! Just the person I've been looking for! I thought I was going to have to call out the National Guard."

The girl's hazel eyes grew huge, and she blanched under the porch light. "I didn't do anything!"

"I'm kidding. But we did miss you at rehearsal today."

"Oh—that."

Leya frowned. "Are you all right?"

"Sure. I'm fine. Why wouldn't I be?" The words were nonchalant, but Holly's arms were wrapped around her body, as if she might jump out of her skin if she didn't hold on tight.

This wasn't the Holly she knew, Leya thought. The daughter Arthur Stroud had asked her to watch over last fall was high-spirited and cheerful. As her designated faculty adviser, Leya knew that some of Holly's other professors found her headstrong and argumentative. Admittedly, she was a challenge in the classroom, where she could always be counted on to champion a minority view. But Leya found her blunt honesty refreshing—even admirable, remembering her own shy and anxious adolescence.

"Come on in," she said, stepping back from the threshold.

"I don't want to bother you. I just…" The girl's voice drifted off uncertainly.

"No bother at all. I could use a break. I was just thinking about a cup of tea. Want some?"

Holly's lips twitched in a fleeting grin. "Earl Grey?" Obviously, she'd endured Mrs. Garibaldi's earnest teatimes, too.

"Do you like Earl Grey?"

"Hate it."

"Good. So do I. Never buy the stuff. Let's see what else we can find."

Still, the girl hesitated, her thick blond curls shimmering under the porch light as she glanced over her shoulder. Leya followed her gaze into the darkened street, puzzled. Nothing. Even the overflow library traffic was gone at this hour. Finally, Holly turned back and stepped into the vestibule. Leya closed the door. "Let me take your jacket," she offered.

"No, it's okay. I…I can't stay long. Really, I shouldn't have—"

"It's all right, Holly, really. I'm glad you came by. Come on, let's go make that tea." The girl followed her down the hall, and Leya cleared a spot on a barstool by the center island. "Sorry about the mess. I'm in the middle of major renovations here. Things are a little tight."

"That's okay," Holly said, perching on the edge of the seat. "I think your house is awesome."

"Why, thank you. I like it, too, but I'm afraid you're the only one who agrees with me."

"No, everyone does. And they think it's cool that you let us come here sometimes."

Leya smiled. At least once each term, she held classes off-campus—a fireside reading of Edgar Allan Poe to coincide with Halloween, or a relaxed discussion over coffee of whatever novel they were working on. "I remember how claustrophobic I used to feel, living on campus," she said, putting the kettle on. "Sometimes, it seemed months would go by before I'd see the outside of Mount Abbey's walls." The young girl nodded, but Leya recalled that Holly seemed to have the campus insularity problem licked—maybe a little too well. "We missed you at *Hamlet* rehearsal."

"I'm real sorry. I called—"

"I found the message on my machine when I got home. I'm glad you called, but that's not the point. Other members of the cast are counting on you, Holly. You have a pivotal role in the play. I know you'll be wonderful as Ophelia, but it won't happen if you don't—" Leya had been pulling out cups and spoons, but she stopped dead when she noticed tears running down the girl's face. "Oh, Holly, I'm sorry! I didn't mean to jump all over you. It doesn't matter about the rehearsal. Tell me what's wrong."

"I think I'm in trouble."

"Trouble?"

She nodded miserably. "Big time. I probably shouldn't be dumping on you, but I didn't know where else to go."

Leya reached out and put a hand on her arm. "I'm glad you felt you could come to me. That's what I'm here for. And whatever it is, I'd like to help."

The girl shook her head, then buried her face in her hands and groaned. "My father's going to kill me!"

Oh-oh, Leya thought, Mrs. G. was right. She's pregnant, and her father probably *is* going to kill her. Arthur Stroud was remote, autocratic and deeply conservative. From what she'd seen and read, his wife, his children, his diplomatic underlings and just about everyone else cowered in his presence. In that respect, he was not unlike her own father. Leya had noticed at last fall's open house, however, that Holly had a knack for teasing smiles and indulgences out of him, and from this, she'd concluded that Arthur Stroud's youngest child was also his favorite. All the more reason why he would not take lightly to her fall from grace. He'd probably disown her and sue Mount Abbey and Leya in the bargain, for gross negligence of the responsibility he'd assigned them.

As she sat down across the counter from Holly, Leya spotted a red cartoon face peering at her from over the opening in Holly's jacket—a Sesame Street character, she realized. Grover? No, the little one with the funny voice. Elmo. "Why don't you tell me what's got you so upset, Holly?"

"You're going to think I'm such an idiot."

"No, I won't."

"Yes, you will. Everyone will. No one's going to believe me when I say I don't know what happened. But I really don't. I'm so scared, Professor Nash. I just happened to be there, that's all, and—"

"Whoa, slow down. You've lost me. Happened to be where?"

"It happened after we left, and we didn't have anything to do with it, I swear."

"With what, Holly?"

"The bomb."

"*What?* What bomb?"

"The one that went off in Newton."

Leya felt the blood drain from her face, and she sat back, stunned. An unplanned pregnancy was one thing, but this— "Holly," she whispered, "you were *there?*"

"Yeah. And now they're looking for me. I heard it on the radio. They've traced my car, and they're looking for me. They think I did it. That Karim and I did it."

Newton, Massachusetts: 9:27 p.m.

Curtis Pullen positioned a chair across the table from Leonard Rickhauser, the FBI's assistant director for criminal investigations. They were in a second-floor meeting room of the Data-Trax employee-services annex, which was being transformed into a temporary command-and-control post for the dozens of FBI, ATF, and local police and fire officials swarming the site.

Around the perimeter of the room, FBI technicians, who'd flown in with Rickhauser, were setting up computer terminals linked by satellite to the J. Edgar Hoover Building in downtown Washington. Over the next few days, as part of the investigation already labeled NEWBOM—bureau shorthand for "Newton bombing"—every conceivable piece of information on the target, the victims and possible suspects would be fed into these terminals. Agents would sift and crosscorrelate each detail, however mundane, searching for connections and known criminal signatures, comparing this bombing to others, ferreting out possible motives for what seemed to be a blatant act of terrorism. With luck, a pattern would emerge sooner rather than later, and the perpetrator or perpetrators could be rounded up before they had a chance to go to ground.

When the headquarters team had arrived—led, to Pullen's astonishment, by the ADIC himself—he'd taken them on a quick tour of the frenzied, nightmarish site. Then, while the forensics people went to work with their tweezers, swabs, and Baggies, he and Rickhauser had moved inside to quieter surroundings for a complete update.

Pullen watched nervously as the ADIC wedged his gargantuan frame into a chair at the head of the table and planted massive fists in front of him. Six foot seven, pushing three hundred pounds, he had steel-wool hair, a broad, mangled nose that had obviously been broken repeatedly, and the predatory, pale yellow eyes of a wolf. In an organization that prided itself on a clean-cut image, Rickhauser was, by far, the ugliest, most intimidating son of a bitch ever to come down the pipe. J. Edgar Hoover, in his day, had personally vetted new recruits, ousting those whose looks he didn't like. Legend had it that when Hoover was introduced to Rickhauser, he'd frozen for a moment, then moved on down the line. "Keep that one," he'd murmured to his aide, Clyde Tolson—his lover, if the rumors were true. "He'll terrify the crooks into surrendering."

Hours earlier, when Rickhauser had told Pullen he was sending a team to work the bomb site, the acting SAC had feared the arrival of a special investigator to wrest control away from him. When the chief himself showed up, Pullen had regretted not accompanying the copter that went to pick them up at Logan Airport. But no, he'd thought on reflection, better to be seen actively working the case, producing early leads. He tried to tell himself Rickhauser's arrival was an opportunity, not a vote of nonconfidence.

When the ADIC fixed his canine glower on him, Pullen struggled to keep his innards still. "Bring me up to speed." The voice was a barely audible growl.

The SAC leaned forward and clenched his fists on the table, mirroring the other man's posture. "What we know so far is this," he said. "At approximately 5:04 p.m., just as the company was shutting down for the day, an explosion destroyed the lobby and collapsed the front portico and part of an underground tunnel. Most of the building's facade was also ripped away, as you saw. Ground zero appears to have been just outside the main entrance."

"Not inside? We're absolutely sure about that?"

Pullen nodded. "We've got that crater next to the drive and a debris pattern that indicates everything radiated from that point. Bad as this is, it could have been worse if it had gone off inside. As it was, some of the explosion's force dissipated in open air. You see, a detonation of highly combustible material causes a sudden, massive expansion of gases that moves out from the point of ignition. Concussive effect gets mirrored and amplified with every hardened surface it encounters, and—"

"I know how a bomb works, Pullen. Next to the drive, you say. Was that lawn, planters, sidewalk, what?"

"Handicapped parking."

"Okay, so we're talking car bomb, probably, which rules out any Unabomber copycats."

"Probably, unless it's a new MO."

Rickhauser shook his head. "No. Guys like that are nerdy losers who get their kicks inciting terror safely, at long range. Then they sit back and gloat over their press clippings, feeling like a man. Haven't got the guts to look their victims in the eye. En route here, I spoke to headquarters. CNN got a call from some animal-rights group an hour ago, saying they did it to protest Data-Trax's use of animals to test its medical scanners. *Boston Globe* says a right-wing militia group called The Minutemen phoned in another claim, while the Bureau got two calls—one from some group styling itself 'The Sword of Allah,' and one from the good old IRA." Rickhauser shook his head disgustedly. "World's full of fucking crazies."

"Well, hang on to that Sword of Allah lead. As a matter of fact, I'm already on the trail of a firm suspect, an Arab, but it's not clear he used a car bomb. We're still combing for vehicle parts, just in case, although with an explosion this size, there wouldn't have been much left. We've got damaged cars out there, obviously, but none with the level of destruction we'd expect, or the kind of pushed-out pocking you get when a bomb's gone off inside a vehicle. Just the opposite, in fact. All the cars we've looked at so far took the force of the blast on the outside first."

"What about this suspect?"

"Right," Pullen said, nodding sagely. "The Arab, the bimbo and the Merc."

"What?"

"We spoke with a company vice-president, who told us

they had a guy in this afternoon for a job interview. A Palestinian, it seems, with U.S. citizenship. Right away, of course, I knew we had to pull out all the stops to find this guy. Problem was, anybody who'd actually seen him was dead, injured or unaccounted for.''

"Main gate have a record of his arrival?"

"Ah, well, that was a problem. Turns out they did, but Agent vanAken took off with the evidence.''

"What do you mean, 'took off'? You get hold of him like I told you? He was here?''

"I did, and he was. Briefly.''

"Where is he now?''

"In Winslow, Massachusetts, far as I know. That's where he was headed, last time he paid us the courtesy of checking in.''

"What's he doing in—where did you say?''

"Winslow.''

"Winslow,'' Rickhauser repeated. "Where the hell is that?''

"Small town, thirty miles or so east of here. Apparently, that's the address on the DMV registration for the car the Arab showed up in.''

"VanAken told you that?''

"Yes, and that's about all he deigned to tell before he hung up on me,'' Pullen said indignantly. "Fortunately, the day guard showed up who'd signed the Arab in at the front gate. He'd been at the dentist and heard about the bombing over the radio there. He came straight back, and was able to tell us about the car the guy arrived in, too.''

"Stolen?''

"Not sure. Some girl drove him.''

"Girl?''

"Cute little blond bimbo, apparently. Guard never took her name, and couldn't remember the Arab's, but the old

Mercedes she was driving had a vanity plate, and *that* he remembered. TUF ENUF, it said. I had it traced through DMV, then put out an APB on it. Car's registered to a Holly Anne Stroud, address in Winslow. I've got agents on the way out there now to check her out.''

"And vanAken?''

"Yes…vanAken,'' Pullen repeated, grimacing. ''Seems after he swiped the security log, he had a patrolman pull the DMV record on the car, then took off. He has the only copy of the log, and no one else knows the name that was on it—except maybe the personnel guy who interviewed this Arab, but he's in surgery. We should be able to get the information eventually from the front-desk logs and the security videos, but they're buried at the moment. Engineers say damaged sections in the building and tunnel could still collapse. Until all the injured are taken out, we can't risk sending a team in there to dig 'em out.''

"Why would vanAken walk off with the log?''

"Because it turns out he knew this guy and wanted a head start at finding him.'' Pullen sat back and let *that* sink in. ''Rickhauser's man,'' indeed!

The ADIC's yellow eyes stared ahead for a moment, then his hammer fists slammed the table. ''Godammit!'' he snarled. He fixed his feral glare on Pullen once more. ''And you're telling me you don't have the name yourself?''

"No, sir, I don't. Agent vanAken declined to share that information.''

12

Disastrous mistakes. Young women make them all the time, Leya thought, listening to Holly's tearful declaration of innocence. Idealism and gullibility lead them blindly into lost causes—and into the arms of men who can only break their hearts. Believing themselves invulnerable, they think they can do anything. Even redeem an incorrigible soul.

Leya had made a similar mistake when not much older than Holly, and she'd gone through her own trial by fire as a result. Eventually, she'd emerged from the ashes, scarred and wary, and gotten on with her life, but not without losing something precious in the bargain. At this time of year, when her thoughts turned reluctantly but inevitably to Peter, she always caught a whiff of something more than spring blossoms in the air. It was a smoky, oppressive scent, and it rose from the charred remains of blind faith in another human being. A naive sentiment, incinerated in the affair with Peter and its aftermath.

Leya passed a box of tissues across the counter to Holly, who withdrew one and blew, noisily but prettily. She was one of those rare, luminous children whose every gesture was appealing, Leya thought, even when she was being difficult. Actually, she reminded herself, Holly wasn't a child at all, but a decently educated, well-traveled young woman. One who, in all likelihood, was working on her second love affair—or more, for all Leya knew. Holly really should have known better than to get herself into this kind of hot water.

But as Leya watched the frightened girl, she sensed a deep, protective instinct rising up in her. A maternal instinct? she suddenly wondered. What did she know about mothering? She glanced around her kitchen and had another sudden insight. Was that what this obsession with the house was all about? Nesting? The human equivalent of some twigs-and-feathers impulse, responding to the silent rhythm of her biological clock, tick-ticking away? What a walking cliché she was.

"Karim and I *were* at the Data-Trax building this afternoon," the girl said. "I drove him there because he was having trouble getting around on his crutches."

"Crutches?" Leya repeated, confused.

Holly nodded. "I gave him Rollerblades for his birthday last Sunday, and we went out to try them. I was showing him how to brake when some kid ran out in front of him. Karim took a bad fall. We thought it was just a sprain, but later, it swelled up, so I took him into Emergency. They X-rayed his foot, and it turned out a small bone was broken. You know how your foot has all these teeny, tiny little—"

"The bomb, Holly?" Leya interrupted. "Why did the two of you go to Data-Trax today?"

"Karim had a job interview."

"So why would the police be looking for you? Did you see anything there?"

"No, nothing."

"Did either of you carry anything in?"

"No, nothing. Except my backpack. And Karim's crutches, of course."

"Are you sure?" Leya pressed.

"Professor Nash, do I look like a terrorist to you?"

"No, of course not. I know you would never knowingly get involved in anything so terrible, Holly, but maybe this Karim—"

She reacted instantly. "No, not him, either! He couldn't. If you met him, you'd know what I mean, Professor Nash. He's quiet and gentle. Karim could never hurt anyone." The girl's hazel eyes were wide and serious. She obviously believed what she was saying.

"So, you drove him to this job interview, and—?"

"And I waited in the lobby while he had his interview."

"How did it go?"

Holly puffed up her cheeks and exhaled. "I'm not sure. He seemed kind of down in the dumps afterward. He didn't think he was going to get the job. I told him he could be wrong, but he was petty discouraged. He really wanted that job. Data-Trax makes medical equipment, and that's a field Karim's really interested in. Which only goes to prove," Holly added, "that he's no terrorist." Ah, Leya thought, to be young and credulous. "Karim's graduating from MIT next month," Holly went on. "He wanted to stay on in the Boston area after graduation to be near…" Her cheeks flushed.

"To be near you?"

The girl nodded. "I wanted him to stay, too."

Leya recalled Mrs. Garibaldi's comment that Holly had been asking about state marriage laws. "But you just met him, didn't you?"

"You sound like my mother." Holly's tone left no doubt that the comparison wasn't meant to flatter.

"You told your parents about him?" That must have

been some conversation, Leya thought. But then, Ambassador Stroud had said on the phone that they didn't know who Holly was involved with. Leya had assumed he was referring to Tyler Newman.

"Not exactly. My mother called last week, and I told her I'd met someone special. I didn't tell her his name, though, or that he was Palestinian. My father would've hit the ceiling. *Will* hit the ceiling when he finds out. He's so hard-line on this whole Arab-Israeli business, you'd think he was Moses himself defending the Promised Land." Holly gave her blond curls an angry toss and looked up at Leya with defiance in her pale eyes. "That's why Karim was so anxious to get this job. He hasn't got any money, Professor Nash, and for sure, my father will cut me off when he finds out. I don't care. I'm going to marry him anyway."

"Oh, Holly! That's an awfully big step to be taking so quickly."

The girl threw up her hands. "You're just like everyone else! You don't understand. But how could you?" she muttered. "At your age, living all alone like this, you've probably forgotten what it's like to fall in love—if you ever knew."

Leya sat back on her stool and arched an eyebrow. "I just turned thirty, you know, which hardly qualifies me as some old spinster recluse. And hard as you may find this to believe, I'm not a nun, either."

"Oh, I didn't mean you were," the girl said, contrite. "I'm sorry. It's just…"

"What?"

"Didn't you ever meet anyone and just *know* you'd love him? That maybe you always had, and that you wanted to help him, no matter what anybody else said?"

Only once, Leya thought, for all the good it did. "I'm

not sure. But we're talking about you, here, not me—you and Karim. What do you mean, 'help him'? Help him do what?''

Holly's shoulders gave a slight shrug. "Help him be free."

Little alarm bells had been pinging in Leya's head all evening whenever her thoughts turned to Holly. They were clanging loudly now. "I don't understand," she said cautiously. "What kind of freedom are you talking about?"

"Karim's a Palestinian, like I said."

"Yes, I knew that."

Holly paused and gave her a curious look. "How? Who's been talking to you about him?" Suddenly, she jumped to her feet, and cried, "Have *they* been here?"

"They? Who? No," Leya said hastily, "no one's been here, Holly. I was at Tyler's earlier this evening, and I asked Mrs. Newman if she'd seen you. She was the one who first mentioned Karim to me."

"Oh," the girl said. She perched nervously on her stool once more. "Joanna's great. I thought it was that man Karim's so scared of."

"What man?"

"There's an FBI agent who's after Karim. And other people, too—other Palestinians. Terrorists. That's why we decided to get married."

Leya stared at the girl across the tiled counter. Holly was bright, but unless her eighteen-year-old mind was capable of seeing connections that escaped Leya, there was a huge gap in logic here. "Let me get this straight— Karim's mixed up somehow with the FBI and with Middle East terrorists, and that's why you and he need to get married?" Holly nodded. Leya shook her head. "This makes no sense at all."

"But it does, don't you see? That's the beauty of it."

"Holly," Leya said sternly, "your father is the American ambassador to Israel. Did it ever occur to you that Karim and these terrorist associates of his might be using you to get at him?"

"No, that's not it at all! You just don't get it, Professor Nash!"

"Well, then, explain it to me, please."

"The terrorists want Karim to work for them. The FBI wants Karim to be an informer. Karim just wants to live in peace, but nobody will let him. If he married me, though, they'd have to leave him alone. My father's a powerful man. The feds would have to back off, and the terrorists wouldn't trust Karim anymore, so they'd go away, too."

They might also kill him, if they suspected Karim had betrayed them, Leya thought. But there was no point in frightening Holly any more than she already was. Leya folded her hands on the countertop to keep them from betraying her nervousness. "All right, I know you're trying to do the right thing here, but I honestly think you're in way over your head."

"But—"

"Just listen, please. I don't know whether what you're planning is the best way to go about helping Karim, presuming he's as innocent as you say."

"He is," Holly said stubbornly.

"Fine. But before anything else is decided, this Data-Trax business has to be straightened out. You're going to have to talk to the police, both of you. You realize that, don't you?"

The girl paled. "I guess so."

"What about Karim? Where is he?"

"He's waiting...somewhere," she said evasively. "He's scared, Professor Nash. When we heard on the radio that they were looking for my car, he panicked. You've got to remember, he comes from a place where they lock people up en masse when something like this happens and practically throw away the key.''

"Well, not here, they don't. If Karim's innocent—"

"He is!" the girl cried again.

"All right, then. You need to make him understand that he has nothing to fear if he didn't do anything. Which, of course," Leya added hastily, "we know he didn't. Look, I'll call the police or the FBI, or whoever, and tell them you're coming in. I'll take you myself, in my car, and we'll pick up Karim on the way. The two of you will explain what you were doing there. They'll probably want to know if you saw anything that might help them track down whoever did this, and that'll be that.''

"I don't know...."

"Holly, there's no way to avoid it. I'm sure it's all just a big misunderstanding, but you've got to go in and clear yourself, or it's going to look like you have something to hide. Same thing for Karim. Surely you can see that.''

The girl started to cry softly again; great, wet tears staining the buttery leather sleeves of her jacket. "I'm so scared, Professor Nash.''

Leya reached out and squeezed her hand. "Don't be. I'll be with you all the way, I promise. We'll just go and get this over with, okay?''

"Okay," Holly said, nodding tearfully.

"What about Karim?"

"I've got the phone number where he's waiting. I need to call him.''

"Here's the phone," Leya said, sliding it over to her. "Go ahead and do that, then I'll call the police. Meantime, I'll grab my coat and purse.''

* * *

He was going around in circles, vanAken realized, his life a downward spiral that had begun accelerating, of late. Physically, socially, emotionally, he'd been isolated for a long time. Old friends and relatives had given up, one by one, after trying unsuccessfully to break through the hard, protective shell he'd built around himself after Beirut. Once outgoing, happiest in a crowd, he'd come to prefer solitude, the better to concentrate on dealing with the demons that plagued his nightmares. He went through the motions of this work he'd somehow stumbled into, but had no enthusiasm for it. Lately, that had been going down the tubes, too, like everything else in his life.

He sat outside the old house for the second time that evening, staring at it glumly. He'd been there just a few hours earlier, as the sun was setting. Now, the house and its whimsically painted turret were outlined against luminous night clouds that threatened snow or rain, depending on how far temperatures dropped. The front light was on, illuminating the broad, welcoming veranda, but Leya's Civic was the only car in the drive.

Maybe she was expecting a late visitor, vanAken thought. At this hour? Who? Anyone coming that late probably wouldn't be leaving before morning. A sudden tightening in his sternum took him by surprise, the anxious reflex as unwelcome as it was unexpected. He didn't have to do this, he reminded himself. One phone call to that idiot Pullen, and some other agent would come out to question her.

But if he did that, vanAken reasoned, he'd lose the head start he'd gained when he skipped off with the main gate's security log. After arriving in Winslow, he'd run down the information on the DMV registration and had learned that the car's owner—Holly Anne Stroud, a Mount Abbey freshman—hadn't been seen all day, according to the house mother at the student residence where she lived.

She'd also told him Leya Nash, Holly's faculty adviser, was looking for the girl.

While taking vanAken on a tour of Holly's room, this Mrs. Garibaldi had provided another piece of information that sent a chill of foreboding down his spine every time he thought about it. Holly Anne Stroud was the daughter of America's ambassador to Israel—and Arthur Stroud, vanAken happened to know, was number one with a bullet on a couple of Islamic-fundamentalist hit lists.

Staring at the turreted house, vanAken sat rigidly, listening to the manic dialogue bouncing back and forth in his brain like in those old Saturday-morning cartoons, where a devil and an angel hover over a character, fighting for control.

"What are you waiting for? Get out of the car and go to the door!"

"What's the point? She has no idea where the girl is."

"You don't know that."

"The girl's on the run with Karim. They're in another state or country by now."

"The Stroud girl might have come here, or at least called. The old lady said she was close to Leya."

"Leya..."

"Aha! See? That's the real issue here."

"There is no issue."

"Bullshit."

"She means nothing to me."

"Double bullshit."

"She's nobody."

"She's Carter Nash's daughter."

"Nash is dead."

"Not yet, he's not."

"He will be. Soon."

"You afraid seeing her will change your mind?"

"Nothing's going to change my mind. I want it over and done with, once and for all."

"You got the guts to look her in the eye before you do it?"

"No problem."

"So?"

"I'm going, dammit!"

VanAken got out of the car. But as he dragged himself up the walk, his feet felt encased in cement, growing heavier with each step. He mounted the front steps, crossed the veranda and reached for the doorbell.

Before he could press the button, a shadow appeared inside the frosted-glass door. Muffled speech reached his ears, the words incoherent, but the voice unmistakable— her voice. She was talking to someone in another part of the house. She wasn't alone. Once again, vanAken felt his solar plexus tighten. Ghostly arms beyond the glass reached up, then came back down trailing a dark, fluid shape that flared around and settled on her form as her arms flung out, one after the other. She was putting on her coat.

He waited, expecting her to open the door, but she moved away again, still talking. He took a deep breath, then leaned on the bell. The voice stopped, and a moment later the shadow reappeared behind the etched glass. The door swung open and her gaze swept over him.

"Yes?" she said.

Her voice seemed distracted, and she looked annoyed by the disturbance. She tugged her hair free of her coat collar, and it tumbled across her shoulders. VanAken found himself mesmerized by the light shimmering on those dark waves. It wasn't really cut all that short, he decided. Close-up, she seemed smaller than he remembered.

They stood face-to-face while she waited, expectantly, for him to say something. And then, finally, recognition dawned. Her dark eyes went wide. Her lips parted in astonishment, but no sound emerged.

"Hello, Leya," vanAken said.

"My God," she whispered at last. "Peter..."

13

Leya stared, dumbfounded, at the man on her porch. She hadn't seen him in a decade—not in person, at any rate. There'd been newspaper pictures, of course, during the period Peter and so many others had been held hostage in Lebanon, human fodder in a war of wills between Islamic fundamentalists and their perceived enemies in the West. Then, a flurry of articles when he'd escaped from his captors and returned home.

But at the time he was kidnapped, their affair was already over. After a brief, incendiary fling, Peter had abandoned her. Then he was taken hostage. In the six years since his captivity had ended, he'd made no effort to contact her. Leya had tried to get in touch after he came home, to wish him well after the ordeal he'd been through, but her attempts had met with silence. Her father had told her, reluctantly and in confidence, about subsequent charges of treason against vanAken and his firm belief they were well-founded. Then he'd had his stroke, and Leya had been preoccupied with that.

In the end, she'd resigned herself to the fact that there were some things she would never understand, and she'd moved on. But from time to time, even now, she caught herself trying to recall warning signs she should have picked up on—hints of the dangerous games vanAken had been playing, and of the double life he'd led. Imagining different endings to a chapter of her life that had always seemed surreal and unfinished.

She'd just turned twenty when she met him. It was in the arrivals hall at Beirut International Airport—a place she had no bloody business being, her father never failed to remind her whenever the subject arose. As Carter Nash's dependent, Leya carried a diplomatic passport, but on that day, it wasn't cutting any ice with the Lebanese immigration officer.

"I'm telling you," she repeated, "my father is trade counselor at the American embassy here." By now, she knew what his real job was, but she'd been drilled on the importance of never deviating from his cover story. *"If you'll just call the embassy, they'll confirm that what I'm saying is true."*

"Then why is your father not here to meet you?"

"He didn't know I was coming. It's a surprise."

"The surprise is yours, mademoiselle. *You require a visa to enter Lebanon."*

"There wasn't time to get one in Athens. When I heard that Beirut airport had reopened, I jumped on the next plane. I was told I could arrange my visa on arrival."

The immigration officer shook his head. "Whoever told you this was mistaken."

"Well, I'm sorry about that, but I'm here now, so—"

"Is there anything I can do to help?" Leya glanced up at a young man who'd appeared at her side. *"My name's Peter vanAken,"* he added, extending his hand.

With a name like that, she would have expected a blond, Dutch-boy haircut and clogs, but this guy didn't fit his

*name. Middling tall—close to a six-footer, she estimated—
he was dark-haired and good-looking, if a little shaggy,
with a heavy mustache that put her in mind of Tom Selleck.
Dressed casually in brown corduroy pants, an open-
necked plaid flannel shirt and an unzipped, scuffed brown
leather jacket, he looked like the kind of guy who'd drive
an off-road vehicle—a Land Rover or a Humvee—and actually leave the highway.*

"Leya Nash," *she said, accepting his firm clasp. No
Dutch clogs, she noted, glancing down at his feet. Sturdy,
lug-soled tan boots that would have done a Special Forces
agent proud.*

*She'd spotted him earlier, watching the arrivals line. By
the interest he seemed to take in the people waiting to be
processed through customs and immigration, she'd assumed he was some local police or militia officer, working
the airport undercover. With its on-again/off-again civil
war, Lebanon was a hotbed of intrigue, and she knew the
place must be crawling with them. But as soon as he spoke,
she realized he was American.*

"I don't suppose you're with the embassy, are you?"

"No, I'm a lecturer at the American University of Beirut. I was just seeing off a colleague." *VanAken turned to
the immigration officer.* "Hi, Bashir. What's up?"

"The young lady has no visa, Peter."

"I see." *VanAken looked at Leya again. His eyes, a
smoldering ash gray, fixed on her with an expression of
bemused curiosity.* "Nash, you said. Are you related to
Carter Nash?"

"I'm his daughter. Do you know him?"

*VanAken nodded slowly, the creases at the corners of
his eyes deepening.* "I certainly know who he is." *Leya
tried to read his ironic expression, wondering if he knew
what her father was, as well. Possibly. The American com-*

munity abroad was small and incestuous, and the CIA station chief was never that hard to spot. His cover was looser than that of other operatives, to allow him to deal with local police and intelligence authorities. Plus, anyone half clued-in would realize that in a country like Lebanon, with its ongoing civil unrest and collapsed economy, there was no work for an American trade official.

But if this vanAken knew Carter Nash's true role here, he wasn't letting on. He walked behind the immigration desk and put an arm around the shoulder of the man named Bashir. Their backs to Leya, the two men launched into a conversation in Arabic, a language in which vanAken seemed fluent. A moment later, Bashir laughed, then turned around, picked up a rubber stamp, and brought it down on Leya's passport with a bang.

"Have a pleasant stay, mademoiselle,*" he said, handing it back to her with a flourish and a wide smile. He winked at vanAken, then waved his hand at the line behind her. "Next, please!"*

Leya moved aside, examined the entry stamp in her passport, then gave her rescuer a puzzled look. "Thanks—I think." She lowered her voice to a whisper. "Did money just change hands here, by any chance?"

"Baksheesh, you mean? Oh, no."

"Because if I owe you—"

"Not a penny, I swear."

"How did you convince him to let me in?"

VanAken shrugged, his gray eyes mischievous now. "We never discussed you at all."

"What were you talking about?"

"His cousin in Baltimore."

"What?"

"Name's Amin, runs a dry-cleaning business. Nice guy.

If you ever need a suit cleaned, you should drop in, say hello from Bashir.''

Leya blinked, then broke into a grin. "Not likely. I'm living near Boston right now.''

"Too bad. Anyway, last time I was in the States, I went to see cousin Amin, who loaded me down with goodies to bring back to Bashir and his family.''

"Ah, I see! He owed you a favor. Well, thanks for stepping in.''

VanAken's shaggy head dipped. "Any time, Miss Nash.''

"Leya.''

"Leya.'' The name slipped experimentally over his tongue as he studied her, the smile in his eyes never wavering. Definitely cute, Leya decided—probably in his mid-twenties, although the mustache made him look older. No rings, she noted as she glanced down at his tanned hands, feeling inexplicably fluttery and ridiculous. "Can I give you a lift, Leya?''

"Oh, no, thanks. You've done enough. I'll take a taxi.''

He grimaced. "I wouldn't recommend it, these days. You never know who's at the wheel, and the airport road's dangerous.''

"But the International Herald Tribune *said things are quiet right now, with the cease-fire and those peace negotiations going on in Switzerland.''*

"Pretty much. It should last, as long as the conference doesn't derail.''

"And if it does?''

"Then all bets are off. Meantime, everybody catches up on their shopping, the backlog of mail gets delivered, and the clubs and restaurants reopen for a few days. You picked a good time to visit.''

Leya shook her head. "I guess you have to be resilient to live in a place like this.''

"It's pretty hairy, but I like the country and the people, in spite of the fact that they need their butts kicked for being so stupid. I admire your gutsiness, though. It's not exactly Club Med around here these days, and we don't get too many tourists." He picked up her suitcase and nodded toward the exit. *"Come on. I'm trustworthy, I promise."*

Somehow, Leya had no doubt about that. *"I was in Greece for spring break,"* she explained, walking alongside him. *"My father was supposed to meet me there, but when I got to Athens, there was a message saying he was bogged down with work and might not make it. Then I read about the airport reopening, so I decided to save him a trip."*

"He doesn't know you're coming?"

"No, and he's probably going to blow a gasket when I walk in. But I've always wanted to see this 'Paris of the Middle East,' and with my father, it's easier to ask for forgiveness than permission."

He shook his head. *"You're even gutsier than I thought—but that explains it."*

"Explains what?"

"Why you've come at a time when he's not even in the country."

Leya stopped in her tracks. *"Are you sure?"*

"Pretty sure. I heard he'd gone to Geneva to monitor those peace talks."

"Oh, no..." she groaned. *"What am I going to do?"*

"Don't panic. He'll probably be back in a few days. Meantime, I'm sure his housekeeper will let you stay at his place. You shouldn't go wandering around by yourself, but if you're interested, I offer my services as tour guide. I've spent a lot of time in this area, and I know some pretty cool places you won't find in the Michelin Guide.*"*

"Oh, I couldn't. You've got better things to do, I'm sure."

"Not really. I have one more lecture to give this afternoon—on the conquest of Phoenicia by Alexander the Great. You can sit in, if you're interested in picking up a little ancient history on the area."

"Ancient history? Is that what you teach?"

"History and archaeology, actually. It's a genetic defect I inherited from my father."

"VanAken! I thought the name seemed familiar. I've heard of him—Lucius vanAken, right? The Smithsonian, National Geographic, and all that? I even saw a picture of you in a magazine once, in full Arab dress, riding a camel in a desert somewhere. You looked about ten."

VanAken winced. *"That's a really old picture. So, what do you say? As of tomorrow, the AUB's on spring break, too. I'd be glad to stand in as guide and bodyguard until your father gets back."*

"Well, it's nice of you to offer, Peter, son of the famous Lucius vanAken, but you're not obliged to baby-sit, you know."

"Listen, Leya, daughter of the infamous Carter Nash," vanAken said, taking her by the elbow and leading her toward the door, *"anybody with the chutzpah to fly into Beirut on a whim hardly needs a baby-sitter. Tough customer like you deserves the full, five-star tour."*

"And you're the one to give it, right?" she said, grinning.

"You bet."

Memory is a strange thing, Leya thought, studying the man under her porch light. For as long and as unrelentingly as Peter had dominated her thoughts, there'd come a time when she could no longer summon up his face. His lean, energetic body, his unruly chestnut hair, his brushy mustache—all those things had remained clear in her mind. But over time, the details of him had become bleached and faded, like a photograph kept too long under bright lights. And for a long while now, try as she might, Leya had not been able to recall the precise color of his eyes. She'd forgotten how they fluctuated between smoke and ash, even a pale, grayish blue when he wore denim, like the shirt and jeans he had on now under his gray tweed sport coat. She'd forgotten the sound of his voice, too, although she remembered that its lowest tones could set off a sympathetic trilling deep inside her, and that his ready laughter had been infectious.

And now, here he was—the mustache gone, the face lined and strained, hair shot with gray, all trace of mischief absent from his voice. Peter, but not Peter. Good-looking, objectively, but with the gaunt, haunted edge of someone who's come through a course of chemotherapy—or, she thought grimly, through physical and psychological torture.

"I'm sorry to bother you so late." The apology was delivered in a monotone, and his wary eyes, after their initial brief contact, seemed reluctant to meet hers.

"Bother?" Leya repeated, still bewildered. "No, it's not a bother, but..." She stumbled, then started again. "It's been so *long*."

"I suppose. I'm surprised you remember me."

"Of course I remember you, Peter. I just...never expected to see you again."

"I'm sure."

There was censure in the way he said it, and Leya felt a stab of guilt. "It wasn't for lack of trying. I got in touch with your mother when I heard you were free."

"I know."

"I was anxious to find out how you were, after…what you'd gone through. It must have been terrible."

"I survived." Lips pressed in a tight line, his gaze was fixed on a point somewhere over her shoulder, as if he'd found a fault in the vestibule's striped ivory wallpaper. It was so unlike the direct, clear-eyed gaze she remembered. And although he'd always been lean, he seemed shrunken inside his clothing now, the collar of his shirt loose and flapping on his neck. Was her memory that flawed? Leya wondered. Was this the same man whose image had so obsessed her that anyone else she'd met in the past decade, including John Merriman, had seemed dull and bloodless by comparison?

Unable to stand the awkward silence, she took a deep breath and tried again. "I was so sorry to hear about your father."

It was his turn to be taken aback, and he nodded slowly. "So was I. It was the strain that did it—the kidnapping, then never knowing whether I was dead or alive. I disappointed him in a lot of ways I never got to apologize for. Now, I also get to live with the knowledge that worry over me finally killed him. He didn't deserve that."

"You can't blame yourself."

"Can't I?"

Leya reached her hand toward his arm, but he recoiled from it. "I called your mother after I heard about your dad's death," she said, "to offer my sympathy, and to see if there was any news of you."

"She told me."

"And then, after you were back home, I called again, to see if there was anything I could do—"

"Like what?"

"I don't know. I was just so sorry—"

"Your pity wasn't needed."

"It wasn't pity. I just—"

"What? What could you possibly have done, Leya? Could you have changed anything? Made those four years disappear? Brought back my father?"

"N-no, I couldn't. Your mother said she'd pass on my message, but when I didn't hear back, I presumed you didn't want to see me." She felt stupid, like some cheery little Brownie holding out a cookie to a Holocaust survivor. "How is your mother?" she ventured.

"She died two weeks after I got back. She'd been sick a long time. Can I come in?"

Already shaken, Leya was truly thrown by his sudden directional shift. "Inside?"

He looked at her as if she were mentally deficient. "Yes, inside."

Leya finally remembered Holly, waiting for her in the kitchen. "Actually, this isn't the best time."

"Were you going somewhere?" he asked, nodding at her coat.

"Yes. I really would like to visit with you, Peter, but there's something urgent I need to do right now. Maybe tomorrow—?"

"This isn't a social call. I'm on official business, and it can't wait."

Leya frowned. "Official business? CIA business, you mean?"

"No, I'm not with the Agency."

"*Anymore,* you mean."

"Not anymore."

"But you *were* in Beirut," she pressed, an old anger finally rising to the surface of all the other turbulent emotions his appearance stirred up. "And all that coy nonsense about just *happening* to know my father—you worked for him, for crying out loud! Why didn't you just tell me what you were?''

"Because it was safer that way, for both of us. Now, can I come in?''

"Depends. Whose dirty business are you doing today?''

He pulled out a leather folder and flashed a gold shield. ''FBI. I'm investigating that bombing in Newton this afternoon. I'm looking for a student of yours who's wanted in connection with the incident—a Holly Stroud?''

Leya stared at the badge, then slumped against the door frame. ''Oh, hell...''

14

Newton, Massachusetts: 10:38 p.m.

The first substantive clue to the bomb's origins came from a fragment of stretched, scorched metal found embedded in one of the concrete pylons that had once supported the glass-and-metal canopy over the entrance to the Data-Trax building. Curtis Pullen watched as an ATF agent carefully dug out the fragment, then handed it with a pair of tongs to Leonard Rickhauser. The Bureau's assistant deputy moved near a portable floodlight to examine it more closely.

"We've located five small samples of the same material scattered around the crater," the ATF investigator said. "Don't know yet if it means anything, but we'll piece together as many as we find, see what it makes."

"Looks like brushed stainless steel," Rickhauser said, turning the fragment under the light. Irregularly shaped, about eight inches in diameter, its edges were feathered and splayed in one direction, like a silvery flower.

"See those striations?" the ATF man asked, pointing out a series of parallel etchings on the fragment. "Leads me to suspect it was close to the bomb. Maybe part of the mechanism itself."

The ADIC nodded and handed the tongs and fragment

back to the investigator, who dropped it into an evidence bag and said, "We'll know more once we subject it to chemical analysis."

"Let's get the lab right on it," Rickhauser said. He turned to Pullen. "Is the evacuation of the building complete?"

"The upper floors are empty," Pullen answered. "Rescue team's still working on the tunnel. We've got six people that we know of still trapped down there. It's slow going."

"What about the lobby?"

"All the DOA's have been centered in that area, not counting the woman coming up the drive who got taken out by flying concrete."

"Is it cleared yet?"

"They've removed six bodies so far, but the dogs just alerted on a couple more, buried in the rubble. The locations are tagged, but they probably won't be dug out till morning."

"Why not?"

Pullen shrugged. "The structure's dicey, and without daylight—"

"We can't wait that long to get into the basement," Rickhauser said. "We need to locate those security videos, see what's on them."

"But the bodies—"

"They're not going anywhere. We'll work around them as best we can."

"The company's not going to like us going ahead before all the victims have been identified," Pullen cautioned.

"We'll get 'em out quick as we can, but I'm not going to pay these victims the ultimate insult by letting their killers escape. I need that videotape." Rickhauser's hulking frame bore down on the nervous SAC, yellow eyes gleaming under the floodlights. "Find out if those blue-prints I asked for have shown up yet. I want a way into that security office, and I want it now."

Winslow, Massachusetts: 10:40 p.m.

Leya stood her ground in the front doorway, her body a barrier to vanAken's passage. Official business or not, she wasn't sure she wanted to set this sullen character loose on the frightened Holly Stroud. He peered over her shoulder.

"The girl's *here?*"

"Yes," Leya said quietly. "She came about twenty minutes ago."

"Alone?"

"Yes."

"All right, let's go."

"Wait a minute. What are you going to do?"

"Take her into custody." He shouldered his way past her. When she reached out to slow him, he fairly leaped past her touch.

"Peter, wait!"

He strode into the living room, scanned it quickly, then turned on her. "Where is she?"

"Let me go in first, tell her I know you, and that it's okay to talk to you."

"She has no choice in the matter. Step aside."

Leya had planted herself under the archway into the living room. He dodged, looking to get around her, but she extended her arms to either side of the frame, determined that he'd have to knock her over before she'd let him swoop down and scare the girl half to death. He looked as if that were fine by him. "Take it easy," she pleaded.

"Move, or I'll arrest you, too, as an accessory!"

Leya stared at him, incredulous. "For God's sake, Peter, what is *wrong* with you? This is Leya! We were…friends, once. Remember?"

"I remember everything, but don't think that gives you any power over me. I'll do what I have to do. If you stand in my way, you'll regret it."

She searched his face for the man she'd once loved, but this was a stranger—one she didn't think she much liked, regardless of what he'd been through. "We're going in together. She's just a kid, and she's scared, so you take it easy on her. I mean it!" She dropped her arms and spun away, heading down the hall, vanAken close behind.

In the kitchen, cups and spoons cluttered the counter where she'd left them, and steam was frothing over the forgotten teakettle on the stove. Holly, however, was nowhere to be seen. Leya turned off the gas under the kettle, then walked toward the powder room off to one side, whose door stood open a crack. "Holly?" she called gently. "There's someone here who wants to talk to you. It's all right, I promise." She pushed cautiously against the door. It swung wide, and when Leya peered inside, the room was empty.

VanAken took his own quick survey of the room. "Well?"

"I don't know. She was here when I went to answer the front door. Holly?" Leya called again, looking into the pantry and the dining room, where her half-read pile of freshman essays still lay scattered across her rolltop desk. "Where are you? Don't be afraid."

She backed into the kitchen and noticed that the chain lock on the back door, fastened earlier in the evening, dangled loose now. Leya stepped out onto the rear landing, peering into darkness. Nothing. She shot vanAken an irritated look. "She must have run off when she heard you threatening. Honestly, Peter! I'd just convinced her to turn herself in.''

He slipped past her onto the stoop, raced down the staircase, then around the side of the house. A moment later, he reappeared from the other direction and remounted the steps, cursing under his breath. ''How did she get here?'' he asked, when he reached the landing.

''In her car, I imagine.''

''Did you hear it?''

''No, but I was working, and I had the stereo on.''

''The only car I saw when I drove up was yours.''

Her eyes narrowed. ''How do you know what I drive?''

''Is that Honda Civic out front yours?''

''Yes.''

''Well, that's the only car I saw. The girl drives an '86 Mercedes, right?''

''Yes. That is, I know it's a Mercedes, her mother's old car, but I'm not sure about the year. It's a banged-up old thing. Holly's a pretty awful driver.''

''She must have parked it next block over.'' VanAken returned to the kitchen, Leya following. He checked around corners once more, then his gaze rose to the ceiling. ''What's upstairs?''

''Empty space, right now. The place is gutted. But she couldn't have gone up there without us seeing her. The staircase in the front hall is the only way up.''

VanAken slumped against a counter. ''All right, what did she tell you?''

Leya settled warily across from him. ''She'd heard on the radio that the police were looking for her car in connection with the bombing.''

''On the radio? I told him not to do that!'' he muttered angrily.

''Who?''

"Never mind. Then what?"

"She was terrified. She said she *had* been at Data-Trax this afternoon, driving a friend to a job interview."

"Karim Khoury?" Leya nodded. "What do you know about him?" vanAken probed.

"Next to nothing. I've never met him."

"You must have." Outside, a dog began to bark. Van-Aken pulled up sharp and walked over to the window, peering out.

"I think I'd remember if I had," Leya said.

Someone whistled—her neighbor a couple of doors down, Leya realized, calling in his yappy terrier. The barking stopped, and vanAken turned back to the kitchen.

"Khoury phoned you."

"What? He never did!"

When vanAken removed a folded piece of paper from the inside pocket of his tweed sport coat, Leya spotted the NYNEX logo on the corner of it. "February twenty-eighth, 7:47 p.m. The call was made from Khoury's landlady's phone to yours."

"But I never—" She held up her hand. "Wait a minute." She went into the dining room and rummaged around her desk until she found her Day-Timer, flipping through it as she walked back into the kitchen. "The evening of February twenty-eighth, you say." She stabbed at the page and held it out for him to see. "*The Joy Luck Club,* 7:00 p.m.—see?"

"What's that?"

"It's a novel by Amy Tan. I had my American Lit 101 class here that night, and that's the book we were discussing. Holly's in that class, and now that I think of it, she did take a call here that night—from a guy." Leya closed the Day-Timer and set it aside.

"Khoury?"

She shrugged. "I don't know. Holly said when she came in that she was expecting an important call, so she'd left my number. I answered the phone, and she took the call here in the kitchen while I went back into the living room with my other students. Holly came back a few minutes later, and I didn't think anything more of it."

"How did she and Khoury meet, do you know?"

"Through people here in town—Holly's former boy-friend and his mother, actually, the Newmans. They run a little restaurant in town called Tyler's."

VanAken nodded. "I've seen the place. They're friends of Khoury's?"

"No. This Khoury guy apparently dropped around their place one day with someone who knew Holly's boyfriend. Holly happened to be at Tyler's house when the two guys showed up, and I guess she and Khoury hit it off."

"Who was the guy he came with?"

"I don't know. Another student, apparently."

"You said 'former boyfriend'? She ditch this guy for Khoury?"

"Seems so. From the way she spoke tonight, Holly is very committed to him. She said—" Leya paused, still unable to believe it.

"What?"

"Holly said she was thinking of marrying him."

"Marrying—!"

"She's a good-hearted kid, Peter, and apparently this Karim's been telling her that he's being squeezed between some extremist group and the government—the FBI, actually," Leya added, studying him more closely. "Do you know anything about that?"

"Is the girl politically minded?" he asked, ignoring the question.

"She's idealistic, in the vague sort of way young people

often are. Championing the underdog in any debate, that sort of thing."

"The underdog—like a displaced Palestinian, maybe?"

"Possibly. But I always got the impression that Holly's views in that regard were more about rebelling against her parents than anything else—especially her father's die-hard conservatism and pro-Israeli stance."

VanAken frowned. "Does Khoury know who the girl's father is?"

"I think so. The ironic thing is that Holly thought being married to Arthur Stroud's daughter would offer Karim some protection."

"Christ! What the hell is he up to?"

"Do you think he's trying to get at Holly's father some-how?"

Again, he ignored her question. "What else did the Stroud girl say? Why were they hanging around a defense contractor?"

"A defense contractor?"

"Data-Trax. They do defense work."

Leya frowned. "That's not right. Holly said they made medical equipment. She said she drove Karim to a job interview because he'd broken his foot and was having a hard time getting around on crutches."

"Did she say how he broke his foot?"

"In-line skating."

"Rollerblades?" he asked incredulously. "Karim?"

"Apparently Holly gave them to him for his birthday, and when they went out to try them last weekend, he took a bad fall. Do you *know* this guy?" Leya asked once more.

"Not well enough, it seems. What else?"

Leya shrugged. "Holly said they had nothing to do with the bombing. They'd left before it happened. I believe her, Peter. She was too shaken up to be lying."

"Why did she come to see you?"

"After she heard on the radio that the police were looking for her, she panicked. I'm her faculty adviser. We've got a pretty good rapport, so she came for help."

"Where were you heading when I arrived?" he asked, nodding at her coat.

"I'd convinced Holly she needed to talk to the authorities, explain what she was doing at Data-Trax and clear her name. I said I'd drive them in. That's what I was getting ready to do when you came to the door."

VanAken seemed to perk up. "Them? Khoury, too?"

"Yes."

"But you said she came alone."

"She did. Karim is in hiding somewhere, waiting to hear from her. She was just calling him when I went to get my coat."

"Calling him—!" VanAken leaped to his feet and grabbed the phone, punching in a number. Eight digits, Leya registered—a toll call, but apparently within the same area code as Winslow. "This is Special Agent vanAken," he said after a few moments. "Patch me through to the SAC, would you? It's urgent." There was another delay, then, "Pullen? I need a call trace on the double—the last call made from this number." He read Leya's number off the base of the phone. "I'll explain later, but—"

VanAken paused, and Leya could hear a loud voice on the other end—grilling him, it seemed.

"In Winslow, like I told you," vanAken said, "but I need an address—what? He's there? Now?… All right, let me talk to him while you get to work on that trace…. Oh, for chrissake, Pullen! Just get me a goddam phone number and an address, and let me talk to Rickhauser, would you?" He smacked the counter irritably.

Leya started at the sound, then froze as she noticed his

hands. Once upon another lifetime, those hands had explored every inch of her, setting off tremors in nerve endings she hadn't even known she possessed. They'd drawn her out, coaxing away shyness and inexperience, teaching her to give and take pleasure in his body and her own. How many times had she kissed those fingers and palms? she wondered. Felt the steady pulse that coursed through those wrists?

Now, the wrists were mangled, wrapped in wide, glistening bands of sinewy scar tissue, the knuckles and fingers bent and misshapen. Peter's hands had once been strong and tanned, their backs bristling with a scattering of dark hair, but the disfigured flesh on them now was as white and hairless as a newborn rodent. Leya turned away, sickened, and busied herself putting away the unused cups and spoons.

"Len?" she heard vanAken say after a minute or so of silence. "Yeah, I know he's pissed off. Sorry, but I had to track that lead myself. It was Karim Khoury." He sighed, then added, "My reaction precisely. I told you he'd vanished three days ago. Turns out he'd planned his disappearance, because I went around to his rooming house, and he'd cleared out, lock, stock and barrel. I don't know where he got to between then and the time he showed up at Data-Trax today, except it looks like this Stroud girl is mixed up in it. Do you know who she is, Len? Arthur Stroud's kid.... Yep, *that* Arthur Stroud. The girl's a student at Mount Abbey College here in Winslow. I got confirmation that she was driving Khoury this afternoon when he showed up at Data-Trax."

Leya looked over at him again, and saw that vanAken was watching her as he listened to the voice on the other end of the line. When their eyes connected, he turned away. Tucking the phone between his ear and shoulder, he tugged at his shirt cuffs. That was it, she realized—the reason he seemed shrunken inside his clothes. He was thinner, but he hadn't wasted away that much. He was wearing shirts a size or so too large in a self-conscious effort to cover his scars.

"That call I gave Pullen to trace was made from the home of one of the girl's professors. She was here, but took off when she heard me come in. Khoury's gone underground, but the girl had placed a call to him.... The professor?" He hesitated again. "Nash—Leya Nash.... Yeah, the same. No big deal. Anyway, Len, could you have Pullen get right back to me with that address...? Thanks. I'll be in touch."

He hung up the phone, then drummed on the countertop, avoiding her gaze. Leya was tempted to ask about that cryptic comment after he'd reported her name, but his expression argued against it. "Well? What now?"

"They'll call back with a name and address on that number she phoned. It shouldn't take more than a few minutes, and then I'll be out of your hair."

"And that's it?"

"For now. Someone might be around in the next day or so with more questions for you."

"Someone? Not you?"

"Probably not."

Leya tried to decide whether that was good or bad. She wasn't sure. Peter vanAken had dominated her thoughts for the past decade, a frustrating, painful old riddle, wrapped now in the enigma of this cold, disturbing man. "I have classes to teach tomorrow," she said.

"Fine. Just carry on with your normal routine."

She shook her head ruefully. "Easy for you to say. What about Holly? I'm worried about her. What if she comes back?"

He reflected a moment, then pulled a scratch pad and pencil from a holder near the phone. As he wrote, Leya found herself mesmerized by his battered hands. "This is the number on my cell phone. Call me right away if she shows up." Looking up, he caught her stare and backed against the opposite counter, shoving his hands into his trouser pockets.

"Peter?"

"What?"

"Your hands—is that from when you were being held hostage?" He nodded. "What did they do to you?"

He hesitated, studying the floor tiles. "Various painful, but fairly unimaginative things. Smashing them with a rifle butt when they thought my attitude didn't demonstrate the proper level of respect, that sort of thing." His shaggy head shook slowly. "The worst, though, was being manacled and chained to a wall for four solid years. You can't imagine what that's like. You live free all your life, and then suddenly..." His voice trailed off.

"Is that how you got the scars on your wrists? From the manacles?"

He looked up, as if curious to see the effect of his words. "No. I did this to myself."

"To yourself? But—how? Why?"

"Don't you know about trapping wild things, Leya? How an animal will chew off its own leg? Sacrifice a limb in exchange for freedom?"

Leya felt the room grow close and stuffy. "You tried to rip off your own hands?" she asked, horrified.

He nodded. "One day, I reached a point where I couldn't stand it anymore. I flipped out, I guess, and by the time the guard looked in and discovered what I'd done, I'd nearly bled to death."

"They didn't let you die, though."

"No, but not out of any kind of humanitarianism. A dead hostage has no value. They were under the delusion that someone actually gave a damn about what happened to me and would trade for my freedom. They were ruthless, you see, but not very bright. Anyway, a doctor, sympathetic to their cause, came in and patched me up."

"And you didn't try it again?"

"Not much point. They put me under closer surveillance and said if I did, they'd just go ahead and amputate my hands for me, then manacle my feet. I knew I had to find another way to escape."

The phone rang. VanAken picked it up, grabbing the paper and pencil once more to note the number and address his colleagues had traced. "Okay, that's that," he said, hanging up a moment later. "I'll be on my way. Call if the girl shows up again."

"I will. But Peter—?"

He was already halfway to the door, but he glanced back distractedly, then stopped. "You're crying—why?"

"Because this is upsetting. The bombing, and Holly, of course, but—seeing you, too." She took a deep breath. "I'm sure you think I'm ridiculous, but what happened between us in Beirut—maybe it was nothing to you, but to me, it was. When you were taken hostage, I was sick with worry the whole time. And after, when you wouldn't see me—" Leya shook her head. "I don't know. I guess I've never had any sense of what my sister the therapist calls 'closure.' The whole business always seemed so gut-wrenching and unfinished."

VanAken shifted from one foot to the other, like all he wanted was to get the hell out of there.

"I wish we could talk," she added hurriedly. "I know it's not possible right now, with your investigation and all, but—"

"You want me to come back."

"Yes, I guess I do. If that's all right. I don't mean to bother you. I realize you must have a whole other life now, and—"

"A life? What—like a wife and kids, you mean? House in the suburbs?" He laughed bitterly.

"Oh. Well…"

"How about you?"

"No—not really. I mean, I have this house, but…"

VanAken began to pace the tiled floor, like a caged cat. "Tell me something," he said finally.

"What?"

"When you left Beirut—when your father came back and blew a gasket, just as you'd predicted, and bundled you onto the next plane out of there—why didn't you get in touch with me like I asked you to? I was ready to leave on a moment's notice, you know."

"But I did! I sent a cable from Athens. I remember exactly what it said. 'Athens Gate Hotel. Come quick. Leya.'"

"How did you send it?"

"On the diplomatic net, from the embassy there. They said the commercial lines to Beirut had gone down again after the cease-fire broke. But by then, I knew you were CIA and could receive an embassy comcenter message. I didn't want to take any chances. I sent it, Peter, I swear! I waited ten days for you to show up. I was almost a week late getting back to school."

He moved toward her, hesitated, then took her chin and tipped her head to the light, like he was looking to catch her in a lie. Leya felt disoriented by the nearness and the scent of him, suddenly and perfectly remembered, and by the rough indifference of his touch, which wasn't at all what she remembered. "I never got the cable."

"But how could you not? My father got one I sent him."

He tapped her chin. "Think about it. It'll come to you." He stepped away and jammed his hands into his pockets once more. "I have to go. But you're right—there *is* unfinished business here. I've been thinking about that myself. So maybe I will come back."

15

Newton, Massachusetts: 10:58 p.m.

Len Rickhauser stared irritably at the flood-lit ruin. He was standing at an upper-floor window in the old mansion annex across the park from the main Data-Trax building, reflecting on the secrets hidden in that twisted pile of stretched steel and pulverized concrete. Fragments and filaments of the bomb mechanism. Chemical fingerprints left by its deadly incendiary compounds. And victims, whose crushed and lacerated bodies would reveal more about the direction, force and nature of the explosion than the victims themselves would have recalled, had they lived to recount what they'd seen. If the investigators were really lucky, they might find images of the explosion itself, recorded by security cameras on microthin magnetic tape. The videotape might even reveal the delivery method and confirm a suspect.

Locating the tape was critical, Rickhauser knew. Eyewitnesses close enough to ground zero to have seen anything significant had paid with their lives for the dubious privilege. The personnel man who'd interviewed Karim Khoury was alive, but in surgery to save his eyesight. It could be another twenty-four hours before agents interviewed him.

Even then, Rickhauser reflected, Rosenberg's testimony would probably reveal little about the suspect that they didn't already know through MENELOP, vanAken's operation to infiltrate the local cell of Hamas. It would tell them nothing at all about any motive or accomplices Khoury might have had—even presuming, Rickhauser reminded himself, that Khoury was their man. Right now, he was the prime candidate, but it was too early in the investigation to rule out other possibilities. Rickhauser could think of a dozen alternative explanations for what had gone wrong here, and one in particular, which had motivated him to come down personally to look the situation over. Every one of those possibilities had to be examined while the evidence was fresh, and while suspects might still be in the vicinity.

But if they could retrieve the videotape—and if it was undamaged, he thought uneasily—it could avoid false starts, and the information it yielded might mean quick closure to the NEWBOM investigation. Reaching it was going to be a bitch, however. Like a game of pickup sticks played by giants, the fragile wreckage had the potential to shift and slide at the slightest misapplication of pressure. The result could be doubly disastrous: the loss of key pieces of forensic evidence, including the videotape, and an increase in the victim count.

Not on my watch, Rickhauser vowed. Bastards have gotten the last notch on their belts they'll ever get.

He turned away from the window to view the temporary command-and-control center, where police, FBI and ATF agents, Data-Trax officials and building engineers were moving in and out. Some were poring over the blueprints that had finally arrived from the Boston architectural firm of Glaser and Rich, which had designed the main building, constructed six years earlier. Data-Trax's own copies of the blueprints, like so much else, were buried in the rubble.

"There are fire exits at either end of the building," the architect, Glaser, was saying. He'd returned with the FBI copter that had flown over to the firm's downtown rooftop to pick up the blueprints. When the diminutive man—five-two, max—had marched in a few minutes earlier carrying the rolled-up plans against his side like a rifle, Rickhauser had had the impression of a toy soldier on parade.

The big sheets were open before him now, spread on the conference table and anchored at the corners by a brief-case, a water jug, a telephone and a Coke can. Rickhauser moved next to the architect and leaned over the plans, planting one massive hand and arm on the table like a buttress to support his off-balance hulk. He squinted at smeary, blue-on-blue lines, while the beefy fingers of his free hand fished in his breast pocket. When he found his reading glasses and slipped them on, the lines came into sharp, precisely rendered focus. He stabbed at a couple of tiny, striped rectangles.

"These staircases next to the fire exits," he said, "they go all the way down to the basement?"

"Yes," Glaser replied. He lifted the Coke can and the water jug, then flipped to another page, his whole arm length required to execute the movement. The next sheet, Rickhauser noted by the corner legend, was the floor plan of the basement. Reanchoring the paper, the architect traced a line from the stairwell at one end to a small square near the center.

"If you want to reach the security office," he said, "the shortest route, aside from the lobby access point, which is obviously a nonstarter, is the exit on the south side of the building. You've got an interior fire door, then...let's see...fifteen, twenty feet of straight hallway, and you're there.''

Curtis Pullen squeezed his way in next to Rickhauser. ''Except,'' he said, ''we already tried that. The exterior door's jammed solid. Engineers say the blast may have shifted the building's foundation a millimeter or two. A lot of the door and window frames are skewed.''

''Can we cut through?'' Rickhauser asked.

''Those doors are two-inch, solid steel, so it'd take some doing,'' Glaser replied, ''but it's possible, yes.''

The Newton fire department's on-site commander, a Lieutenant Ealy, stood across the table from them. ''One slight problem—with the weight of the building redistributed, we've got to shore up everything we touch. We've already gone through our supply of foundation jacks, trying to get at the victims in the lobby and the tunnel. We've put a call out for more, but—''

''What about the exit at the north end?'' Rickhauser interrupted, tracing the path of a double line on the blueprint. ''It's open, isn't it? The route's farther, but—''

Ealy shook his head. ''It's open, all right. That's how most of the upper-floor occupants were taken out. But the basement behind the interior fire door is flooded by a broken water main, and blocked by fallen beams and debris at about the twenty-foot mark. Some of my men were down there, checking for victims, but they had to turn back until we could secure the ceilings.''

''Damn!'' Rickhauser cursed, the table jumping as his fist slammed down. Only the architect's quick reflexes prevented the Coke can from toppling and spilling over the blueprints. ''Sorry,'' the ADIC muttered. He straightened and addressed the group. ''Okay, then, people, we need to cut through that exit on the south wall. When are those jacks expected?''

"Within the hour," Ealy said.

"Can we make it quicker?"

"I can try."

"Please do. Meantime, let's see if we can rig some temporary support so the guys with the torches can get to work on that door." As the firefighter and others bustled out, Rickhauser turned to the acting SAC. "Boston field office has one of the new surveillance vans equipped with a satellite uplink to headquarters, doesn't it?"

"Yes, sir," Pullen said, nodding. "Received it about six weeks ago. It's a beauty—long-range video and audio recording and editing, real-time satellite transmission and reception. We're using it on a Russian-mob stakeout at the moment."

"Not anymore. I'm reassigning it."

"Sir?"

"Get it over here. The minute we get our hands on that security video, I want to review it together with the lab boys at Quantico—do a frame-by-frame analysis. If," Rickhauser added soberly, "the damn tape's not damaged. If it is, we'll have to ship it up to them physically, see what they can salvage."

Pullen nodded eagerly and jumped for the nearest free phone. "I'll have the van here within the hour, sir."

Winslow, Massachusetts: 11:32 p.m.

She needed to talk to someone, Leya decided, dialing the number of her half sister in Albany. It was only when Susan's phone began to ring that she noticed the clock on the wall, and berated herself for calling so late. "Did I wake you?" she asked anxiously when Susan, gravelly voiced, finally picked up.

"Oh, Leya, hi! No—well, yes, actually, but it's okay.

I'm glad you did. I was lying on the sofa, reading, and I dozed off. I hate that, don't you? Now I'll be prowling for hours.''

"Where are Mike and the kids?"

"Erin's sleeping over at a friend's, and Mike and Will went to a hockey game. The kids are on spring break this week," Susan said, yawning, "so they don't have to get up for school. I was wondering if you'd gotten my message.''

"I would have called earlier, but I had a date with John. I had to cancel in the end, though. That bombing in Newton shut down the Mass Turnpike and there was no way I could make it in on time. Just as well. Things got a little crazy after that.''

"Oh! The bomb—I saw a report about it on the news, but it didn't click that you'd be affected. It's awful, isn't it? Those poor people, heading out the office door, looking forward to dinner and putting their feet up in front of the tube. Then suddenly, boom! None of them will ever be the same again. The survivors, the families, the rescue team— they're all going to live with this for the rest of their lives.''

"I know. You think you're invulnerable, then some random act of violence touches you, and..." Leya's voice drifted off. Random acts, she thought. Bombs. Guns. Kidnapping.

"I hear they're looking for some Palestinian."

"Yes, and a young woman who drove him to that building. It turns out she's a student of mine.''

"You're kidding!"

"No, and what's more, she showed up here at my house tonight, then disappeared when..." Leya hesitated. Maybe she wasn't supposed to be talking about this. Peter hadn't said not to, but maybe she was leaking confidential information, and— She caught herself, and shook her head. No doubt about it, she thought. Life as Carter Nash's daughter had left her marked by his habitual paranoia. If Susan had escaped the curse, it was probably only because she'd had so little contact with their father.

"You okay?" her sister asked.

"I'm fine. It's been an stressful night, that's all."

"Missing your date with John, and all."

"It's not the date."

"It's not? So, how do you feel about that?"

Leya smiled, in spite of herself. "Now there's a real shrink-type question."

"Oops, you're right," Susan said sheepishly. "Sorry. The kids hate it when I do that."

"I forgive you. But to answer your question, I feel fine about it. I wasn't really looking forward to the evening, but I didn't have much choice about going."

"Of course you did."

"Not really. John bought those season tickets—"

"For you. I know. Last Christmas, right after you tried to tell him you wanted to see less of him, wasn't it?"

"So what are you saying?"

"You tell me."

"He suckered me into spending more time with him, instead of less?"

"I don't know. What do you think?"

Another shrink question, Leya thought. The poor woman probably couldn't help herself. "I think— No, I know," she amended, "that he could have given me the tickets to use as I wanted if they really were a gift and not a bribe."

"Very good."

"So what does that make me? Codependent? An enabler?"

"Those words will never cross my lips. Anyway, you're off the hook, this time."

"Not quite," Leya said.

"How so?"

"He's coming over tomorrow night. That's progress, actually. I'm the one who usually has to drive in. I live in a cultural and culinary wasteland, according to John Merriman." Leya sighed again. "Listen to me—I don't know why I complain so much. John really is a nice man. Even Dad likes him."

"Oh, high praise indeed! Look, Leya, I've never met John Merriman, and maybe he's the greatest, but your enthusiasm seems so underwhelming whenever you mention him that I have to wonder, that's all."

"Maybe the problem's not John, Susan. Maybe it's me."

"What do you mean?"

"Well, that's why I called."

"You didn't call about Easter?"

Actually, Leya had forgotten all about the invitation. "I haven't got an answer for you on that yet."

"Don't tell me—Dad's waffling."

"It's not that he's not eager to see you guys," Leya hedged, embarrassed and frustrated that her father's intransigence had put her in this position—again. "He's just on a rampage these days."

"So what else is new? What set him off this time?"

"My house. I caught him this afternoon, trying to intimidate my contractor."

"I thought this guy you hired comes highly recommended."

"He does, but you know Dad."

"Yes, and I know he's going to continue to try to run

your life, Leya, until you put your foot down and tell him to butt out."

"I've tried, but he gets so worked up that I'm afraid—"

"That he'll work himself into another stroke. Don't you see? That's what he wants you to think. It's his way of maintaining control."

Leya sighed and rested her forehead in her hand, sighing deeply. "I've been walking around in circles here, Susan, working myself into a complete lather."

"Why? What's he done?"

"It's not Dad. You'll never guess who showed up here tonight."

"You mentioned that student of yours."

"Holly, yes. She ran off before I could try to help, and I'm awfully worried about her. But someone else was here, too. A ghost from the past."

The line between them crackled for a second or two. Then, Susan ventured, "Not Peter...?"

She was nothing if not astute, Leya realized. "Yes."

A year earlier, when she and her half sister had both ended up in New York for simultaneous academic conferences, they'd spent a long evening together, talking through dinner and several glasses of wine—the longest conversation they'd ever had without their father hovering nearby. After dealing with awkward issues like their divided family, their respective mothers, and the irascible, domineering Carter Nash, they'd launched into more conventional sisterly subjects, like the men in their lives, past and present. And that night, Leya had told Susan about Peter vanAken.

"Oh, my," Susan said. "I can see why you're in a lather. So, how was he?"

"Very, very strange. Not what I remembered at all."

"Physically, you mean?"

"Partly that. It's been ten years, of course, but he's so worn-out looking. Scarred—externally, but internally, too, I'd say."

"That's not so surprising, is it, after what he went through? Four years of confinement, torture—my God, that would damage anyone."

"He said the worst part was being shackled, day and night. Peter was such a free spirit when I knew him, Susan, that I have to believe it. He said it made him crazy."

"I can imagine."

"No, I mean *really* insane. He tried to rip off his own hands to be free of his shackles. Nearly killed himself." Leya heard Susan's shocked murmur. "I haven't heard a word from him in all these years, and now, suddenly, he shows up out of the blue. But he seems so changed. So angry."

"Not toward you, surely?"

"Toward everyone and everything, including me."

"But why you?"

"I couldn't figure it out, at first," Leya said, frowning. "But as he was leaving, Peter asked why I hadn't contacted him after Dad made me leave Beirut that time. I sent him a cable, Susan, I really did, but for some reason, he never got it. I think he feels I betrayed him. And in a way, maybe I did let him down. If he'd followed me out, he might not have been taken hostage."

"But wasn't he kidnapped several weeks after you left? You would have been back at school by then, anyway."

"Yes, but when we were in Beirut, he told me he was thinking of leaving." Leya's finger traced the squares of the blue tile countertop. "I could be wrong, but at the time, I thought he might move back to the States, to be closer to me. If we'd had more time together, maybe—"

"Leya," Susan said sternly, "it's *not* your fault Peter was taken hostage. You know that, don't you?"

"He didn't get my cable. He must have thought I'd changed my mind, that I didn't want to be with him, so he delayed."

"And so it's your fault?"

Leya sighed. "No, I guess not. But that seems to be where he's coming from. He was so cold to me."

"But this is crazy! I mean, I'm sorry the guy went through such a terrible ordeal, but to blame you..." Susan was silent for a moment, and when she spoke again, Leya heard something firm and clinical in her voice. "Why has he shown up now? Do you think there's any chance he's been watching you?"

"Watching? You mean, like stalking?"

"Yes. He sounds disturbed, Leya—which wouldn't be surprising. The kind of trauma he's been through would throw anyone off-balance. I don't want to frighten you, but I think you need to be very, very careful around this guy."

"You think he's dangerous?"

"Potentially. People who harbor festering grudges can snap unexpectedly. Does he have a family?"

"No. His parents are both dead, and he mentioned that he wasn't married."

"Inability to form bonds of trust and love," Susan said, as if reading from one of her case files. "Sounds like a textbook example of post-traumatic stress syndrome."

"Oh, no, you're reading this all wrong," Leya said hastily. "It's not like he's a derelict, you know. He works—"

"Don't they always? 'He seemed like such a quiet, hardworking fellow.' Isn't that what the shocked colleagues always say whenever some guy cracks and goes berserk?''

"That's not Peter. If you'd known how he was, Susan. Brilliant, fun-loving, warm—''

"And as a therapist, I'd love to have a go at the man, Leya, and try to help him work through his problems. But as your sister, I have to warn you that the Peter you once knew is probably gone. And also, that your memories of him could be a little distorted.''

"Distorted? How?''

"Just stop to think for a minute. You were a sheltered, inexperienced young woman when you met him—this handsome, Indiana Jones character who sweeps you off your feet, reads you Arabic love poems in the middle of a war zone, and makes love to you under a full moon in an ancient ruin. The frigging Temple of Jupiter, for crying out loud! That alone would pack an emotional wallop. But then, this same guy—who's actually leading a double life and has lied to you, and maybe to a lot of other people, too—vanishes, is held hostage and tortured by fanatics for four years, emerging from the ordeal a hollow, angry shell of the man he once was.''

"He was a good man,'' Leya insisted, "even if he didn't tell me he was one of Dad's covert operatives. And I could never fathom that treason business. There had to have been some mistake.''

"Maybe,'' Susan said, her voice dripping with skepticism. "But even so, you have to realize that your own memories of Peter are clouded by powerful emotions. This angry man you saw tonight, ten years and a million miles of experiences after that brief time you spent with him, is an altogether different person. Potentially a dangerous person.''

Leya ran her fingers along the telephone receiver, the

same one he'd used a short while earlier. She inhaled, trying to pick up his scent. "Maybe I can help him," she said quietly.

A sigh whistled down the line. "Oh, Leya! If I had a dollar for every good woman who thought she could save a disturbed man, I'd—" Susan paused. "Well, I'd probably still do what I do, but I'd come home to *much* fancier digs."

"You think I should forget him?"

"You'll never forget him, but for your own well-being, I really don't think it's wise for you see him again."

"That could be difficult."

"Why?"

"Because in the first place, he's with the FBI now, and he's working this bombing case. That's what brought him here tonight. He's trying to find that student of mine."

"Great! A potentially psychopathic G-man," Susan muttered. "You said 'in the first place.' What else?"

"In the second place, I asked him to come back and see me when he's off the case."

"You didn't."

"I'm afraid I did."

Tuesday, March 28, 1995—Day Two

A Sea of Troubles

16

Greek kings and Burger Kings, vanAken thought, sighing wearily as he scoped out the fast-food restaurant.

He'd named the operation to infiltrate the Hamas terrorist group MENELOP, after Menelaus, the Greek monarch who'd built the Trojan horse. Karim Khoury couldn't have known that, but he seemed to be laughing in vanAken's face, anyway, leading him on this merry chase—first to the Cambridge Burger King, which had been the phone number he'd left his landlady, then here, to the Winslow branch of the same restaurant chain, whose pay phone turned out to be the number Holly Stroud had dialed from Leya's house.

VanAken hunkered down in the driver's seat while he surveyed the place, trying to conserve body warmth as the outside temperature plummeted—punishing himself by refusing to turn on the car heater. The restaurant was at one end of a strip mall. He'd parked in shadow under a spruce tree in a far corner of the lot so as to have an overview of the entire area. The Burger King had closed at midnight, and the teenage counter staff was cleaning up, between games of pitch-the-catsup-pack. VanAken watched their antics as he sipped the extra-large coffee he'd loaded down with sugar, Middle-East style, for an added energy boost.

How the hell, he wondered grimly, does an archaeological historian who spent the first half of his life bouncing across Middle Eastern plains on camels and in Land Rovers, seeking lost temples, golden cities and ancient civilizations—a guy who knows more about Phoenicians than forensics—wind up like some pulp-fiction gumshoe, his life an endless series of stake-outs of strip malls, rooming houses, greasy spoons and all the other nondescript, colorless places where criminal scum conceal themselves?

Some people loved the game, he knew—the stalking, the chase, and, if they were lucky, the capture. He just didn't happen to be one of them. He'd drifted into federal police work almost by accident, after it became clear that a future in Langley was out of the question—not that he'd been the world's most eager intelligence officer, either. But he'd turned out to be a round peg in the FBI's square hole, too. He knew it, and so did everyone else in the Bureau he'd ever dealt with.

He should have moved on long ago, except that there was nowhere to go—no career, place or person he could bring himself to give a damn about. He was like a bug after an encounter with a spider. Beirut had sucked him dry, and now he drifted weightlessly, carried wherever the winds of fate saw fit to toss him.

He pulled out his cell phone and punched in the number of the Boston field office. "This is Agent vanAken," he said, when the night-duty agent picked up. "Patch me through to Assistant Deputy Rickhauser, would you? He was out at the Newton bomb site with the SAC, last I knew." VanAken waited while the duty agent tracked him down. He'd met Rickhauser six years earlier, and at this point, the ADIC was about the only human being with whom he had a civil relationship.

After escaping his captors in Beirut and returning to the States, vanAken had walked smack into a hornet's nest at Langley. The CIA had gone through a series of scandals and embarrassing revelations over illegal activities during the time he'd been held prisoner. The President had appointed a federal judge, who'd spent several years as FBI director, to take over the Agency and try to clean up its act. The judge had drawn an old bureau agent, Len Rickhauser, into the CIA inspector general's office. It was Rickhauser who'd led the investigation into charges that vanAken had been involved in a terrorist bombing causing sixty-three deaths at the U.S. Embassy in Beirut—charges brought by Carter Nash, chief of station at the time.

Nash versus vanAken. It had been a hopeless mismatch from the start, given the former's reputation and credibility inside the Agency. Nash was the heroes' hero. For a quarter-century, he'd led some of the Agency's most audacious covert ops, snatched agents from the jaws of certain death, and never left a man in enemy hands—except him, vanAken thought bitterly.

He'd spent a mere two years as a CIA area specialist before his capture. In that time, he'd bucked his station chief, fought the Agency's policy line on Lebanon, and, in general, not played the game by company rules. He had no allies in Langley. And when he'd first set eyes on Rickhauser, vanAken had been convinced that his goose was well and truly cooked.

But, incredibly, the old wolf had saved him from the Allenwood Federal Penitentiary cell that had looked to be his inevitable next stop. An outsider with a stolid cop mentality, Rickhauser had been neither swayed by the evidence, awed by Carter Nash, nor intimidated by the CIA old-boy network that had arrayed itself against vanAken. When he'd eventually left the Agency to return to his FBI home turf, Rickhauser had scooped vanAken and taken him along. Not letting this man down had been vanAken's last remaining personal commitment. Now, it looked as if that link was disintegrating, too, right alongside Operation Menelaus.

A gruff voice came across the telephone line. "Rickhauser."

"It's Peter, Len."

"Where are you?"

"Outside the Winslow Burger King. Khoury was here when Holly Stroud called him. I hung around to see if they'd show back, but it looks like the trail's gone cold."

"You're sure he was actually there?"

"Yeah. I staked the place out for a while and finally went inside, looked around. No Karim, but when I pulled out a picture, a kid at the counter said he's seen him in there a few times, including earlier this evening—which doesn't surprise me."

"How so?"

"Kid gets stressed, first thing he does is eat. Whoppers are his comfort food—that and Reese's Pieces, believe it or not. I can't tell you how many I've watched disappear during debriefings over the past couple of years." The amazing thing, vanAken thought, was that Karim was thin as a rail, the evidence of his junk-food compulsion concealed by a hyperactive metabolism—jump-started, he suspected, by a good measure of fear.

"Bullet doesn't drop the kid, clogged arteries will," Rickhauser said. "What about the girl?"

"Disappeared, as well. I think I spooked her when I showed up at the house."

The ADIC was silent for a moment. "You haven't seen her before tonight, have you?"

"The Stroud girl?"

"No, you know who I'm talking about—Nash's daughter. Have you seen her since Beirut?"

"No."

"And? You okay?"

"Fine. You know," vanAken said, changing the subject, "this is the second time Karim's left a trail to a Burger King. That dummy number he left his landlady when he disappeared in Cambridge turned out to be the Burger King there."

"So what's your point?"

"That phone in Cambridge was one of our contact points when we needed to set up a meet. I think it's a message. I think Karim's letting me know he knows I'm on his trail."

"Cocking his snoot at us—defiant little bugger."

"Yeah, maybe."

"You don't think so?"

"I'm not sure. Maybe he's just saying he wants out of the game."

"Kind of coincidental, him showing up at Data-Trax today, don't you think? Bomb's a funny way to say good-bye."

"Yeah. Shit, Len, I don't know. He was a reluctant recruit, but I thought he was with us, I really did."

"Don't beat yourself up over it. Maybe he was playing a double hand from the start. Or maybe, he got turned later. Who knows? One way or another, Pete, that operation's gone south. I've got agents out rounding up all the Hamas suspects on the MENELOP file before they disappear, too. I don't know if we've got anything there to nail 'em on, but if there's a link to NEWBOM, I don't want 'em getting away on us.''

VanAken slumped lower in his seat. Despite his lack of enthusiasm for the work, he'd gone through the motions, knowing the assistant deputy had taken a chance on him when others would happily have seen him shot—trying not to insult Rickhauser's faith in him by fucking up. Looked like he had, anyway. "What do you want me to do now?"

"You should crash for a while. You slept at all in the last three days?"

"Some. I'm okay."

"Pullen sent a few agents out to Winslow after they got the DMV info. They were back at her dorm after you were there, and some of her other haunts."

"Leya's?"

"No. I told him you had that one covered for now. We'll fan out with additional manpower at first light if we haven't located the Stroud girl and Khoury by then."

"The girl's key, Len. I'm sure of it. She and Karim have got some kind of cockamamy alliance going on here."

"There's another possibility, you know. That Khoury's using the girl to get at Arthur Stroud. I think she's in very serious trouble here."

"I know." The cold shiver vanAken felt had nothing to do with his stoic refusal to employ the car heater. "It's been worrying the hell out of me since I found out who the girl was. But I would have sworn Karim wasn't capable of violence, Len, especially not against a girl like that, no matter who her father might be."

"Maybe he's got no choice. Maybe he's just a pawn in Hamas's game."

"Yeah, maybe. Or, more likely, I'm a lousy judge of character."

The line was silent for a moment. Then Rickhauser said, "Get some rest, Peter."

"I'm going to stick around Winslow, keep an eye out for them."

"Get some sleep. That's an order. You're no damn good to me as a walking zombie. Check back in the morning, at 0700, and we'll see where we're at."

VanAken sighed. "Roger."

He pressed the cell-phone button to end the call, then watched the Burger King staff finally emerge and lock up the place. As the last car pulled out of the lot, he downed the sticky dregs of his coffee, gone cold now, and considered his next move. Sleep was not an option. The problem was, he seemed to be fresh out of alternatives.

Leya was right. Fool that he was, he'd spooked the Stroud girl by barreling in and stomping around the house like some jackbooted stormtrooper. He hadn't meant to be so heavy-handed. He just hadn't anticipated how off-balance he'd be thrown by going into that house. He shook his head. It wasn't the house. It was her. Seeing her again. Inhaling a scent that he thought he'd forgotten and redis-covering what it did to him. Standing next to her. Touching her with his scarred, ugly hands. Shaken by the whole experience, determined not to let her see it, he'd grumbled and blustered—like a drunk angrily insisting on his sobri-ety.

VanAken popped his coffee container into the cup holder and turned the key in the ignition, grimly resolved to forget her and focus on the hunt for Karim and Holly. When moving forward isn't an option, he thought, you go backward, retracing steps. As he'd told Rickhauser, it was unlikely they'd gotten far since she'd left Leya's—not with the girl so terrified, knowing every cop on the eastern sea-board was watching for her green Mercedes with its vanity

plates bearing the shallow boast, TUF ENUF. Which
meant there was a good chance they were still in Winslow.
Obviously not at the Burger King, but this was the girl's
territory, so they may have slipped back to someplace she
knew and felt safe. The Mount Abbey campus, in all likelihood. Unless, vanAken thought uneasily, they'd circled
back to Leya's house once the coast was clear.

Cruising up and down the streets of Winslow, he tried
to imagine what was going through Karim's head. How
had he missed the warning signs that the kid was getting
ready to bolt? Admittedly, Karim had been a reluctant recruit. But it was payback time, vanAken had argued.
Karim owed America for taking him in and giving him a
home. When the young man had still resisted wading into
the alligator swamp of Middle East politics, vanAken had
pushed harder, invoking the personal debt Karim owed
him, as well, for arranging his immigration in the first
place.

It was strictly business, vanAken had told himself, as
he'd bulldozed over Karim's fears and objections, a matter
of national security. In time of war, including the war
against terrorism, it was sometimes necessary to draft reluctant soldiers. Karim's number had come up, and he'd
been drafted. Tough luck. So had vanAken's, at the same
age as Karim, and he'd paid the price—a high price—for
his patriotism. Why should Karim be any different?

Except, vanAken was now forced to admit, he had been
a willing draftee, and patriotism had had little to do with
his motives. When he'd been approached to work undercover in Beirut, he'd been a twenty-three-year-old with a
freshly minted doctorate—specializing, like his father, in
the history and archaeology of the Middle East—and an
academic career ahead of him that everyone predicted
would be brilliant, because he was, after all, the gifted son

of Lucius vanAken. But as he'd contemplated the prospect of following a road already well-trod by his father, he'd felt overshadowed and bored. And so the young Peter van-Aken, fool that he was, had jumped at the opportunity to play spy games.

It had seemed such a lark. He'd moved through his CIA training in weapons and covert communications with the same precocious ease that had already allowed him to assimilate several languages and cultures. At his initiation into the secret-ops brotherhood, he'd been told that former friends were "sources" to be exploited. He learned to hold himself aloof and suspicious, trusting only his fellow undercover operatives. For a time, he closed his eyes to the fact that most of them were cynical, ruthless and hopelessly bigoted. That they held in contempt everyone outside their secret caste, foreigners and Americans alike. That they screwed indiscriminately with women they couldn't bring themselves to respect. That they drank excessively to drown self-doubt and the certain knowledge that, in setting themselves up as their own personal gods, they had fallen into the ugliest of cults.

In Lebanon, he soon discovered, they put their own biased spin on every cable back to Washington, until official policy became sunk so deep in quagmire and contradiction that disasters like the embassy and marine-barracks bombings became inevitable.

But by the time vanAken had realized he wanted out of the brotherhood, it was too late.

Karim Khoury, by contrast, had been born in the midst of intrigue and factional violence. While at his age van-Aken had craved adventure, Karim had seemed to want nothing more than to be the all-American kid, finding his own quiet way in his adopted country. He loved Whoppers, Reese's Pieces and baseball. He memorized starting

lineups and earned-run stats. Karim had worked his tail off
to gain admittance to MIT, then slogged his way for four
years toward an engineering degree.

Had he now abandoned all that? vanAken asked himself
for the hundredth time since reading the name on the Data-
Trax security log. Had Karim given himself over to violence and fanaticism, after all? Or had his Hamas contacts
simply blackmailed him more effectively than vanAken
himself had done?

Recalling Leya's report of how Holly Stroud had tried
to teach him in-line skating, vanAken shook his head at a
mental picture of gangly, shy Karim on Rollerblades. Then
he felt a stab of guilt. The skates had been a birthday
present, Leya said. VanAken hadn't even bothered to note
his young agent's birthday, despite the fact that Karim had
no one else who'd mark the occasion—except Holly, as it
turned out. Holly had also plotted to shelter Karim by marrying him, believing no one would dare touch Ambassador
Stroud's son-in-law—presuming a man like Arthur Stroud
would even stand by and let such a marriage go unchal-
lenged. The girl was painfully naive, vanAken thought. He
only hoped it wasn't too late to save her from herself, even
if Karim turned out to be a lost cause.

VanAken cruised Winslow's main drag, scanning side
streets, peering at knots of young people strolling out of
closing bars and hangouts like Tyler's. Reaching the edge
of town, he turned in at the college's big stone gates and
headed down a tree-covered alley toward Escott Hall.
When he'd been there earlier in the evening and the housemother had taken him up to search Holly Stroud's room,
he'd found nothing significant, except a collection of
stuffed teddy bears, closets jam-packed with expensive
clothes, and walls covered with Amnesty International
posters—the retreat of a privileged child with a budding

social conscience. The dresser top had been covered with everyday toiletries, and under the bed, vanAken had found what seemed to be a full set of luggage, the pieces nested one inside the other. Whatever else Holly Stroud had planned for that day, skipping town hadn't seemed to be on her agenda.

Now, back at the residence, he saw that her second-floor window was unlit, as were most of the others in the building, including the housemother's. Another dark-colored Ford Taurus was parked across the road from the residence—one of Pullen's agents, vanAken noted, catching a glimpse of a close-cropped head in the driver's side window. They nodded to one another, then vanAken continued on through the quiet grounds of the college, looking for coves or corners where Holly and Karim might have hidden the conspicuous vehicle. There were plenty of possibilities.

Tucked in the gently rolling hills of eastern Massachusetts, the Mount Abbey campus was well treed and idyllic, with a network of roadways and walkways that threaded between ivy-covered brick buildings. VanAken found himself wondering in which of these Leya spent her days. At a fork in the road, a set of signposts pointed, variously, to the Field House and Pool, the Theater, and the Admin, Physical Sciences, and Fine Arts buildings. VanAken took the road toward the theater. It twisted between bicycle paths and tennis courts, ending at a small lake, surrounded and overshadowed by towering evergreens and denuded maples and oaks.

He brought the car to a stop and leaned back wearily in the seat casting his gaze across the lake. On the far side, towering majestically over it like a transplanted Parthenon, stood a flood-lit white Greek Revival edifice. Over six fluted Doric columns, the words Elizabeth Wilkins Theater were etched deep into a frieze topped by a simple, peaked cornice. From the pillared facade, broad steps stretching the entire width of the portico ran down almost to the water's edge. In summertime, he thought, the building would be reflected on the water, picturesque as hell—the kind of view featured on student-recruitment and alumnae fund-raising brochures.

Rolling down his window, vanAken leaned out and inhaled a clear, cold breath, then watched it billow before him as he exhaled. He rested his head against the door frame, cold steel easing the throbbing in his temple, as he studied the theater, the serene beauty of its design handed down from the ancients. It would be hard to imagine a more peaceful setting, yet it inspired in him only a dry, hollow melancholy. Deep in his gut, he felt again the gnawing sense that, a long time ago, his life had taken a fatally wrong turn.

Now, trapped in dark thickets, the path behind him overgrown and impassable, all he could do was hack his lost and bloodied way forward. Anger was his shield and his weapon, revenge his only conceivable refuge.

17

Newton, Massachusetts: 1:13 a.m.

Len Rickhauser stepped outside the Data-Trax annex and glanced up. Large, feathery flakes of snow had begun to waft over the bomb site, drifting and dancing against a backdrop of emergency floodlights, lending an obscenely festive air to the scene. Flipping up the collar of his overcoat, he headed down the front steps and along the path to check on the progress of the search for the security video.

But before he was halfway across the compound, his big barrel chest was heaving. He cursed his out-of-shape body. Wendy, his wife of thirty-two years, did her best to keep his diet limited to fruits, vegetables and steamed fish, convinced her commonsense cooking would sooner or later undo the damage wrought by too many desk jobs, around-the-clock investigations, and take-out meals. But Rickhauser, who'd never been small, knew that every bomber, serial killer, kidnapper and paranoid, armed-to-the-teeth nutcase out there would add a few more pounds to his bulky frame, until he retired from the Bureau or dropped in mid-hunt.

On the path ahead, he spotted a cloaked figure standing motionless, staring at the devastation. Earlier in the evening he'd spoken to the man, a computer analyst who'd been on the fourth floor of the building when the bomb went off. The man's pregnant wife had worked downstairs in the lobby, at the Data-Trax reception desk, and she was still missing.

A shimmer of sympathy for the young man's grief ran through him, and Rickhauser swallowed hard. He'd called his own wife a couple of hours earlier at their Maryland home, just outside Washington. Throughout their long marriage, no matter where in the field the job had taken him, not a day had gone by that they hadn't spoken to one another. He couldn't imagine life without her.

Len Rickhauser had met Wendy Nakamura when they were both juniors at UC Davis. Rickhauser had attended the central California college on a basketball scholarship. Not that there was anything graceful about his playing style. It was a little like watching the running of the bulls at Pamplona: once he'd worked up a head of steam, you didn't want to stand in his path.

Wendy had shown up at a postgame party with a couple of her girlfriends one night, and Rickhauser had been smitten the minute he set eyes on the lithe, black-eyed beauty with the shy smile and a rope of silky, waist-length hair that begged to be touched. He was plug-ugly, with his yellow eyes and battered nose, and he knew it. But there were plenty of center-court groupies sufficiently impressed with his size and his team letter to overlook his face. Not Wendy, however.

Rickhauser had pursued her for two years, going so far as to join the San Diego Police Department after graduation, because Wendy had moved back down there to teach third grade and be near her family. He'd spent most of his off-duty hours hanging around Hiroshi Nakamura's fruit-and-vegetable fields, helping her father and brothers lug heavy flats to county farmers' markets. Finally, late one night, as he and Wendy were out walking in the berry fields, he'd asked her to marry him. From that moment on, the flavor of strawberries had become linked in Len Rickhauser's mind to the unbelievable feeling he'd had when she'd said yes, and to the memory of making love to her in a cool, loamy furrow, and tasting their sweet juices on her mouth. Even now, he never ate strawberries in public for fear of embarrassing himself at the erotic response they aroused in him.

When the ADIC lumbered next to him, the young man on the sidewalk glanced up, then turned his gaze back to the wrecked building. Rescue workers had given him a blanket to keep warm while he maintained his vigil, and it was wrapped around his shoulders, hunched forward and down in a posture of grief and defeat. "No word yet, Mr. Pirelli?" Rickhauser asked quietly.

Alec Pirelli spread one arm wide, the movement sending snowflakes tumbling from the coarsely woven blanket. Underneath, Rickhauser saw, he was clutching a scuffed and torn black leather sack. "They found her purse about an hour ago," he murmured. "They say it could be a while yet till they can get to Angie." He closed his arms again, gently cradling the battered handbag under the blanket, like a child.

"Why don't you go inside, son?" Rickhauser said gently. "Warm up a little. I'll make sure someone comes for you, soon as there's any news."

Pirelli shook his head, glistening eyes fixed on the scurrying rescue team. "No, I'll wait." His Adam's apple slid up and down his neck. After a moment, he asked huskily, "You ever put together a crib?"

"Yeah. Long time ago."

"How many kids do you have?"

"Three, but they're all grown-up now."

"This was going to be our first. I finally got the baby's room finished this past weekend. Those cribs, though—they're hell to put together, aren't they? What with all those safety catches and everything?"

Rickhauser nodded, and they fell silent while he considered the crib, destined to remain empty now. How would Alec Pirelli react, he wondered, if he knew Rickhauser had woken up Monday morning, knowing a bomb would go off that day? Certain it would happen, but unable to guess where, much less why. Helpless, therefore, to do a damn thing to prevent the Pirellis' nursery from becoming a shrine to vicious, senseless loss.

"You get 'em," the younger man said suddenly. He turned to the ADIC, and when he spoke again, his voice was raspy hard. "You make sure you get the bastards who did this."

Rickhauser nodded grimly. "I will. I promise you, Mr. Pirelli, I *will* get them."

Winslow, Massachusetts: 2:15 a.m.

Leya reread the paragraph for the fourth time, then gave up and closed the essay, ripping off her glasses in disgust. Elbows on the desktop, she pressed the heels of her hands into her burning eyes. It was hopeless. She couldn't concentrate. She'd spent the past two hours since talking to Susan alternately pacing and trying to address the piles of paper on her desk, knowing sleep was impossible until she'd found some way to exhaust herself beyond the mind's power to torture with unanswerable questions. It wasn't working.

She sighed and leaned back in the carved oak chair. The Hemingway essays would just have to wait, and her *Ham-*

let cast would have to do one more script run-through without their Act V stage positions blocked. Without their Ophelia, too, she thought, stomach plummeting as she tried again to imagine what had been going through poor Holly's mind when she'd bolted from the kitchen like that. Had she heard Peter say he was taking her into custody? Had she heard him bullying, threatening Leya with arrest?

Who is he? a voice in the back of her brain agonized. *What's he become?*

Had Holly gone into hiding with Karim? Or to try to convince him to turn himself in? Would Karim hurt her? Or take her hostage, offering up Ambassador Stroud's child in exchange for his own freedom?

Hostage. *"Don't you know about trapping wild things, Leya?"* Peter had asked.

Holly, where are you? Leya telegraphed anxiously.

Pushing back the chair, she stood, tugged down the sleeves of her sweatshirt, and walked out of the circle of light cast by the gooseneck lamp on the desk. Barefoot, she paced back and forth in the small space between the desk, the computer table, the bed and the door, feeling full of trepidation for Holly Stroud—and for herself. Because no matter what Susan might say about hyped emotions, distorted memories and a victim's anger, she knew she was as drawn to Peter vanAken now as she had been a decade earlier, in spite of his strange, angry demeanor. A tide to his lunar gravitational pull.

Lunar. Lunatic. Moonstruck insanity. There'd always been a measure of that in him—especially in the reckless ease with which he'd dodged between and behind the myriad factional lines of that violent, beautiful land where they'd met.

* * *

They spent five days together in Lebanon, during a pe-

riod of rare but welcome calm in the country. Over those five days, as she felt herself falling under his spell, Leya watched Peter weave it on others, as well—encouraging his students, charming the friends he seemed to have everywhere, easing his way past Shiite, Druze, Christian, Israeli and Syrian checkpoints that bristled with weapons and nervous young zealots.

That first day, driving into Beirut along the airport road where so many Westerners had already been abducted, they passed easily through several checkpoints. As Leya watched bombed-out buildings flash between swaying palms and dusty, gray-green olive trees, Peter tried to put the civil conflict into perspective for her.

"It's always been a fragile country. A community of communities, mutually distrustful. Christians and Muslims are the largest groups, and then you've got the small Druze sect thrown in for good measure."

"Is that what the fighting's about? Christians versus Muslims?"

He sighed. "If only it were that simple. No, there are divisions within each—Maronite versus Orthodox Christians, Shiite versus Sunni Muslims, the Druze constantly shifting alliances—all of them occupying their own little fiefdoms, isolating themselves from one another, following warlords obsessed with personal power, even if it means sacrificing their country."

"A kaleidoscope."

"That's it. And every time you start to see some order to the place, someone shakes things up again. You've got Palestinians, for example, driven out of Israel. The Jordanians and Egyptians won't have the refugees on their territory, but Lebanon can't resist the onslaught. Then, the Israelis invade and bomb the southern regions to retaliate against cross-border attacks from the PLO. That pushes

out the Lebanese Shiites who live there, sending them crashing north into the other sects.''

''And all these Syrian soldiers?''

Peter grimaced. ''Ah, yes—the other neighbors. They stir the pot, dividing and conquering whenever the locals show signs of uniting for peace. Syria doesn't accept the very concept of Lebanon, you see. As far as they're concerned, this country is part of 'Greater Syria,' which historically also included Israel and Jordan. Will again,'' he added ominously, ''if the Syrians have their way.''

''And the Westerners who've been taken hostage? Who's holding them?''

''Mostly Shiite Muslims, operating with Syrian complicity, under the religious direction of Iranian ayatollahs. The ayatollahs, of course, despite their 'holy war' rantings, have their own agenda—mostly, they want arms and the Iranian assets that have been frozen in the West since the overthrow of the Shah.''

Head spinning, Leya gazed out the window at the battered city, its cream-colored, tile-roofed buildings nestled between the sparkling Mediterranean on one side and the snow-capped peaks of the Lebanon Mountains on the other. ''It's so beautiful,'' she said sadly.

''It was.''

Later that afternoon, sitting in on Peter's lecture at the American University of Beirut, listening to him describe the invasion of this territory by Alexander the Great, Leya gained an even greater appreciation of the country—and of Peter vanAken.

''It was the Greeks who named this region Phoenicia,'' he said, ''derived from phoinikos, the Greek word for 'purple.' Archaeological digs here in Beirut have uncovered piles of murex shells, industrial waste from the rich purple dye made here that was so coveted by the Greeks. The *artifact record also shows Indian spices, Chinese silk, Arabian perfumes, all passing through these ports. Then, as now, the Lebanese—because 'Lebanon' was what the locals called it—were brilliant traders, culturally as well as economically rich. It was they, for example, who spread the alphabet throughout the known world.*

"But," he added darkly, "the Phoenician city-states fought among themselves, weakening the country, leaving it ripe for picking by outsiders."

He paused for effect. The modern parallel was only too obvious, Leya thought.

"When he conquered Phoenicia in 333 B.C., Alexander knew he'd acquired a jewel for his empire, even if the Phoenicians themselves didn't sufficiently value what they had to work together instead of bickering. And the same was true of Lebanon's other conquerors, in turn—Assyrians, Babylonians, Persians, Romans, Arabs, Ottomans, French. But keep in mind that, for five thousand years now, Lebanon has regained its independence over and over, throwing out foreign despots. Beirut is a Phoenix, rising from its ashes and rebuilding itself, again and again. As a historian," vanAken added, "I think it's pretty safe to say the last chapter of this story hasn't yet been written."

His mischievous smile was returned by his students, who seemed intrigued by an optimistic, longer-range perspective on the unhappy little country. But later, as young people crowded around him at the lectern, Leya noticed a scowling, bearded man at the back of the hall, watching Peter closely. Suddenly, the man spun on his heel and walked out. A shiver of fear ran down her spine, and she turned back toward the charismatic prof. What kind of risks was he running, staying on here, helping keep the university open, despite the chaos all around them?

"Aren't you afraid?" she asked him later. They were

standing on the balcony of his apartment, overlooking the pretty American University campus and the blue-green Mediterranean beyond. Since 1866, the privately funded university had stayed open through good times and bad. It was the most respected institute of higher learning in the Middle East. "Some of your colleagues are among the hostages, aren't they?"

"Yes. And the last AUB president was murdered right outside his office door."

"So why do you do it?"

He shrugged. "When I was growing up, my father's research took our family all over the Middle East, but Beirut was always home base. My dad taught here himself at various times. I hate to see what's happening now. The Lebanese have been horribly served by their leaders. In the long run, only dialogue and tolerance—and education—will solve their problems. But if we let the bad guys force us to close," Peter added, tapping Leya's forehead, "shut down minds and take away these kids' right to think—well, then, the bad guys win, don't they?"

"I guess. Still, it's amazing the university can function, given the level of anti-American sentiment in the country."

"It's our government people have problems with, Leya, not Americans per se. Washington's taking sides here."

"The wrong side?"

"There is no wrong or right side. There are atrocities and heroes all around. Washington and Israel are backing the right-wing Christian Phalange, and that doesn't sit well with the others. The Phalange are as murderous as anyone else, and they're busy making new martyrs to the Islamic cause. At the AUB, things are different, though. Muslims and Christians work and study together. They squabble—a lot—but at least they look each other in the eye and hear the other guy's point of view. It's easy to *hate people you don't know, but not so easy when you sit down together and talk. Compromise and free speech— that's what we do here. It's messy, but it sure beats the alternative.''*

"I think your students see you as a hero, Peter.''

"I'm no hero. I'm not even sure I'm doing the right thing these days. But,'' he added quietly, "I'm glad you came, Leya.''

"To your class? So am I.''

"No, to Lebanon. To see it for yourself.'' He was standing very close, and the combination of his nearness and sudden weary expression was having an unsettling effect on her. "Anyway, class is dismissed. Come on, let me show you this beautiful country.'' He reached out, and Leya slipped her hand into his. But it was her heart she felt him closing in on.

In the end, she never did stay at her father's empty house.

Her pacing had led her into the darkened, overcrowded living room. Winding a path between stacked packing cases, the sofa piled high with linens and curtains from upstairs, a Bentwood rocking chair and antique tables groaning with books, Leya made her way to the window and leaned against it. The beveled glass felt cool and damp on her forehead, the air around it chilling the tears running down her cheeks.

Knowing what she did now, she thought she understood the doubts vanAken had expressed that day about whether he was doing the right thing. It wasn't the teaching. His commitment to his students, and the love and respect they returned to him, had been all too apparent. What he'd been agonizing over was his *other* role. The secret role. The role of spy.

Which of those roles had betrayed him, in the end? she wondered, recalling the angry man at the back of the lecture hall. The teacher, encouraging his students to think for themselves and work for another vision of their country? The covert operative of a feared and overconfident superpower, whose shortsighted policies were alienating so many of the local players and making so many enemies? Or some other role? How could he have done it? Didn't he realize the schism inherent in those roles? The damage it would do to him? The price he would have to pay?

Wiping her cheeks with the back of her hand, Leya took a deep breath. Then, looking out at the quiet street, she spotted it. The car was back—the same, dark Taurus her father had been watching so intently earlier that evening.

18

Winslow, Massachusetts: 2:36 a.m.

Rummaging in the dark through shoes and boots on the floor of the front hall closet, Leya found an old pair of sneakers and slipped them on her bare feet. Her hands fumbled through clothing that she'd transferred from the dismantled upstairs bedroom and jammed temporarily into the downstairs coat closet. When she finally located her coat, she tugged it off its wooden hanger and pulled it on over her sweatshirt and jeans. She reached up to unlock the dead bolt on the front door, then thought better of it, and moved to the kitchen and out the back door.

Treading carefully down the wooden staircase made slick by a lightly falling snow—spring delayed yet again, she thought, frustrated—Leya descended to the back walkway. At the side of the house, after a quick glance down the drive, she sprinted over to the garage, passing behind it and coming out on the far side of the yard, which abutted the street fifteen feet or so behind the Taurus. Sliding along the perimeter fence of weathered pickets, she paused in the shadows of a spruce tree at the edge of the road, inhaling its Christmasy scent while she caught her breath. Then, dropping into a crouch, she slipped behind the car and peered around the fender at the driver's side rearview mirror.

The sedan's windows were tinted, obscuring the interior, but suddenly, an inside light flashed on, and she caught a reflected glimpse of shaggy dark hair. Nodding, her suspicions confirmed, Leya rose and walked up to the driver's door. Inside, gnarled hands were flipping through a small spiral notebook. She rapped on the window and was perversely pleased when vanAken nearly jumped out of his skin.

He shoved open the door. "Jesus, Leya! What the *hell* are you doing?"

"I was going to ask you the same thing."

He'd swung his feet out onto the road, but he exhaled sharply and slumped in his seat, one hand on the door. "I've been driving around town, trying to spot the girl and Khoury."

"No luck?"

He shook his head. "I checked out the place she'd phoned from your house. Karim had been there, but he'd already left."

"And Holly?"

"I'm not sure. I was hoping she might come back here."

"Thought you'd take another shot at frightening her to death, did you?"

He frowned. "I didn't mean to."

"So much for subtle technique. What about this?" Leya asked, waving at the parked car. "Is this how they taught you to do surveillance at The Farm?" The name was insider shorthand for the CIA's training center at Camp Peary, Virginia. Officially a military base, its real function was the worst-kept secret in the intelligence community.

"I took the short course," vanAken said.

"Obviously."

"Karim doesn't know this car," he added defensively, "and I doubt the girl would have noticed it among all the others on the street when she took off like that."

"Are you planning to sit here all night?"

"If necessary. If they haven't shown up by dawn, I'll move to Plan B."

"Which is—?"

VanAken shook his head again. "Damned if I know."

"Well, in case they do show up, why don't you move the car behind my garage, just to be on the safe side? I'd let you park it inside, except my contractor's got his tools and building supplies locked up in there."

"The view of the street's good from here."

"It's even better from inside the house, and you can watch the back from there, as well."

He gripped the door frame. "Inside?" He eyed her suspiciously, as if she were the witch from *Hansel and Gretel*, Leya thought, trying to lure him into her gingerbread cottage. *Try Granny's nice cookies, little boy. Hee-hee!*

"Unless you'd rather freeze to death out here. Come on, Peter, move the car. If there's any chance Holly might return, I want to make sure she's not scared off again. The back door's open," she added over her shoulder, walking away.

A few minutes later, he joined her warily in the kitchen. Leya shrugged out of her coat and draped it over a chair, conscious of him following her every move out of the corner of his eye as he gave the place a careful once-over—checking to see if she'd stoked the oven, no doubt. "Can I get you anything? Something to eat? Coffee?"

"No. You go back to bed. I'll stand watch."

"I wasn't in bed. I was working."

"This late?"

"Well, to be honest, I wasn't getting much work done. I was a little distracted, all things considered."

His glance landed on her briefly, then slid away. "I won't keep you. Can I watch from upstairs?"

"It's gutted and not very comfortable."

"Doesn't matter."

"Up to you," Leya said, shrugging. She opened a kitchen drawer, withdrew a flashlight, and handed it to him. "Here, you'll need this. I'll get you some pillows to sit on and a blanket. There's no heat up there right now. Come to think of it, this isn't going to be much of an improvement over sitting in the car."

"I'll be fine."

Leya pulled the bedding out of a box in the corner. As he reached for it, his jacket draped open, and Leya spotted the butt of the gun holstered under his arm. She froze momentarily, and their hands collided. VanAken grabbed the bedding and stepped back.

"Peter?" He'd been turning to go, but stopped. "You were out there earlier this evening when I was leaving with my father, weren't you?" His eyes narrowed. "It *was* you. What were you doing?"

"Tracking down those numbers Khoury had called from his landlady's—yours and the residence over at Mount Abbey."

"So you knew it was me who lived here. But you didn't come to the door then—only later. Why?"

For a moment, it didn't look like she was going to get an answer. But then, his voice low, vanAken said, "Because *he* was here."

"My father?"

A shadow flickered across his jaw as the muscles locked, but he said nothing.

"I think he spotted you," Leya said.

Something ominous crossed his features, then disappeared before Leya could even swear she'd seen it. "Was he worried?"

"Worried? I wouldn't say that. I'm not even certain that he saw you." She leaned back against the counter and folded her arms across her chest, studying him. "Tell me something."

"What?"

"Did the two of you always dislike each other? Or was it only after I showed up?"

"Why don't you ask him?"

"My father's not one to discuss his feelings, on this or anything else."

Arms loaded with bedding, vanAken stood there looking decidedly uneager to enter this conversational territory. "You knew he was furious about us."

"About some of the places you took me, sure. Fit to be tied. He said we could have been killed." Leya sighed. "I guess I really messed up your working relationship with him, didn't I?"

He shook his head. "It was just the final nail in the coffin. He and I never saw eye-to-eye, not from the first minute he set foot in Lebanon. We didn't agree on anything—who we should be talking to, what position we should be taking, what we should be reporting back to Washington. Carter Nash didn't like me or trust me, full stop. And then, I went and committed the ultimate sin. I seduced his little girl."

Leya felt her face go warm. "He didn't know that for sure."

"Oh, grow up, Leya! He knew everything. Where we went, what we did. The fact that you stayed with me the whole time. I wouldn't be surprised if my bedroom had been bugged. Christ Almighty, girl! Why do you think I never got your cable? And why you didn't get my letters?''

''You wrote to me?''

''Of course I did! But I sent the letters through the diplomatic bag, because the postal service was so unreliable. Cables came through the embassy comcenter. Turned out Nash was intercepting all my mail and messages.''

''But—why would he do that?''

''He was the post security officer,'' vanAken said darkly, ''and I'd been cited as a security risk.''

Leya felt her nerve ends tingling, like a premonition of lightning. ''What exactly were you accused of?''

''He didn't tell you?''

''Not in detail. He never discussed operations with me. But he did say you were responsible for sixty-three deaths. I never understood how such a thing could happen.''

''They said it was because I was dealing with terrorists.''

''Were you?''

''Obviously. That was my job—to make inroads with the different sects and factions, anywhere and everywhere I could. There were no innocents there, Leya, but I would have talked to the devil himself if it would have helped find a way out of the mess that place was in. How do you think I was able to take you to the Bekaa Valley and Baalbek, to show you the Temple of Jupiter? That area was under the control of Iranian Revolutionary Guards, for crying out loud—the hunters of foreigners. Half the Western hostages were held there.''

Feeling chilled, Leya remembered the trip they'd made to the inland valley. How Peter's way had been eased through tense checkpoints. How he'd asked her to wait in the anteroom of a house in the ancient city of Baalbek, watched over by men with guns who muttered among themselves in Farsi, while he spoke with a somber man inside. Peter had told her he was seeking permission to visit an old Roman temple on whose conservation his father had worked. His request, she recalled, had taken a very long time to discuss.

Carter Nash had been apoplectic when he'd found out that vanAken had taken his daughter to the Bekaa. The fact that the trunk of Peter's car had been filled with food, blankets and baby formula, which they'd delivered to friends who'd been caught in the crossfire for months, had done nothing to lessen her father's anger or change his assessment of vanAken. And who knew? Leya thought now. Maybe those people had been agents and informants, not friends.

"That trip was business, not pleasure for you, wasn't it?" she said coolly.

The look he gave her was almost pained, and Leya felt guilty for her doubts. They *were* friends. The affection they'd shown him—and her, by extension, because she was with Peter—was unaffected and sincere. "I could have gone anytime," he said, "but I wanted to show you the temple. It's a special place to me, and it was a gift I wanted to give you."

Leya closed her eyes as the memory rolled over her— of strolling with him in brilliant sunshine through the old ruin, up and down its broad steps, around weathered columns, over the remnants of intricately tiled floors. Watching Peter's animated features as he wove stories of Jupiter, ruler of the Roman pantheon, dispensing justice, virtue and thunderbolt fury. And of Minerva, his favorite daughter, patron of warriors and the arts, who'd sprung fully formed from her father's head. They'd stayed with a family who lived not far from the site, that of Peter's father's former research assistant.

In the middle of the night, Peter had come to Leya in silence and woken her. Hearts pounding, they'd slipped out of the house, stealing through dusty, rubbled streets, past armed patrols, back to the Roman temple. It was an insane risk to have taken, but when Leya had seen the temple's gleaming white marble columns illuminated by the full moon—tall, radiant sentries keeping silent watch through the ages—she knew it was the most wondrous moment she'd ever lived, or could ever imagine. And the night would have been magic, even if she and Peter hadn't made love in the shadows—quietly, urgently, mindful of the danger, but overcome by the intensity of their need to touch one another. As it was, the heat of his skin on hers had burned the experience deep into Leya's mind and heart. Nothing in her life, before or since, had ever matched its luster.

"It *was* a gift," she said quietly.

He shook his head. "It was stupid! I was so goddam cocky. I thought I was charmed—that nothing could touch me because I was one of the great bloody vanAkens of Arabia. And so nothing could hurt you, either, as long as you were under my protection."

"Peter, don't do this—"

"I was wrong, all right? Dead wrong. But no matter how stupid and arrogant I was, Leya, I was never a traitor. I was not responsible for those deaths your father blamed on me!"

She reached out, but he shoved her hand away. Leya backed into a corner, cowed by his mercurial temper. His eyes were ringed with dark shadows, and deep crevices around his mouth hinted at stresses she couldn't begin to imagine. With his disheveled hair and the dark stubble on his cheeks and chin, he could easily be mistaken for the fanatics he hunted—and who'd once hunted *him*.

Somewhere at the center of all the horrors Peter had seen and endured, Leya realized, her father figured prominently. She knew they'd clashed, but until now, she hadn't realized the depth of their mutual animosity. How could she have known? Peter had been absent from her life for years, and among all the emotion-laden subjects she and her father had never been able to discuss, Peter vanAken was top of the list. "You really hate him, don't you?"

The speed of the hissed reply left no doubt about it. "Yes."

"And me, too?"

Glancing away, vanAken said nothing for a moment. Then, he shook his head slowly. But when he turned back to her, his eyes were cold, and she knew that the wall between them, briefly breached, had gone up again. "I don't hate you," he said, "but I can't abide being near you, Leya—because I can't look at *you* without seeing *him*."

Newton, Massachusetts: 2:47 a.m.

Len Rickhauser peered into a jumbled cavern of broken concrete. Human shadows scurried back and forth, grunting like slaves in some ancient stone quarry. Lamps on hard hats bounced light across the tangle of steel rebars and cracked, dripping walls. Water supply to the Data-Trax building had been shut off, but not before a damaged main had flooded the basement cavity, further weakening the already precarious structure. Sump pumps chugged noisily, trying to drain the space so the investigators could more easily wade through the wreckage to get to the security office. But it was slow going.

"How long?" Rickhauser asked. He was tempted to grab a hard hat and jump into the pit himself, except he knew he was too big to squeeze through the tiny crevices of the damaged structure, and that his presence would only make the others nervous and prone to mistakes.

"Another hour, maybe more," Curtis Pullen replied. "We're trying to get through as quick as possible, but we need to be careful not to trample evidence in the process. The team'll go back over the site more carefully, soon as we get daylight. Make sure we don't miss anything."

Rickhauser nodded. That was the problem with bombs—their exasperating tendency to destroy evidence crucial in identifying their builders. Since his first bomb case a quarter century earlier, when four members of the radical Weather Underground had blown themselves and their Greenwich Village brownstone to smithereens, Rickhauser had worked on dozens of criminal cases involving explosions—most of them smaller than this one, but always with the same damned result of covering the suspects' tracks. What tiny clues remained were scattered over a radius of thousands of yards. Arrests and convictions depended on minute shreds of forensic evidence, which no one but a skilled investigator would even recognize.

Rickhauser knew it was a risk, pushing the team so hard to get to the security tape now instead of waiting for the light of morning. But he also knew in his bones there was something special about this case, and that some critical physical evidence had already been identified—the crater in the handicapped parking space, and the blast-marked bits of brushed steel that the ATF man had found, which might shed light on the bomb's construction. With luck, they could even yield a latent fingerprint or two.

Within hours, the ADIC expected a chemical report on the steel fragments, which had been shipped to the scientific analysis section of the FBI's crime lab, located on the fifth floor of the Hoover Building in downtown D.C. The lab was actually a series of offices, crowded with benches, Bunsen burners, fume hoods, microscopes and computers. One room featured a battery of mass spectrometers, freezer-size devices capable of detecting any chemical compound through the unique pattern on the light spectrum produced by its individual elements.

The World Trade Center bombing had been the result of ANFO, an explosive mixture concocted from large quantities of ammonium nitrate fertilizer and fuel oil. But with no oversize delivery vehicles reported at Data-Trax at the time of the blast, Rickhauser was reasonably certain that the chemical residues in this case would point to a plastic explosive, like C-4. Beige, odorless, insensitive to shock but simple to detonate, the putty-like material was the explosive of choice for organized terrorists and amateur anarchists alike. It was easy to manufacture, and almost as easily stolen from military stocks, it seemed, given annual explosives-ordnance theft reports filed with the FBI. One-third more powerful than TNT, with a detonation velocity of over twenty-six thousand feet per second, C-4 was capable of producing a deadly shattering effect on anything in its path—steel, concrete, glass, or flesh and bone.

"You don't mind me asking, sir," Pullen ventured.

"What?"

"This rush to get the security video—you think it's wise? I mean, we've pretty much got our suspect nailed, right? Now that we know about that Arab wangling himself a job interview? The guy vanAken was tailing and lost?" Pullen added, his expression turning smug.

Rickhauser let out a weary exhale. Obviously, vanAken had made himself another enemy. "Possibly."

"Possibly?" Pullen repeated, head shaking. "I know it's going to look bad for the Bureau, sir, if it gets out one of our people had Khoury under surveillance and the guy went and did this right under the agent's nose. I've already started damage control, but if you don't mind me saying so, I think vanAken should be reeled in, before he embarrasses us any further. I figure if we can show quick progress on this case, it'll help neutralize the damage he's done. That's why I decided to announce that we had our suspect.''

"I wish you hadn't talked to the press. In future, all releases will be precleared through me."

Pullen's face twitched. "Of course, sir. I just thought—"

"Putting out the police APB on the car was fine, but announcing the Stroud girl's name really raised hackles over at the State Department and the White House. They tell me the ambassador's on his way back to the States as we speak, and he's going to run smack into a media frenzy when he arrives. He's not going to be a happy man, Curtis. If you think the Bureau's going to be in hot water over Karim Khoury, it's nothing compared to the heat we'll feel when Arthur Stroud demands to know who was responsible for publicly naming his daughter as a suspect this early in the game."

Even under the spotty lighting conditions around the bomb site, the blanching of Pullen's features was evident. "We didn't know who the girl was when we released the DMV information, sir," he said nervously.

Rickhauser arched one eyebrow. Suddenly, it was "we." Bureaucratic ass-covering, he thought, disgusted. To his way of thinking, you assessed a situation, you took a stand, and if your judgment turned out to be wrong, you took your lumps. He'd taken his fair share of flak during a long career, including the controversy over his decision to offer a haven to Peter vanAken when others in Washington were prepared to leave the guy twisting in the wind. He'd take it again this time, if it turned out he'd fucked up. But he wasn't prepared to concede that yet.

"I think there's a lot here that *we* don't know," he told Pullen gruffly.

19

VanAken stood at the top of the stairs, peering into the darkened space, waiting for his eyes to adjust and to get his bearings before moving forward. Waiting, too, for the pounding in his chest and the shaking in his hands to ease. At this point, he could barely maintain a grip on the flashlight, much less turn it on.

In the kitchen, he'd experienced a sudden, almost physical sensation, like something cracking deep inside. Not trusting his voice or himself, he'd spun around and walked out, leaving Leya staring after him. Now, like a dam with a hairline fracture, he felt his wall of self-control threatening to buckle under the strain of emotions surging against it.

He forced himself to focus on his immediate surroundings. The gutted upper story of her house smelled musty, like decrepit wood and rubbery linoleum, overlaid with the piney smell of sawdust and virgin lumber. Different altogether from the downstairs, which was imbued with scents of fresh paint and varnish—and of Leya. A cologne she wore, maybe. It always put vanAken in mind of vanilla and oranges, and it lingered in her rooms with the same stubborn determination that it had lingered in his memory.

The scent had walloped him like a sledgehammer when he'd walked in the front door earlier that evening. He should have realized right then that his equilibrium was in peril and turned around and left her to others.

Wind in the rafters echoed his own weary exhalation as he glanced around. What little illumination there was came mostly from the front of the house, the glow of streetlamps weeping through cobalt blue and copper-colored diamonds of stained glass in the turret's windows, which subtly transformed the light into something soft and melancholy. He made out a broad and open space, without interior walls. Deep vertical shadows striped the perimeter, whose surface had been peeled back to reveal a scabrous wooden substructure. Fissured, curled and dusty linoleum covered the floor. The place was cold as a tomb.

Opposite the staircase, near the back wall, a pile of two-by-fours was stacked, the clean, white pine gleaming in the dark. VanAken had seen enough restoration of ancient sites to know that when the new material was transplanted into the body of the structure, replacing its worn and eaten parts, this eccentric old "Painted Lady" of a house, strengthened and rejuvenated, would stand proudly for another hundred years or more. Still, it was a daunting task, resurrecting the dead and dying. Not a mission for the fainthearted or easily discouraged.

As the pounding in his chest throttled back a little, vanAken crossed the open space to the turret, set the flashlight down on the knee-high windowsill and dropped the bedding on the floor. The exterior walls defined a circular alcove about six feet in diameter, with five long windows that ran vertically from a couple of feet above floor level to within a few inches of the coved ceiling. In the center of each window was a clear rectangle of glass, bordered all around by those diamond-shaped panes of cobalt and copper, each one held in place by a ribbon of lead solder.

VanAken looked out, casting his gaze up and down the quiet street, then walked around the floor and peered through the other windows. Huge spruce trees, taller than the house, spread deep shadows across the yard. Black patches of earth hid under the skirts of their branches, sheltered from the lightly falling snow. A weathered picket fence, leaning drunkenly in spots, stood guard around the property. The roof of the garage, he noted, was missing a few shingles.

As he expected, there was no sign of Holly or Karim. The only footprints in the faint dusting of snow vanAken could make out were the ones Leya had made when she'd gone out to his car, and the ones he himself had left as he trailed her reluctantly back to the house. Even they were rapidly disappearing. But Leya had been right. The view was good from up here, and if Holly and Karim decided to come back, he would spot them easily. Chances were, they wouldn't. But if not here, then where?

Something had been nagging at him from the moment he'd discovered Karim had returned to Winslow with Holly after the Data-Trax bombing. If Khoury and his Hamas associates had been responsible, why hadn't they organized an escape route? It wouldn't have been necessary, of course, if the mission had been intended as a suicide bombing. But Khoury, the girl, and, presumably, the car had all gotten away intact.

Karim was unsophisticated and socially inept, but he wasn't stupid. As a trained engineer, he was certainly capable of building an explosive device sufficient to do the kind of damage vanAken had witnessed in Newton. For that matter, any illiterate *mujahedeen* guerrilla could have done as much. But unless he was opting for an immediate martyr's rendezvous with his Maker, even an illiterate terrorist would have planned a better getaway.

VanAken moved back to the turret and crouched against the base of one wall, staring gloomily out the opposite window. And what about the Stroud girl? Was she some Patty Hearst clone, a rich kid brainwashed or seduced by the dubious glamour of the outlaw life when she met Karim? How well did she understand Khoury's balancing act between the two sides pulling at him? When had she learned of his apparent decision to betray his FBI handler and throw his lot in with the terrorists?

Or was Holly the instigator here? VanAken suddenly thought. Conning Leya with her tearful protests of innocence? Was the spoiled ambassador's kid playing at revolution, urging a gawky, love-struck young Palestinian-American to prove his oppressed credentials by doing something defiant and sexy, like blowing up a few people, just to demonstrate contempt for her old man and his politics?

Fathers and their offspring, vanAken thought, ruefully—the theme of so many ancient dramas. Modern ones, too. Holly and Arthur Stroud. Himself and his own father. Leya and Carter.

Leya.

He recalled the morning at Beirut International Airport when he'd first set eyes on her. He'd been seeing off his neighbor, Larry Kenyon, a professor of agriculture at the AUB whose family in Pennsylvania had been pleading with him for months to leave Lebanon. When a mortar shell had come through Kenyon's bedroom window one morning, moments after he'd gotten up and gone into the bathroom to shave, he'd finally given in to the fear and submitted his resignation.

Kenyon had boarded his plane, and vanAken had been on his way out of the airport when he spotted a girl waiting in the arrivals line. She'd come in on the same Olympic Airways 737 on which his friend and neighbor was about to leave. Wearing a soft white blouse, a long, jewel-colored skirt, and old-fashioned, laced suede boots under an open tan coat, she was striking—not precisely beautiful, but close enough, vanAken had thought, admiring the mahogany-colored hair that spilled down her back, and her equally dark, arresting eyes. Her coloring suggested Mediterranean roots. She could have been French, Greek, Spanish, Israeli—even Lebanese.

But when she approached the immigration desk, van-Aken saw the blue and gold cover of an American passport in her hand, stamped Diplomatic. He'd watched, intrigued, as the girl and his old buddy Bashir launched into a quiet argument. She was nervous, he could see, but stubbornly holding her own. Bashir's color was rising, and he looked flummoxed, more in need of rescuing than she did. Van-Aken hadn't been able to resist stepping into the fray.

When he'd found out who she was, and the fact that she'd flown unannounced into Beirut, he'd been doubly astonished. And wary. He and Carter Nash were already at loggerheads. The last thing he needed was to be seen aiding and abetting his station chief's insubordinate kid. He certainly hadn't set out to seduce her, much less fall in love with her. But given that this was Beirut, neither did he dare abandon her to fend for herself. Although, vanAken had thought, she probably would have survived just fine. Carter Nash's daughter was tougher than she looked. Not surprising, given the genes she carried.

He exhaled sharply, the white vapor of his breath turning to blue, then gold, under the colored light of the turret windows.

If there are no atheists in foxholes, neither are there many celibates in a civil war zone. When death can ride in on the next stray mortar or chunk of shrapnel, social inhibitions and coy rituals have a tendency to go by the board, and chance encounters take on a level of intensity they might not otherwise possess. Within a few hours of her arrival, both he and Leya had known they weren't going to shake hands and say goodbye at her father's door that night.

What if he had walked away and let Bashir deport her for not having a visa? Would things have turned out differently? Or had his fate been a preordained drama, as the ancient Greeks believed? If so, vanAken thought grimly, then the last act was about to unfold.

Newton, Massachusetts: 3:17 a.m.

By their crimes ye shall know them, Rickhauser mused. It was the profiler's credo. The weapon, the victim, the setting, the timing—every minute detail formed a trail that led directly back to the perpetrator, if you knew how to interpret the signs.

The ADIC stood in shadow near the main Data-Trax gate, watching the straggling crowd still gathered, despite the hour, beyond the yellow police barriers. One of the first things he'd done on arrival was to ensure that a surveillance camera was mounted and trained at all times on the onlookers outside the compound. This was the second time Rickhauser had wandered over for a look-see during a lull in the action inside.

He passed his gaze along the line of reporters, TV cameramen and others milling around, searching for a face that might betray the bomber's telltale characteristic—secret pride. Invariably, bombers were closet megalomaniacs, their god-complexes stoked by the frenzied activity that always followed an explosion.

By their crimes ye shall know them. Murders involving knives were, most often, intensely personal acts of rage and retribution—a suspect who knew his victim well, and whose inflamed mind felt justified in meting out a terrifying, in-your-face payback for some perceived insult. Gun crimes tended to be more detached, the victims dehumanized in the killer's mind, mere obstacles to be dispatched on the road to some other, more pressing personal objective.

But bombers—especially serial bombers—were among the coldest, most calculating bastards Rickhauser had dealt with in his long career. He reserved for them a special, tortured place on his wish list of ideal punishments. Smart enough to construct an explosive mechanism without killing themselves in the act, they were also fanatic enough to persevere for as long as it took to select a target, calculate optimum damage, obtain materials, manufacture an appropriate device, then plant it without being detected.

More often than not, bombers reasoned in the abstract terms of obsessive causes which, in their minds, called for murder on a mass scale—the more innocents, the better, in order to drive home the message, whatever it might be. Some serial bombers—not all—issued communiqués from time to time, taunting the authorities, placing each new act of violence in the context of some broad mission. But over time, their aims tended to become more vague, their messages more disjointed. In the end, the addictive, dangerous thrill of the act itself became motive enough to go back to the workshop and start tinkering again.

Rickhauser studied the faces outside the gate. They were reporters, mostly, talking quietly among themselves, stamping their feet and blowing on their hands to keep warm. His eyes narrowed, as a prematurely balding fellow in a duffel coat walked up carrying a cardboard carton and started handing out plastic cups of hot coffee to the cops on duty. The ADIC distrusted overeager, Boy Scout types at crime scenes. Ingratiating themselves with the cops, probing for inside dope on the investigation—it was classic suspect behavior, trying to find out if the authorities were on to him.

The balding guy handed the last cup to a cameraman, then set the empty box down on the pavement. When he rose, Rickhauser spotted the CNN logo on his jacket. He snorted. Classic hack behavior, too, he thought, bribing the cops with coffee. The cameraman balanced his heavy equipment on his shoulder with one hand, while the other brought the steaming coffee to his lips.

Rickhauser puffed up his cheeks and exhaled sharply. Wasn't technology just fucking great? he thought. Why would a suspect even bother standing out here, freezing his ass off, when he could sit in front of the tube and watch as the disaster he'd created was replayed and updated, over and over, on the hourly news?

Disgusted, the ADIC swung his bulky frame around and lumbered up the drive.

Winslow, Massachusetts: 3:52 a.m.

Leya was awakened by a cry, deep and guttural. Her first thought was of a wounded animal hit by a car. But then, it howled again, and she realized the sound was coming from inside the house. She threw off the duvet and dropped her feet to the floor, her whole body tensed, listening.

Nothing.

She shivered. The house was cold, her legs bare. The oversized T-shirt she wore to bed had twisted itself around her body. Leya untangled it and tugged it down over her thighs, but it didn't do much to warm her. She considered retrieving the jeans she'd stuffed in the laundry hamper before she'd crawled into bed and sunk into troubled sleep, but before she could move, a thundering bang sounded.

She jumped to her feet, heart pounding, trying to locate the source of the noise. There was another bang. Definitely inside, she decided. Then, a yell and a series of pummeling thwacks, coming from the front of the house.

Padding quickly to the glass doors separating the dining room from the living room, Leya slid them open. In the pale glow from the streetlights, she made out the myriad shapes of jammed-together boxes and furniture. Nothing seemed to be moving. She stepped forward cautiously, until another hoarse cry halted her advance. Upstairs.

She looked to the ceiling just as scuffling broke out overhead. And then she remembered—Peter. He'd gone up a couple of hours earlier, after storming out of the kitchen, leaving her alone and alarmed at the depth of the malice he bore toward her father. But who was he fighting now? A burglar? Karim Khoury?

She shivered again, but not from cold. Her eyes swept the living room, searching for something to use as a weapon. A baseball bat would be a practical accessory for a woman living alone, she decided, or one of her father's heavy canes or walking sticks. Finding nothing, she ran into the front hall, heading for the stairs. At another thump, she paused to grab a small African sculpture from the hall table. Carved from dense black ebony, it was heavier than it looked—and as a defensive aid, better than nothing.

She gripped the figurine tightly and her bare feet took the steps, one by one, ears straining to hear through the absolute silence that had fallen over the house.

20

At the top of the stairs, a wail of agony made Leya's blood run cold. Once more, she thought of a wounded animal. Peering through the gloom, her eyes made a quick circuit of the dimly lit open space. She could clearly make out the tinted bay windows in the turret, but vanAken was nowhere to be seen.

As a groan drifted across the floor, Leya's gaze dropped to a mound of shadows at the base of the window. A foot kicked out from the lumpy mass and crashed into the opposite wall. She breathed a sigh of relief. He'd fallen asleep in the little alcove among the pillows and blankets, and he was having a nightmare.

She tiptoed over and crouched next to him. "Peter?" she said gently. "Wake up! You're having a bad dream." He was lying on his side, twitching and moaning, legs tucked up into himself again. "Peter?" she said, louder this time. Her hand reached to shake him by the shoulder.

She never saw the fist that exploded out of the shadows, only a brilliant flash as it connected with her left cheek. The blow sent her sprawling backward across the floor, the ebony sculpture flying out of her hand and skidding noisily on the cracked linoleum. As her head smacked against the

floor, her brain registered an observation. Stars, she
thought. You really do see stars. She lay there for a second,
then rolled dizzily onto her side, lifting herself onto one
elbow. Her other hand went to her cheekbone, which was
already sending up a painful throb. When her vision
cleared, Leya looked up at the turret—and froze, heart
leaping.

"Peter, don't!" she cried. "It's Leya!"

VanAken was on his feet, silhouetted in the circle of
windows, arms fully extended, light glinting off the steel
barrel of the gun gripped tightly in his hands. His body
was trembling fiercely, but his hands were rock steady. His
pale eyes glistened in the light—mad, wide and seemingly
blind.

Leya skittled backward, crab-style, then pulled her knees
into her chest, never taking her eyes off him or the barrel
that bore down on her. "Don't shoot!" she pleaded, terrified. "Peter, *please*—it's Leya!"

They stared at each other for what seemed an eternity.
Finally, he wavered and blinked. "Leya?" he said, uncertainly.

She let out a long exhale. "Yes." Never, she resolved,
would she *ever* sneak up on him again.

VanAken's arms dropped to his sides, and he stood still,
breathing heavily, watching her. Then, his chin dropped in
his chest. "Jesus! Leya..."

Her eyes closed, and she huddled into herself, shaking,
now that the immediate terror had passed. Her hand went
again to her cheek, and she felt it swelling.

The floorboards under the linoleum creaked as vanAken
knelt beside her. "What are you *doing* up here?" he demanded angrily.

"You were having a nightmare, thrashing around. It
woke me. I thought you were fighting with someone."

He slipped the gun back into his shoulder holster and reached out with one hand to push back her hair, while the other peeled a wet strand off her cheek. "Here, let me look," he said, lifting her chin, turning her face to the light. He shook his head and exhaled. "I'm sorry. Shh, don't cry. I don't think it's broken. Does it hurt?"

She nodded. "A little."

His fingers stroked the swollen cheekbone, and he apologized again. "I was exhausted." He glanced back at the bay of windows. "I guess I conked out and got myself wedged in there—I—I'm claustrophobic. I was dreaming I was in the hole again. I thought—" His voice drifted off.

Leya watched his tortured face, remembering the dread she'd felt after he was abducted, and during the four long years that followed. Four years during which she'd carried on numbly, living in dull fear and apprehension over where he was and what might be happening to him. Terrified every time she opened a newspaper that she'd find out he was dead, yet unable to resist the urge to scan for his name. Depressed when it wasn't there, discouraged when it was, because all the reports ever said was that he was still among the missing in Lebanon.

Leya reached up and covered his hand with her own. She felt his muscles tense, and she expected him to yank it away. But he didn't. Shuddering at the memories that pressed down on her, she turned her head, burying her face in his palm, breathing deeply, feeling the warmth of his skin and rediscovering the scent of him—never forgotten, she realized. It didn't matter that all they'd ever had was five days together a decade ago. In that brief space of time, he'd become part of her, and his absence ever since had left her with a dull ache, like that of a phantom limb.

He held himself absolutely still. He seemed to have stopped breathing.

Without thinking, Leya kissed his palm. Her lips moved to his wrist, brushing softly, back and forth, against the rippled scar tissue. She took up his other mangled wrist and kissed it gently, as well.

"Leya—don't."

She heard him, but couldn't bring herself to let go. All the years he'd been held prisoner, she'd waited in lonely silence for some word of him. Her father had rebuffed every mention of Peter's name and refused to say if his sources had any news. There was no one else who knew about her and Peter except Mrs. Garibaldi, but Leya had moved on to graduate school in New York soon after the kidnapping, and in any event, sweet as the old house-mother was, Leya couldn't endure her sympathy for long. Platitudes and Earl Grey tea did nothing to ease her grief.

She laid Peter's hands in her lap and looked up at him, backlit against a halo of light from the windows. He appeared as haunted as she felt.

When she'd read in the paper about the death of his father, Leya had suddenly realized that there was at least one other person she could talk to about Peter, one person who was grieving terribly and missing him, too. She had called his mother in Chicago to express her sympathy and support. It was from Mary vanAken that Leya had first received word of Peter's escape, but the older woman had never hinted that she herself was dying. She'd managed to hang on, Leya realized, just long enough to see her son once more.

After coming home, Peter had never called Leya, but she'd comforted herself with the knowledge that he was safe and free at last. But *was* he free? Could anyone ever feel free after such a horror?

Now that the pounding pulse in her head was beginning to subside, the hard, nagging voice of reason was clamoring for attention. This man was a stranger, it said, and a disturbed one at that. A troubling memory from long ago, maybe, but one that had nothing to do with her life now. Worse, he was hostile to it, since it necessarily and inevitably included her father. And yet—

Leya closed her eyes, struggling for balance, and for a truce between the instincts warring inside her.

"Are you all right?" he asked. "Do you feel dizzy? Maybe you should—"

She sighed and opened her eyes. "I'm fine." She looked up at him. "But what about you, Peter? Are *you* all right?"

He hesitated, then half turned away. "No—I guess not. Not for a long time now. I just…" His voice faded, and he shook his head.

Leya lifted herself to her knees. When she put her arms around him, his body went rigid. She felt it and knew she should back off, reestablishing space between them, for his sake as much as for her own. It was all too much, too quickly, for both of them.

She should pull away, but instead, Leya found herself drawing him closer, protectively, into the circle of her arms. "I'm so sorry for what happened to you," she murmured. "But no one can hurt you anymore, Peter. You're home."

She stroked his hair, her fingers combing the muss of his curls. His body was trembling, and his hands settled lightly, nervously, on her hips. Slowly, Leya began to sway from side to side. After a moment, he moved with her, and gradually, she felt a little of the tension drain from him, like a slow thaw. His arms slipped all the way around her. He held her close, and as his lips burrowed into the crook of her neck and shoulder, she heard him breathe her name. "Leya…"

Cupping his face in her hands, she rested her forehead against his. They swayed together, bodies locked in a slow dance of remembering. Her lips were touching his cheek. After a while, they moved to the other. Then to his eyelids, one by one. Then his mouth. Like a starveling, famished beyond the ability to take what he most needed, he was unresponsive at first. But slowly, he began to return her kisses. Uncertainly. Then hungrily.

Suddenly something erupted, and his mouth was grinding into hers. Leaning into her, Peter forced her into a backward arch until Leya felt herself losing balance and tumbling. He caught her at the last second and lowered her to the floor, then fell on her, his hands brusque and impatient, pushing up her T-shirt, grabbing at her thigh, pulling her leg around him as his mouth moved over her body. Leya winced at the weight of him grinding her bones into the gritty linoleum.

"Peter," she gasped. "Easy—"

He squeezed her leg roughly, and she cried out with pain as his teeth found her breast. He let up, but his breathing was rapid as he grunted and grappled at her. A ripping noise echoed in the emptiness, and Leya felt a sharp, abrasive burning on her leg as he tore off her underwear.

She squirmed and tried to pull away. "Peter, please!" she cried.

He lifted his head, but held her pinned to the floor, breathing hard. "You want it. I know you do."

She hesitated and considered denying it, but it was ridiculous. She did want him. She had, from the first minute he'd walked through her door. And he knew it. "Yes, dammit—but I need you to slow down."

She reached up to touch his face, but he reared back, wedging her head between his hands. "Say it!"

"What?"

"You *know* what. Say it!"

His fingers tangled in her hair, and Leya winced as he clenched his fists, the roots pulling tight against her temples. From out of the darkness came echoes of cautionary voices—Susan's, she realized, and her father's, never neutral on the subject of Peter vanAken. But although their warnings resonated in her brain, it was Peter's weight that pressed down on her. His face that filled her field of vision. His need and her own that she felt—the ache that only heat can ease. They exerted a far more powerful force on her than prohibitions ever could. Always had.

"I love you," she said quietly.

"You mean that?"

"Yes."

"No matter what happens?" He loomed expectantly.

Happen? What could happen? Then Leya felt his heart pounding against her ribs, and she sensed his need for one truth that endured beyond loss and betrayal. She understood her own need, as well, to acknowledge it, once and for all, after all the years spent denying, minimizing, trying to forget him.

"No matter what. I've always loved you, Peter, more than anyone I've ever known. I always will."

The tension in him gave way at last, like a broken dam, and he loosened his grip, kissing her deeply, over and over. And for a while, at least, it seemed as if he really had come home.

Newton, Massachusetts: 4:42 a.m.

It was inconspicuous—or as inconspicuous as a thirty-foot-long, nine-foot-high GM van could be, Curtis Pullen thought, as he sprinted across the Data-Trax parking lot toward the surveillance van Rickhauser had ordered in from the field. For the Russian-mob stakeout it had been assigned to, they'd had it painted orange, which might have seemed counterproductive—except that was the color of the Boston municipal fleet. The Water and Sewers crest slapped on its side completed the illusion. The watchers in the van could flip up a manhole cover, drop down a couple of traffic cones and Men Working signs, and people would walk past the thing for days and never notice it. No one would suspect that the mud-splattered, ordinary looking service vehicle bristled with several million dollars' worth of state-of-the-art receivers, transmitters, cameras, directional microphones and digitized video and audio recording and enhancement devices.

Clutching three mucky videotape cartridges under one arm, Pullen opened the van's rear door and climbed inside, scanning the interior. Four or five agents and technicians were milling around Len Rickhauser, all of them watching a television screen that flickered with black-and-white images of brick buildings on a grungy city street—somewhere in the greater Boston area, Pullen guessed.

"Close that door," Rickhauser snapped.

Pullen quickly did as he was told. Rickhauser had shed his overcoat and suit jacket, and his gargantuan, shirt-sleeved frame was squeezed into one of three swiveling armchairs bolted to the van's floor. Mark Leung, one of the Boston field-office technical specialists, sat in a chair to one side of the chief, while a local agent sat on the other—Blume, Pullen registered, a Russian-speaker assigned to the field office a few months earlier. Before them was arrayed a bank of monitors, buttons, slides and playback devices that took up every available inch of space in the van's cargo area.

Blume and Leung nodded to the acting SAC, but Rickhauser never looked up from the monitor in front of him. Its light danced off his wolf eyes, which were fixed on the screen as intently as if it were the target of his next kill.

Pullen went over and stood behind him. "What have you got there?"

"Surveillance tape from the Russian-mob stakeout," Blume explained. He pointed at a figure walking across the screen. "Boris Baklanov, point man for the extortion, illegal gambling, theft, prostitution and drug ring we've been tracking. We caught him on tape yesterday, discussing a hit on a bar owner who was balking about paying protection. Best stuff we've gotten yet. Too bad," the agent added, glancing nervously at the ADIC, "that we had to pull out."

Rickhauser turned away from the screen and leaned back in the chair. It creaked in protest. "Hopefully, I can let you get back to it in short order. This is good work, Blume."

The agent's face twitched as he suppressed a proud beam. "Thank you, sir. This is good equipment."

Probably thought he was hot stuff, Pullen thought grumpily, just because the number-three man in the whole damn Bureau knew his name. Big deal. He held out the black plastic cartridges he was carrying. "I've got the security tapes, sir."

Rickhauser looked up and almost smiled. "All right! Intact?"

"Cartridge on one is cracked, but the tape itself looks good. I just hope these particular tapes are the ones we need. When we finally managed to dig through to the security office, we found the ceiling collapsed. The video storage units were smashed. Most of the previously re-corded tapes are shredded. The only ones that survived intact were the ones actually in the recorders, where the hardware provided a little extra protection. Thank God there wasn't much of a fire, or we'd have been shit out of luck."

"Okay, let's take a look."

Pullen waved Blume out of his chair and settled in next to the ADIC, then snapped a finger at Leung, the techni-cian, to remove the Russian video. "There were recorders for each of the twelve surveillance cameras around the compound," he said, "but I figured the tapes we're most interested in are the main gate, front entrance and lobby."

Rickhauser nodded. "Let's start with the one from the front of the building."

Pullen shuffled the videos and found one labeled Main Entrance. He handed it to the tech, who inserted it in one of the playback machines. "You want me to rewind it to the beginning, sir?" Leung asked.

"How long is it?"

The tech glanced at the other two videotapes, then at the one in the machine. "They look to be three-hour jobs. This one here's stopped about two-thirds of the way in."

"Let's see what it was recording just before the system went off-line," Rickhauser said. "We can work backward from there."

The tech hit the Rewind button and let it run for a couple of seconds. Then, as he hit Play, the monitor above their heads shifted from a pattern of gray snow to a wide-angle shot of the semicircular drive in front of the main Data-Trax building. The counter in the bottom right-hand corner gave the date and the time—5:04:21 p.m.

They saw a stream of employees walking out of the building and heading toward the parking lot. At 5:04:29, a Nissan minivan pulled up to the front walk. A man with a bald patch on top of his head, caught by the overhead camera, opened the front passenger door and climbed in. He leaned over to kiss the woman at the wheel, and just before the door closed, two small pairs of arms popped into view from the back seat. The van's door shut, and at 5:04:47, it drove off. Safe? Pullen wondered. Did they get far enough away before the blast? He couldn't remember whether a Nissan van had been among the damaged cars out front.

"Watch the handicapped spot," Rickhauser said, pointing to one of three parking slots next to the sidewalk, posted with the blue-and-white wheelchair symbol. All three were empty.

At 5:04:49, another group of five or six employees passed down the walk, cut across the handicapped zone, and disappeared out of sight in the direction of the parking lot.

At 5:04:55, one of the group who had just vanished from the top edge of the screen reappeared—a young woman, early twenties, with cropped platinum-blond hair and a black trench coat. She walked back up the sidewalk toward the building, frowning, rummaging through her purse as she went, then tapping her coat pockets. Misplaced her keys, Pullen guessed, gut churning as he resisted the impulse to call out a warning.

"Shit," Rickhauser muttered. "I saw her body in the morgue." The blonde passed under the surveillance camera and disappeared into the building.

At 5:04:59, another car pulled up, a white Honda Accord, and sat idling, waiting. Pullen remembered the Honda, but by the time he'd seen it, it was a burned-out shell, flipped on its roof and lying ten yards away from the building. The only reason he'd known it was a Honda was because its H-shaped insignia had blown off and considerately landed nearby the wreck, helping investigators to quickly identify the make of the car.

At 5:05:11, a middle-aged, chunky woman approached the Honda and reached for the passenger-door handle. When the counter reached 5:05:12, a bright light erupted on one side of the television screen. A split second later, several objects, including the woman and the car, began to lift off the ground. Before the counter on the video recorder could reach 5:05:13, the picture on the screen turned to snow.

The occupants of the surveillance van were silent for several seconds as they stared at the blizzard. Then, as if on cue, each person in the cramped space exhaled, uttering a low oath.

Rickhauser turned to the technician. "Okay—I want you to take it back to just before the flash and run it for me again, frame by frame."

Leung nodded and rewound the tape to 5:04:55. They all watched, fixated, as the doomed blonde who'd forgotten her keys and the chunky woman at the Honda drifted in slow motion toward their fates. At the frame where the first glimmer of light appeared, Rickhauser snapped, "Freeze it! Now, back up a couple of frames."

The woman at the Honda pulled her hand away and rolled back on her heels, stopped, then started inching forward again as the tech advanced the image, one frame at a time. At the first sign of light, he backed up two frames, froze the action and glanced expectantly at Rickhauser.

"Can we enlarge that corner?" the chief asked, pointing to the handicapped parking spot.

The tech nodded. His hand moved to a computer mouse, and as he moved it across the mousepad, a dotted square appeared around the area Rickhauser had indicated. Leung hit a key on the board in front of him, and the square expanded to fill the entire monitor.

The ADIC frowned. "I can't make anything out."

"I can try doing a pixel enhancement, sir—break the picture down into its individual components, then rebuild it in greater detail. It's not ideal, but the computer can extrapolate from the information here and try to guess what's missing. That might give us a hint as to what the device is."

Rickhauser nodded. "Go ahead."

The tech focused in tighter on the blacktop immediately in front of the concrete curb, directing the computer to examine the image, micromillimeter by micromillimeter, until the area was transcribed into a blurry gray grid. The cursor passed over the grid, square by square, as the computer assessed and modified. Then the tech hit a button and the image pulled back a little.

Rickhauser's great forefinger stabbed the screen. "There!" he exclaimed, his voice triumphant. Half-a-dozen bodies leaned forward, eyes peering, as he traced a faint curving line just visible over the top of the curb. "Can you take out the curb? Extrapolate from this line, try to see what this is?"

The tech nodded and went back to work on the image, pixel by pixel, like a photo retoucher, airbrushing out unflattering moles and wrinkles. In a couple of minutes, the curb was gone. Then, based on what little information it had, the computer filled in the blank spaces with its best estimate of the object that had been mostly hidden up till then. When the image pulled back again, the investigators in the van were left staring at the grainy, indistinct representation of what appeared to be a large dinner plate. Rickhauser leaned back in his chair, frowning.

"A hubcap?" Blume ventured.

Pullen shook his head dubiously. "Most cars don't come with hubcaps anymore. They pretty much all have bolted-on wheel covers."

"The '86 Mercedes 310 had hubcaps," Rickhauser said. He turned to the technician. "Save this picture. Then I want you to rewind the video until we get to the last car parked in that handicapped spot. That's where the device was detonated—obviously a time-delayed initiation. I want to see how it was delivered. And let's hope the hell," he added grimly, "that it's on this tape, and not on one of those shredded ones back in the security office."

21

The radio alarm clicked on. Leya's first instinct was to groan and curse the morning, come far too quickly. Instead, she smiled as she recognized the music—Gato Barbieri's tenor sax, growling out the smoky, erotic passages of "Europa." Quite possibly, she mused, the most sensuous piece of music on the planet. How appropriate.

Peter stirred in the bed. Leya was lying with her back to him, her body spooned into his under the feather-soft duvet. His arms enveloped her. As the dusky jazz slid over and around them, his hands began to move on her skin, soft lips and scratchy whiskers nuzzling her shoulder. He drew her body up tight against his own. He was definitely waking up.

"You put in a special request for this song, didn't you?" Leya murmured, reveling in his touch and the sax's gritty warmth.

"Do I seem that organized to you?" he whispered into her neck.

She shrugged lazily. "Mood music would be a piece of cake for a guy who arranges for full moons over the Temple of Jupiter."

He rolled her onto her back and lifted himself on one

elbow, frowning. But when he saw her smile, the creases in his forehead eased. His expression was sober, however, as he touched her left cheek.

With her eyes open, Leya noticed that her view was compressed on that side and that her cheek felt fat under his fingertips. "How do I look?"

"Like a poster child for the domestic-abuse hot line," he said glumly. "I'm really sorry."

"Don't be. It was an accident." He gave a rueful shake of his head and started to apologize again, but Leya stopped his mouth with a kiss. "Shh," she whispered, pulling him close. "It doesn't hurt. I feel wonderful."

And for the third time since she'd courted death by waking him out of his nightmare in the turret, they made love. The first time, on the dusty linoleum of her gutted second story, had been furious, primitive and quick. The second, when she'd convinced him to come downstairs with her, had been a slow, intense, exploratory voyage of rediscovery. Third time was a charm, deep and warm. Leya felt as if she, too, had come home from a long period in exile.

The WFNX deejay capped it several songs later with another appropriate, if eccentric, musical selection, Bobby McFerrin's goofy "Don't Worry, Be Happy." Peter collapsed on the pillows, arms splayed, shaking with silent, but almost-easy laughter. Leya watched him and smiled. In the space of a few hours, he seemed to have shed layers of something ugly and confining, like a cocoon, and the Peter she remembered was reemerging.

She laid her head on his shoulder and stroked his chest contentedly. But as she did, her fingers discovered again, as they had in the dark, that the mat of hair was bare in several places, the skin pocked. Burn scars, she realized, examining the round, purplish marks more closely in the light. These hadn't been self-inflicted, any more than the stripes she'd found on his back. Blind rage welled up inside her against anyone who could do this to another human being.

She tried not to let him sense the change in her mood, but when she glanced at him, he was watching her soberly. "I have to go."

Leya sighed and nodded. "My carpenters are going to show up any minute. Things are not always this chaotic, you know," she added.

He glanced around. "Good thing. The place is a mess."

Leya punched him lightly in the shoulder, smiling again. "I know that. Will be, too, for a few more weeks. I'm surprised you didn't have any more nightmares," she added quietly. "This isn't the best spot for someone with claustrophobia."

"Didn't seem to bother me." He kissed her one last time, then rolled over with a groan and dropped his feet to the floor. "Can I take a quick shower before I leave?"

"There is none, at the moment. I'm going over to the Mount Abbey Club for mine—it's the athletic facility in the field house on campus. Do you want to come with me? There's a men's locker room there, for visitors."

VanAken shook his head and retrieved his pants from the floor. "No, it's all right. I've got a hotel room in the city. I need to run in, anyway, check with my people, see what's happening. Doesn't look like Karim or Holly are going to show up now." He stood, zipped his pants, pulled on his denim shirt and started tucking himself together.

"I'll call you if I hear from her," Leya said. He nodded. As he backhanded his unruly hair into some semblance of order, she remembered seeing that morning gesture before, long ago and far away—although it wasn't quite as graceful now, she realized, given the strange angularity of those once-fluid hands. He shrugged into his leather shoulder harness and checked his gun.

"Peter?" He glanced over, but she hesitated, loath to tread into sensitive territory so soon.

"What?"

"Working for the FBI now—it means you were cleared of the charges against you, doesn't it?"

His expression hardened, and his lips pressed into a grim line. He shook his head.

"But you must have. The Bureau has a reputation for being even more stringent about security clearances than the CIA. They would never have hired you if—"

"I wasn't cleared. And I wasn't convicted. There was an internal CIA investigation, but they had insufficient evidence to prosecute, so I was left in limbo. Most people in the Company still think I'm guilty."

"But someone must have believed you, or you wouldn't be doing what you are."

He nodded slowly. "One person did."

A noisy muffler rumbling up the drive announced the arrival of the carpenters' pickup. Aggravated by their brilliant timing, Leya pulled on her T-shirt, stood, walked over and put a hand on his arm. "Two," she said. "At least two people believe you, Peter. I do, too. I believe *in* you."

"You mean that?"

"Absolutely."

The front doorbell rang. VanAken glanced toward the hall, then turned back, studying her. Finally, he nodded brusquely and reached for his jacket. The bell rang again. Leya cursed, grabbed her jeans from a box on the floor. Hopping on one foot, then the other, she shimmied into them. "Let me get the door. Don't run off yet, okay?"

"I need to call in."

She indicated the phone on the rolltop desk. "There's an extension there," she said, heading for the front hall.

When she opened the door, Ernie Latouche was sorting through his massive key ring, and his nephew was behind him, slouched against a post on the veranda. They both did a double take when they saw her face. "Professor!" Latouche exclaimed. "What happened to you?"

Duncan whistled. "Some shiner!"

Leya's hand went to her check. "Oh! I...uh...I tripped over some boxes in the dark last night. It's nothing. Come on in." They followed her into the hall.

"I was wonderin' whether you had a spare key for that padlock on the garage. Dingbat here," Latouche said, cocking his thumb at Duncan, "was supposed to lock it up before we left last night, but he forgot. I see you caught it, though. Thanks for that. Only now, Duncan can't remember what he did with the key, neither. I think he might have left it inside the garage."

"But I didn't lock it up."

Latouche shrugged. "Padlock's closed. You think you might have an extra key for it?"

Leya nodded slowly, her mind swirling with uneasy possibilities. She glanced at Duncan. Scowling from his uncle's criticism, he was shifting his weight from one baggy-jeaned leg to the other. His eyes were red, bleary and lined with dark circles. He looked like he'd gotten as little sleep as she had, although from the boozy ether rising from him, Leya guessed that his late-night carousing had included copious amounts of alcohol.

Duncan returned her stare defiantly from his safe vantage point behind Latouche, until something in the living room seemed to catch his attention. He glanced away, then turned back to Leya, a slow smirk rising on his face. Curious to see what had caused it, she saw Peter in the dining-cum-bedroom beyond the glass doors, standing next to the rumpled bed, his back to them as he spoke on the phone.

"Oh," Latouche said, flustered, also noticing. "You got company."

"It's all right. He's just heading out." Leya ignored Duncan's leer, but suddenly remembered, horrified, that her underwear, torn off in the initial frenzy with Peter, was still lying on the floor upstairs. Just what the little twerp needs to see, she thought. She held up a finger. "I think I do have a spare key for that padlock, Ernie. I'll get it in a second. Wait here, would you?"

Leaving them standing in the front hall, she sprinted up the stairs and immediately spotted the scrap of fabric lying where Peter had tossed it. As she stuffed it into the pocket of her jeans, Leya saw against the wall the ebony sculpture she'd carried up for self-defense when she'd thought he was wrestling with an intruder, instead of his demons. She picked that up, too, and then her gaze fell on the tangle of bedding in the alcove. She hesitated, then waved her hand dismissively. The hell with it, she thought. It'll give them something to wonder about.

Peter was coming into the front hall as she reached the bottom of the stairs. All three men gave her quizzical looks when she deposited the African carving on the hall table. "Peter, this is Ernie Latouche, my contractor, and his nephew, Duncan. This is Peter vanAken," she added to the others. "He's an old friend of mine."

Latouche held out his hand. Leya saw the getting-ready-to-bolt look on Peter's face, but after a glance at her, he recovered and shook hands with the older man. When he turned to Duncan, the youth held up a bandaged right palm and shrugged, stepping back.

"What happened there?" vanAken asked.

"Cut my hand on some glass."

"Foolin' around last night, as usual," Latouche added. Duncan shot his uncle a dirty look and slouched against the wall, hands in his pockets.

"Peter," Leya said, ignoring their squabble, "Ernie tells me they left the garage open by mistake last night. It's locked now," she added significantly, "but *I* didn't lock it."

He frowned. "The lock was on the first time I was here last night, when I did the circuit of the house. I'd better go take a look."

"I can open 'er up myself, you wanna gimme the key," Latouche said. "No need for you all to go runnin' out in the cold."

"I'll do it," vanAken repeated. Leya started to move, but he grabbed her arm. "Wait here."

"I want to be there, Peter, in case she's inside." He shook his head, but she had no intention of backing down. "I'm coming."

"All right, but you stay behind me. I'll check it out first—alone."

"Fair enough. Let me grab my coat. My keys are in the pocket."

"Somebody wanna tell me what's goin' on?" Latouche asked.

Leya pulled her coat out of the closet and glanced at vanAken as she shrugged into it, uncertain how he wanted to handle this.

Up front, as it turned out. "I'm with the FBI, Mr. Latouche. I've been tracking some suspects in connection with yesterday's bombing in Newton. One of them is a student of Professor Nash's. She was here briefly last night, then disappeared again."

"The ambassador's girl, the one who goes to Mount Abbey? I heard that on the news. No kiddin'—she was

here? I was gonna ask if you knew her," Latouche added
to Leya.

"Cool!" Duncan said. "Shoot-out at the professor's!"

"There's not going to be any shoot-out," Leya said irritably. She pulled on her sneakers, then turned to van-
Aken. "Let's go."

"This way," he said, heading for the back of the house.

They went through the kitchen and down the steps, then
crossed quietly over to the garage, the same way Leya had
gone the night before when she'd approached his car. She
hadn't even bothered to look in the garage, thinking it was
locked up with Ernie's tools and building supplies. Had
Holly been hiding there all along?

At the side of the old wooden building, vanAken forced
her head down under the window, then peered in cautiously. Leya heard a stone crunch and turned to find Duncan creeping up behind her.

Frowning at the boy, vanAken ducked again and withdrew his gun. "Stay right here," he warned them. Duncan
grinned, eyes wide with excitement.

"Peter, what are you doing?" Leya whispered. She
waved at the gun. "Is that really necessary?"

He held out his free hand. "Give me the key," he said
in an undertone, "and don't make a move until I tell you
it's safe."

"But—"

"I mean it, Leya! Her car's in there. They might have
locked the door so as not to raise suspicion, then climbed
back in through a window. Now, give me the damn key
and stay down. You, too," he added, pointing a finger at
Duncan.

Heart thumping, Leya separated the padlock key from
her ring and handed it to him, then held back as he inched

along the side of the garage and around the corner, holding himself low, the gun cocked beside his head.

"Cool," Duncan exhaled, his breath warm and sour next to Leya's face.

"Back off, Duncan!" she whispered fiercely.

"I know this chick, you know. What a ditz, gettin' herself mixed up with some fuckin' raghead!"

Leya eyed him, curiosity getting the better of distaste. "How do you know Holly?"

"Seen her around town in that ol' Benz of hers, an' over at Tyler's place, coupla days ago."

"I didn't know you were a friend of Tyler's."

"Newman's got lotsa friends. I see you do, too, eh, Professor?" he added, grinning.

"I told you to back off, Duncan."

"Sure thing. Wouldn't want to get in FBI-Man's way. Likes it rough, don't he?" he added, his forefinger flicking her swollen cheek.

Leya smacked his hand. "You want to see rough?" she whispered furiously. "You open your foul little mouth once more, and I'll grab that gun of his and use it on you! You've only lasted this long because I like your uncle, Duncan, but you so much as glance at me with that smarmy look on your face again—much less *breathe* on me—and I'll bounce you off my property so fast it'll make your head spin! You understand, you little jerk?"

"Jeez! I was just kiddin'—"

"You're too obnoxious to be humorous, Duncan. Now, shut up and get the hell away from me!"

Leya watched him slink off, back to the house. Then, inching toward the front of the garage, she peered around the corner. VanAken was easing the padlock off the hasp between the big double doors. As he folded it back, he caught sight of her and scowled, then held up a warning finger. She nodded and pulled back a little. He pressed himself against the right-hand door, gun raised, while his left hand inched the other door open a few inches.

"Karim? Holly?" he called out. "This is Peter van-Aken. I'm a federal agent. Come on out, let's talk."

Silence. He tried again.

"I'm a friend of Professor Nash, Holly. No one's going to hurt you. I want you to come out now, so we can talk." They listened. Nothing. "Come on, Karim! You can't stay in here forever. Let's get this straightened out. Don't play games, or someone's going to get hurt. Put your hands where I can see them and come on out."

Complete, ominous silence. Peter glanced back at Leya and motioned to her once more to duck down and stay put. She did, biting her lip as he opened the door wide, waited a second, then swung around and dropped into a crouch in the opening, gun trained on the interior. "Karim! Come on out, man!" Cautiously, he stepped forward, then disappeared inside the garage.

Leya waited, listening, for what seemed an eternity. Then, when she could stand the suspense no longer, she moved around the corner. Keeping low, under the level of the windows on the door, she crept along the front of the garage. At the opening, she paused, then put her head around the door—only to come face-to-face once more with Peter's gun. This time he pulled it up immediately.

"Dammit, Leya! I told you to wait back there!"

She stood cautiously and glanced around the garage, shrugging. "I couldn't anymore."

He shook his head, exasperated. "And it's still easier to ask for forgiveness than permission, isn't it?"

She fought back a grin. "Yep. They're not here?" Holly's battered green Mercedes sat in the middle of the dirt floor, license plate defiantly proclaiming TUF ENUF.

"No." He holstered his gun, then used his elbow to push the other door wide. "Looks like they stashed the car, then took off. Don't touch anything," he warned. "The forensics guys will want to go over everything. I'll have to call them in right away."

"Are you sure that's necessary?"

"Yep."

Leya's heart sank. "Why, Peter? What did you find out?"

He glanced behind her. "Where's the skinhead?"

"I sent him back to the house. What did you find out?" she repeated.

He exhaled heavily. "I talked to my chief. They've recovered the tapes from the Data-Trax security cameras, and there's no doubt about what happened. The whole thing was captured on film. This is the vehicle that carried the bomb, Leya. Holly and Karim delivered it."

Newton, Massachusetts: 7:09 a.m.

Curtis Pullen could not believe his ears.

Leonard Rickhauser, FBI assistant director in charge of the Criminal Investigative Division—the man who'd personally ordered investigators to bulldoze their way through an underground nightmare to reach the Data-Trax security office, who'd kept agents up all night, viewing and reviewing the precious taped evidence, frame by frame, over and over, who'd found the telltale shadow of the bomb device on the tape, who'd backtracked until he found recorded evidence that the Stroud girl's car had delivered it, who'd also, it turned out, had her friend the Arab under surveillance for the past two years because of his links to Hamas—this same hard-boiled, slave-driving, never-satisfied, pain-in-the-ass, glory-stealing, son of a bitch

ADIC was now standing in front of the assembled press corps, *downplaying* the likelihood that the Data-Trax bombing had anything to do with Arab terrorists or Islamic fundamentalist fanatics!

As he stood on the sidelines, watching Rickhauser field questions, Pullen's teeth crunched—hard—on his fifth antacid tablet in as many minutes.

They had called the press conference for 7:00 a.m., thirty minutes after the last two bodies, those of the Data-Trax receptionist and security chief, were pulled out of the destroyed atrium. Barring additional deaths among the hospitalized victims, some of whom were still critical, the final toll from the incident stood at nine dead, forty-two injured, several dozen treated and released, and God only knew how many millions of dollars' worth of damage to the Data-Trax facility.

The only bright note—and that, Pullen thought, was a strictly relative term—was that none of the fatalities, miraculously, had included children, unless you counted the receptionist's full-term fetus. When access to the collapsed underground tunnel was finally gained, medics had been forced to amputate the crushed leg of one four-year-old to free her from a fallen concrete wall before she bled to death. They'd found several other children and parents with broken bones, cuts and scrapes, but on the whole, Pullen thought, it could have been worse. Much worse.

Now, with the press clamoring for an update, Rickhauser had agreed to meet them in the conference room of a U.S. Post Office building, several blocks from the bomb site. After hoping he would be lead investigator on this case, Pullen found himself relegated to playing the role of faithful hound dog to the ADIC's master hunter. Watching Rickhauser, Pullen ripped yet another Tums off the roll he'd been munching to quell the fire in his gut.

"Are you saying this wasn't Arab terrorists, sir?" Mort Syngen, from the *Boston Globe,* asked. "Definitively?"

"I'm saying it's too soon in the investigation to eliminate other possibilities," Rickhauser answered.

"Surely you're not suggesting the explosion was accidental?" Syngen harrumphed. Pullen groaned inwardly, knowing the *Globe's* coverage was going to crucify the Bureau.

"No, I think I can safely say this was no accident."

"How do you know?" CNN's Boston correspondent piped up.

"We've got top explosives experts from the FBI and ATF here. Between them, they've investigated over ten thousand bombings—that's how I know," Rickhauser said. "We've collected chemical samples and physical evidence that should allow us to establish the mechanism in short order. But determining the cause of the explosion is only one of three stages in an investigation like this. The second stage, which is already under way, involves intelligence work—identifying every individual or group who might have had a motive for bombing the Data-Trax facility."

"Data-Trax is doing federal-government defense work, isn't that true? Wouldn't that make them a target for foreign terrorists?"

"Government contractors are targeted by foreign and domestic terrorists alike. We're also looking at an animal-rights group that has protested the use of animals in some of the company's medical work. And there's always the possibility of a personal motive, as well—a disgruntled former employee, or an ex-spouse, or—"

"Oh, come on!" a voice called from the back of the room. "Don't you already have your suspects? Ambassador Stroud's daughter? And her Palestinian boyfriend?

That's her car Special Agent Pullen announced you were looking for, isn't it?''

Rickhauser's yellow wolf eyes never blinked or wavered from the pack in front of him, but Pullen could have sworn the man had a second set, so palpable was his feeling of being glowered at. He felt his skin bristling and his stomach churning, and he popped one more Tums into his mouth.

"The field is wide-open. That said," Rickhauser added, raising his voice above the ensuing commotion, "we *are* looking for Holly Anne Stroud and another individual, based on information that places them at the Data-Trax compound yesterday afternoon, not long before the explosion took place."

"What about the Arab with her?" someone shouted. "What's his name?"

Rickhauser hesitated for a second. "The individual we believe accompanied Miss Stroud," he said, obviously deciding the name wasn't going to stay secret for long, "is a naturalized American citizen of Palestinian extraction named Karim Khoury. I stress, however, that Miss Stroud and Mr. Khoury are being sought only as material witnesses, at this point. It's possible they have information that could help us."

A half-dozen voices spluttered, "But—"

"I said," Rickhauser added loudly, "that an investigation like this has *three* phases. The third phase, also in motion as we speak, is hard-slogging detective work. Interviewing every eyewitness, including those in hospital. Anyone who may have seen or knows anything, no matter how insignificant. It's gumshoe stuff, folks, but it's how we avoid jumping to conclusions prematurely, and maybe letting bad guys slip through the net."

The room was in an uproar now, and if it weren't for

the need to keep up the appearance of bureau solidarity, Pullen would have been tempted to tear out his hair. *What the hell is the man doing?* he thought. Any academy freshman could see what this bombing had been about—Middle East terrorists targeting a prime strategic-defense contractor involved in developing the next generation of spy satellite. If rumors were true, the Guardian satellite, when launched, would be capable of counting the hairs on an ayatollah's beard, through dense cloud cover, at that, from a geostationary earth orbit of four hundred miles. No way the opposition wanted to see that baby get off the ground.

Pullen felt a tap on his sleeve, and he turned to find Agent Wilf Berger standing beside him. Not for the first time, it occurred to him that these new recruits were getting younger and younger every year. The kid showed no fatigue and only the faintest stubble of beard, despite having been at it all night, like the rest of them. Disgusting, the SAC thought.

"What are you doing here? You're supposed to be interviewing witnesses."

"I was, sir, but then I was sent over to deliver a message. Field office said they didn't want to radio it, in case somebody was listening," Berger added quietly, nodding in the direction of the press.

"What message?"

Berger moved closer. "Agent vanAken called."

"Oh, joy," Pullen said, rolling his eyes. "To what do we owe the honor?"

"He's located the vehicle."

Pullen pulled up sharp. *"What?"*

"Holly Stroud's vehicle, sir. Agent vanAken found it."

"Shit!" Pullen seethed, fist punching his thigh.

"That's good, isn't it?"

"What? Oh, yeah, sure. Great. Where is he now?"

Berger handed him a slip of paper. "He's at this address in Winslow. With the car."

Pullen glanced over at Rickhauser, who seemed to be wrapping up the press briefing. "All right," he said, turning again to the young agent. "You head back to the crime scene now."

"Do you think maybe I could—"

"That'll be all. Back to work!"

"Yes, sir," Berger said, crestfallen.

As the young agent trudged off, Pullen glanced at the paper in his hand, then stuffed it into his pocket. Rickhauser was disengaging himself from the makeshift podium at the front of the room. Pullen decided to wait until they were back in the car to tell him about vanAken and the Stroud girl's vehicle.

But as the ADIC lumbered over, Pullen recalled Arch McCreary's comment about Peter vanAken: *"He's Rickhauser's man, Curtis. Give him what he needs, and leave it at that."* Maybe McCreary had gotten it backward, Pullen mused. Maybe vanAken was running Rickhauser.

A few hours earlier, liaising with the CIA's counterterrorism desk, and bringing them up to date so they could pulse the system and see what their own people abroad could dig up, Pullen had mentioned that the prime suspect in the Data-Trax bombing was an Arab whom Agent vanAken had had under surveillance. At the mention of vanAken's name, Pullen's CIA contact, Bill Lavin, had given a contemptuous snort, then passed along a choice bit of inside dope on the former spook. "You want to watch that one," he told Pullen.

"You know him?"

"Only by reputation. He was one of ours for a while. Ran Arab agents in Beirut a decade ago. When our embassy there was bombed, they said vanAken had leaked information on gaps in the embassy's physical security, giving the terrorists a blueprint for maximum damage.''

"He sold out?"

"Apparently. He's an Arab-lover, you know, like his old man. Word is, vanAken's loyalties were always suspect."

"So, how come he's still running around free?"

"Because vanAken himself was burned in Lebanon. His cover got blown, and he was taken hostage. We'd already lost a former station chief there, and vanAken was written off for dead, too. But four years later, he escaped. There was an internal agency investigation, but the evidence trail in the embassy bombing was cold by then." Lavin chuckled. "You guys got suckered, big time, when you hired that guy."

And now, Pullen thought, following Rickhauser out the door, they had another bombing on their hands, another suspect linked to vanAken, and an FBI assistant director trying to cover up the traces. Who owned who around here?

22

Leya realized her carpenters would have an unexpected day off. She watched vanAken circle Holly Stroud's car in the garage, examining it, but taking pains not to touch it. Ernie Latouche's tools and supplies had been unceremoniously shoved against the wall. Had Holly done that on her own, Leya wondered, or had Karim been here with her?

"No one touches a thing until the forensics guys are done," vanAken repeated. He peered through the windows of the Mercedes, then exclaimed, "Hello-o, Karim!"

Leya stood on tiptoe, trying to see over his shoulder. "He's in there?"

"Not in the flesh. Just his spoor."

"Spoor? What are you talking about?"

VanAken pointed at the front passenger seat. "See those Reese's Pieces wrappers on the seat? The mark of Karim Khoury. The guy's addicted to them—and to Burger King Whoppers. They're his comfort food."

"You're kidding."

"No. He told me once that he'd seen *E.T.—The Extra-Terrestrial* about twenty-five times. Remember how the kid in the movie befriended the alien with Reese's Pieces?

Karim's loved the stuff ever since. Says it's 'friendly American food.'"

Leya shook her head, then frowned. "You seem to know him awfully well, Peter."

"I'm not so sure." He led her out the door and resealed the garage, and they started back to the house.

"You're the FBI man Holly said he was afraid of, aren't you?"

He frowned. "What exactly did she say about that?"

"Nothing, really."

He stopped walking, his features tight. "She said *something*. What, Leya? Think."

Leya wrapped her arms around herself. "Nothing much. She just said Karim was being harassed by an FBI agent, who wanted him to inform on some Palestinian terrorist group, but he wanted out of the whole business. And what is this?" she added. "The third degree? Am I a suspect, too? Are you going to arrest me as an accessory, after all?"

He hesitated, then backed off. "No, sorry. I'm on edge. Look, I have to wait for the investigators, but there's no reason why you can't go to your classes."

"They won't need me here?"

"I doubt it. If they do, I know where to find you. Just don't leave town."

"Oh, Agent vanAken, I'll bet you've always wanted to say that to someone," Leya kidded, anxious to break the tension that seemed to erupt far too quickly in him. She was rewarded when he almost smiled. She looped her arm through his. "Come on. I'll put on some coffee before I go and find you something to eat."

Back at the house, she told the carpenters they could leave, and while vanAken warned them to keep quiet about what they'd learned, she put coffee on to brew and toasted a couple of bagels. Taking hers into the dining room, she made the bed and gathered her papers, briefcase, clothes and toiletries. In the powder room, she washed up and brushed her teeth, then changed into a skirt and her favorite sweater, a gold cashmere turtleneck that she thought brought out the gleam in her dark brown hair and eyes. She debated clipping back her hair until she could get to the field house and take her shower, but decided to keep it down.

While she brushed it to a high shine, Leya studied herself in the mirror. Turning the right side of her face forward, she noted that her color was elevated, even without makeup, and that her eyes were bright. It was the face of a woman in love, and exhausted by it, she reflected, smiling. She experienced a guilty flash at the thought of John Merriman. She'd never looked like this after a night with him. Turning the other way, however, she saw that the swelling in her cheek had turned a riveting shade of magenta, complemented by a pool of navy blue collecting in the hollow under her eye. Definitely a domestic-abuse poster child, she thought ruefully, dreading the curious questions she would face all day.

When she came back to the kitchen, vanAken was sitting at the center island, drinking coffee, eating his bagel and cream cheese, and flipping through the *Boston Globe* as casually as if he did this every morning. She walked over and scratched the blue stubble on his cheek. "You look a little worse for the wear, fella. Are you sure you don't want to come over to the field house with me? You could shower and shave, and be back in half an hour."

He glanced up, then did a double take and straightened in his seat, putting down his cup. "No, I have to keep an eye on the garage. I've got a razor out in the car. I'll make do here."

Leya combed his hair with her fingers. "You'd better.

You wouldn't want your colleagues thinking you've gone to seed."

"They already think that." He swiveled on the stool, then reached out and pulled her close, trapping her between his legs. His finger touched her cheek. "You should try to keep ice on this today."

"It doesn't hurt, honestly." She leaned into him and they kissed. Once, twice—then a third kiss that went on and on, until they were at serious risk of total meltdown, right there on the blue-and-white tile floor. "I have to go," Leya said, pulling back breathlessly.

He held her tighter. "Stay a little longer," he whispered.

"I can't," she protested, even as her brain calculated whether she could. "I've got a class at nine. I have to shower before that, and run by the drugstore to pick up my father's prescrip—"

VanAken stiffened and dropped his arms. Sliding the stool away from her, he turned back to his newspaper. Leya watched him, stunned. Her father, she realized. No matter how far they'd come in the past few hours, Carter Nash still stood between them—the elephant in the room that nobody was supposed to mention.

"Peter," she ventured, "I know you and my father—"

"No, you don't. You have no idea. Go on, Leya. You do what you have to. That's what I intend to do." He took the paper, snapped it flat and bent over it, ignoring her.

Leya moved away uncertainly, slipping into her coat, gathering her briefcase and the backpack that held her toiletries. Her chest felt tight, and her stomach was churning as she made her way toward the front door. Then she stopped. She was slinking out of her own house, goddammit. She spun around and stomped back down the hall to the kitchen. "Peter!"

He looked up, startled, then wary. "What?"

"You can't do this to me. It isn't fair!"

"Fair?"

"You can't ask me to choose between you. I'd do almost anything for you, but don't ask me to hate him. He's my father. Father, mother—the only family I've ever had. He raised me and loved me. He could have shuffled me off, let other people—one of my grandmothers—raise me after my mother died, but he didn't. He sat up all night next to my bed when I got pneumonia, and stayed home to nurse me through chicken pox."

"Swell."

"And now he's old and tired and sick, and he needs me."

"Fine. Then there's nothing more to discuss, is there?" It sounded casual enough, but his mouth was set in a hard line. His skin had paled, and his scarred hands rolled into tense balls.

"Peter, please—"

"Go on, Leya. Go where you're needed."

"I'm needed here, too," she said quietly.

"No, you're not. You'll just be in the way when the team gets here."

"I'm not talking about the investigation. I'm talking about you."

"Me? What makes you think I need you?"

"I don't think it, Peter. I know it."

He leaned back on the stool. "My God, woman, you have an inflated sense of yourself, don't you? This may come as a shock, but I do not feel particularly drawn to you."

"Really? Then what was the last few hours about?"

He gave a derisive snort. "You know exactly what it was about."

"And you don't feel a thing about what happened here

between us—again?" The slow smirk that rose on his lips reminded Leya of Duncan, but she decided to ignore it. "Peter, don't do this. Don't shut down. Let me—"

He grabbed her by the wrist and pulled her to him. "You want to go one more round? Come on—we can do it right here on the countertop."

"Stop it!"

"It's a little late to be coy, isn't it? You were begging for it earlier."

Leya shoved him away. "You really are a shit, you know that?"

"Aha! There it is. *That's* Daddy's girl talking."

"Go to hell."

He shrugged. "Been there. Didn't like it."

Leya stared at him. She really didn't know this man. He was an angry stranger with an FBI badge who bore a superficial resemblance to someone she'd once loved. And yet... "Peter, tell me why you hate him. I know the two of you had your disagreements, and that my arrival didn't help matters. But that's no reason—"

"You want to know? Fine. I'll tell you. He tried to kill me."

"What?"

"Your father sent me into a trap. I told him I was quitting, but he insisted I meet a new contact before I went. He knew damn well that the source I was supposed to hook up with had no bona fides. Worse yet, he sent me in there knowing that my cover had already been blown. Once I'd been made as CIA, my chances of getting out alive were nil."

"He would never do that."

"He would, and he did."

"No way. Anyone else, maybe, but not my father. If

there was one thing he was known for, it was protecting his men.''

"Ah, yes," Peter said bitterly. "That unassailable Nash reputation. When he dies, they're going to have him bronzed and mounted in the lobby at Langley, right next to the stars on the memorial wall. 'The heroes' hero, who never left a man in enemy hands.' Bullshit!''

"If there'd been any way he could have gotten you out, don't you think—''

"He could have! Even after he sent me into that trap, he could have sprung me. A month after I was taken, the Israelis went to him with information from an *oter*—one of the Arabs they ran—detailing exactly where I was being held. Mossad even offered to help mount a rescue, payback for previous CIA favors. Nash turned the offer down and never even reported it to Langley. Then, when the situation got too hot in Lebanon and the embassy closed down, he turned out the lights, sailed away and left me there to rot.''

"No—''

"So don't tell me what a hero he is, Leya, because that man nearly destroyed me. What happened to me *did* destroy my parents. And when I refused to cooperate and die for him—when I came back from the dead—he set out to annihilate my name and my reputation, instead, with a bunch of trumped-up allegations of treason, when all I'd done in Lebanon was the job I was sent there to do.''

"But *why*, Peter? Why would he do such a thing?''

"Don't you think I've asked myself that a thousand times? You tell me! Tell me why that man was so obsessed with you that he would see me dead rather than let me touch you. Tell me again about all those cozy nights he spent next to your bedside. You did say *next* to it, didn't you, Leya? Or did the two of you—''

She slapped him, hard, across the face. Then, yanking

open a drawer, Leya withdrew a key and threw it on the island countertop. "Lock the front door when you go, and leave the key under the mat on the veranda."

She wheeled away and walked out on him.

Newton, Massachusetts: 7:30 a.m.

Reinforcements had arrived—twenty-three additional agents from the FBI's Boston field office, another sixteen pulled in from headquarters, plus four more ATF bomb experts, all of them reassigned to the NEWBOM investigation. Rickhauser roamed the area at the front of the main hall of the Data-Trax mansion annex, addressing sixty-eight investigators sitting on folding chairs, bringing them up to date, breaking the search down into half-a-dozen discrete assignments they were to focus on for the next forty-eight hours.

Also standing at the front of the room, once again off to the side, the Boston acting SAC, Curtis Pullen, watched the ADIC with a mixture of envy, awe and irritation. Neither of them had slept in over thirty hours. Pullen felt like shit, despite having grabbed a shower and a quick shave in the locker room downstairs. It was all he could do to remain vertical. Rickhauser, on the other hand, looked alert as a werewolf under a full moon.

"Team number one," he said, nodding to an agent in the front row whom he'd already named as its leader, "you've got the crime scene. Now that we've got daylight and all the victims out, I want you to work with the ATF people, go back over the ground, inch by inch, searching for bomb components or other evidence we can track to the source." He turned to Pullen. "How soon do we expect the lab to get back on the chemical analysis from those steel fragments they found last night?"

"End of the day," the SAC said.

"Lean on 'em. We need it yesterday. Team two," Rickhauser said, addressing another agent, "I want you to reinterview employees, see if anyone's remembered anything more since last night. Not just about the blast itself. I want details on every protest group or individual who's ever uttered a threat against the company—foreign crazies, bunny huggers, right-wing paranoiacs, left-wing paranoiacs, ex-employees, disgruntled spouses, spurned lovers, business partners—anyone and everyone. Then I want each and every one investigated and their movements for the last seventy-two hours accounted for."

The agent nodded smartly. Rickhauser continued walking, then stopped in front of yet another agent. The man sat up straighter. "Team three—I want you to pay attention to company management and major shareholders— who are they? What organizations are they active in? Israel Defense Fund? IRA/Sinn Fein links? Cuban exiles? The mob? The CIA? Any major movements of company stock lately? Unhappy business partners? What about that government contract for the Guardian satellite system? What press coverage did Data-Trax get, and who might have seen it? Who did they beat out for the job? How's the competition been doing since?"

Curtis Pullen raised a hand, impatience finally getting the better of him. "Sir? What about the Stroud girl and Karim Khoury?"

The big man at center stage nodded. "Right. Teams four and five are with me. We're going out to Winslow to examine the car and bring it in, and fan out the search for Khoury and the girl. We'll hook up with Agent vanAken and have him bring us up-to-date."

"But sir—!"

"That's it," Rickhauser told the assembly. "You have

your assignments. No talking to the press. I want updates submitted twice daily through Curtis Pullen here, who'll handle command and control. Teams four and five, I'll meet you outside in two minutes. Dismissed."

Seething, Pullen held back as the hall cleared. He was going to be left behind, cooling his heels, paper shuffling. Admittedly, Rickhauser had made it clear that he was in charge of command and control. That was good. On the other hand, there was no doubt the ADIC intended to stick around to oversee the case—not exactly a vote of confidence. Not only that, Pullen fumed, but Rickhauser and bloody vanAken had the car and would probably nab the girl, the Arab and the glory.

Or not, he suddenly thought.

"Len," he said, stepping forward, his voice firm, determined not to let this wolf intimidate him, "I have to protest the way this investigation is being handled. We should be putting more resources on Khoury and the girl, not chasing phantoms. They delivered the mechanism. You know that. You found it yourself on the video. They were the last ones to park in the handicapped spot, and they left the bomb behind when they left."

Rickhauser nodded. "I know."

"Well, then, why—"

"They're mules, Curtis."

"What?"

"Mules," Rickhauser repeated. "Bomb carriers—maybe even unwitting ones—but not builders, I'm betting. Not operations planners."

"But how—?"

"I've called down a file from headquarters, told them to copy it to you. Get some rest till it gets here, then read it. And go back to the surveillance van, look at the video again. I've got the tech working on a hunch of mine. If I'm right, and he finds what I think he will, then all bets are off as far as who planned this bombing.''

23

Leya stood before a mirror in the Mount Abbey field house, ripping a brush through her damp hair. *This is insane,* she thought. *What have I done?* Her traitorous body was in a state of febrile shock, alternately giddy and overwrought by the highs and lows of meeting Peter again, after all these years. Her brain, meanwhile, was reeling from his accusations and his anger. He was still back at her house, waiting for his FBI colleagues to arrive. Logically, she thought, there was a good chance she would see him again before this business with Holly Stroud was resolved. The anticipation of it filled her with both dread and yearning.

Be careful what you wish for, she thought, because you just might get it. Maybe what she was going through now was the process of closure she'd been looking for after the abrupt and wrenching split with him so long ago. She didn't want to spend the rest of her life like the last ten years, feeling incomplete, always wondering where he was and what was happening to him, whether the bond between them had been real or illusion. But if she'd known that achieving closure was this difficult, she might have been content to live with the problem.

For a decade now, the memory of Peter had run through her like a subterranean river, eroding and undermining every relationship she'd had with any other man—like the widowed classics professor she'd gotten involved with at Columbia. Peter had been held hostage for almost a year when Leya met the prof after a campus theater production of *Oedipus Rex*. Loneliness and mutual grief—his for his dead wife, Leya's for Peter—had drawn them together, but Leya had pulled back after a few months, when the older man began to talk of marriage. Then there was the Reuters foreign correspondent, a Brit she'd met at a Kennedy Center concert. And the burly carpenter she'd had an affair with when she was working as assistant director in a little summer-stock troupe in the Poconos, after the Reuters man was reassigned to Beijing and Leya declined to follow him, having had enough of the nomad's life.

Each of those relationships, each of those men, she realized, had been a substitute for some aspect of the man she'd lost to Lebanon—for Peter's intellect and warmth, his worldliness, his physical energy. But individually and collectively, they hadn't been enough to help her forget him. And every time things had started to get serious, she'd withdrawn, a nagging little voice in her head telling her, *Peter's the one. Peter will be back.*

With a pang of guilt, Leya thought again of John Merriman—a steady, reliable fellow, ready to commit, the kind of man her single-women friends lamented couldn't be found anymore, just before they reminded Leya again that she was bonkers for not grabbing him with both hands. But what she felt for Merriman was a pale shadow of what she knew she could be feeling. What she *had* felt, and did feel—but not for Merriman.

What was it about Peter, she thought irritably, that he'd held such sway over her for so long now? All they'd ever had was five days, for crying out loud! Five days that had left her romantically dysfunctional and spoiled for anyone who followed. Five days that had produced nothing but a broken heart—and, Leya recalled sadly, an unplanned pregnancy.

No one but Mrs. Garibaldi had ever known about that. Leya had been six weeks along, the day she saw the newspaper report of Peter's kidnapping. A few minutes later, she'd fainted on the Arts Building staircase, taking a flight-and-a-half tumble that had brought on a miscarriage that night. Not having worked up the courage to write and tell her father about the pregnancy, Leya had sworn Mrs. Garibaldi to secrecy, and cashed a savings bond to pay for her brief hospital stay so it wouldn't show up as a claim on his health-insurance plan. Then she'd tried to pick up the pieces of her life and move on.

Now Peter was back, and all the memories and raw emotions of that long-ago spring had come rushing in on her again. Why was it that he touched her so deeply? What, objectively, did he do for her that the others didn't?

Her body, of course, had a ready answer, but Leya mistrusted its eager enthusiasm. Great sex was no antidote to high stress, volatile emotions and no sleep. But was that really all it was about? Hormones, pheromones, or whatever chemistry it was that turned rational, competent human beings into quivering, mindless idiots? If her brain had been addled at two in the morning, when she'd found Peter on the street and invited him into her house, and then her bed, that was nothing compared to the conflict she was feeling now, knowing he hated her father—the man who had raised her, sacrificed for her, been her only family—with a fury and for reasons that left her breathless.

And although loath to give credence to his accusations

against her father, Leya knew very well that Carter Nash had never had any use for Peter vanAken.

When he finally arrived back in Beirut and got wind of the fact that his daughter was in-country, staying with Peter vanAken, Carter Nash had burst unannounced into the young prof's apartment on the American University campus.

Leya and Peter were cross-legged on the living-room floor, starting a game of backgammon—fully dressed, fortunately, but only just. One look at her father's face, white with rage, and Leya knew there would be no reasoning with him until he calmed down. She gathered her things and left with him quickly, before the situation came to blows. Later, at his embassy-owned house, Nash planted the first seeds of doubt in her mind about Peter, seeds that grew into a tangled, weedy garden, where her blossoming passion was very nearly choked. Nearly, but not quite—stubborn obsession that it had proved to be.

"Are you out of your mind?" her father bellowed. "The Bekaa Valley, for chrissake? He could have gotten you killed!"

"But he didn't. If anything, Peter's kept me out of harm's way, Dad. I had no idea you wouldn't be here when I arrived."

"You had no business coming! Do you know how many Westerners have been taken hostage in this country? How many have been murdered?"

"Probably not as many as are murdered every year in the streets of New York."

"Don't get smart with me, young lady!"

"I'm sorry. But I missed you, and I wanted to see Beirut. You didn't raise me to spend my life hiding under a bed,

*did you? There's risk everywhere. Isn't that what you told
me, when I worried about you coming here?''*

"It's not the same. I'm trained to take care of myself.''

Conditioned by him to expect that walls had ears, Leya
lowered her voice to a choked whisper. *"You're a prime
target, Dad! Don't you think I know that your predecessor
was kidnapped and tortured to death?''*

His face softened when he saw her fear and her tears,
and he took her in his arms. *"I have tight security arrangements, honey. Nothing's going to happen to me. But
you! To put your trust in vanAken, of all people...''*

*"He's been great. He's a terrific teacher, you know—I
went to one of his classes. And he has friends everywhere,
people he's known all his life. When we went up-country,
he carried food and blankets and baby formula. I never
felt in danger for a minute while we were touring around,
and I learned so much about this country.''*

Her father shook his head. *"You don't know him.''*

"What do you mean?''

Nash hesitated, then took her out into the garden, where
the wind and traffic noises beyond the high stone walls
would muffle any words that passed between them. He sat
Leya down next to him on a bench under the swaying,
silver-green leaves of an olive tree. Then, having come this
far, he was seized by his usual reticence. He leaned forward, elbows on his knees, fists clasped together, and
stared ahead, thick brows knotted in a frown, thumbs tapping against one another.

Leya examined the liver spots on the ropy backs of his
hands. And his hair—it had been gray for as long as she
could remember, but had acquired heavy white streaks at
the temples since the last time she'd seen him, nearly eight
months earlier, when he'd driven her back to Mount Abbey
after summer vacation. They hadn't been able to spend

Christmas together. Fighting in Beirut had kept him hun-kered down, and Leya had spent a lonely holiday season with the family of one of his Langley colleagues, who had stepped in when her father couldn't get out of Lebanon. Now, she sensed how much this stressful posting was tak-ing out of him. He'd always seemed huge and invincible. It had never occurred to her that he would one day be an old man. For the first time, Leya found herself wondering how much longer he could survive in what he always called "the game."

"You wanted to tell me something, Dad."

He glanced at her, then straightened. "VanAken works for me, Leya."

Her jaw dropped. "He's CIA?"

"Theoretically, but I'm going to have him yanked. He's out of control here."

"How so?"

"I can't give you details, you know that. But believe me, the list of his security infractions is as long as my arm. He doesn't follow orders. He goes places he's not sup-posed to, consorts with people he has no business dealing with. Disappears for days on end. He's a womanizer—" *Leya must have blanched, because her father scowled. "Don't tell me you think you're in love with him?" When she said nothing, Nash snorted contemptuously. "You and half the women in Beirut. But no way is he getting near you again. He's dangerous. Just being in the same room with that guy is dangerous, given the kind of game he's playing here. He's a bad apple, mark my words, and he's going to fall—hard."*

And that was as much as he'd been willing to tell her. Early the next morning, still sick with confusion, Leya said goodbye to her father at the airport and boarded a Swiss-

air flight back to Athens. No sooner had she buckled her
seat belt than a stewardess approached.

"Are you Leya Nash?" When Leya nodded, the atten-
dant handed over an envelope, smiling. "I was asked to
give this to you."

Inside was a note.

> Leya
>
> I called, but your father wouldn't put you on the
> phone. I also came to the house, but no luck—his
> goons had orders not to let me in. He is not a happy
> camper, is he?
>
> I need to see you. We have to talk. I'll come to you,
> anytime, anywhere. Please, please, cable me c/o the
> American University of Beirut and say yes.
>
> I love you.
>
> Peter

It took only the duration of the flight from Beirut to
Athens for Leya to make up her mind. When she found out
that the commercial lines to Lebanon were down again,
she went straight to the American embassy and had the
comcenter there send her cable via the diplomatic net.

Athens Gate Hotel. Come quick. Leya.

The cable he never got, Leya thought, as she packed her
shower things and closed her field-house locker. Shoving
her feet into the brown loafers she'd opted to wear, in spite
of the light dusting of snow on the ground, she reached
for her coat. She'd waited ten days in Athens for him to
show up and never heard a word. Finally, late for the beginning of spring term, she'd returned to Boston and
Mount Abbey, resigned to the belief that her father had

been right, determined to put all thought of Peter vanAken behind her. But it hadn't turned out to be as simple as that.

"Professor Nash! What happened to you?"

Leya turned to see Allison Velotta, one of her freshman AmLit students, standing next to her, bathing suit dripping.

"Hi, Allison. Swim-team practice this morning?"

The girl nodded. "What happened to your face?"

Leya hesitated, uncomfortable with the position her bruises put her in. It didn't matter that Peter had struck her unconsciously. The situation forced her to make excuses that sounded too much like a battered woman in denial, and she didn't like the way that made her feel. "I had an accident," she said reluctantly. "My house is being renovated, and there are a lot of building materials underfoot." It wasn't the truth, but it wasn't a lie, either—just irrelevant.

"Ouch! Looks painful."

"No big deal. Just one of those fluky things."

"Did you hear about Holly Stroud?"

"Yes, I did. You haven't seen her, have you, Allison? She's still missing."

The girl shook her head. "Not for a couple of days. But I met that Arab friend of hers—the one they say planted the bomb? It's so awful. Poor Holly! I can't believe she let herself get dragged into something like this."

"When did you see this fellow?"

"A couple of times. First time was over at the theater, two or three weeks ago, during *Hamlet* rehearsal." Allison worked set design in Leya's campus theater troupe.

"I don't remember seeing him," Leya said, frowning.

"Maybe not. You were out front, in the auditorium. He was backstage, hanging out with Holly while she waited for her cues to go onstage. She got him to help shift some backdrops I was painting, and that's when she introduced Karim.''

"Did the two of them seem…close?"

"I think Karim really had the hots for her. He hardly ever took his eyes off her. Holly was all attentive, too, but at first, I thought he was just her latest cause. You know Holly," the girl added, eyebrow arched. "One week, she's on a save-the-rain forest kick, next thing she's, like, going on in poli-sci class about the poor Palestinian refugees. But then later, I decided there must be something between them."

"Why's that?"

"We were all heading over to Tyler's after rehearsal, and I asked Holly if they were coming. But she's all, 'No, I don't think so.' I figured she didn't want to take this Karim guy there. Holly and Tyler Newman were…you know…."

"So I gather."

"Anyway, Karim didn't say more than about three words the whole time he was backstage that day, but I *never* figured the guy was a terrorist, you know? I mean, he seemed pretty normal and all, for a foreigner. I guess you can't ever tell, huh?"

Leya sighed as she pulled on her coat. "Maybe not. So Tyler must have been pretty upset when Holly gave him up for this other guy."

"For a few days maybe. But you've seen Tyler, right?"

"Sure."

"Well, it's not like he'd be desperate for company or anything, is it? I mean, life goes on, you know."

Leya noted the girl's blush and gave her a curious smile. "Are you seeing Tyler, Allison?"

"Oh, just kind of hanging out, that's all. But it's okay," she added, hurriedly. "I mean, it's not like I'm going behind Holly's back or anything. They're friends again now. Platonic, you know.''

"I see. Well," Leya said, gathering up her things, ''I have to run. I'll see you in class later?''

"Yep. Bye, Professor Nash. Watch your step, okay?'' the girl called after her.

Leya left the field house and threw her things into her car, then climbed in, heading for the pharmacy in town, her mind once again on Holly Stroud.

It takes two to tangle—another of Bhu's, her old *ayah's* garbled sayings. Holly had sworn she knew nothing about the bomb, but if Karim was responsible, then he'd had a willing dupe. The girl was young and idealistic, and Leya hoped, desperately, that she'd be all right. But as Ambassador Stroud's dependent, she would have had briefings from her parents and from government agents on security risks and precautions, just as Leya had. When she'd hooked up with Karim Khoury, Holly had defied every warning she'd ever received. How could she have done that? Leya gave her head a rueful shake. She knew exactly how. She knew all about the blind hearts of young women.

Pulling into a parking spot near Haddad's Pharmacy, she turned off the ignition and leaned wearily against the steering wheel. *It takes two to tangle*. Her father and Peter. What had really gone on between those two? And what was she doing, getting herself caught again between them?

The sound of breaking glass pulled her out of another fruitless cycle of frustration and self-recrimination. She looked up to see Haddad, the old pharmacist, knocking a shard of glass out of the drugstore's big front window. It fell to the sidewalk, shattering into smaller pieces. Most of the window was already lying on the pavement or in the display case, but a few sections still clung precariously to the caulking. It was these that he was cleaning out with the claw end of a hammer, which he held in heavily gloved hands, apparently clearing the opening for the plywood sheet that was leaning against the corner of the building.

Frowning, Leya got out of the car, her gaze shifting to the druggist's wife. Salt-and-pepper curls shaking, Mrs. Haddad was scrubbing furiously at the brickwork, where a message had been spray-painted in red: Dirty Arabs— Go Home!

The scrawled, unevenly spaced letters were an ugly gash on the noble old building. The drugstore was located on Winslow's renovated central square, which surrounded a parklike common, dotted with wrought-iron benches and an old-fashioned, trellised bandstand. Haddad's, with its gingerbread woodwork and striped blue-and-white awnings, was one of the prettiest properties on the common. Directly opposite, on the far side of the green, stood the tall spires of the old Congregationalist church. That church and its belfry were the pride of Winslow, boasting twin bells cast by Paul Revere. Tyler's was a couple of buildings down from there.

Leya approached the door. "Mrs. Haddad?" she ventured. The tiny woman glanced at her, but went on scrubbing. Leya put a hand on her shoulder. "Who did this?"

The older woman paused, large brown eyes bright, lips pressed tightly together. She shook her head, then went back to her work. Leya turned to her husband, who put down his hammer and gloves. His kind old face, which always bore a ready smile, was grim now.

"It happened early this morning," he said, waving his hand disgustedly at the damage as he walked toward Leya and his wife, broken glass crunching under his shoes. Looking down, Leya saw scattered bits of gold foil, remnants of the Gothic lettering that had been embossed across the plate glass: Haddad's Pharmacy. "The police said somebody called in a report about some skinheads rampaging around town in a pickup." Haddad pointed toward a building across the green, just down from the church. "Someone in the second-floor apartments over there said they heard glass breaking about five this morning, but they couldn't see through the bandstand what was going on."

"I'm so sorry. This is dreadful."

He nodded, glancing at the brickwork, which was running red as Mrs. Haddad's frenzied scrubbing turned the graffiti to a smear. "'Go home,'" he read bitterly. "Home *where?* Nada and I have lived in Winslow for thirty years. Our children were born here. The village in Palestine where we were born doesn't even exist anymore! Where are we supposed to go?"

"Nowhere," Leya said, firmly. "This is your home, and it's a better place for having the two of you in it."

The lines in his face evened out a little. "Thank you, Professor Nash. I guess it's because of that bombing yesterday," he added resignedly. "But how could anyone think we had anything to do with such a terrible thing?"

"'Think' is not the operative word here, Mr. Haddad. Thinking is way beyond the capability of morons like this."

"You're right, but still..."

"Can I do anything to help?"

"No, no, we'll be fine. I'll call the glass place this morning, and the sign painter. We'll get it fixed up quickly. They don't discourage us so easily, do they, Nada?" He put his arm around his wife's shoulder.

The old lady ventured a wan smile. "No. But all the same, I wonder—what does it take to belong? What do you have to do, before they stop treating you like a stranger?"

Leya squeezed the woman's arm, and shook her head.

"Did you need something, Professor?" Mr. Haddad asked. "For that bruise, maybe? I don't know, maybe ice is best...."

Leya's hand went to her cheek. "Oh, that—it's nothing. A stupid accident, that's all. Actually, I came to refill my father's Capoten prescription, but maybe this isn't a good time."

"No problem. In fact, it's all ready. I tried to call Mr. Nash yesterday. I thought he must be running low by now, and he shouldn't stop taking this medication suddenly. I left a message, but he didn't call back."

"He wasn't home. He was at my house," Leya added wryly, "running roughshod over Ernie Latouche."

"I heard you were having some work done on the old place."

Leya nodded, but at the thought of the carpenters, she had a sudden recollection of Duncan's bandaged hand. What did he say had happened? He cut it on glass? *Plate* glass, maybe, like from a storefront window? She debated whether to mention it, but decided there was no point in upsetting the pharmacist and his wife any more than they already were. She could pursue the matter herself. "Next time, feel free to call me about my dad's prescription if you can't reach him, Mr. Haddad. I'll make sure he gets his refill."

The old pharmacist shrugged. "I thought maybe you were taking it somewhere else."

"Not a chance," Leya assured him, smiling.

He brightened, then turned to his wife, kissed her cheek and took the scrub brush from her hand. "Go on, Nada. You get the prescription for Professor Nash. I'll finish up here."

Leya stood outside her father's apartment door, listening

in vain for his step. He was normally an early riser, but
the morning paper sat uncollected on the doormat. She'd
already knocked and rung the bell twice, without success.

No more nasty surprises, she prayed silently. Not today.

Opening her purse, she fished in a side pocket for her
spare key to his apartment, then inserted it in the lock.
"Dad?" she called, opening the door. "I picked up your
pills for you."

She took the *Boston Globe* from the mat, stepped into
the apartment and glanced around. Nothing out of the ordinary. His stereo and television were off. The previous
day's paper was folded on the table next to his favorite
armchair, where he read it first thing every morning. Setting down the Tuesday edition, she noticed the TV guide
next to the paper. It was open at Sunday's listings, suggesting he hadn't touched it the previous day. He usually
spent most of his evenings in front of the tube. Leya often
saw its blue light flickering in his window in the wee hours
of the morning, when she was coming home from a late-
evening date in the city with John Merriman.

She walked into the kitchen and inhaled the smell of
stale, overheated coffee. The light on the coffeemaker was
on, but from the brown sludge encrusting the sides of the
glass carafe and the tiny black puddle in the bottom of it,
Leya knew it was yesterday's brew. She switched off the
unit and ran the carafe under hot water. Leaving it to soak
in the sink, she walked back across the living room, her
heart taking up a nervous beat as she started down the hall
toward the bedroom.

"Dad?" she called, approaching the half-open door.
"Are you okay?"

Silence.

24

A line of drool trickled down the side of his chin. When Curtis Pullen snapped awake, he felt the wet trail on his neck, as well as the cold, clammy spot where it had soaked into his collar. He closed his mouth hurriedly and wiped his face on his sleeve, glancing around, embarrassed and disoriented. He was in the surveillance van, he realized, sprawled in one chair, his legs propped on another. What had woken him was a triumphant exclamation from the tech working the video-playback system. The SAC dropped his feet to the floor, wincing at the stiffness in his back and neck.

Leung glanced over. "Sorry. I didn't mean to wake you."

"It's okay," Pullen said groggily. "You find something?"

"Yeah, I think so."

The SAC changed seats, moving next to the computer board and monitor where Leung had been working. "Show me."

The tech pressed a rewind button. "Rickhauser asked me to try to pinpoint the exact moment when the bomb was removed from the Stroud girl's vehicle. I've been going back and forth over the video, from the moment her car pulled into the handicapped spot until it left. You know that thing on the road that he found that looks like some sort of disk? It's definitely there from the moment she and the guy drive off.''

''But not before they arrived—so we know they planted it.''

''Yeah, but how?''

Pullen waved a hand. ''Minor detail. Useful in building an airtight prosecution, but not critical. The essential fact remains—the Arab and the Stroud girl were responsible for the bombing.''

''Maybe not.''

''How do you figure?''

''Well, in the first place, I examined their movements, frame by frame. It was tough, given the angle of the surveillance camera. We're looking down at the front of the car, right? But from slightly to one side—the driver's side. We can see the girl's movements clearly from the time she opens her door until she moves back to the trunk to get the guy's crutches out, but not so well when she comes up the passenger side and hands them to him.''

''One of our people interviewed Khoury's landlady last night,'' Pullen told him. ''She said the guy broke his foot. Local hospital confirmed he'd been to the emergency ward last weekend.''

Leung gave him a quizzical look. ''If you were a terrorist, wouldn't you postpone a bombing until you were fully mobile?''

''Not necessarily. If I were a fanatic, and I had an accomplice and a narrow window of opportunity, I might risk it.''

The tech shrugged. ''Well, anyway, it's hard to see their precise movements before they reach the sidewalk, but nothing in what I *can* see suggests they planted that thing coming in.''

"On the way out, maybe?"

Leung shook his head, advancing the film until the couple were seen exiting the building. Night had fallen by then, but the area at the front of the building was brightly lit. He hit the Slow-Motion button, and Pullen watched the couple's pace drop to a crawl. The car's headlights blinked lazily when the girl aimed her key fob at it. As video frames inched forward, she and Khoury opened their respective doors, and he slipped his crutches into the back seat before they got in. The tech was right, Pullen thought. They weren't doing anything remotely unusual or suspicious here.

Just as the car started moving, Leung froze the action. "Look! There, see? Those black marks on the pavement? She laid rubber when she peeled out."

"In a big hurry. Looks pretty guilty to me."

The tech advanced the video a few more frames, then stopped at a full side view of the Mercedes in the split second before it moved out of the picture. "See the right front wheel? Hubcap's missing."

Pullen squinted at the picture, then examined the car's rear wheel, which still had its cap attached—brushed stainless steel, by the look of it, like the metal fragments the ATF investigator had shown them the night before. "Was the front hubcap on when they pulled in?" The tech nodded. "Okay, so that's where the bomb was. Maybe her key-chain remote activated a release mechanism."

Leung shook his head. "Nope. That's not when the hubcap came off. I've checked it over and over." He rewound the tape again to the point where the car first began to back out of the parking spot. "See how the tires start spinning when she guns it? Now watch—I enhanced this." He made a few computer keystrokes, and Pullen saw a still close-up of the car's lower-right front fender and the pavement. He followed the line of the tech's finger, tracing a shadow on the ground. "Here—this is where the hubcap fell off."

"*Fell off?*"

Leung nodded. "You can't see the wheel itself, but you can see a shadow on the ground as the cap falls. After this frame, it's on the pavement, next to the curb, just where Assistant Deputy Rickhauser spotted it." He rewound the tape at high speed to the moment when the car first pulled into the handicapped slot. Its front tires hit the curb, and the Mercedes bounced before coming to a complete stop. "I think that's when it started to come off. The force of acceleration when she peeled out later would have been enough to finish shaking it loose."

"But if the hubcap came off *accidentally*—" Pullen paused, then sat back in his chair, scowling. "No way. I don't believe it."

Winslow, Massachusetts: 8:14 a.m.

It didn't take a genius to read the evidence, Leya thought—the uncollected morning paper outside his door, the day-old coffee, the unslept-in bed. Her father hadn't come home the night before.

As soon as she pulled up in front of Tyler's, her suspicions were confirmed and she breathed a sigh of relief. He was sitting at the same corner table where she'd left him the previous evening, drinking coffee and still wearing the same clothes. But he surely hadn't stayed there for fourteen hours straight. Leya shook her head wryly. Apparently, she wasn't the only Nash who'd had a busy night.

He seemed moderately discomfited when he spotted her

coming through the door. His gaze jumped reflexively toward the oak counter, where Joanna Newman was ringing up a customer's bill. Glancing up, the older woman also did a double take, then froze. "Leya! Whatever did you *do*, dear?"

It was on the tip of Leya's tongue to say: "The same as you and my father, I suspect," but then she realized it was her battered face Joanna was referring to. She shook her head. "Had a tussle with an open door. I lost." Inwardly, she groaned. An open door? Pathetic.

"Poor girl! That looks painful. Come in, come in! Your father's here."

"So I see." Leya gave the other woman a smile that she hoped was reassuring and noncompetitive. But treat him right, she prayed.

"Will you join him for breakfast?"

"Just coffee, thanks." Leya moved to the far corner, glancing as she passed at the television set over the bar. Volume up, it was set to the CNN news. Her father was already on his feet, pulling out a chair for her. His moment of self-consciousness had passed, and he was frowning at her swollen cheek. "No door did that," he said darkly.

Leya sat down, patting his arm as he followed suit. "Relax, Dad. It looks worse than it is, and I'm embarrassed enough over my stupidity. I don't need any more grief. So," she added, forcing a smile and sidestepping an interrogation she wasn't ready to face, "What have *you* been up to, you devil?"

"What's that supposed to mean?"

She held up a hand. "Oh, nothing! None of my business. I dropped by your place with your prescription, that's all. When I didn't find you there, I thought I'd check here." She pulled the package from Haddad's out of her purse and laid it on the table.

Nash snatched the bag and stuffed it into his pocket, glancing again at the front counter. "Thanks," he mumbled.

"You won't forget to take them, will you?"

He shot her an irritated look and whispered, "*No*, Leya, I won't forget."

"Okay, okay—sorry. I didn't mean to nag. Did you already eat?" she asked. The place mat before him was clean, except for a few crumbs and a half-filled coffee cup.

"Yes. What's this about the FBI being at your house?"

She pulled up sharply. "Who told you that?"

"Your contractor and that nephew of his were in here for coffee. They just left."

"That nephew of his," Leya repeated, shaking her head. A large *latté* appeared on the table in front of her, and she turned to Joanna Newman. "Thanks."

"You're welcome." The older woman settled into a chair between Leya and her father, leaving her waitresses to work the breakfast rush.

Well, here we are, Leya mused, looking at the two of them in turn—a happy little family. Until Dad finds out who's in town. At the thought of Peter, her stomach did a nervous flip. She studied her father more closely, trying to imagine him doing the things Peter had accused him of. He looked the same as always, except for the fact that he needed a shave, and his color was better than she'd seen in a while.

Joanna's vivid blue eyes were also brighter than usual this morning, and her energy level seemed, if anything, to have surpassed its usual high peak. "You look tired, Leya. And your poor face!"

Leya nodded. "It's been a busy night." She recalled how, that morning in the mirror, her own face had been as animated as Joanna's. She'd positively glowed, until

Peter's acrimony and his accusations had stripped the shimmering gleam off their reunion.

"Ernie and Duncan said the FBI found Holly Stroud's car in your garage."

Leya frowned. "They weren't supposed to talk about it."

Joanna waved a hand airily. "Telling Ernie Latouche to keep a secret is like telling the *National Enquirer*. And even if he hadn't said anything, young Duncan certainly couldn't keep quiet about news like that."

"Great. It'll be all over town by now. I wish they—" She stopped mid-sentence as her father's hand, which had been lifting his cup to his lips, banged down on the table. As coffee splashed, Joanna grabbed a wad of paper napkins from the dispenser and dammed a rivulet rushing across the table. It was heading directly for Leya.

"Yikes!" Leya pushed her chair back, but the paper barrier had already done its work.

Her father glanced at her. "Sorry! Cup slipped."

"It's okay. It missed me. I—" His frown was focused on the TV. Leya swiveled in her seat. On the screen, a very ugly man in a suit and tie was standing at a podium, big hands gripping either side of it as he spoke. In the top corner of the screen, next to the CNN logo, were the words Press Briefing on the Massachusetts Bombing—Recorded Earlier. The man's name and title were noted over a red line that bisected his chest: Leonard Rickhauser, FBI Assistant Deputy.

Joanna finished mopping, then turned her attention to the screen, as well. "I've been watching this," she said. "They've been running stories all morning on the bombing in Newton. They let a press-pool camera inside the Data-Trax compound a little while ago. It's incredible. You wouldn't believe the damage!"

The three listened as the assistant deputy answered questions from the assembled journalists. Holly Stroud and Karim Khoury, he said, were wanted for questioning, but investigators hadn't ruled out the possibility that someone else could have been responsible for the blast.

"He's playing games," Nash muttered. "They haven't got a clue."

"Why do you say that, Carter?" Joanna asked.

He said nothing for a few minutes, only scowled as the assistant deputy wound up the press briefing. When the screen changed back to the Atlanta anchorman and a shot over his shoulder of the devastated Data-Trax building, Nash turned to what was left of his coffee, dropping a curtain over his features. Leya had seen that expression before. After she'd learned what he did for a living, she'd come to think of it as his Don't-ask-me-questions-I-can't-answer face. "I've dealt with the FBI. They couldn't investigate their way out of a wet paper bag." He turned back to Leya. "So why were they at your place?"

"Holly showed up there last night."

Joanna leaned forward. "You *spoke* to her? Oh, dear! Is she all right? What did she tell you? What about Karim?"

Leya hesitated. Ernie and Duncan might be indiscreet, but she had learned from an expert the importance of playing cards close to the chest. "I only saw Holly. We talked for a while. She told me a little about what's been going on with her lately."

"What about the bomb?" Nash asked.

"I don't think she had anything to do with it, Dad—not consciously, anyway. But I think there's a chance she's been played for a patsy here."

"What does the FBI think?" Joanna asked.

"Well, despite what that man just said, apparently

they're convinced Holly delivered it. They traced her to
Mount Abbey by her car's DMV registration. When the
housemother at Escott Hall told them I'd been looking for
her last night, an agent dropped around to ask me some
questions. Unfortunately, Holly was in the kitchen when
he arrived, and when she heard him identify himself, she
disappeared out the back way. And that was the end of
that.''

"They didn't catch her?"

"Not yet, I don't think."

"Why would she run?"

"She panicked."

Nash frowned. "Or maybe she knows more than she's
letting on. So how is it that Latouche found the FBI still
at your house this morning?" His expression was unread-
able—would make a formidable poker opponent, Leya
thought. Had Ernie and Duncan mentioned the agent's
name? No way, she decided. He wouldn't be so calm if
they had. "They decided to keep my house under surveillance, in case Holly came back."

Joanna frowned worriedly. "Maybe Holly knows, deep
down, who's responsible for this. She's a very bright girl."

"I wouldn't be surprised," Leya agreed. "All the more
reason why she needs to come in out of the cold, before
somebody decides she's a threat and should be silenced."

Back at the house, vanAken had washed and shaved in
the tiny powder room off the kitchen. He was pacing restlessly, waiting for Rickhauser and his team to show up,
feeling buzzed from lack of sleep, one too many cups of
coffee, and the intense, conflicting emotions playing crack-
the-whip with his gut.

In the crowded dining room, he stopped and stared at
the bed, inhaling the lingering scent of Leya and their love-

making. There hadn't been a day in the past decade when he hadn't thought about her. Imagined a reunion. Wanted to see her and touch her again. In the four years he'd been a prisoner, vanAken calculated, he must have made love to her a thousand—no, ten thousand—times in his mind. It had been his only comfort, and he'd clung to it like a life preserver. Whenever his beaten body and mind had begun to sink, the thought of seeing her again had kept him afloat, despite believing she'd buckled under her father's disapproval and walked away from him.

Now, he knew she'd never given up on him. She'd even said she loved him. But it was too late. Years too late.

Moving into the living room, vanAken studied her cluttered possessions. "Artifacts of a life," his archaeologist father would have called them. He'd always said you could read anyone, dead or alive, by the objects they valued. Lucius vanAken had been a board member of the Smithsonian Institute and the National Geographic Society, and director of the Oriental Institute at the University of Chicago. He'd roamed the Middle East for years, wife and young son in tow, leading digs, lending his expertise to conservation efforts, working to ensure that ancient sites and treasures weren't lost to future generations. By the time Peter was in first grade, his Arabic and Farsi had been as fluent as his English, and he could already distinguish pre-Islamic from post-Islamic pottery shards at a glance.

Examining Leya's things, vanAken read signs of a life that had been, if anything, even more nomadic than his own. She had ebony carvings from Africa, shadow puppets from Indonesia, prayer rugs from Iran and Turkey, brass pots from India—all the magpie gleanings of a wandering life, tucked into this nest she was making for herself. VanAken could understand her need for permanence, evidenced by the effort she was putting into fixing up this place. He, too, had grown up with a father who was comfortable everywhere, and at home nowhere. Of course, there were major differences between Lucius vanAken's wanderlust and Carter Nash's. The two men, he suspected, would have had little use for one another.

Anticipating their reaction, vanAken had been reluctant to tell his parents when he was recruited by the CIA. But his father, no fool, had quickly put two and two together when his son went from a period of mysterious training in Virginia directly into the American University of Beirut.

"This is *wrong*, Peter," he'd fumed, the day of Peter's departure. "The CIA's part of the problem in Lebanon, not the solution. The country's a delicate balancing act, but they're trying to tip the scales in favor of their Phalange and Israeli clients. That can only lead to disaster."

"I can help, Dad. I can make sure they have a pipeline into the other sides, as well."

VanAken Senior had shaken his shaggy, pure white head. He was tall and thin, and when he was upset, his whole body seemed to rattle inside his baggy pants and cardigan. "It won't happen. I know the mentality of the people you're dealing with. Don't you think they've approached me, too? Tried to get me to spy for them, co-opt agents for them? They're arrogant fools! Their clumsy shortsightedness is just making enemies for America in the Middle East. And you!" he thundered. "To compromise the neutrality that the AUB's worked so hard to maintain. You put not only yourself but every other person there at risk if you're found out."

"I *won't* be, Dad," vanAken had replied stubbornly.

It was the last time he ever saw his father, and they'd parted badly. How many times since then had vanAken wished he could see him just one more time—this thoughtful old academic, who'd spawned his only child late in life, but who'd always been his son's hero. Who'd carried him on his shoulders, past pyramids and through old Roman temples. Taught him to read the dramas and foibles of human history as revealed in its ancient artifacts and hieroglyphs, and to respect and value the best in people, wherever he found them.

Impatient and brash, the young Peter vanAken had, for a time, considered his father archaic and timid, especially compared to the dynamic Carter Nash. By the time he realized that the old man had been right, and that he didn't want to be part of this covert brotherhood—that, as a junior operative, he couldn't even sway one pigheaded station chief, let alone reverse single-handedly the clumsy course of CIA misadventures in the Middle East—it was too late to save himself, much less ask for his father's forgiveness.

VanAken threaded his way over to the mantel, where he examined a clustered display of framed photographs. His eye landed first on a studio portrait of a woman with Leya's coloring—her South American mother, he concluded. Next to it was a snapshot of the same pretty woman, standing in front of the glittering white domes and spires of the Taj Mahal, beaming at the camera—at Carter Nash, presumably, who must have taken the picture. Wearing white silk pants and an intricately embroidered Indian tunic and scarf that draped her rounded stomach, the woman was very pregnant. Never suspecting, obviously, that she would be dead within weeks, and that the baby girl she was carrying would have to grow up without her.

When Leya was with him in Beirut, she'd told vanAken about the time, when she was five years old, that her father had reluctantly allowed his in-laws to take her to meet the family in Venezuela. But once they had Leya safely with them, her well-connected relations had convinced a local judge to strip Nash of his custody rights. Unwilling to wait for a diplomatic solution to regain his daughter, he'd recruited a couple of fellow covert operatives and pulled off a snatch in broad daylight in downtown Caracas. Washington had turned a blind eye to his caper, despite official Venezuelan protests, and Leya had said it was the last she ever saw of her maternal relatives.

VanAken's gaze moved down the line of photographs, taking in those of Nash, alone and with her, in various locales and at various stages of her life. Was it love or obsession, he wondered, that made a man ruthless? Or simply knowing he had the unchecked power to get away with it? Stealing back his five-year-old child was one thing. VanAken could see himself doing the same, under similar circumstances. But setting out to destroy a man with whom his *adult* daughter had fallen in love demonstrated possessiveness of an altogether different—and very sick—order of magnitude.

From the moment he was abducted, vanAken had wrestled with the suspicion that Carter Nash had sent him into a trap, but for a long time, he'd been unwilling to believe it. No matter how many operational disagreements they might have had, Carter Nash had the ironclad reputation of never leaving his men in captivity, much less sending them there deliberately. Only after his escape had vanAken discovered the full extent of the man's treachery. Racking his brain to understand how such a thing could have happened, he'd finally been forced to conclude that his real crime in Carter Nash's eyes was daring to compete for his daughter's affection.

It was an unseasonably hot day in late March, five weeks after Leya's departure from Beirut, that vanAken had signaled his desire to meet with the station chief. A coincidental encounter had been arranged for the Commodore Hotel's pool-area bar, a common gathering place for Beirut's foreign community. To protect his cover, van-Aken kept his distance from "official" America, rarely approaching the embassy. Neither, for independence and security reasons, did most of his American University colleagues.

The two men struck up an apparently casual but very subdued conversation at one end of the bar.

"Did you have anything to do with the message I just got from Langley, reassigning me to Saudi Arabia?" vanAken asked.

"You've been in Beirut long enough. It's time you moved on."

"I'm not going to Saudi."

"You have no choice."

"Yes, I do," vanAken countered, slipping an envelope across the counter. "This is my letter of resignation." He watched Nash take it and slide it into his pocket without looking at it.

"Are you quitting the AUB, as well?" Obviously, the man wasn't going to waste his breath expressing regret, or trying to talk him out of his decision.

"I'm not sure. I'm going to take some leave and go home to think about it."

The station chief fell silent for a while, watching the pool, where several kids were splashing around. "Are you planning to see Leya while you're in the States?" *he asked. His expression was neutral, his voice a low monotone. VanAken trusted neither.*

"I'd like to." *What he didn't say was that he'd already booked his flights and that Boston was his first stop.*

Nash took a sip from his drink and went on watching the children, as if there were secrets to be deciphered in their squeals. But when vanAken made a move to get up and leave, the chief held him back. "There's a job I need you to do."

VanAken settled onto the barstool once again, but shook his head. "I don't—"

"It's important. I wouldn't ask if I had anyone else who could handle it, but you're the best Arabic speaker in the station."

"What's this job? I don't have much time—"

"Please. It won't take long. Just one meeting with a source we've gotten wind of, who apparently has information on the whereabouts of Terry Anderson and Ben Weir that he's willing to sell." Anderson, the AP bureau chief in Beirut, and Weir, a Presbyterian minister, were two of the Americans being held hostage by militant Shiites. "I just need you to find out what his terms are, and whether he's on the level. If so, you'll set up a second meet, and I'll take it from there."

VanAken hesitated. They'd had leads on the hostages before, none of which had ever panned out. There was no reason to think this one would prove to be any different. On the other hand, if he were being held captive, he'd want every effort made to free him. "All right. Tell me when and where."

In the end, of course, there was no "source," only a two-car ambush in a blind alley, led by a psychopath called Ali, who knew vanAken's name and exactly what he was. The only thing Ali didn't realize at first was that vanAken spoke fluent Arabic.

After they had shoved vanAken into a back seat, trussed

*him, blindfolded him, and stuffed his mouth with oily rags
that made him gag, he heard a victorious cackle as the
car sped away. "What a day, when the nest of spies sends
us one of their own!"*

"We kill him, yes?" another voice asked.

*"Eventually. First, we'll see what he's worth, in money
and in information."*

*VanAken heard another loud cackle. Then, a kick to the
head sent him spinning into darkness.*

He stood before the mantel in Leya's living room, staring at Carter Nash's face smirking back at him from a
photograph. Suddenly a hand, scarred and mangled,
reached out and swept the picture off the shelf. It landed
on the brick hearth with the splintering sound of broken
glass.

25

"Don't tell me you're not tempted," Kerry Nyland said, propping his feet on Leya's desk and tipping back the chair into which he'd plopped himself after trailing her from the parking lot. Leya had spotted the history prof on the road ahead of her as she'd turned in at the Mount Abbey gates, his fox gray ponytail streaming from under his helmet, the wheels of his motorcycle slipping and sliding on snow-dampened pavement. Hell-bent on turning his kids into orphans, the big dope. She'd slowed her car, hoping to duck an encounter. No such luck.

"I'm not remotely tempted, and get your muddy boots off my desk, please," she said distractedly, rummaging through her briefcase. She had nine minutes to get to her American Lit class all the way across campus, and she'd misplaced her lecture notes on the Edith Wharton story they were supposed to be starting that day. The last thing she needed was a debate on the merits of abandoning New England's changeable weather and moving to Arizona.

Nyland had raised the subject as they were walking into the Arts Building—although not before commenting on Leya's bruised face, prompting yet another creative lie on her part, this time involving a car door. Fiction-writing was a definite career option, she decided.

"The University of Arizona has fall-term openings in its history *and* English departments," Nyland had said, pulling out an advertisement from a learned-societies bulletin. "What do you say we blow this pop stand, gorgeous, and head out for warmer parts?"

"And anyway," Leya added now, searching her file cabinet, hoping the Wharton notes were there, "what about your children? You don't really want to be so far away from them, do you?"

Nyland hesitated, then shrugged. "No, of course I don't *want* to—but they could visit. They'd love it out there. I'd get a place with a pool. Sometimes," he added lamely, "a man's gotta do what a man's gotta do."

Leya glanced at him as she closed the cabinet drawer. Today, under the black leather jacket, he had on his white ribbed sweater, the one with the off-center coffee stain that always made her think of a nipple that was lonesome for its mate. Another time, as Nyland was leaving her office, she'd noticed he had the stain facing backward, a sort of out-of-sight, out-of-mind approach to grooming that she found eccentric but endearing. It occurred to her, however, that men who lived alone shouldn't wear white unless they were up to speed on the fine art of stain removal.

Suddenly, Leya had a mental image of a coffee cup sitting on top of her Wharton file on the computer table at home, next to her rolltop desk. She'd moved it there the previous evening, when she was digging for her Day-Timer to prove to Peter that Holly had been at her house the time Karim Khoury had telephoned. In the midst of that morning's excitement, she'd overlooked it when she was packing up to head out. "Damn!" she muttered.

"What?"

She waved a hand. "Nothing. Forgot my lecture notes, that's all."

"Not having a banner day, are we?"

"Tell me about it." She ran a finger along her bookshelf until she located her copy of *Ethan Frome*. She tossed it into her briefcase and snapped the locks shut. "Guess I'll have to wing it. Gotta go, fella," she said, nudging him out of his chair.

He sighed as he got to his feet. "The woman is always chasing me away." Leya was buttoning her coat when she glanced at her phone. "Coming?" Nyland asked.

"In a sec. I want to check my voice mail." She lifted the receiver, punched in her access code, then drummed her fingers impatiently on the desk. *"You have—one—new message,"* the digital voice droned. Leya entered the code to retrieve it, and frowned when the same tedious voice told her the message had been recorded at 5:33 a.m. Who on earth would be calling her office at that hour? She had to strain to hear the whispered, panicky message that followed.

"Professor Nash? It's Holly. I hope you get this soon, because I haven't got any more change for the pay phone. I'm at the Lizzie. I think I know what happened, but— Oh, God! Please come, and bring help!"

The message ended abruptly, and the virtual secretary's bland tone announced, *"End of messages."* Leya wanted to strangle that voice for its cool efficiency, which took no special note of a child who sounded frightened for her life.

"Problem?" Nyland asked.

Leya spun around, startled. "What? Yes—something I need to take care of right away. Would you do me a huge favor, Kerry?"

"Sure. What?"

"Go over to Bingham Hall, Room 126, and tell my

AmLit 101 group that I have to cancel today's class? Tell them they're to go ahead and read the first ten pages of *Ethan Frome* before Thursday, would you?''

"*Ethan Frome,* first ten pages—got it. Anything else?''

"No, thanks. You're a doll.''

He cocked a finger at her, grinning. "Yes, I am, and don't you forget it!''

Leya returned his smile, but hers faded as soon as Nyland's ponytail disappeared down the stairs. She started to follow, then paused. Turning back to the desk, she picked up the phone. Her hands were shaking as she dialed her home number.

Listening to her phone ring at the other end, Leya studied her bulletin board, where she posted programs and reviews from campus theater-group productions. Their pre-Christmas offering had been *Little Women,* with Holly Stroud type-cast as the irrepressible Jo March. In a group photo taken opening night, Holly stood in the center of the troupe, beaming, her frizzled blond hair tamed into a nineteenth-century chignon. A flowing blue gown covered her lithe form, and her arms were slung merrily around cast members on either side of her—typical, Leya thought. From the first moment she'd arrived on campus, Holly had become the heart and life of the little troupe, her enthusiasm infectious, her energy unflagging. How could anyone think of hurting such a sweet kid?

After the fourth ring, Leya heard her own voice as her answering machine clicked on. She cursed and started to hang up, then realized Peter could be screening calls. Or, she thought, he might be preoccupied with the car in the garage, in which case he'd never think to check the messages. But just in case— "Peter, it's Leya,'' she said, after the beep. "I just found a message from Holly Stroud on my office voice mail. She said she's—''

The phone picked up. "I'm here." His voice was flat, impersonal.

Leya's heart thumped, and she stammered, "I was afraid you wouldn't get this."

"I was outside when the phone rang. The forensics team just arrived. What did she say?"

"She called about five-thirty this morning and said she was at the Lizzie—"

"The what?"

"The Elizabeth Wilkins Theater, here on campus. She had a key, dammit! I should have remembered that when we were trying to find her last night. That must be where they went after they stashed the car in my garage."

"Is Karim with her?"

"I don't know, but Holly sounded terrified. She says she thinks she knows what happened—the bombing, I suppose she meant. I'm heading over there right now. You can—"

"No! You stay put. I'm on my way."

"But—"

"Stay there, Leya. I know where the theater is. I've got backup, in case there's trouble. We'll go right now and pick her up. I promise not to play bogeyman again, but you're not to go near the place, understand?"

"All right," she said reluctantly. "But Peter? I'll be waiting to hear, so—"

"I'll call you as soon as we've got her."

"Please."

But as she hung up the phone, it occurred to Leya that the theater would be shut tight at this hour on a Tuesday morning. Holly had a spare key because she'd volunteered to lock up the previous week, when a scheduling conflict had forced Leya to leave rehearsal early. Holly, always helpful, had stepped into the breach and offered to close the theater for her.

If the FBI arrived, sirens screaming, bullhorns blaring, Leya thought, they could easily scare the terrified girl away again—especially if they started breaking down doors. And even if they were more subtle, they'd waste precious time trying to round up someone from campus maintenance to open the building.

To hell with Peter and his imperious commands, she decided, grabbing her key ring. She bolted from her office, slamming the door behind her. Weaving through the crush of students on the granite staircase, she ignored curious looks as she dashed out of the Arts Building and down the path toward the theater.

Newton, Massachusetts: 8:53 a.m.

The encryption keys on satellite data transmissions between FBI headquarters and its four hundred field offices and resident agencies had been changed at 8:00 a.m., Eastern time, as they were every day. But Mark Leung, preoccupied with the Data-Trax video search, had forgotten to switch the surveillance van's computers to a corresponding decryption key, as per technical protocol. So when Curtis Pullen moved away from the video screen at last, and settled in to read the file Rickhauser had ordered transferred to him via internal E-mail, what he pulled up was running columns of letter-digit combinations that could have been Urdu, for all the sense he could make of them.

Leung had just run out to grab breakfast, but Pullen paged the tech back. "Sorry about that," Leung said when he arrived, scrambling to punch in his access codes to call up and install the day's key.

When he was done, Pullen tried again, and was rewarded by good, old American English. He flipped through his E-mail until he found the lengthy document forwarded from the ADIC's office—a file on an investigation code-named ANNIBOM. He'd never heard of it, but this was relatively small potatoes as serial cases went, he noted, scanning the pages. The Unabomber had already racked up sixteen actual or attempted hits. The ANNIBOM-file summary listed just four incidents, stretching back over a number of years, in locales as far-flung as New York, Detroit, Seattle and San Francisco. Not for the first time, Pullen asked himself why Rickhauser seemed so intent on muddying the waters.

Admittedly, of the four incidents grouped under the ANNIBOM file, three were bombings, and one was an attempted bombing that had failed because the device was discovered in time to be disarmed by bomb-squad personnel. There had also been two cases of uttered threats, delivered in rambling letters from the old left-wing radical group, the Weather Underground. The communiqués, full of revolutionary, antigovernment gibberish, had been linked back to the bombings because they contained details that had never been released to the public.

Pullen frowned at the terminal. Street gangs, the mob, petty extortionists, terrorists and nuts with grudges planted bombs every day in America. It was beyond him why he should be looking at these particular cases, instead of at several dozen active FBI files on Hamas, Hizbollah, or any of the other fundamentalist Islamic groups with a track record of violence—including, he suddenly thought, the file on the operation that vanAken was allegedly running when he'd had Karim Khoury under surveillance. MENELOP was the name on that file. Where was *it?*

The targets of the bomb incidents in the ANNIBOM file were as disparate as their locations, he noted. An army recruiting office, a college professor, a post office— where a letter bomb had exploded prematurely, obscuring the actual target—and an upper-middle-class suburban Detroit housewife, who was on her way to drop her son at his Grosse Pointe preschool when her car blew up, killing them both.

Pullen's sleep-starved eyes itched as he flipped through screen after screen of dry investigative material, with its inconclusive evidence and speculative theories on the connection between these various targets. Only one link was immediately evident—all of the incidents had taken place on the same date, March 27. Yesterday's date. Obviously, if the same bomber was responsible, he was marking the anniversary of something—hence ANNIBOM, the Anniversary Bomber. But what?

Two of the incidents had been cited in Weather communiqués—the army recruiting office, where a sharp-eyed corporal had spotted a suspicious-looking box left at the front door and called out the bomb squad, and the letter bomb to the Columbia University professor, which had missed its target and injured a secretary instead. Professor Lionel Monk, who taught African-American history, had a long history of radical rhetoric and protest, it seemed, dating back to the Vietnam era, the Weathermen and the Black Panthers. Pullen snorted. Guy seemed a more likely perpetrator than victim of something like this.

The premature post-office explosion, in which most of the evidence had been destroyed, had been linked to the letter bomb sent to Professor Monk because a piece of its padded envelope had survived, and both envelopes had turned out to have come from the same discontinued line of stationery.

The car-bombed woman in Grosse Pointe, Ellen Fraser, had once been a student of Professor Monk's, although her murder had taken place five years before the bomb was sent to his office. Only later was it linked to the Annibomber, because of the date it occurred and the Columbia University connection—which all seemed a little tenuous, as far as Pullen was concerned. When interviewed after the attack on his own office, Monk had claimed no memory of Ellen Fraser. Her husband, a prominent Detroit pediatrician, had been investigated but had come up squeaky-clean. In the absence of any other less baroque explanation for the murder of the woman and her son, the presumption of an Annibomber connection had stood.

But what, Pullen wondered, did any of this have to do with a Palestinian-American engineering student, already under suspicion because of his links to the radical group Hamas? Or with an uppity ambassador's kid, who had volunteered, or been conned or seduced into helping him deliver his deadly package?

Winslow, Massachusetts: 9:01 a.m.

At the stage entrance to the Elizabeth Wilkins Theater, Leya used a boulder from a nearby rock garden to prop open the heavy, self-locking door, hoping Peter would spot it when he arrived. Then she went inside. Her eyes struggled to make the adjustment from daylight to the gloomy interior, while her hand groped for the switch that she knew was on the right-hand wall, just inside the door.

"Holly?" she called, flipping it on. "It's Professor Nash."

No answer.

The stage door accessed a long hallway, whose unpainted cinder-block walls were always a drab surprise to newcomers expecting something more dramatic, given the classical elegance of the building's exterior. But this was the working part of the theater, where illusions and magic were born. Doors lining the hall opened onto prop rooms, dressing rooms, rehearsal studios, costume storage, and set-design workshops. The smell of sawdust and grease-paint permeated the air, odors linked forever in Leya's mind to memories of opening nights, when she'd stood on one side or the other of the footlights, with butterflies in her stomach, first as student actor, now as resident director of the little Mount Abbey troupe. Rarely, she recalled, had her father been in the audience to see her perform, although since moving to Winslow, he'd seen all the productions she'd directed.

As a Mount Abbey undergraduate, she'd spent four years in the same campus troupe she now led, taking to drama like a duck to water after years of reinventing herself in one new place after another. If most young actors find it daunting to swallow their fear before curious strangers, it was second nature to Leya, part of the bag of tricks she'd acquired to cover her natural shyness—a survival tool she carried alongside water purification tablets, chloroquine, foreign phrase books, and a passport smile. She'd learned from a master, after all, a man who'd cloaked himself in dozens of false identities over a long career. An actor might risk the occasional killing review, Leya reflected, but her father had played his roles on a dangerous international stage, where the difference between a good and a bad performance literally spelled life or death.

As she made her way along the corridor, Leya poked her head in at each door, calling softly for Holly, thinking the girl might have fallen asleep as she cowered in the dark and waited for rescue. Stepping into the wardrobe storage area, her heart leaped at the sight of a looming figure. She flicked on the light. It was a dressmaker's dummy, draped in the leaf-strewn gown that Holly was meant to wear for Ophelia's drowning scene. In the play, driven mad after being torn between her scheming father and hostile lover, Ophelia throws herself into a pond and is dragged to her death by the weight of her sodden garments. The way things were going, Leya thought grimly, she might be looking for a pond herself, before long.

Turning off the light and reclosing the wardrobe room, she continued down the corridor, calling. The only answer was silence.

At the end of the hall, a set of twenty-foot-high double doors, extra-wide to allow for the passage of scenery flats, accessed the stage area proper. Pulling one of the doors open and propping it with the rubber hinged foot at the bottom, Leya called out again. "Holly? Are you here? It's Professor Nash. It's safe to come out, I swear. I called for help as soon as I found your message, and they'll be here soon."

She entered the wings at stage right. Deep shadows fell across the stage itself, cast by the "ghost light" that was kept on at all times. Leya flipped the lid of the electrical panel on the wall and turned on the backstage lights. Most of the house- and spotlights were controlled from a booth high above and to the rear of the banked seats in the auditorium. But the lights in the wings were controlled by a panel of rheostats, allowing them to be set on bright during rehearsals and set construction, but dimmed during performances, leaving just enough illumination for the actors to follow reflective-tape outlines on the floor that marked the boundaries between the wings and the acting areas visible to the audience.

For the *Hamlet* production now in rehearsal, a cyclorama had been hung at the rear of the stage, covering three sides of it. From where she stood, it partially blocked

Leya's view of the actual stage area. Featuring an ominous skyscape that suggested the stormy climes of northern Denmark, the cyclorama was suspended from the fly space high above the stage by five of the many ropes attached to the counterweight system of lines and pulleys, located throughout the steel-beamed gridiron under the roof. The block-and-tackle arrangement allowed for the quick raising and lowering of heavy scenery flats and backdrops, so that the ramparts of Elsinore, for example, where Hamlet first spies his father's ghost, could quickly be converted to a castle interior, or to the Danish plain where he finds Yorick's skull in an open grave—the same grave into which he later leaps to embrace his dead Ophelia.

Moving around the cyclorama and onto the upstage area, Leya walked down the raked incline toward the lower area near the footlights. When she reached the apron, she stood for a moment, shading her eyes against the glare of the ghost light, she peered into the orchestra pit, then out into the dark auditorium, calling softly. Nothing. Tiers of plush velvet seats sat empty and silent, eerily lit by the pale red glow of exit signs around the perimeter.

Leya sighed in frustration. Turning back upstage, she was heading for the exit behind the cyclorama, when out of the corner of her eye, she caught the movement of a shadow at stage left. She crossed over and passed around one of the rear legs masking the wings on that side. Suddenly she tripped and stumbled. Something clattered as she dropped to one knee, landing painfully on what turned out to be aluminum tubing. No, not tubing, Leya realized, pulling it toward her—a crutch. She spotted something small and dark on the floor a foot or two away. A shoe, lying on its side. Frowning, Leya got to her feet and picked it up. A man's shoe, black.

A shadow moved again, and she felt a faint breeze and

caught a whiff of something vaguely familiar. Her gaze rose. High overhead, a stockinged foot dangled in midair. Another foot, also shoeless but oversize, hung next to it. Leya gasped. Swinging ever so slightly, the body of a man hung suspended from a rope connected to the gridiron overhead. Leya was too horrified to cry out or even breathe. She stared at the dark, suited form, its arms dangling limply. At the ends of the arms, long-fingered hands flopped like dead squid from the rumpled sleeves of a white shirt, cuffs gleaming in the dim light. And as her gaze moved higher, Leya could barely make out the head, pale and lolling, half hidden in shadow but for two terrified, dead eyes that stared down at her.

She finally screamed and stumbled back—right into a blow that dropped her to her knees once more. The shoe tumbled from her hand as Leya reached out to break her fall. Before her hand could touch the floor, a rope whipped around her neck and yanked her backward, off-balance. Leya tried in vain to steady herself with one hand and get the other underneath the thick hemp line, but before she could get a grip, the noose tightened, cutting off her air. Slowly, the rope lifted her. Rising, she choked and gasped, tearing frantically at the coarse fibers, still scrambling for footing.

The rope pulled her up onto the tips of her toes, but when her feet left the floor, her own weight conspired to turn the struggle against her. Rising higher, suspended in midair now, Leya twisted and pivoted, bumping again and again into the body strung from the rafters. Clawing at her neck, she fought vainly for air. Pressure built in her face and eyes, and her skin felt as if it were exploding. Her body gyrated, but exertion and lack of oxygen sapped her strength, and her futile digging grew weak. Leya felt herself losing consciousness, and her arms flopped to her sides. Spinning slower now, her body turned toward the auditorium.

The last thing Leya saw, before everything went black, was the pale red glow of an exit sign.

26

Someone was screaming. Screaming and screaming, over and over, a piercing, insistent wail that was as grating as it was distracting. Also, the image of a wolf kept intruding on her thoughts, its yellow eyes gleaming, intense, fierce, predatory. A wolf's head on a man's broad shoulders, barking and growling—but not necessarily at her, Leya realized. At shadows floating around them, hovering, scurrying.

She wished they'd all just go away—the shadows, the wolf, the screamer—because she'd been dreaming that Peter was kissing her, and it wasn't something she cared to do in public. After protecting every intense thought and memory of him for so long, holding them close, like some rare and fragile thing, she loathed the idea of exposing what passed between them to the glare of casual, curious scrutiny.

In the dream, his mouth would close over hers, briefly, but then he would pull away, his face contorted by a ferocious emotion she couldn't read, his face wet with tears. And then he would kiss her again, desperately. Leya wanted to reach out and hold him. Tell him he had nothing to fear—that he was home now, and she was there and wouldn't let anyone hurt him, ever again. Except this noise and confusion kept distracting her, and she couldn't seem to work up the energy to move.

Then it was too late, and Peter's kiss was gone, and so was he. Also the shadows, the wolf, the dream—all gone. All except that damned annoying screamer, Leya thought, irritated. She frowned and opened her eyes.

"She's coming around!"

The unfamiliar voice came from somewhere near her left ear, but when Leya tried to turn her head, it wouldn't budge. Her forehead was bound tight, and her neck was rigid. Her elbows were clamped against her sides, and under her fingers, she felt a scratchy cover on her immobilized lower body.

"Leya? Listen to me," the voice demanded. "Don't move. It's important that you not try to move."

She shifted her eyes to the left, and a stranger came into view. About her own age, she guessed, muddy-blond hair clipped short, he wore a blue nylon jacket. When he moved to adjust her restraints, she spotted a red patch of some sort on his shoulder. And that was about all she saw, between the bindings that restricted her movement and something else over her face that partially obscured her view. A clear plastic mask, she realized, covering her nose and mouth.

"Can you hear me, Leya?" the stranger asked loudly.

Abundantly, she wanted to tell him, so could you pipe down? And while you're at it, could you tell whoever's screaming to shut up?

"Do you understand what I'm saying? Blink if you do."

Leya blinked.

"Good girl! You're in an ambulance, and we're on our way to the hospital. You may have a spinal injury, so we've immobilized you until they can check it out. I need you to keep very still, okay?''

She blinked again. Ambulance. Siren—the screaming voice. That's it, she thought. She watched the paramedic adjust an IV line running down into her arm. As he took her blood pressure, Leya's gaze shifted to shadows bouncing off the interior walls of the ambulance. Idly, groggily, she studied built-in slots holding clear storage bins, filled with dressings, syringes and other medical supplies. She looked up at the vehicle's ribbed metal ceiling, then down toward the back door, where bare trees were flying by a window with a red cross painted on it.

As her gaze shifted once more, Leya spotted Peter sitting near her feet. His eyes, fixed intently on her, were puffy, and his face was grayer than she would have thought possible for living flesh. His lips were pressed together in a taut line. Leya tried to give him a reassuring smile, but felt the mask again and the flow of cool, heady air passing over her nose and lips. He seemed to take no note of her attempt, because his grim expression never varied. Reaching under the constraints that bound her arms, Leya stretched out her left hand. When Peter wrapped it in his own, she gave him a squeeze.

"Movement in the upper extremities—that's a good sign," the paramedic said, taking note of her effort. Peter nodded soberly. "Leya, can you squeeze with your other hand, too?" the attendant asked, reaching across to take her right hand in his. She did. "How about your toes? Can you move them?"

Of course she could. Why wouldn't she? Leya wiggled her feet and felt a blanket against her stockinged toes. "My shoes—?" Her voice was a croak under the oxygen mask. Her throat hurt. Funny, she didn't remember feeling a cold coming on when she'd got up that morning. That's what lack of sleep will do to you, she thought ruefully. Still, a little sore throat hardly called for all this commotion.

"I've got your shoes right here," Peter said, holding up her brown loafers. "Just lie still."

Leya watched his worried face and tried to tell him she was fine, that this was all unnecessary. Wasn't there something they were supposed to be doing? What? She racked her brain to remember. And how, exactly, had they ended up in an ambulance?

"Peter?" she ventured, straining against the wail of the siren. But before she knew whether he'd heard or not, the ambulance pulled under some sort of archway and came to a halt, the insistent wail echoing loudly for a moment, then dying away, at long last. "We're here," the attendant said.

The rear door flew open, and they pulled her out on the stretcher. Disoriented, Leya watched lights and ceiling panels flash by overhead. Then she was in a bright room, and more faces were hovering over her, tossing information back and forth about vitals and blood gases and elapsed time. She was jostled once more as they shifted her—strapped to a board, she realized—off the stretcher and onto an examining table.

"Sir, you'll have to wait outside," she heard someone say.

Peter's voice replied from somewhere beyond Leya's line of sight. "No. I'm Special Agent vanAken, FBI. I'll stay out of your way, but I'm not leaving."

A gray-haired woman standing next to the gurney, wearing a disposable smock over hospital greens, glanced at him briefly, then shrugged and turned her attention to Leya. Lifting the plastic mask from her face, she helped another pair of hands slip a tube around Leya's head and under her nose, then shone a light in her eyes, one after another. "Pupil dilation and movement normal." Like the paramedic's, her voice grew overly loud. "Miss Nash? Leya? Do you know where you are, and what day this is?"

"Hospital," Leya croaked. "It's—um—Tuesday?"

"That's right. This is Winslow Memorial, the emergency room. I'm Dr. Allenby. I imagine your neck and throat are hurting, so don't worry about talking just yet, okay? Lie very still." The doctor loosened the cervical collar around Leya's neck, and her fingers began probing gently underneath. "Were you there when she was found?" she asked, glancing up as her fingers passed over Leya's spine, vertebra by vertebra.

"I took her down," Peter said.

"Suicide?"

"No, murder."

The physician went on with her examination, not missing a beat. Tough old bird, must have seen everything by now, Leya thought, wondering idly who they were talking about. The doctor listened to her chest, then Leya felt the straps being loosened around her legs and the blanket being lifted off. Something sharp ran along the soles of her feet, one after the other. Her feet twitched and Leya tried to pull up her legs. Someone held them down.

"Lie still, Leya, that's a girl," Dr. Allenby said, patting her arm. She glanced again in the direction of Peter's voice. "Murder? You sure about that?"

"Yes. She was one of two."

The doctor moved back to the head of the table, opening Leya's mouth gently and peering down her throat with a scope. "Two victims? The other one—?"

"Coroner's got him," Peter said.

Suddenly, it came back. Leya's heart took up a frantic hammering, as an old nursery rhyme repeated itself in her head. *One shoe off and one shoe on, Diddle, diddle dumpling, my son John.* She was at the Lizzie, onstage. A pair of legs dangled over her head, one foot shoeless, one clad in something bulky. Then she remembered being lifted into the air. Choking, gasping. Terrified fingers ripping at her neck. Swinging. Bumping in the dark against something soft. A glowering red exit sign, mocking—this way out. Then nothing.

She cried out, but it emerged more gasp than scream. Peter pushed his way around a nurse and grabbed her hand. "Shh, it's all right, Leya. You're going to be okay." She held on to him, searching his face for an explanation.

"Leya?" Dr. Allenby asked. "Are you in pain?"

She blinked away tears. "No."

"You're sure? Any pain at all? Anywhere?"

"No, not really," Leya whispered. "My throat, that's all."

"Okay. I need you to stay calm—absolutely still, understand? You're looking real good here, aside from some rope abrasions, but we're going to take X rays of your neck and spine to be sure. Also your larynx—your voice box. I think it's only bruised, not crushed or fractured, but I'd like a closer look." Leya blinked. Allenby turned to Peter. "How long had she been hanging when you found her?"

"I'm not sure. Not long, I think. She was still swinging, and we cut her down right away. We got a faint heartbeat, but her breathing had stopped. I gave her mouth-to-mouth. It seemed like forever until she started breathing on her own again," Peter added, his own voice fading. "But I think it was probably only about a minute."

Allenby exhaled sharply, shaking her head as she palpated Leya's neck once more, then refastened the cervical collar. "You're one lucky lady that the agent here found you as quickly as he did, Miss Nash. And that you're a lightweight. You could easily have ended up with a broken neck, or worse, but I think you may walk away with nothing more than some bad bruises. You might need to wear the collar for a while.'' She touched Leya's cheek, probing lightly. ''Looks like they walloped you good here. There's no break, though.''

Leya glanced at Peter, who shifted uncomfortably. She tried another smile, but the effort failed miserably. He looked not in the least comforted. Leya turned back to the physician and whispered, ''Hit me on the head.'' She lifted a hand to the back of her skull.

''You took a blow to the head from behind, too?'' Leya nodded, and the doctor palpated her skull. ''Okay,'' Allenby said to a nurse across the table, ''we'd better get an MRI, too, rule out subdural hematoma. But have them do a cross-lateral X ray of the neck first. I want to see that, stat.''

Everything started moving as they prepared to wheel her out, but Leya gripped vanAken's hand tighter. ''Wait, please! Peter—''

''I'm here, Leya. I'll stay with you. Just relax.''

''Who was it?'' she whispered. ''The hanging man?'' VanAken hesitated, glancing around. ''Tell me, please!''

He leaned close, his voice low. ''It was Karim Khoury.''

Len Rickhauser glanced disbelievingly at young Agent Wilf Berger. Berger was driving, while the assistant deputy sat in the front passenger seat of the bureau car. Pulling out of the Elizabeth Wilkins Theater parking lot, they were following the ambulance carrying the body of Karim Khoury. An FBI medical examiner had come down from headquarters with Rickhauser the night before to work the Data-Trax bombing site, and he was on his way over from

Newton. They were scheduled to rendezvous at the county coroner's office, where the bureau ME would oversee the autopsy—theoretically a shared jurisdictional effort, although, given Khoury's link to the Data-Trax case and the county's limited forensic facilities, the Bureau would lead on the examination and handle all the lab analyses.

"You think Khoury committed suicide, Agent Berger?" Rickhauser echoed. "So tell me, how did he manage this trick of hiking himself ten feet into the air, then tying off the loose end of the rope to a cleat on a wall fifteen feet away? Did you see something I missed on that stage? A chair, maybe, or ladder, or anything else he could have launched himself from once the noose was around his neck?"

"No, sir."

"And what about Professor Nash? You think she found Khoury, and was so overcome by grief that she decided to off herself, too?"

"No, sir," Berger repeated sheepishly. "Same problem there—how would she have tied the rope? Plus, what motive would she have, really?"

"Right. And so?"

"And so, we're looking at a third party. Coroner said he figured Khoury had been dead at least a couple of hours, so I guess our guy did him, then waited for Miss Nash, knowing Holly Stroud had called her, and that she'd probably show up at the theater sooner or later."

"Right again on the third party. But why do you say it's a guy? It could have been a woman, you know. Holly Stroud herself, for example. She set Miss Nash up, after all, with that phone call."

"Yeah, but the physical description from Holly Stroud's driver's license puts her at five-five, a hundred and eight pounds. Khoury looked five-ten or -eleven and must have weighed, what? One-forty or -fifty, maybe? Would've taken another guy to string him up.''

Rickhauser shook his head. "Not necessarily. Those ropes were designed to lift stage sets. They're on a pulley system, which gives a mechanical advantage for hoisting heavy loads. Comes in handy, I guess, at an all-girl school. Holly Stroud's familiar with the theater's setup, don't forget, and she's still missing.''

"So she's our prime suspect?''

"Looks like. We might know more after they finish the crime-scene examination. We're looking into her political affiliations. Maybe she's got militia or terrorist connections.''

Berger nodded as he slowed near a campus crosswalk, making sure the way was clear before proceeding. Curious Mount Abbey students held back at the sound of sirens, peering at the passing ambulance and bureau car. A crowd had gathered at the theater, too, restrained by a local police cordon.

Rickhauser had followed the first stretcher bearing Leya Nash, handing her shoes to vanAken as the latter jumped into the ambulance, just before the door closed. The student bystanders had sent up a collective gasp when they realized it was one of their professors being carried off. Sometime later, when the bagged body of Khoury had been removed, another cry had gone up from the crowd, as well as exclamations of curiosity and fear over who might be inside. Their shouted questions had gone unanswered, however, because Rickhauser had ordered a total clampdown on information.

"Sir?" Berger ventured.

"What?"

"Agent vanAken seemed real shook-up over Miss Nash. She a friend of his?"

''They've got some history, yeah.''

Berger nodded and fell into silence again. Rickhauser stared at the road ahead as they pulled out past the big stone gates at the main entrance to the Mount Abbey campus. ''Shook-up'', he thought, didn't begin to describe what he'd seen in vanAken's eyes when they'd walked onto that stage and found Leya Nash swinging next to the body of Karim Khoury. VanAken had let out an unearthly bellow, and before Rickhauser's brain had fully registered the horror of what they'd found, vanAken already had the woman by the legs and was lifting her to take the weight off her neck.

''For Christ's sake!'' he screamed. ''Get the rope!''

Rickhauser dashed over to where the end of the rope had been loosely wound around a cleat on the wall and whipped it free. Berger helped vanAken lower her to the stage, while Rickhauser untied the other rope holding the hanging man. This knot was tighter and had been fastened with more care. It took longer to undo, but from the appearance of the victim—his tongue distended, his face terrified, eyes bulging whitely in the dim light—Rickhauser knew the delay would make no difference to the outcome. When the body was also lowered to the stage, the ADIC got on his radio and barked an order for backup and ambulances. Then he yelled at his men to fan out. ''Suspects could still be in the vicinity. She hasn't been up long. Find 'em!''

All the agents scrambled except Berger and vanAken, who were preoccupied with the female victim. VanAken had already started giving the woman mouth-to-mouth. Berger had a finger on her carotid artery. ''She's got a pulse. Faint, but it's there.''

Rickhauser crouched next to the other victim, loosening the noose around his neck and feeling for a pulse. Nothing, of course. It was only when he rifled through the man's pockets and located a wallet that the ADIC realized who they had. Inside, he found an MIT student ID card for Karim Khoury. He studied the photo on the card, then the body before him. There was no doubt it was the same person. They'd found their man.

"Damn!" Rickhauser muttered. He glanced over at the dark-haired woman lying on the stage, who obviously was not Holly Stroud. "Is that Leya Nash?"

VanAken nodded between breaths. Just then, she coughed—once, twice—and finally, drew a deep, rasping breath. Berger released a low exclamation of relief, but vanAken's panicked expression never varied, and his intense gaze stayed locked on her face.

Rickhauser watched him closely. After bringing him into the Bureau, he'd ordered vanAken to undergo psychiatric counseling, worried about the load the guy had to be carrying after his long hostage ordeal and subsequent rough treatment at the hands of his former CIA colleagues. The bureau shrink had reported him to be uncooperative, but Rickhauser had decided not to push it. VanAken kept his feelings tightly bottled, but he carried out his duties competently—even brilliantly, at times. Still, he was isolated, emotionally and socially. Other than cold anger, Rickhauser had never seen the man express an honest sentiment, or known him to have a friend, man or woman. Except maybe himself, and even that only went so far, given the wall vanAken had built around himself.

Knowing what he did about their history, Rickhauser had always suspected that this lady on the floor was the one person who might have breached that wall. Under the circumstances, however, that had seemed pretty unlikely to happen. Now, he mused, maybe it had. It was pretty obvious that vanAken was still in love with her. But that just meant there were land mines ahead. Last Rickhauser had heard, Carter Nash was still alive and kicking. There was no telling what would happen if those two came face-to-face again.

"An ambulance is on the way," he said. "You want to keep her real still, Peter, avoid any further injury to the neck and back." The ADIC glanced at Berger. "I saw some sandbags backstage. Grab 'em, so we can immobilize her neck, then go to the door and direct the paramedics this way, soon as they arrive."

Berger leaped to his feet. "Yes, sir!"

After he was gone, Rickhauser moved next to vanAken. "You okay?"

VanAken nodded slowly, but he didn't look at all okay. He was stroking the woman's hand, watching her closed eyes, tracking every rise and fall of her chest. His face was damp, although he probably didn't realize it. "I told her not to come here, Len. Why did she have to go and walk into this, when she said she wouldn't?"

Rickhauser put a hand on his shoulder. "Hang in there, fella. She's gonna pull through, and then you can ask her yourself. Meantime," he added, "looks like we found Khoury."

VanAken finally tore his gaze away and glanced at the other victim. He closed his eyes and groaned. "Shit! I don't get it. What the hell is going on here?"

"I don't know," Rickhauser said, "but I damn well intend to find out."

27

Whenever a terrorist bomb exploded in Israel, Len Rick-hauser knew, there were deeply religious, Orthodox Jewish men whose self-appointed mission was to climb telephone poles, rappel high-rises, and crawl on their bellies along the ground, wielding scrapers and tweezers, gathering every minuscule shred of flesh they could find in an effort to ensure that the victims' bodies were buried in their entirety, if not intact, before the next setting of the sun.

Much as he respected the incredible commitment and deeply held convictions of these holy men, Rickhauser had always found this devotion to dead tissue incomprehensible. Philosophies that drew a clear distinction between body and soul made more sense to him. In his thirty-three years of law enforcement, he'd seen thousands of corpses, and every single one reminded him that when the spark of life had been snuffed out, the flesh was pretty damned insignificant. You could imagine that you loved the eyes, lips, or hands of another person, but it the end, it was the human spirit that counted. Take that away, and we were all just so much meat.

He heard a rustle, and glanced down at young Agent Berger, standing at his side. Like the ADIC, Berger was decked out in disposable paper cap, gown, slippers and mask. The two of them were next to a steel water table at the county morgue, watching the local coroner and the FBI medical examiner begin their autopsy of Karim Khoury. The deceased's clothing had already been removed and packed in labeled evidence bags, ready for shipment to the FBI forensics lab, along with Khoury's crutches and the Velcro-fastened, fiberglass cast he'd been wearing on his broken foot.

Above his mask, Berger's eyes looked glazed. "You okay, son?" Rickhauser asked.

"Yes, sir. I think so, sir."

"First autopsy?"

"Yes, sir."

"Well, if you get to feeling queasy, look away or sit down."

"I think I'm okay. It's the smell that's getting to me, I guess. Kind of like an abattoir in here, isn't it?"

"Yeah, but the physical reaction disappears in a few minutes. Sense of smell's the brain's early-warning system for danger. If you ignore the panicky messages, after a while it gives up and stops sending them. You could step out of the room for a break, but when you walk back in, the sensory alarms will just start up again. Best to tough it out, if you can."

"Yes, sir. Actually, I think it's passing."

"Good man. So, what do you think, Jorge?" Rickhauser asked, turning to the bureau ME. Dr. Jorge DaSilva, forensic pathologist, had been with the FBI even longer than Rickhauser. Sixty-two years old, short, rotund, and bald as a baby's butt under his surgical cap, DaSilva was addicted to the *New York Times* crossword and five-thousand-piece jigsaw puzzles, the kind that came with no picture on the box to guide you. One lab bench in his Quantico office was always taken up by his latest puzzle, sent, inevitably, from one grateful colleague or another whose case the medical examiner had helped crack. For Dr. DaSilva, a murder victim on a slab represented another irresistible brain-teaser.

His rubber-gloved hand reached between the cadaver's legs. Withdrawing a rectal thermometer, he peered at it through half-moon glasses. "Body temperature 88.1 degrees Fahrenheit." He peered over the glasses at Rickhauser. "You said he was found indoors?"

"Yep. In a theater. Heated to fifty-five, maybe sixty degrees."

The ME laid aside the thermometer and moved up to the head, where he prodded at the neck and face. "A little rigor setting in here." He straightened and glanced at the clock on the wall. "So I'm putting death at around 6:00 a.m., give or take an hour. Do you agree?" he asked, turning to the county examiner, who seemed intimidated by all the high-priced help. DaSilva was invariably considerate of local sensibilities. It was only one of the things Rickhauser liked about him. The coroner nodded his agreement. "Okeydoke," DaSilva said cheerily, eyes smiling up at Rickhauser. "That's how the two of us are calling it, Len—six-ish."

The ADIC nodded, then glanced at Berger, who was looking confused. "Body temperature after death drops a couple of degrees every hour, unless it's been submerged in cold water or otherwise exposed to extreme temperatures."

"And rigor mortis?"

"Caused by the postmortem buildup of lactic acid," Da-Silva explained. "Muscle rigidity starts to appear about six hours after death. It starts with the smallest muscles, like the facial ones here—see?" He prodded the stiffening cheeks. Berger nodded. "The rigor then builds in the larger muscles in the extremities, then the upper and lower trunk, until finally, the whole body's rigid. After twenty-four hours, when the cells start to decompose, rigor starts disappearing, at about the same rate and in the same order as it first appeared—smallest muscles first. Understand?"

"Yeah, I get it. So, between body temp and extent of rigor, you can figure time of death?"

"That's the idea, for the first forty-eight hours, or so. After that, it gets a little trickier."

"Can you confirm asphyxiation by hanging as the cause of death, Jorge?" Rickhauser asked. "Any chance the guy was killed someplace else, then strung up later?"

DaSilva wiggled his fingers in the air as he gave the body a quick once-over. "Well, let's see. Distended eyes and tongue, slightly engorged face." He stopped to examine the neck, which rested on a wooden block. "Ligature marks, abrasions. More pronounced at the front than the back of the neck," he added, lifting the head and crouching to peer underneath. He laid the neck back on the block, picked up a pair of tweezers and withdrew a fiber that had stuck to a bloodied, rope-burned area. He peered at it under a light, then glanced at the ADIC. "You save the rope?"

Rickhauser nodded. "On its way to the lab."

"Hemp or sisal?"

"One of those. Not synthetic."

The ME nodded, then turned to the local coroner. "Could you pass me one of those evidence bags, please?" he asked. He took the bag offered and dropped the fiber in, then sealed the bag and labeled it.

Moving to the victim's right hand, DaSilva removed the paper bag that had been secured over it with a rubber band and examined the fingers. "Looks like we've got the same fibrous material under the nails. The fingers are pretty raw, and he's got scratch marks on his neck. Odds are, lab'll find his blood on the noose. I'd say our boy here was struggling to get the rope off before he died. Would you mind?'' he added, holding the dead hand out to the other examiner.

"No, not at all." Obviously eager for something to do, the man began scraping beneath the fingernails, depositing what he collected inside the bag that had protected the hand while it was being moved from the crime scene to the morgue. When he was done, he moved around the table and did the same for the other one. In addition to rope fibers, there would be skin cells, Rickhauser knew— Khoury's own, given that he'd scratched up his neck trying to get out of the noose, but with luck, maybe his killer's, too, if they'd tussled before the guy strung him up.

While the other man was working on the hands, DaSilva picked up a 35-mm camera and walked the length of the autopsy table, snapping more pictures of the body from various angles. They'd taken shots at the crime scene, plus others of the body before it had been disrobed. When the fingernail scrapings were complete, DaSilva reached under the shoulders and rolled the cadaver sideways, letting the other man hold it while he examined and photographed the back and buttocks.

"Lividity nil on the backside areas. All concentrated in the head and feet." He put down the camera, and they settled the body on the table once more. "Lividity," Da-Silva explained, looking up at Berger. "That's blood settling after the heart stops pumping. The noose constricted the major veins and arteries in the neck, you see, so some of the blood volume was trapped in the head area, prevented from flowing back down. But except for situations like that, gravity generally settles the blood in the area of the body that's lowest, and that's where it stays, as long as the body's not moved before it can clot.''

He pointed to the victim's feet, purple and swollen. The color was mottled and less pronounced moving up the leg, and those areas of skin from thigh to shoulder not covered by black body hair were pale as milk. It looked as if a vampire had sucked the young man dry. Clearly, he'd died in a vertical position and hadn't been moved until cut down from his swinging perch.

Khoury had been twenty-three years old, Rickhauser recalled—the same age he himself had been the year he joined the San Diego PD as a ploy to stay near Wendy Nakamura after graduation. But at an age when his own life, like most people's, had just been getting under way, Karim Khoury's was already over.

He studied the body. It was lanky, the stomach deeply concave below the rib cage. The long bones of Khoury's arms and legs were connected by thick knots of knees, elbows, wrists and ankles. The fingers were attenuated and delicate. "Sensitive hands," a woman would call them. The boy had been thin, but he had a virile mat of dark chest hair and signs of what would probably have been a thick beard, if he'd ever missed a day or two of shaving. Although you couldn't prove it by the distended face here on the morgue table, Rickhauser knew from FBI photographs that Khoury had been a good-looking fellow—attractive enough to seduce a pretty ambassador's daughter.

Rickhauser's eye traveled to the genital area and its uncircumcised penis, as he fought a losing battle not to think about where that organ had probably been, and how sad it must be, knowing it wasn't going there anymore. Sick thoughts, he reflected, but what the hell—it was a sick job sometimes. Then his gaze narrowed, and he peered more closely. "Hey, Jorge?"

DaSilva had zeroed in on the area, too. "Yeah, I see." He combed through the pubic hair, which seemed sticky. Semen traces, Rickhauser guessed. DaSilva withdrew and bagged a few lighter-colored hairs that probably came from another person—Holly Stroud, more likely than not. That wasn't what had caught the assistant deputy's attention, but he quickly realized that DaSilva was on the same track he was.

After saving the evidence of Khoury's recent sexual activity, the ME bent closer to examine the flaccid penis, then probed underneath and between the testicles. He turned to the coroner. "Could we get a razor and some shaving cream, please?"

"Sure thing." He produced a Bic disposable and a can of "sensitive-skin" Gillette—as if the dead appreciated a little pampering. DaSilva went to work, removing all trace of pubic hair. The scent of lime permeated the room, but it wasn't enough to overpower morbidity's perfume. Rickhauser glanced again at Berger, but the young agent seemed to have recovered from his squeamishness and was watching the proceedings with interest. When DaSilva was done with the razor and the area had been rinsed, it looked like the smooth crotch of an overendowed little boy—but one who had been viciously abused. Every man in the room winced and squeezed his thighs reflexively at the sight of Khoury's bruised and swollen genitals and pubic bone.

"Ouch," Berger said sympathetically.

"Ante- or postmortem?" Rickhauser asked.

DaSilva bent over the wounds. "Both, I'd say. From the amount of swelling and bruising, at least some of these blows were inflicted while the guy was still alive and his heart was pumping. But see these marks?" His finger traced several red marks and depressions over the pubic bone. About an inch and a half in diameter, the marks were variously circular or moon-shaped. "Abraded tissue and broken blood vessels, but hardly any bleeding. I'd say these were induced postmortem. By what, I couldn't say. These circles look too big to have been made by something like a gun barrel. And there's no major tissue breakage, so I'm thinking something softer than metal."

Rickhauser straightened and looked up at the ceiling, stretching one arm overhead, picturing how they'd found Khoury and Leya Nash, swinging from the theater's gridiron. Khoury had been hoisted a foot or two higher than the woman. "His feet were eye level to me. Even somebody my size couldn't have reached his groin very easily."

"His crutches, sir," Berger said. Rickhauser dropped his arm and looked at the kid. "They were lying on the stage, remember?"

"That's right, they were. And I'll bet those round marks are a perfect match for the rubber caps on the bottom. Whoever did this kicked the crap out of the guy before stringing him up, then used a crutch to give him a few more jabs in the balls for good measure. Which means there's a chance we'll find two sets of prints on the crutches. Good thinking, Berger. We'll make sure the forensics guys dust 'em closely."

Berger nodded, looking proud of himself.

"These marks are the only sign of assault, aside from the lynching itself," DaSilva said. He had taken up the camera again, and was photographing the genital wounds. "This is real up-close and nasty stuff, Len."

"Personal."

"Sexual anger. Maybe this Khoury fellow raped someone, and this was payback."

Rickhauser thought about that. "Not the professor, obviously. Khoury had to have been long dead by the time she arrived on the scene. Given those lighter hairs, I'd guess the Stroud girl, although relations between the two of them were consensual, from what I gather. Or not. Who knows? Maybe they had a fight.''

''A girl wouldn't do something like that to a guy's privates,'' Berger said, head shaking.

Rickhauser's gristly eyebrows rose above his mask. ''Remember Lorena Bobbitt?''

Berger winced again. ''Yeah.''

''Anything's possible.''

''You're right, sir. Dumb comment.''

DaSilva put down the camera and picked up a scalpel. ''Can we continue here?''

''Yeah, sure. Carry on.'' Rickhauser turned to his young colleague as DaSilva made the Y-incision down the victim's chest. ''I need to get going, Berger, but I'd like you to stick around, let me know if anything else interesting turns up.''

Berger tore his eyes away from the table, where the two MEs were attacking the freshly exposed rib cage with a pair of heavy steel snips the size of garden shears. Shiny beads of sweat had popped out on his forehead, but he nodded gamely.

''You sure you're up to it?'' the ADIC asked.

''Yes, sir. I'll be fine.''

''Good man. Give me the car keys. You can head back later with Dr. DaSilva.'' Berger lifted the paper gown and fished in his pockets for the keys to the bureau car they'd come in. ''Thanks for your cooperation,'' Rickhauser said to the local coroner. He took the keys from Berger and turned to the bureau ME. ''Catch you later, Jorge.''

DaSilva paused in his cutting and looked up over his mask. ''You gonna hang around to oversee this case, Len?''

"Don't know yet. Depends what develops. This one's been bugging me from the get-go."

"Why?"

Rickhauser exhaled sharply. "'Cause I knew a bomb was going to blow yesterday, only I didn't know where."

"You *knew?* How?"

"Goddam ghost told me," Rickhauser muttered. "I gotta go."

Leaving three astonished pairs of eyes behind him, the ADIC headed out through the automatic sliding door and yanked off his mask, pausing to deposit it, along with the cap, gown and slippers, in a hazardous-medical-waste bin outside. Just before he left, he glanced through the autopsy-room window once more. The two examiners had gone back to work, and Berger looked pained as DaSilva excised the stomach from the open body cavity and set it in a stainless-steel pan, where its contents would be examined to see what Khoury's last meal on earth had been. A Whopper and some Reese's Pieces, Rickhauser guessed.

Winslow Memorial Hospital was staffed entirely by aging Amazons, Leya decided, from the formidable Dr. Allenby in the ER, to the Brunhilda clone who ran the radiology department, to the Nurse Ratchet look-alike who was now giving Peter so much grief.

"I don't care who you're with!" she snapped. "This patient has been through major trauma. You can talk to her later."

Leya tried to intervene. "I'm really quite all right," she protested—except it came out hoarsely as, "wee-wee kwite ow-white." Elmer Fudd with laryngitis. They'd given her something to ease the pain of her bruised larynx and relax her savagely wrenched neck muscles, and the drugs were kicking in with a vengeance. For someone who rarely took so much as an aspirin, it was like stumbling into a Shanghai opium den.

"I'll stay," vanAken insisted. These turgid refusals to be ejected had been his only utterances since arriving at the hospital. He stood on one side of the bed, Nurse Ratchet on the other, irresistible force confronting immovable object. The two of them glared across Leya's draped and prostrate form. She'd been put into a private room after they'd finished taking pictures of her head and neck. When they'd wheeled her in, Leya had noticed a cop planting himself on a chair outside the door.

Leya patted the nurse's arm and chose her words carefully this time, steering clear of the Fudd zone. "It's okay," she whispered. "I want him here."

"The doctor wants you to rest."

"I need to talk to him." And fast, Leya realized. Her body felt weighted down, like Ophelia, sinking under petal-strewn waters. At the image, her blurry mind pulled into focus once more—Holly! "Please," she added urgently.

"All right," Ratchet grumbled. "But only for a few minutes. And then, you let her rest," she added, stabbing a finger at vanAken. She rammed the stiff bedsheets fiercely under the mattress, then lumbered out the door.

Head movement limited by the thick collar binding her neck, Leya shifted her whole body in the bed to see him better. His chestnut hair was more disheveled than usual, the hollows under his somber eyes deeper and blacker. Strain showed in the lines around his mouth, and his shoulders slumped wearily. He looked as if every fiber of body and soul had been stretched beyond the limit. Leya reached out to him. "You should climb in here with me. You look like you need rest more than I do." He hesitated, then took her hand between the two of his, studying her fingers as he massaged them distractedly. "Have they found Holly yet?" she asked.

"No."

"Any sign of her at all?"

"She'd been at the theater. I made a quick call while you were in X ray. Apparently they found her jacket and backpack near the pay phone. The surveillance videos showed her wearing a leather jacket when she went to Data-Trax yesterday."

Leya nodded. "She was wearing it when she came to my house last night."

"They also found some long blond hairs caught on a hinge to a trap door under the stage."

"Her grave."

"What?"

"Holly was cast as Ophelia in a production of *Hamlet* I'm directing. We're using the space under the trap door for the grave Hamlet jumps into during Ophelia's funeral scene."

"She might have hidden there at some point. If she were in a hurry, she might have caught her hair on the hinge. Was it open when you got there?"

Leya shook her head, wincing at the pain in her neck. "I passed over it twice, on the way to the apron, then back again. It would make a good hiding place, I guess. If someone didn't know about the trap door, they could easily miss it."

"What *did* you see?"

"I had checked out all the workrooms, then the auditorium. I was just heading backstage again when I tripped. Over a crutch, as it turned out. I fell and saw a shoe, then I looked up. That was when I saw him—Karim," Leya added, shuddering.

"And?"

"I froze for a second. Panicked, I guess. And then I stumbled backward. Someone had come up from behind, and they hit me over the head. Next thing I knew, there was a rope around my neck, and I was going up."

"Did you see who it was?"

"No."

"Any sense of his size."

"All I remember was Karim's body, then being hit and strangled—and the sheer terror I felt. But it all happened so fast."

"Anything else?"

Leya frowned. "A smell," she recalled, "but I can't place what it was."

"That trap door," vanAken said. "Apparently it connects to a passageway under the stage?"

Leya nodded stiffly, and her chin scraped the foam collar. "Leads to the backstage area, near a fire exit."

"Is the exit alarmed?"

"No," Leya said wearily, an overwhelming lassitude sneaking up on her.

"Holly would have known that. She probably slipped right out from under our noses," he muttered.

Leya's eyes opened wide. "You don't think Holly attacked me, do you?"

"That's exactly what I'm thinking."

Leya shook her head. "Not Holly. She wouldn't do that to me—much less to Karim."

"I wouldn't be so sure."

Leya's head felt stuffed with cotton, and her tongue was getting thicker by the minute. "No way. Think she loved him." She fought her drooping eyelids, in vain.

"Maybe," he said, laying her hand down gently. "Anyway, get some sleep."

"Will you stay?"

"There's a guard outside your door."

She opened her eyes again. "That's not what I mean. You can't go on like this, Peter."

"I know," he said, turning away.

"You saved my life."

He glanced at her again, irritated now. "I wouldn't have had to, if you'd damn well stayed put, like I told you to!"

Ah, Leya thought, there's fire in the old boy, yet. She smiled and settled deeper into the starched pillow. "Some cultures say if you save a life, it belongs to you. Not that it makes a diff'rence," she mumbled, losing her battle against the drugs and her cement eyelids. "S'been yours for a long time, anyhow."

Somewhere, far off in the distance, Peter's voice murmured a reply, but Leya was asleep before she knew what it was.

28

"I just spoke to the lab at headquarters," Curtis Pullen said. He was slouched over his temporary desk at the Data-Trax command-and-control center, forehead propped in his hand, phone clenched to his ear, feeling neither in command nor under control. "They've reconstructed a piece of the hubcap, and found RDX chemical residues on it. They're thinking plastic explosive."

"C-4?" Rickhauser asked. He'd phoned in for an update on the bombing investigation and to report that Karim Khoury had been found murdered on the campus of Mount Abbey College. A professor, apparently, had narrowly escaped the same fate after stumbling onto his body. Once again, Pullen felt he was bobbing on the backwater of this case and that the main action was passing him by—a fact made all the more galling by the realization that vanAken was right out there in the middle of it.

"Might have been C-4," he conceded, "but it'll be a while until the workup's complete." He had a sudden, horrifying thought. What if Rickhauser was grooming that white-haired boy of his to be parachuted into Arch Mc-Creary's SAC position, heading up the Boston field office when the slot formally came open? Now, *that* was a scary thought. He'd end up working for that smug ass. A suspected traitor! No way. Couldn't happen. Could it?

"Your guys find any trace of a detonator or timer?" the ADIC asked.

"Yeah, as a matter of fact. One of the ATF guys just came up and showed me a watch crystal he'd found with—"

"—a hole drilled in the face?"

Pullen frowned. "That's right. How'd you know?"

"The crystal's plastic, right? A Timex?"

"It's plastic, all right. Not sure about the brand, yet. It's warped out of shape, so—"

"Did you read the ANNIBOM file?"

Pullen hesitated. "Most of it." Actually, he'd skimmed the old file, decided it was irrelevant to the Data-Trax bombing, and gone outside to lean on the investigative team to speed up the search for hard evidence. But come to think of it, he mused, wasn't there a reference to a watch delay-timer in one of the incidents cited in that file? It was in—"

"Grosse Pointe, Michigan. March 27, 1975," Rickhauser said. "Ellen Fraser and her five-year-old son were killed instantly when her booby-trapped car exploded. A piece of the timer survived the blast—the hour hand of a Timex watch that cost eight dollars and ninety-five cents back then, and was sold in about two million drugstores across the country. Had a plastic crystal. It's a classic timing device—bomber makes a hole in the crystal with a heated nail, threads a screw in, sets the hour hand, connects everything to a battery and a detonator, and packs it all into explosives. Come zero hour, watch hand touches the screw, closes the circuit and boom! Low-tech, but effective."

"I remember reading that on the file, but—"

"Explosive was C-4, and it was packed into the hubcap of her car." Pullen sucked air through his teeth. "Ellen Fraser was the ex-lover of a guy named Michael Gore," Rickhauser added. "Gore was the father of her kid. They were involved in radical, left-wing politics, although he disappeared in 1970, and she married her pediatrician. Meantime, the Weather Underground had built up a large stash of C-4, stolen out of military inventories from Pennsylvania to California. Stuff showed up in a slew of bombings all over the country. Several, like the Ellen Fraser murder, happened on March 27."

"What's so special about the date?"

"That was on the file."

"I think I missed that page."

Rickhauser grunted. "It's the anniversary of an incident in New York City. March 27, 1970. Twenty-five years ago yesterday. The FBI had surrounded a brownstone in Greenwich Village, where four members of the Weather Underground—Michael Gore, Kyle Pierce, Jerry Bernstein and Annabelle Deaver—were reported to be holed up, plotting an attack on a federal armory. Negotiations for surrender broke down. When shots were heard inside the building, a bushy-tailed agent decided to lob in a stun grenade—only it turned out the place was a powder keg, and it blew sky-high. The four inside were killed, and about a dozen people outside were injured by flying debris. Major property damage, too. Not the Bureau's finest hour."

"You've got quite an interest in that old ANNIBOM business, haven't you, sir?"

"You could say that. I was the bushy-tailed idiot who lobbed in that stun grenade."

"Oops."

"No kidding."

"But this Michael Gore character—he was in the brownstone. I thought you said he'd disappeared?"

"Well, see, that's the problem. All that was left of the four people inside were tiny pieces, so the ID was dicey. A Weather communiqué said Michael Gore was there with Pierce, Bernstein and Deaver, but the Bureau didn't buy it. He stayed on the Most Wanted list for fourteen years, and was the prime suspect in those other ANNIBOM jobs."

"I see. And besides the coincidence of the date, the connection to Data-Trax is—?"

"MO's similar to the Ellen Fraser case. Most of the intended victims in the other bombings were somehow connected to Deaver and the others, and— Hell! I know what my gut tells me, and I'm damn well going to put it all together!" Rickhauser exhaled heavily. "Anyhow, good work on the investigation, Curtis. Keep at it."

"You bet. I'm right on top of things here, Len." Pullen rolled his eyes. Timex watches? Left-wing radicals? Anniversary bombs? *Hello-o? The Arab terrorists your boy was supposed to be tracking? Remember them, assistant deputy?* It was the damn Arab who bombed Data-Trax— they had it on videotape, for chrissake! Maybe the old wolf was coming down with Alzheimer's.

"I'm going to need a half-dozen more agents out here, to beef up the search for the Stroud girl," Rickhauser said.

"She your suspect in Khoury's murder and the attempted murder of that professor?"

"Possibly."

Time for a reality check, Pullen decided. "You don't think maybe Khoury's Hamas buddies decided to stifle him before he could get himself caught and give them up, as well?"

"That's also possible," Rickhauser said. "One way or

another, Ambassador Stroud's little girl is in deep shit, right up to her pretty eyeballs. If she's not already dead, I'd like to find her before somebody decides *she* should be stifled, too.''

Winslow, Massachusetts: 2:47 p.m.

She looked small and defenseless, vanAken thought. The white sheet and blanket rose and fell in a steady rhythm as Leya slept, dark hair spilling across the pillow and down the thick collar strapped around her neck, lashes brushing the purple bruise on her cheek. Her right hand lay where he'd placed it a few hours earlier, palm up, on the bed.

VanAken shifted his weary body, crunched into a hard vinyl chair that he'd backed into the farthest corner of the room, and he waited. He'd planned to leave as soon as she fell asleep, but an agent had shown up at the hospital with a message from Rickhauser, ordering him to sit tight until he got there. This enforced inactivity, vanAken suspected, was the ADIC's not-too-subtle way of obliging him to take some downtime. Or, more likely, Rickhauser was warehousing him, having concluded that his professional usefulness had about come to an end, given his botched handling of Khoury and MENELOP. So much for his brilliant career in the FBI.

Still, there was a kind of release in all this. Hunched in his corner, marking time, listening to Leya's steady breathing and the sounds of other people's medical dramas being played out beyond the door, vanAken felt suspended in time and space—detached, like a phantom gazing down on the imminent closing of another chapter in his own turbulent life. The final chapter, he thought gratefully.

He'd felt a debt of loyalty to Rickhauser, but the time

to repay it had passed. Without that objective to drive him through each day, there was nothing to hold on to, no reason to continue this hollow facsimile of a life he'd led since Beirut.

Even his desire for revenge was gone. When he'd walked onto that stage and found Leya hanging, the long-smoldering anger he'd carried inside him had died, snuffed out by an explosion of terror far worse than any he'd felt during all the years of his captivity. Watching her now, vanAken knew that Carter Nash had won. The old bastard held the ace card. Always had.

Leya heard deep, murmuring voices drifting toward her, emanating from somewhere beyond the far reaches of consciousness. Lulled and torpid, she floated on waves of soft bass tones, registering only half of what was being said.

"Hamas conspiracy…?"

"Rounded up…airtight alibis…"

"Khoury tried…wanted out…"

One voice was Peter's, Leya registered. She stirred and smelled bleached cotton. Her hand rolled over and closed on soft, woven fabric, and the voices fell silent. She opened her eyes. A lean, shaggy-topped silhouette at the window turned toward her, its outline tinged with a blue aura—sunlight on denim. Peter had taken off his jacket. A glint of smooth leather across his shoulder reminded Leya that she'd watched him dress that morning, then shrug into that holster. It seemed a long, long time ago.

Next to him, another shadow perched on the wide window ledge—a huge, broad-beamed shape of a man, with legs like sprawled tree trunks, and a burred head that came level with Peter's, even though the big man was sitting and Peter was on his feet. When Peter approached the bed, the giant rose and followed a few paces behind. Away from the bright window, Peter's features came into view, his expression subdued and guarded. Closed off. His hands remained in his pockets.

"Hi," she said.

"How are you feeling?"

She took a quick internal inventory. "Dopey. A little stiff and sore. Otherwise okay."

"Sorry to wake you."

"It's all right. What time is it?"

He glanced at his watch. "Almost four."

"Any word on Holly?"

"No. We were hoping you could answer a few questions."

Leya nodded, her gaze shifting to the man behind. Now that she could see him clearly, she felt the urge to recoil. Dressed in a rumpled tan topcoat, dark suit and tie, he loomed massively over Peter, who was no midget himself. But even more intimidating than the older man's size was his face. With a mangled nose and fierce, glittering eyes, it was something right out of a Grimm's fairy tale. If he had snarled and shown fangs, Leya wouldn't have been surprised. And yet, she realized she'd seen this man before. Where?

"This is FBI Assistant Deputy Rickhauser, Leya. He's up here investigating the Data-Trax bombing—as well as Karim Khoury's murder, now, and the attack on you."

"Miss Nash," the giant grunted, giving a brusque nod. "You're feeling better?"

"Yes, thanks," she said nervously. Suddenly, she remembered that she'd seen him that morning, on the television at Tyler's. But somewhere else, too. She worried at it for a moment. Then Leya recollected a dream about a wolf. "You were there, too, weren't you?"

"At the theater? Yes."

"He helped cut you down," Peter added.

"Then I owe my life to you, as well. Thank you."

"Glad we got there in time."

"Believe me, so am I." Leya ventured a rueful smile, but the two stone faces never cracked.

"Do you feel up to answering questions?" Rickhauser asked.

"Anything."

"Good. Can you tell me what, exactly, Holly Stroud said in the message you found at your office?"

Leya took a deep breath to clear her fuzzy head. "Just that she was at the Lizzie—the theater—and that she had an idea what had happened. She sounded scared."

"She was calling from the pay phone?" Rickhauser asked.

"Yes. The box office has the only other phone, but it was out of order. Peter said you found her things?"

The assistant deputy nodded. "Do you know if Khoury was with her?"

"I'm not sure. I think she said '*I'm* at the Lizzie.'"

"It could have been just a turn of speech," Peter noted. "Doesn't necessarily mean he wasn't. He was killed around six. Didn't you tell me she'd called just after five?"

Leya nodded. "Five-thirty, I think. The message should still be on my voice mail at work, if you want to hear it. I didn't take the time to delete it before I took off for the theater."

"Why did you go there?" vanAken asked testily.

"Because I knew the place was locked, and I had the key."

"You had no business entering the building."

"I thought you'd be right along behind."

"You could have waited outside."

"Yes, I could have, and all things considered, I guess I wish I had. I blew it. So shoot me."

"Don't tempt me."

Rickhauser eased Peter aside, interposing himself between them. "We *will* be taking that message off your voice mail," he warned. Did he think she was lying about it? Leya wondered. "Agent vanAken tells me you had a conversation with Miss Stroud last night, and she told you about her relationship with Karim Khoury."

"That's right," she said.

"How long had they known one another?"

She looked to vanAken for a little reassurance. This was beginning to feel like the Spanish Inquisition. "I told Peter—"

"Tell *me*," the big man growled.

Her gaze snapped back. "A month maybe? I'm not certain, but I can give you the name of someone who would know for sure."

"I'll want that name. Meantime, the girl and Khoury—were they intimate?"

"Possibly. I'm not sure."

"She's only eighteen," Rickhauser pointed out.

"That's true, but Holly's precocious, in many respects. Again, I can't be certain, but I think there's a good chance they may have been sleeping together."

"You told me she had another boyfriend that she dropped for Karim," Peter noted.

Leya nodded. "Tyler Newman."

"This Tyler Newman, is he from around here?" Rickhauser asked.

"Yes. He and his mother run a small bistro in town, and they live on a farm at the edge of town. Bethany Hill, it's called. It's just beyond the western boundary of the Mount Abbey campus. That's where Holly and Karim met.

It was Tyler's mother, Joanna Newman, who introduced them.''

"How did that come about?"

"Joanna could give you the details."

"We'll talk to her. Right now, I want you to tell me what *you* know."

Leya frowned. He was treating her like a hostile witness. It wasn't as if she didn't have a personal stake in solving this, too, especially now that she'd nearly been killed for her efforts to help Holly. "Apparently Karim came to the farm one day with a friend of Tyler's, someone who attends MIT. Holly was there, and Joanna introduced them."

"And then?"

"They hit it off, I gather, and continued to see one another after that."

"Khoury knew her father was ambassador to Israel?"

"Yes."

"And the girl knew it was a potential security risk for her to be dating a Palestinian refugee, but she did it anyway?"

"Holly has a mind of her own."

"So it seems. Quite the little troublemaker."

"I don't think that's a fair assessment, Mr. Rickhauser. Holly's a sweet kid."

From his scowl, Leya concluded that her judgment was in serious doubt. "The other boyfriend—how did he react when the girl dumped him?"

"I'm not sure."

"Was he upset? Upset enough to go after Khoury?"

"Go after him?"

"That's what I said."

Leya blanched. "Murder him, you mean? *Tyler?* You can't be serious."

"I'm extremely serious, Miss Nash." Rickhauser exhaled impatiently. "Look, somebody kicked the bejeesus out of Khoury before he was killed, and they didn't stop there, because his corpse took a beating, too. The way he was beaten suggests either an angry lover or a jealous one—someone who didn't like the idea of someone else having the Stroud girl. Add to that," he said, his voice dropping dangerously, "the fact that your sweet young friend and her lover delivered the bomb that destroyed Data-Trax, killed nine people, and injured several dozen more. Call me crazy, but I'm guessing there's a link between these events that's more than coincidental. Whoever murdered Khoury and tried to kill you probably knows something about that bombing. I'd like to get to the truth here—*if* that's all right with you!"

Peter touched the big man's sleeve. "Len," he said quietly, "this isn't her fault."

The assistant deputy glanced at him, then pulled back, and nodded. "It's been a long day. And night. Sorry," he added curtly to Leya.

She nodded her acceptance of the apology, rote though it seemed. Something was off, here. This Rickhauser was a professional and a senior official, and he knew better than to antagonize a witness. But she was picking up vibes from him, and his harsh, appraising looks suggested a reaction beyond fatigue and the stress of a difficult case. For some reason, the man had taken a dislike to her.

As Peter's gnarled hand slipped back into his pocket, it dawned on her. This was the one—the man who'd stood by him when no one else would. If the assistant deputy believed his version of what had gone down in Beirut, then of course he'd have no use for anyone related to Carter Nash.

"I'm not sure what Tyler's reaction was," she said. "I wasn't following Holly or her love life that closely. Before last night, I didn't even know about Karim. As far as I knew, she and Tyler were still an item. Except…'' She frowned.

"What?"

"Ambassador Stroud called me from Israel yesterday afternoon, looking for Holly. He and his wife had gotten some ambivalent messages from her, it seems, and were getting a little antsy about what she was up to. I promised I'd track her down and get her to call them. That's when I found out she and Tyler had split. But depending on who I spoke to, I got several different versions of how they were getting along lately, ranging from spitting nails, to not speaking, to the best of platonic friends." Leya turned to vanAken. "Remember Duncan, my contractor's nephew?"

He nodded. "The skinhead."

"That's the one. Apparently he's a friend of Tyler's, which was news to me. He told me this morning, when we found Holly's car in my garage, that he'd seen her at Bethany Hill a couple of days ago." She grimaced. "He also made some racist remarks about her involvement with what he called 'a raghead.' And by the way," Leya added, "a drugstore in town was vandalized last night, and the front window was smashed. Someone reported it was skinheads in a pickup truck who did it."

"That Duncan character said he'd cut his hand on glass," vanAken recalled.

"Yes, he did, didn't he? The pharmacy's owned by an old Palestinian-American couple, the Haddads. They were pretty shaken up, especially by the graffiti the vandals left behind. Do you think maybe you could drop a hint to the Winslow police, tell them they might want to have a chat with Duncan?"

"I think I'd like to have a chat with him myself," van-Aken said. Rickhauser nodded.

Just then, the door swooshed wide, and the woman Leya had nicknamed Nurse Ratchet charged in, head down. She pulled up fast when she saw the two men in the room and planted a hand on her ample hip. "I thought we agreed to let the patient rest?" she said to vanAken.

"It's all right," Leya reassured her. "I slept for quite a while. I feel much better."

The nurse clumped over and popped a thermometer in her mouth, then picked up Leya's wrist to take her pulse. "Just the same, this isn't a convention center," she muttered to her wristwatch.

"We'll leave soon," Rickhauser promised.

Nurse Ratchet grimaced, then grabbed the chart from a rack over Leya's head and made a notation. "We just had a call at the desk from someone who said he was your father."

Leya nearly swallowed the thermometer. "My favver?" she mumbled.

"Yes. He just heard about what happened. You'd think *somebody* would have notified your next of kin before now," she added, glaring at the others. "Anyhow, he said to tell you he'll be here shortly." Rickhauser and vanAken exchanged glances, then vanAken walked over, picked up his sport coat from the chair, and shrugged into it. The nurse removed the thermometer, read it, and made another notation on the chart. "How's the pain? The doctor left instructions that you could have something every four hours, if you need it."

"No, I don't want anything, thanks," Leya said, "except to go home. I'm fine, really. A little stiff, that's all."

Nurse Ratchet shook her head. "The doctor left orders that you were to stay overnight for observation."

"I'd rather not—"

"Stay *put*, Leya!" It was vanAken.

She glared at him. "I'm fine."

"Agent vanAken is right, Miss Nash," Rickhauser said. "Whoever tried to kill you this morning could try again. I've arranged for an officer to stand guard at your door. You should stay where you are."

"Dr. Allenby will be up to see you later," the nurse added. "Meantime, you should be resting." She glowered at the two men once more, then walked out.

"I'll go and talk to that Duncan character," vanAken said to Rickhauser.

The assistant deputy nodded. "I'll follow up on the old boyfriend."

VanAken turned to Leya. "Do you know where Duncan lives? Or his last name?"

"No, neither. It's not Latouche—that would be his mother's maiden name—but I'm not sure what it is. Ernie Latouche is in the phone book, though, and he lives over on Emerson Road. He could tell you where to find Duncan."

VanAken headed for the door, nodding to Rickhauser as he went by. "Catch you later, Len."

"Peter?" Leya called. He turned, one hand on the door. "Will you come back?"

It was the longest wait of her life, but when he finally did answer, her heart plunged. "No, I won't be coming back." He took a deep breath and added quietly, "Bye, Leya. You take care, okay?"

29

Leya stared at the closing hospital-room door, trying to assimilate the fact that Peter was gone. Just like that. Out of her life once more, less than twenty-four hours after his sudden reappearance had thrown her tidy little existence into turmoil, revealing it for the fraud it was. Distress and fury ripped at her insides, like hyenas scrapping over fresh kill.

She'd already forgotten the assistant deputy, and his voice startled her. "I'll be off, too."

"Wait! Could I talk to you for a minute?"

Rickhauser paused. "You remembered something else?"

"No, it's about Peter."

"Agent vanAken? I don't—"

"Please—I know you're in a hurry, but it's important."

His yellow wolf eyes were wary. "What is it?"

"He told me about Beirut and about my father—that he thinks my father was responsible for what happened to him. He also told me that nobody believed him, except one person. That was you, wasn't it?"

The eyes narrowed. "Yes."

"Then I can understand why you don't think much of

me, or want to have anything to do with me. But I'm caught here, and I don't know what to do. You see, I know my father, and I know how dangerous Lebanon was, so it's hard for me to credit Peter's version of what went on over there.''

His big hand tightened on the door handle. ''You really should talk to your father about this, Miss Nash. I—''

''Have you ever met him?'' Leya asked, exasperated.

''Your father? Yes, we've met.''

''Then you know what a nonstarter that suggestion is.''

''Well, I'm sorry, but I don't think it's up to me to—''

''I think Peter considers you his friend, Mr. Rickhauser. You may be the only person in the world he still trusts.''

He seemed taken aback. ''If that's true, then I'm glad of it.''

''And if Peter trusts you, so do I. I happen to care a great deal for that man. In fact, fool that I am, I think I'm probably in love with him. And I'm worried about him.''

The assistant deputy's brow wrinkled. He stepped away from the door, and his fist thumped the foot of her bed. Finally Leonard Rickhauser's big shoulders heaved up and down under the weight of a sigh, and he perched himself on the end of her mattress. Leya had to shift position to keep from rolling downhill. ''He got a raw deal, Miss Nash.''

''Leya.''

''Not only did he lose four years out of the prime of his life, Leya, stuck in that hellhole, but when he came home, he found his father dead, his mother dying, and his former colleagues trying to take away his good name and his reputation.''

''Was there any truth to what they said about him—that he compromised the embassy's security and opened the door for that terrorist bomb?''

"Not that I could see. Our embassy in Beirut was bombed twice, in fact, and the marine barracks were destroyed in another hit. We were a prime target there. There was a civil war going on, and we were hardly neutral. After the bombings, everyone was looking for scapegoats, but there were blatant security lapses and plenty of blame to go around. As for vanAken, far as I could tell, he did the job in Lebanon that he was sent to do. Maybe he did it too well, infiltrating circles nobody else could get close to, before or since. That alone made him suspect, in some people's eyes."

"You think professional jealousy played against him?" Leya tried to shift for a better view of him, then decided she'd had enough of lying down. But getting up was a little more complicated than she'd counted on, with her neck immobilized. After a second or two of watching her struggle like a flipped turtle, Rickhauser reached out a hand and pulled her to a sitting position. Leya crossed her legs and tucked the blanket around her waist, smoothing her hospital gown, trying to recover a modicum of dignity. "Thanks."

"You're welcome. I think rivalry was part of it. Plus the fact that vanAken's an independent thinker. Thinkers don't make the world's best foot soldiers. They're lousy at following orders."

Leya smiled. "You give him a long leash, don't you?"

"It's the only way, with the ones like him."

"Is he a good FBI agent?"

The assistant deputy pursed his lips, thinking about that. His appearance was interesting, Leya decided. She didn't know why she'd found him repulsive. His face, canny and weathered, looked like it would distrust popular opinion and easy answers. Like it belonged to a man who considered things carefully and agonized over old-fashioned concepts like justice and virtue. A man whose trust would be difficult to earn, but, like most things of value, worth the effort.

"VanAken's heart isn't in this work," Rickhauser said at last. "But then, I don't think it's been in anything for a long time."

"Did you know him before his hostage experience?" He shook his head. "He was a different person," Leya said. "Enthusiastic, committed, inspiring. He inspired *me*. Peter's the reason I became a teacher. He's the one who made me see how important it is to work with young people, help them grow into thoughtful, responsible adults. That's where his heart was, too, before he lost it completely—or had it ripped away," she added grimly. "What about my father?"

Those boulder-size fists took to drumming again, on mammoth thighs this time. "Are you sure you want to hear this from me, of all people?"

"What do you mean, 'of all people'?"

"Don't you know how your father had his stroke?"

"I know he was at work when it happened. His secretary at Langley called me in New York afterward."

"He was in my office. I was CIA inspector general at the time."

"It was you who investigated Peter?"

"That's right. And the day your father heard about my decision to close the inquiry, he came to my office spitting nails. That's when he collapsed."

"Oh, my God..." Leya's bruised throat constricted as she recalled her panicky flight to his hospital bedside. Her fear at the thought of losing him. Her shock at seeing him tubed and restrained, a confused, drooling old man. Her anxiety over whether he'd ever recover. Then, as he'd fought his way back, the depression, rages and paranoia.

Finally, it all made sense. Taking a deep breath, she propped her elbows on her knees—in for a penny, in for a pound. "And what about Peter's countercharges that my father set him up in Beirut, then abandoned him?"

"All true."

She gasped at his matter-of-factness. "How do you *know?*"

"At the time, I didn't—not for sure. But my gut told me vanAken was being harassed on trumped-up claims. Then, one day, a year or so later, when I was back at the Bureau, a Mossad agent walked in the front door of the Hoover Building and asked for asylum."

"An *Israeli* defector?" Leya asked incredulously.

"Even friendlies become disillusioned with their governments sometimes. It's embarrassing, diplomatically— State Department hates it—but that doesn't mean we won't hear them out and take a look at whatever files they decide to bring us."

"And this Mossad agent—?"

"Brought records of their intelligence operations in Lebanon, including reports of a warning to the CIA station chief—your father—that one of his deep-cover operatives had been blown." Rickhauser shrugged. "It happens, sometimes. People get spotted in action or dealing with other known operatives."

"So it wasn't my father who blew Peter's cover?"

"I don't know. But regardless of how it happened, van-Aken should have been pulled out of there immediately, for his own safety. And, in fact, there *was* a plan afoot to send him to Saudi Arabia, but that was still too close. Standard operating procedure is for a burned operative to be kept out of the field for at least five years, to let the heat die down."

"My father told me when I was in Beirut that he wanted Peter yanked because he didn't trust him."

"He made that abundantly clear to headquarters, but he *didn't* report that vanAken had been made. And then," Rickhauser added, "Mossad warned him that a Shiite named Ali had put out an offer to deal on the hostages, but that the guy was probably bogus. Nash sent vanAken to meet the guy, anyway, with predictable results. A month after he was taken, Mossad gave your father a detailed report on where vanAken was being held, right down to a plan of the building, and offered to help spring him."

Leya shook her head, disbelieving. "Are you sure this Israeli defector's information was legit?"

"My counterpart in Tel Aviv subsequently verified it. The Israelis had no reason to deny the facts. They hadn't done anything wrong. On the contrary, they'd tried to do us a favor. But neither, mind you, were they trying to disparage your father. They've got a lot of respect for him. In the end, they left it to us to sort it all out."

"How did they get their information about this Ali character?"

"Israeli intelligence in the region is pretty impressive. Seems this guy was so unpredictable, he even gave his *own* side the willies. They wanted him neutralized, so they ratted on him. Of course, if he met a martyr's death at the hands of the Israelis or us, so much the better, for their propaganda purposes."

"Only my father never took the Israelis up on their offer. He just left Peter to rot. Oh, God…" Leya's vision went blurry, and she covered her mouth with her hand, rocking back and forth.

Rickhauser sat hunched at his end of the mattress, looking utterly embarrassed. Finally, he put a hand on her arm. "I'm sorry," he said. "Look, Leya, by all accounts, your father was a solid intelligence officer. I don't know why he delayed having vanAken pulled out of there, and maybe it was just a case of incredibly lousy judgment when he sent him to that meet. But then, he made matters worse by trying to cover his tracks and shift the blame.''

"Why didn't—" Her voice broke, but not because of her bruised larynx. Rickhauser waited patiently while she recomposed herself. "Why didn't Peter fight back, once he knew the truth? Surely he could have had him brought up on disciplinary action."

"Worse than that. Nash could have faced criminal charges. *Should* have, far as I'm concerned."

"So what happened?"

"VanAken refused to have anything to do with it. Believe me, I tried—hard—to change his mind. His testimony would have ensured a conviction in federal court, but without his cooperation…" Rickhauser shook his head. "In the end, all I could do was go to the CIA director and insist that your father be retired. Carter Nash was allowed to leave the Agency honorably, for health reasons, with his reputation intact and a generous pension. Which is a hell of a lot more than he was prepared to grant Peter vanAken."

"But *why?*"

"Why did vanAken let Nash off the hook, when he obviously despises the man? I wondered about that myself, but every time I pressed for an explanation, vanAken clammed up on me. Eventually, I gave up trying. I've always had my suspicions, mind you, but it was only this morning, in that theater, that I knew for sure."

"Knew what?"

Rickhauser shrugged. "That he did it for you."

As he trudged the eight blocks from Winslow Memorial

Hospital back to the Mount Abbey campus to retrieve his bureau car, vanAken's lug-soled hiking boots beat out a refrain. *Do the job. Close the case. Do the job. Close the case.*

He focused on the hypnotic rhythm of the chant, while bracing, late-afternoon air cut through a residue of medicinal odors and swirling emotions that fogged his mind. The previous night's snowfall had melted under a warm spring day, one that had completely passed him by while he'd been pacing antiseptic corridors, hovering reluctantly near the one person with the capacity to make him feel. Too much. Now the day was shutting down, the sky's darkening hurried along by thick cumulus clouds rolling in off the eastern seaboard.

Do the job. Close the case. Call it quits. He walked quickly, motivated by the prospect of silent calm that lay at the end of the road, once the job was finished and his obligations were met. Empty, blessed peace.

An image flashed in his mind—Karim Khoury on a frigid slab at the county morgue—and a tremor of guilt ran through him. He recalled the sick sensation he'd experienced when he'd found Karim's name on the Data-Trax entry log and thought he'd been betrayed, yet again. But *had* his young recruit betrayed him? Or had Karim, too, been set up?

Like him, Karim had been swept into a dangerous life of parallel illusions, where nothing was what it seemed. Then he'd fallen under suspicion for playing the game too well. Full of self-doubt, infatuated with a girl and dreams of a simple life, Karim had tried to walk away, only to discover, as vanAken had, that he was caught in the belly of a beast that rarely disgorged its prey intact.

The bombing of Data-Trax and the murder of Karim Khoury—two crimes tied together in a tangled knot of players. The common thread, vanAken realized, was Ambassador Stroud's daughter, who'd been present at both. But was she perpetrator, coconspirator or, ultimately, a victim like Karim, her body even now waiting to be discovered?

By all accounts, Karim and Holly's meeting had been a chance encounter, their subsequent relationship a function of mutual sympathy and youthful hormones. But what if Karim's radical Palestinian contacts inside Hamas had gotten wind of it and grabbed the opportunity for a double strike—at the American defense community, through Data-Trax, and, simultaneously, at the hated-but-well-protected Ambassador Stroud, Israel's staunch ally? Undermining him by ensnaring his daughter in their schemes?

A sudden realization dawned on vanAken, and he felt another chill. Rickhauser had said that the explosive device used in the Data-Trax bombing was a timed mechanism. Karim had ostensibly gone to Data-Trax to apply for a job, but his interview had been cut short when the personnel man had decided Khoury wouldn't pass security muster. The bomb, packed in the wheel well of Holly Stroud's car, had accidentally dislodged as the young couple left the compound. All of which meant that Karim was never intended to survive the bombing. Nor was Holly Stroud.

Had it been planned as a suicide bombing? Or had Hamas decided Karim was untrustworthy and expendable, and set him up? And what about the locals—Holly's spurned boyfriend, who may have had reason to want Karim and Holly dead? Or even the bigoted punk, who had it in for "ragheads"? Each thread, vanAken thought, had to be taken up and followed to see where it led. He owed that, at least, to Karim.

Turning in at the Mount Abbey College gate, he glanced across a broad expanse of wet, brown lawn and saw the young agent who'd picked him up in the FBI helicopter the previous evening. Wilf Berger was walking down the steps of a multistoried, red brick edifice, its walls entwined by a forest of bare ivy vines. Over the entrance, the words Arts Building were carved into a stone plaque.

Berger had also spotted him, it seemed, because he picked up his pace along the walkway. As he approached, he nodded a greeting. "How's the professor?"

"Okay. No permanent damage, by the look of things."

"That's great. I was just in her office," Berger said, cocking his thumb over his shoulder. "I'd been over at the morgue, observing the autopsy on Khoury. After they finished there, I checked in with the ADIC, and he told me to drop back here, take a dupe of Holly Stroud's message from the professor's voice mail." He pulled a cassette tape out of his overcoat pocket.

"Anything helpful on it?"

Berger shrugged. "Just what the professor told Mr. Rickhauser, I gather. Miss Stroud said she was at the theater and figured she knew what had happened. She sounded scared."

"What about the autopsy? Rickhauser mentioned that Khoury's balls had been used as a punching bag. Anything else?"

Berger slipped the cassette back into his pocket. "Nope. They found a few more bruises, indicating a struggle, but the ME put the cause of death as asphyxiation by hanging. Only other thing was that the guy'd had some recent sexual activity, and there was what looked like a burger and some peanut butter and chocolate in his stomach. Pretty gross."

"A Whopper, probably, and Reese's Pieces."

"How do you know?"

"I'd had dealings with this kid in the past. Khoury was

a big fan of American fast food. We also found wrappers in the Stroud girl's car.''

Berger nodded sagely. ''One of those fanatics who hates our guts, but deep down, is envious of all the good stuff we've got here.''

VanAken shook his head. ''I'm not so sure about that. Khoury actually bought into the whole American Dream thing. He wanted to fit in, only he found out that being accepted took more than a citizenship certificate.''

''So he got all bitter and twisted, and decided to hit back?''

''Maybe. We won't know for sure till we put all the pieces together. I've got to go,'' vanAken added, turning away.

Berger hustled up and started walking alongside him. ''Your car's still here, right? You left it behind when you rode over with Miss Nash in the ambulance?'' VanAken nodded. ''Could I get a lift?'' The young agent flipped up his collar, peering nervously at the sky. The wind had risen, and rain was beginning to spit on the shoulders of his crisp, beige topcoat.

''Where's your ride?''

''Lost it to the ADIC. The bureau ME dropped me here before he headed back to Newton. I'm supposed to meet Rickhauser at six, at a place called Tyler's, over on the town common. I've got time to kill, so if you've got something else you need to be doing, I'd be glad to tag along.''

VanAken sighed. ''All right, come on. I need to track down a skinhead.''

''We destroyed it, I'm afraid,'' Dr. Allenby said.

Leya stepped back from the wardrobe next to the bed, and she winced—from the pain in her neck, and from the memory of her beautiful gold cashmere sweater.

"We had to cut it off in the emergency room so we could work on you, remember? We managed to save your skirt, though," the doctor added hopefully.

Pulling the skirt off a hanger, Leya stepped into it. After Rickhauser had left, she'd removed the cervical collar and got out of bed, determined to get moving. "That's right, I forgot. I realize you had no choice."

"I am sorry. It was a beautiful sweater."

"One of my best Filene's Basement finds. Oh, well." Leya sighed. "Can I borrow this gown to get home in? I'll return it, I promise."

"No problem. But I'd rather you got back into bed, Leya. You've had a serious trauma, physical and psychological, and you need to take time to recuperate. You should stay here, at least overnight."

Leya tucked the stiff blue gown into the waistband of her brown wool skirt and buttoned it. Her underwear had also fallen to the emergency-room knife—second time that day she'd had her skivvies ripped off, she thought wryly. It was going to be a drafty trip home. A person could get pneumonia doing this Sharon Stone routine in chilly New England.

"There's an officer outside the door," Dr. Allenby added. "I'm guessing the police would rather you remained here, too."

"I'm not under arrest, you know."

"Nevertheless, you should reconsider."

Leya had pulled her loafers out of the closet and was slipping her bare feet into them, but she paused and looked up at the older woman. "I'm really grateful for everything you and the staff here have done for me, Doctor, but I just can't lie around any longer. I want to go home." No, she amended to herself. First to Mount Abbey to pick up her car and purse, then a quick trip home to change, then—

Her father's boom interrupted her calculations. "Oh, no, you don't! You get right back into that bed and stay put, like the doctor said!" He filled the open doorway—stealing up on her, as always. She realized that there was anxiety behind his bluster, but she perceived it hazily, as if through a curtain. For thirty years, this fierce old man had been her hero. Now, he seemed half a stranger.

"Is she going to be all right?" he asked, turning to Dr. Allenby.

"Just fine. And you are—?"

He dipped his gleaming white head. "Carter Nash, Leya's father."

"Well, Mr. Nash, your daughter is a very lucky lady. If those FBI agents had found her a minute later—"

"FBI?"

"Assistant Deputy Rickhauser," Leya said, her voice cold, "and Peter vanAken."

He blanched noticeably. "Rickhauser and vanAken—?"

"It was Peter who stayed at my house last night, Dad. He saved my life this morning." She waited for the inevitable explosion, but her father was speechless. Leya turned to the other woman. "Is there anything I need to sign before I leave, Dr. Allenby?"

The doctor sighed. "I'll leave the papers at the desk."

"Thank you."

"Take the collar, Leya, and try to wear it for a few days, to give your muscles a chance to heal. If you have any problems at all, come and see me."

"I will. And thanks again for all you've done."

Allenby nodded to them both, then slipped past the door that Leya's father held open for her. As he closed it, Leya reached into the closet, pulled her coat off a hanger, and shrugged into it, desperate to be away from him. It was as if someone had replaced the air in the room with acid. It was eating away at his image, sluicing off the surface membrane of loving, protective father, revealing something dark and appalling underneath. Leya felt the acid-air burning her, too; stripping away truth as she'd known it, leaving her raw, exposed and in pain.

"Hold on, now." His voice was strained, and when she looked at him, he had one hand on his walking stick, leaning heavily. But he scowled, and his free hand stabbed in the direction of her bruised cheek. "Now, I understand. It was vanAken who did that to you, wasn't it?"

"I have to go."

"No! Don't you go running after him!"

"That's none of your business, Dad."

"Oh, yes, it is—it most certainly is. That bruise isn't all he did to you, is it?" His voice dropped. "Did you think I didn't know he got you pregnant?"

She froze. "How did—?" Then she knew. "Oh, great! Mrs. Garibaldi told you, didn't she? Well, no, Dad, as a matter of fact he didn't get me pregnant. We *both* did. I wasn't raped. I was a willing participant in what happened between the two of us in Beirut."

"You were a child."

"I was an adult, fully responsible for my own actions, and you had no business—" Leya gasped. "My God! Is *that* why you did it?"

"Now look here, Leya, whatever they told you—"

"Dad! Read my lips! Peter saved my life this morning. Do you realize what that means? If you had succeeded in Beirut—if he hadn't managed to survive against all odds—you wouldn't even *be* here right now. You'd be down at the morgue, ID-ing my body."

A muscle in his cheek twitched. "You just listen—"

She held up a hand. "No. You listen to *me*, for once in your life. I do not want to talk to you right now. I mean that. There may come a time when I'll be able to stomach whatever explanation you have for what you did to Peter, but not today." As he came toward her, Leya sidestepped him. He stumbled, dropping heavily onto the edge of the bed. In spite of her anger, she asked, "Are you all right?"

"I—I'm not sure. Sit here with me while I catch my breath. You need to calm down. We both do. And then, we can—"

Leya shook her head and opened the door. "If you're going to collapse, Dad, you're in the right place. Take the bed, if you want. I'll ask the nurse at the desk to come and look in on you. Right now, I need to go and find someone who needs me more than you do."

30

The middle-aged woman who opened the door to van-Aken and Berger looked as worn, gray and weathered as the cedar shingles on her saltbox house. Located in an old, un-Yuppified part of town, the house backed onto a sluggish tributary that fed into the Charles River basin. A tumbledown boat shack leaned precariously on the bank of the stream. Near the boat shack stood a battered camper, round-topped, like an old toaster. About ten feet long, the pre-Winnebago relic might once have trailed an Edsel down American highways. A long, orange extension cord spilled out one of its windows and snaked across the muddy lot to an electrical outlet on the side of house.

VanAken nodded to the woman on the stoop. "Mrs. McCaw?"

She crossed one arm over her chest, while her other hand clutched her black cardigan to her throat. "Yes?" Underneath the cardigan, she wore a red-and-white-striped tunic over black knit pants and scuffed white Keds.

"I'm Special Agent vanAken, Federal Bureau of Investigation. This is Special Agent Berger. We're looking for Duncan McCaw. I believe he's your son?"

The woman peered at his badge, then at Berger's, also

held out for inspection. "He's my son, all right. FBI? What's he done now?"

"We'd just like to ask him some questions. Is he at home?"

"I'm not sure. I just walked in the door myself. I work over to the Red Barn restaurant, just off the I-90."

"Could you see if Duncan's in, please, ma'am?"

"Yes, sure," she said uneasily, stepping back from the threshold. "Come on in, then."

VanAken and Berger entered the house and were immediately pummeled by the twin odors of stale cigarettes and beer. They were in the living room. A beige, seat-sprung couch and matching armchair, cushions stained and askew, were positioned opposite a television on a metal stand. On the wall behind the sofa, a framed print of fluo-rescent palm trees and rolling breakers had been knocked off-kilter. Crushed beer cans and overflowing ashtrays cluttered scuffed oak tables. One beer can lay on its side next to the couch, having spewed a dark spot onto brown-speckled wall-to-wall carpet.

"I worked the evening shift yesterday," the woman said defensively, catching the direction of their gaze. "Duncan had some friends in, and I didn't have time to clean up before I left for work this morning."

Housekeeping was the least of the poor woman's prob-lems, vanAken thought, given the inconsiderate slob she lived with.

She moved to a back hall, looking one way, then the other. "Duncan? You here?" When there was no answer, she turned to the two agents and shrugged. "He's probably still at work. He's doing a renovation job with his uncle—my brother."

"They had the day off."

"They did? How do you know?"

"I spoke to your brother a few minutes ago," vanAken said. "Mr. Latouche gave me your address. He said Duncan was with him until about eleven, picking up lumber and supplies, then he let him go for the day. Any idea where he might have gone after that?"

"I'm not sure." She clutched her sweater nervously to her throat once more. "Is this about that lady professor that got attacked this morning?"

"Why? Do you know anything about that?"

"No. I heard about it over to work, is all. And then— well, that renovation job Duncan's doin' with my brother? It's her place they're fixin' up. So maybe some people might think…" Her voice trailed off.

"Might think what, ma'am?" Berger asked.

The woman glanced almost resentfully at the apple-cheeked young agent, then turned back to vanAken, whose scruffy edges seemed to offer her more reassurance. "Duncan wouldn't of had anything to do with that. He's had problems, sure, but it ain't easy, you know. His dad walked out on us five years ago, and with me workin' long hours—"

"We just want to talk to him, Mrs. McCaw."

She bit her lower lip. "They said somebody got murdered over to the college where that lady professor was attacked."

"We just want to talk to him," vanAken repeated gently. "We're interviewing a lot of people around town, gathering information. Do you think you could check and see if he's been home? Maybe his room?"

She shook her head. "He don't use his room these days."

"How's that?"

"Most of the time, he stays in the trailer out back. Just comes in to eat and use the bathroom, or watch TV. He's eighteen, and, well, you know how it is with young fellows. They wanna be independent. Duncan found that ol' trailer down to the dump, dragged it home, an' fixed it up, put in a space heater. He sleeps out there mosta the time. I'm not allowed to go inside. I'd rather he was in the house, mind, but at least he's close by.''

''You think he might be there now?''

She shrugged again. Berger was already edging toward the door.

''Go see,'' vanAken told him, then turned to the woman. ''Mrs. McCaw, what time did you get off work last night?''

''Midnight.''

''And when you got home, what time was that?''

''Half past, maybe.''

''Was Duncan here when you got in?''

''Yeah. Him and a couple of his friends. But I was beat, and I told Duncan I was goin' to bed, and I didn't want them hootin' it up half the night in here.''

''What happened then?''

''I went to bed. They all left.''

''Right away?''

Outside, they could hear Berger rapping on the trailer door. They paused for a moment, listening. Plucking nervously at her sweater, Duncan's mother turned back to vanAken. ''I'm not sure exactly what time they left. I fell asleep. I woke up later, about three. All the lights were on, but the house was quiet. I never heard them leave.''

''Did Duncan leave with his friends, or did he go to the trailer?''

''With his friends, I figure. They dropped him back here later. I heard a truck in the drive when he came in, and voices.''

''Do you know what time that was?''

"Quarter of six. I know, 'cause I looked at my clock radio when I heard 'em comin' up the drive. I wasn't too happy Duncan'd been out so late when he had work this morning. I knew Ernie'd be real teed off about it, too. He came by about six-thirty, and he had to really pound on the door to wake Duncan up."

They both paused again as voices drifted across the yard. "Looks like Agent Berger found him," vanAken said. "Excuse me, Mrs. McCaw. Thanks for your time."

Before she could say another word, he was out the door and down the front steps. He saw Duncan slouched in the doorway of the trailer, baggy jeans hanging perilously from his hipbones and puddling around his bare feet. He was shirtless, and his chest shone pale and waxy in the twilight. VanAken noted puffiness around the kid's eyes and deep creases etched into one cheek, giving it the appearance of a discarded burger wrapper. If the kid'd had any hair, it would have been mussed. Berger had obviously woken him up from a deep sleep.

When he spotted vanAken, Duncan scowled. "You! I shoulda figured she'd sic you on me."

"What do you mean?"

"Professor Nash. The bitch hates me." Duncan folded his arms, tucking his fists under his biceps to pump them up. His right hand was still bandaged, the wrap grimy now. On one shoulder, VanAken spotted a crudely drawn black swastika tattooed over the initials W.A.R.

"Now why would Professor Nash hate a fine, upstanding fellow like you?" vanAken asked.

"How the hell should I know?"

"You're awfully defensive here, Duncan. Why are you so defensive?"

Duncan's eyes narrowed. "Bitch tried to hustle me,

okay? I turned her down, and she's had it in for me ever since.''

Wilf Berger's eyebrows shot up to somewhere in the vicinity of his well-tended hairline. "Professor Nash tried to seduce *you?*"

"Yeah, but I don't do old broads, see? I got all the action I can handle already." Duncan shook his head, indignant. "It figures she'd try to pin it on me when somebody jumps her. But I got a witness. I was with my uncle mosta the morning, and I been right here, sleepin', ever since. I know my rights. This is sexual harassment."

VanAken jammed his fists into his pockets and shook his head. "Nobody's accusing you of anything, Duncan. We've already spoken to your uncle, and we know you were with him when Professor Nash was attacked, so you're in the clear on that. Can we come in?"

Duncan glanced behind them, as if he suspected they had troops massed just over the horizon. "What for?"

"Just to talk. It's freezing out here. You don't want to catch cold, do you?"

Duncan nodded toward the house. "We can talk in the—"

"Thanks." VanAken pushed past him and stepped up into the trailer.

"Hey! I didn't mean here, I meant—"

But vanAken was already circling the cramped, cluttered space. Like the house, it smelled of beer and cigarettes, overlaid with a ripe miasma of body odor, dirty sheets and mildew, all of it cranked up to a stifling temperature by the glowing space heater on the floor. The walls around the rumpled bed in one corner were papered with staple-punched centerfolds of nudes in none-too-subtle poses. But what really caught vanAken's attention was a black-and-white poster—a grainy, blown-up photo of a group of men in camouflage gear, standing in a wooded area, brandishing AK-47s. Above black kerchiefs, only their eyes were visible. Keep America Pure! the message at the bottom exhorted. White Aryan Resistance.

On a shelf below the poster were a cassette player and a scattered collection of tapes—mostly heavy metal, he noted, picking up a couple and examining the labels. Turning away from the bed, vanAken walked over to a litter-and magazine-strewn table that folded down from a wall. He flipped through an eclectic collection of porn, militia tracts and gun catalogs, then turned back to the kid at the door. Berger had stepped up into the trailer behind him.

"Nice place you got here," vanAken said dryly.

"This is private property. Nobody's allowed in here uninvited. You keep your mitts offa my stuff and get the hell out!"

"Relax, Duncan," vanAken said, clearing a spot on the table. He perched himself on the edge, but as he settled, his boot scraped noisily on the black linoleum floor. Frowning, he lifted his foot and propped it on his knee, inspecting the thick sole. A piece of glass had embedded itself in the nubby tread. Pulling out a penknife, vanAken pried the fragment loose and examined it under the table lamp. A speck of gold glittered at one corner. He crouched low, peering along the floor and under the bed until he found the black combat boots he recalled Duncan wearing that morning. Hefting the steel-toed weight of them, he flipped them over.

"What do you think you're doing?" Duncan took a step forward, but vanAken raised a finger and shot him a warning glance. The kid stopped in his tracks.

Turning back to the boots, vanAken dropped one, then used his knife to dig a glass fragment out of the arch of the other, just in front of the heel. "How exactly did you cut that hand of yours, Duncan?"

"What's it to you?"

"Just answer the question."

"I accidentally broke a beer bottle last night, okay? I cut my hand while I was cleanin' up the pieces."

VanAken glanced at him skeptically. "Cleaning up?" He dropped the boot and studied the two glass fragments, side by side. "What kind of beer was it?"

"What kind? How the hell do I—wait! It was Red Dog, that's right."

"And this happened over there in the house, in your mother's living room?"

"Yeah. And she's a witness, too. She saw me there with my friends last night."

"Did you break that bottle and cut your hand before or after she saw you? Think, now, Duncan, because I'm going to ask her."

"It was, uh, after. I cut it after she went to bed."

"I see." VanAken frowned. "Agent Berger? Is my mind going on me, here? Did you notice any bottles in that mess Duncan left for his mother to clean up? Or just cans?"

"I only saw cans."

"Me, too. Good. I thought I was losing it there for a minute. See this piece of glass I just pulled out of his boot?"

"Yes, sir."

"Even though we didn't actually see any bottles in the house, would you agree that it *could* have come from a beer bottle, like Duncan here says?"

Berger peered at the fragment. "Uh, actually no, I wouldn't. It's clear. I'm not sure about Red Dog, but in general, beer is bottled in dark bottles—brown or green, usually. Light spoils the brew.''

"I think you're right about that," vanAken said, nodding. He looked back at the kid. "There's some gold foil on these pieces of glass, Duncan. Do you suppose that a crime lab could match them up with the plate-glass display window that got smashed when the pharmacy on the town common was vandalized this morning? Maybe match up your blood to some splatters over there, too?''

The kid took an aggressive step forward. "Okay, that's it! I want you two outta here now, or I—!''

"*Sit down!*''

Duncan collapsed onto the bed like someone had kicked his feet out from under him. Berger, too, glanced around for a place to sit, until he realized vanAken didn't mean him.

Carefully, vanAken set the glass fragments aside on the table. "Now," he went on, his voice affable once more, "in just a minute, Duncan, Agent Berger here is going to give the Winslow Police Department a call, since that vandalism over at the drugstore falls within their jurisdiction.'' He paused, wrinkling his brow. "Unless it comes under the category of hate crime. What do you think, Agent Berger? That would put the ball in the FBI's court, wouldn't it?''

"Yes, sir. Hate crimes and civil-rights violations are federal offenses.''

Duncan hesitated, looking from one to the other. Then his shoulders slumped, and he leaned back slowly, glancing longingly at the bed, as if he would like nothing more than to be left alone to go back to his nap. But when vanAken spotted his hand sliding toward the pillow, he planted a boot on it and pushed the kid facedown on the mattress. Berger jumped to his aid.

"Cuff him!" While Berger slapped on the handcuffs, vanAken reached under the pillow and withdrew a pistol. "What have we here? Looks like your basic Saturday night special, wouldn't you say, Agent Berger? You expecting trouble, Duncan?"

"It's for self-defense," he mumbled with some difficulty, given that his face was pressed into the mattress.

"Right. And I'm sure it's properly registered, too. You got any more goodies like this around here? Sit him up," vanAken added. The young agent pulled Duncan to a sitting position while vanAken began flipping open cupboards. In a wardrobe closet, he found six baseball bats. He lifted one out and examined its scratches and chips. "You play a lot of ball, Duncan? Into spring training these days? Use that drugstore window for a batting cage?"

Duncan sneered up at him. "Go ahead and laugh, asshole, but me and my friends, we're on a war footin' here. It's us against the conspiracy."

"What conspiracy is that?"

"Don't play dumb with me, FBI-man. You think we don't know about your plans?"

"Plans?"

"Yeah. Your secret black helicopters, and how you put microchips under people's skin whenever they go into a hospital, so you can track us, turn us into slaves."

"I'm lost. Are you lost, Agent Berger?"

Berger shrugged, and vanAken turned back to the kid on the bed. "Clue us in, Duncan—who exactly is behind this conspiracy?"

"You know damn well who! You feds, that's who. The government, controlled by Jews, niggers, ragheads, faggots, an' feminists."

"That's quite a coalition."

"They're just shovin' white men aside, takin' all our

jobs and our land. But you're not gonna get away with it. There's an underground army formin', and it's growin'. Us white guys ain't puttin' up with this shit anymore. Country belongs to us, and we're takin' back what's ours!''

VanAken shook his head. "Gee, Duncan—last time I checked, I was a heterosexual Caucasian male. You, too, Agent Berger?"

"Me, too."

Duncan spat on the floor. "You guys are race traitors! You ain't part of the solution, you're part of the problem. You're gonna find that out, real soon, but by then, it's gonna be too late for *you*, assholes!"

VanAken perched on the table once more and massaged the tops of his eye sockets. A severe headache had been simmering for hours, and it was hammering at his skull now. "The problem *I* see, Duncan," he said wearily, "is lazy, dumb shits like you, who figure the world owes them something for nothing. But, hey, what do I know? I'm a little slow on the uptake. Why don't you tell me more? Like, for example, who else around here is part of this underground army of yours, fighting the good fight against a couple of old shopkeepers on the town common?"

"I'm not tellin' you nothin', asshole!"

"You tell these men what they want to know, Duncan!"

Three heads spun toward the door as Mrs. McCaw gripped the frame and pulled herself up into the trailer. As she glanced around at the decor, her face was a shifting mask of disgust, anger and fear.

"Get outta here, Ma!"

"Don't you *dare* raise your voice to me!" she snapped. "I've put up with that about long enough, I'd say!"

"They got no right—"

"I shoulda horsewhipped you and thrown you out on

your ear long ago! There I am, workin' my tail off, and
your Uncle Ernie, too, tryin' to help you make somethin'
of yourself, and what are you doin' but hangin' out with
those deadbeat friends of yours, gettin' into more mischief
and talkin' garbage! Now, you do like they tell you, Duncan, before you find yourself in a whole lot more trouble
than you already are. That happens, don't you go thinkin'
I'll bail you out. No more! You understand?''

"Jeez, Ma—''

"Tell them!''

Newton, Massachusetts: 5:57 p.m.

"What the hell—!'' Curtis Pullen leaned toward the terminal in the FBI surveillance van, still parked at the Data-
Trax bomb scene. Slack-jawed with disbelief, he read the
E-mail on his screen for the third time. Then he pulled up
the old case file that Rickhauser had insisted he look over
that morning, skimming pages until he found the photo
and background data on the subject cited in the E-mail
message. "I don't believe this!''

Mark Leung turned from his position at another monitor
nearby. "Believe what, sir?'' the tech asked.

"I just got a message from the fingerprint-ID division.
They nailed that latent print we found on the watch crystal.''

"Was it Khoury's?''

"No, dammit! The old wolf was right. We got a goddam
ghost at work here! See if you can get him on the horn
for me. He was still out in Winslow, last time he checked
in. We need him back, on the double.''

But half an hour later, after Leung had spoken to several
of the bureau agents swarming over the small college
town, hunting for Ambassador Stroud's daughter, picking

over her car, and collecting evidence on the murder of
Karim Khoury, the assistant deputy still hadn't been located. Dr. DaSilva, the medical examiner, arrived back at
the Newton crime scene during this time, but said he
hadn't seen Rickhauser in hours.

"What about vanAken?" Pullen asked.

"Haven't been able to raise him, either," Leung replied.
"He's got an office ride, but the radio's out of range."

"His cell phone?"

"Dead battery, maybe. I can't get through."

"More likely the asshole's ignoring it or turned it off."

"You want me to keep trying, sir?"

"Of course I want you to keep trying!" Pullen shouted.
"Find the ADIC, goddammit!"

31

Len Rickhauser's cell phone bleated from the pocket of his rumpled overcoat, but he was in no position to do anything about it. He'd gone down like a giant redwood at a blow struck from behind—something wooden, he'd sensed in the nanosecond between the crack on his skull and the buckling of his knees. Felt like a telephone pole. The ringing of the phone brought him around again, but he had no idea where he was or how long he'd been out. All he knew was that he was lying on his left side, and that he was uncomfortable as hell.

The noise in his pocket finally died away, but the echo lingered, buzzing between his ears. His head ached like the worst hangover of his life. He wanted to cradle it in his hands, but when he tried, he discovered that his arms were immobilized, yanked tight behind his back. Vinyl tape over his mouth stretched his skin from one ear to the other. The acrid smell of it filled his nostrils, overlaid by something pungent and pissy-smelling, like cow manure in a gas station. Feeling grit under his cheekbone, Rickhauser sensed he was lying on bare ground, but not outside. It was cold, but the air was close and windless. He opened his eyes to dim shadow. What little light there was seemed to be seeping in from overhead.

Trying to shift position for a better look at his surroundings, Rickhauser discovered that his legs were bound behind him, linked to his wrists. Struggling against his constraints brought searing pain to his head—and worse, fierce nausea. His stomach heaved. Severely disoriented, in throbbing pain, Rickhauser had just enough presence of mind to understand that he was in big, big trouble. That tape across his mouth was stuck tight to his face. If he upchucked now, he'd aspirate the vomit and he'd die.

Eyes closed again, he forced himself to breathe deeply and carefully through his nose, willing down the queasiness. His wife's face flashed through his mind, and he tried to focus on her. He should have called her by now. What time was it? It wasn't right that she should have to worry about him. He thought about how much he'd always despised the idea of Wendy getting the late-night knock at the door, opening it to those sober suits with their lousy news. He'd had to deliver news like that a couple of times, and it was the pits. And for her to have to be told that he'd drowned in his own puke? No way, Rickhauser thought grimly, taking another deep breath.

Gradually, the pain and the nausea subsided. Sweat-drenched, he held himself as still as possible, dreading another onslaught, doubting he could resist it a second time. For sure he had a concussion. Maybe even a skull fracture. Which meant he needed to get out or get help, sooner rather than later. But where was he? And how had he got here?

He opened his eyes once more and stared at the space before him, until finally he made out a rough earthen wall lined with heavily laden shelves. It almost resembled a root cellar, he thought. The kind that farmwives had once stocked with home-made preserves and tuberous vegetables to see their families through long, harsh winters.

That's it! he thought. *A farm!* He was on a farm just outside Winslow, Massachusetts. He'd gone to interview Holly Stroud's former boyfriend at work, but the waitress at the little joint named after him had said Tyler Newman had called in sick. She'd given Rickhauser directions to Bethany Hill, the old farm just beyond the Mount Abbey campus. And then—

Then what? What happened after that?

Rickhauser winced. It wasn't just his head that hurt. His shoulders, back and thighs were cramping wickedly. He'd been hog-tied, wrists and ankles yanked together behind his back. Even if his busted noggin had allowed him to move, he thought, he still would have had a time trying to sit, kneel or roll, given the way he was tied—not to mention the fact that his size and his late-middle-age lack of agility also conspired against him.

Lying on his side, breathing hard like some old hound dog who's been run too fast, he recalled a police convention he'd attended in Las Vegas once, where eight hundred federal, state and local cops had been treated to a performance by David Copperfield. This pickle he was in now would have been a piece of cake for the contortionist, Rickhauser thought. Guy would have folded himself inward and flipped his arms around his head to loosen the ropes. Putting slack in the rope—that was the key. After that, a couple of quick twists, and you were home free. Problem was, unlike the skinny Copperfield, his own girth didn't lend itself to easy manipulations.

As another cramp seized his fettered arms, an image of vanAken flashed through his mind, shackled in a Beiruti pit for four long years. All the contortions in the world wouldn't have freed vanAken from the chains that had bound him to that wall. For the first time, Rickhauser understood—really understood, beyond simple human sympathy—the horror of what had been done to the man, and what had been taken from him. And as the ADIC lay in the gloom, bound, gagged and beaten, he felt the terror that preys on pain and helplessness.

Think! his mind bellowed. There had to be a way out of this. He peered once more at the shelves on the walls. They held stacked bags of some sort, forty- or fifty-pounders, by the look of them. There was printing along the sides of the bags, but he couldn't decipher the letters. He squinted. An *A?* Some *M's,* or *N's?* An *O?* Nope. Couldn't make it out. Giving up the effort, Rickhauser dropped his gaze to a lower shelf, where wooden boxes stood beside metal jerricans lined up in a row, like fat soldiers on parade. Tidy bugger, this Tyler Newman, he thought grimly.

His heart began to pound, and his eyes leaped back to the bags on the upper shelf. Ammonium-nitrate fertilizer! And fuel oil! *Shit!* The place was storage for a fucking homemade bomb factory! He'd bet his pension that those boxes held stolen blasting caps.

Then Rickhauser felt an eerie chill run the length of his spine, as he recalled what had brought him to Massachusetts in the first place. Was *that* what those vibes had been about? A premonition of some sort of weird cosmic justice? Of his own death in the same kind of blast he'd set off a quarter century earlier, when he'd lobbed a stun grenade into that Greenwich Village powder keg, vaporizing four young people seduced by the glamour of violence?

Suddenly he recalled what he'd been doing just before he'd taken the crack that had dropped him. After a minute or so of knocking at the door of the farmhouse, he'd walked across the yard to the weather-beaten barn. No one had answered his hails there, either. When he'd ventured inside to look around, Rickhauser had found empty stalls and, near the barn's other door at the far end, a tack room, which was heavily bolted. He'd given the padlock a routine yank, presuming it wouldn't give. It didn't. He'd studied the padlocked door, dying to know what it was hiding, running his fingers along its rough wooden boards. Then, after a quick glance around, Rickhauser had pulled the car keys out of his pocket and used the point of one to dig at the space between two planks, gouging a tiny peephole. It was when he'd been squinting through the hole, trying to make out the room's interior, that he'd felt the crack on his head.

Was that where he was now? Rickhauser wondered. Still in the old barn?

Steeling himself, he decided to chance another survey of the gloomy space. He took one more deep breath, then slowly, carefully, arched his neck. No good. The movement brought a knife blade of excruciating pain slicing through his brain. Rickhauser felt his body go rigid, then begin to convulse. But at the last split-second, just before he lost control and consciousness, he glimpsed a small lump huddled against a wall, six or eight feet beyond the top of his head. A lump with terrified, staring eyes, and a halo of pale, frizzled hair.

VanAken placed his hand on the hood of the BMW 750 parked in Leya's driveway. It was warm to the touch. He glanced at the agent standing next to the Bimmer who was admiring it—Collins, he'd said his name was. "Her fiancé?" vanAken repeated.

"Apparently. Nice wheels, hey? What are we doing wrong, we can't afford wheels like this?" Collins bent to peer through the BMW's windows, the fluorescent block letters on the back of his dark windbreaker gleaming under the streetlights. He was one of two FBI agents still at the house, keeping an eye on things and waiting for the truck that was coming to tow Holly Stroud's car to a security impound. "Name's John Merriman," Collins added, straightening again. "Just showed up with flowers and wine. Guess he and Miss Nash had a hot date planned for tonight. Hadn't heard about what happened. I had to tell him she was in hospital."

"He's inside now?"

"Yeah, had a key. Said he wanted to give her old man a call, then he'd head off to see her. He was pretty shook-up. I figured it was all right to let him go in." When vanAken didn't respond, the other agent glanced at him. "The professor's going to be okay, isn't she?"

"What? Oh—yeah, she'll be fine."

"Maybe you should talk to the poor guy, let him know?"

VanAken nodded distractedly, turning toward the house. He'd left Berger with the local cops to handle Duncan's arrest and questioning while he caught up with Rickhauser. But when he realized he didn't have his cell phone, he'd decided to drop by Leya's house to collect it and the few other things he'd left behind that morning.

Now, standing at the opaque window of the front door, he hesitated. He had no desire to speak to some guy who claimed to be her fiancé. He didn't even want to know such a person existed. It was just one more detail in a day that had already produced too many unwelcome surprises. But neither, vanAken reflected, did he want to wait around until this guy left—much less come back later. He slipped Leya's key into the lock.

"FBI," he called, rapping on the door as he opened it. "Hello?"

"Back here," a deep voice replied.

In the kitchen, vanAken found a man about his own age and height, standing at the center island like he owned the place. Bespectacled but fit-looking—a blond Clark Kent in search of a telephone booth—he wore an open black overcoat, plaid-lined, the collar flipped up over a pin-striped shirt and dark tie. He was holding Leya's phone to one ear, while his free hand rifled a brown leather case that vanAken recognized as his own shaving gear. A huge spray of red roses lay on the counter, wrapped in clear cellophane and tied with silver ribbon—two dozen, vanAken estimated. Next to it, bright beads of condensation glistened on a bottle of white wine, obviously chilled and ready to be cracked open.

"That's my kit," vanAken said curtly.

"Oh! I wondered…" The other man hung up the phone and pushed the case across the counter. "I was trying to reach Leya's father, but there's no answer at his apartment. John Merriman," he added, thrusting out his hand. "And you are—?"

"Special Agent Peter vanAken, FBI." He watched Merriman's face, but the name evoked no reaction. Obviously, Leya had never mentioned him to this character. Fair enough, since she hadn't mentioned Merriman to him, either. In fact, when the subject arose last night, hadn't she said she was unattached? She was her father's daughter, after all, vanAken reflected, her life carefully compartmentalized. Not that it mattered, at this point.

The two men exchanged firm handshakes, but when Merriman's brown eyes dropped, vanAken pulled away and slipped his hands into his pockets. The guy's hairline was wispy, receding over an already high forehead. He'd be bald in five years, vanAken thought, taking some satisfaction from the idea.

"You mind telling me what's going on here, agent? The fellow outside said Leya was hurt."

"Somebody jumped her over at Mount Abbey this morning, inside the theater. She's going to be okay, though."

"Who did it?"

"We're not sure. It's under investigation."

"Does this have anything to do with that bombing last night? I heard on the news that Ambassador Stroud's daughter was involved, and I know she's a student of Leya's."

VanAken nodded. "We think there may be a connection. The girl was here briefly yesterday evening, then disappeared. That's her car in the garage they're getting ready to tow. We kept the house under surveillance all night, in case Miss Stroud returned, but she never did. Leya—Professor Nash—was out looking for the girl this morning when she was ambushed."

"You had her house under surveillance all night? Is that why your shaving kit is here?"

VanAken nodded. "I camped out upstairs, standing guard. That's my overcoat on the stool there, too. I just dropped by to pick up my things and return the house key Miss Nash left for us when she went to work this morning."

Something shifted in Merriman's expression. "I see. Well, is there anything else you people will be needing? If not, I'll take that key off your hands. I'm going to see her now, and I want to lock up the place before I go."

VanAken handed it over. "I'm finished here. I think you'll find Miss Nash's father at the hospital with her. She's at Winslow Memorial on the second floor, west wing."

"No, I'm right here," her voice said, from the hall behind them.

"Leya!" Merriman sprinted around the counter and past vanAken, who turned and watched as the other man scooped her into his arms. She allowed herself to be held, but her gaze traveled over Merriman's shoulder to him. "They said you were in the hospital!" Merriman said.

"I checked myself out." The cervical collar was tucked under her arm, vanAken noted, and her purse was slung over her other shoulder. She must have gone by the college to get it and her car.

Merriman pulled back and touched her cheek. "Oh, sweetie, look at your face! What did they do to you?"

She finally looked up, venturing a smile, and patted his arm. "I'm fine, John, really. You two have met?"

"Yes. The agent here told me they staked out your house last night. Obviously, you should have had full-time protection."

"This was no one's fault but my own, John. I walked right into it."

"We did put a guard on her hospital room," vanAken said. "Now that she's home, I'll make sure someone stays on duty outside until we find the Stroud girl and determine who was responsible for the attack." He debated asking why the hell she'd left the hospital, against all advice to the contrary, but that was someone else's concern, not his. Gathering up his case and overcoat, vanAken patted its pockets, then frowned and glanced up at her. "You don't recall seeing my cell phone, do you? I've misplaced it."

"Your phone?" Leya said. "No, I don't."

"Must have dropped it at the theater. I'll track it down later." VanAken nodded to Merriman as he edged around them and headed toward the door. "Nice meeting you."

He had almost made it to the door when Leya caught up to him. "Peter, wait! Where are you going?"

He stopped, reluctantly. "To find Rickhauser. He was supposed to be at Tyler's, but I drove by and didn't see his car. I think he might have gone out to the Newman place. By the way, Duncan's been arrested."

"You're kidding! What happened?"

"He tried to pull a gun on me. Turns out he was part of the gang that smashed that pharmacy window early this morning. He's into some idiotic militia shit—pretty small potatoes, I think, but he gave us Tyler Newman's name, among those of his buddies."

"Tyler was with that gang of vandals?"

"No, but apparently these kids are using the Newman farm for their soldier games. I was going to call and give Rickhauser a heads-up, until I realized I didn't have my phone. I just dropped by here to get it and leave your key, but I have to run now."

"All right, but come back later, okay? We need to talk."

VanAken sensed John Merriman watching from the hall. "I think what *you* need, Leya, is to rest and spend some time with your fiancé. He's really worried about you, and—"

"My *what?*" Leya spun around.

Merriman flushed slightly. "That's what I told the agents, so they'd know it was all right for me to come inside when you weren't here. It's practically true, and—"

"Oh, John, no!" She shook her head wearily, and turned back to vanAken. "Peter, listen, I—"

He held up a hand. "I don't have *time* for this. How do I get to the Newman place?"

She exhaled sharply and put a hand to her forehead. "Hancock Drive. Go past the Mount Abbey main gate, then take the first road on your left. I think it's about a half mile down.''

VanAken nodded, then left before she could come up with another pretext to hold him there. Pulling away from the drive, he saw her silhouette in the open doorway, the tall shadow of John Merriman hovering close behind. She'll be all right, vanAken told himself. He should never have intruded. The sooner he was out of the picture, the sooner her life could get back to normal. Somebody had to move on. Let it be her.

He'd been sick after all, Rickhauser sensed. He smelled the sour odor of it and felt a damp patch under his cheek. By all rights, he should be dead—but dead couldn't possibly be this foul. He felt wet, weak, and as helpless as a newly hatched bird.

Opening his eyes, he was startled to see fingers just inches from his nose, wriggling to shake loose a wadded strip of silver duct tape. Flexing his jaw, Rickhauser found that the binding was gone from his mouth. He studied the slender fingers, the nails short and shining pale. They were the small hands of a girl. Like him, she was lying on her side, her blue-jeaned, booted legs lashed together and pulled behind her. Her arms were clad in a white long-sleeved shirt, and they seemed as tightly bound as his own. A mass of blond curls tumbled over her shoulders and along the ground.

''Holly Stroud?'' Rickhauser croaked, bile eating at his throat and nose. The hands stopped moving, and he heard a whimper of confirmation. ''Thanks for getting that tape off my mouth. That was real smart. You probably saved my life.'' She whimpered again. ''Can you turn yourself around to face me?''

She tucked up her knees a little, pulling against her

ropes. A gap of skin appeared between her jeans and her shirt, as the girl scooted around on her side, wriggling in a counter-clockwise circle until she was facing him—but upside down, her head to his knees. A bright red Sesame Street character grinned at Rickhauser from the middle of her chest. The girl's mouth was covered with silver duct tape, as his had been, and above it, her eyes were terrified and tear-filled.

"You did good, Holly. I'm grateful," he said, mustering what he sincerely hoped was a reassuring smile. For sure, his face wouldn't be doing much to quell the poor kid's terror. "My name's Len Rickhauser. I'm with the FBI. It's nice to finally meet you, though I'm afraid we're in a bit of a mess here—in more ways than one," he added ruefully, wrinkling his nose. A fresh stream of tears spilled into her hair as she nodded. If she went on crying like that, Rickhauser thought, she was going to be in as much trouble as he'd been. "Holly, listen to me—don't cry. We're going to be okay, but if you cry, it just gets you stuffed up and makes it hard for you to breathe. First order of business here is to remove your tape, too. Problem is, my head hurts like the dickens. I'm afraid if I try to move, I'm going to pass out again. Do you think you can make your way around to my hands?"

She nodded once more and started working her way past his bent-up knees, pumping along like some prehistoric teenage invertebrate. A moment later, Rickhauser's spine tingled, as he sensed her behind him. His fingers stretched, and he touched something fluffy—her hair. She moved in closer, and he tamped his way down her cheekbone until he felt the edge of the duct tape over her mouth. Picking at it, he loosened a corner and started to tug. Holly yanked back, trying to help, but the tape slipped out of his weak, hammy fingers. His left hand felt numb—lack of circulation, Rickhauser thought. The girl maneuvered close to him again.

"Let me get a good grip," he said. "Okay—now, pull!" This time, she gasped as the tape came free. Rickhauser lay still, panting, exhausted by the minimal effort and by the severe pain it brought.

"Are you all right?" the girl whispered.

"To tell you the truth, Holly, I'm not feeling real great."

"I think you were having a seizure a little while ago. He must have hit you awfully hard."

"Was that Tyler Newman?"

"Yeah. He dumped you down here. He came after me, too. I called him at work late last night to see if he'd help us. Karim was terrified about turning himself in, because he figured you all'd just quit looking for the real bomber once you had him. That is, if you guys didn't shoot him first," she added scathingly.

"And Newman?" he asked, ignoring the crack.

"When I called, he kept asking where I was and if Karim was with me. All of a sudden, I got this sick feeling that he *wanted* to see Karim arrested. I hung up on him. But I'd already told him I was in Winslow, and that I didn't have my car anymore. Obviously, I couldn't go back to the rez. I guess it was just process of elimination after that. I was trying to call one of my profs early this morning when Tyler showed up at the theater. I waylaid him before he realized Karim was there, and he dragged me off. Poor Karim," Holly added worriedly. "He's probably still hiding, terrified, thinking I ran out on him."

Rickhauser let that pass. No need to get her upset now. She'd know about Karim soon enough. "Did you know you were carrying the bomb into the Data-Trax compound yesterday?"

"We didn't!"

"Yes, you did. It was in the hubcap of your car, and you left it behind when you pulled out of the parking space. The whole thing was recorded on security cameras."

"No way!"

"You really didn't know?"

"No, I swear! It's a mistake. I'd never—"

"What about Karim?"

"Not him, either, honest! If you knew him—"

"Okay, okay. I believe you."

She fell silent for a moment. "You do?"

"Yeah. Most people wouldn't, mind, but I do. Listen, do you know where your ropes are tied?"

"Near my ankles, I think."

"Can you move again, try to get them close to my hands? I'll see if I can work you free, so we can get out of here."

"That's a great idea, Mr.—"

"Call me Len."

"Okay, Len." He heard her grunt and shuffle again, backing around until her boots were against his hands.

Fighting the pain in his head and the cramping in his body, Rickhauser stretched out his fingers, trying to locate a loose end of rope. "Move in a bit more."

She inched closer to him. "Did you come here looking for me?"

"The town's full of people looking for you, and now. they'll be looking for me, too, I imagine." Rickhauser finally located a stub of rope. He followed the loose end until his fingers found a knot and attempted to worry it loose.

After a minute or so, Holly exclaimed, "My tires— that's it!"

"That's what?"

"Tyler said my tires were wearing and needed to be rotated. He said he'd do it before I drove Karim in for his interview." Holly fell silent again, then, *"That's* how he got into the Lizzie this morning. I thought he must have broken in. But I left him my key ring with the car. The stage-door key was on it. He could easily have copied them."

"Did Tyler know Karim had an interview at Data-Trax?"

"Yeah. Karim had been hiding out here at Bethany Hill, in the barn, after he ran away from Cambridge. That's when Tyler was still pretending he wanted to help. Karim had been working for you," Holly added accusingly.

"I know."

"He wanted out."

"Khoury was helping us keep tabs on Hamas, a radical Palestinian group that's been responsible for a number of terrorist attacks abroad. We were concerned they might strike here. You're absolutely sure he hadn't decided to go over to their side?"

"No way. Karim is apolitical—he has less interest in that stuff than I do. Not only that, he also happens to love this country. He did what you people asked because he was grateful to be here, but if he'd wanted to fight, he'd have gone back to the Middle East."

"Some people think striking at America is the best way to hurt Israel."

"Not Karim. He hates violence. He says it just leads to more violence, until people become so obsessed with revenge that they forget what they were fighting for in the first place. He's already lost his parents and the rest of his family. Karim's grandfather used to have dreams about Karim dying a violent death. That's why he sent him away.

Karim had promised him he'd never get caught up in that stuff here."

"What about Tyler?"

"*He's* something else. People think he's just some cappuccino stud, but he's not. He's political, antigovernment, big time. At first, I thought it was cool—'cause of my father. I can't stand his politics. When I found out Tyler was having these meetings out here at Bethany Hill and doing militia training, I thought that was kind of neat— like the thirteen colonies, struggling against an oppressive government—you know?"

Irritated, and unable to hide it, Rickhauser gave her ropes a sharp yank—but that was a mistake. A wave of pain hit him, and the unwieldy knot slipped from his grasp.

"Hey, are you all right?" Holly asked anxiously.

His breath came in short, shallow gusts until the wave passed. When he could speak again, he asked, "Do you think it's possible Tyler Newman set Karim and you up?"

"Yeah, that's what I was beginning to think must have happened. See, when I broke up with him and started seeing Karim, Tyler pretended to be okay about it. But he was all weird when he found out we were..." She hesitated.

"Sleeping together?"

Holly sighed. "Yeah. I wouldn't with Tyler. Which was bad enough for his precious ego, but then, he walked in on Karim and me two nights ago, in the hayloft. Tyler never said a word, but he had this *expression* on his face. And I could tell he was really pissed off. He pretends to be this supercool, easygoing guy, but where girls are concerned, he's not used to losing—especially to a 'raghead.' That's what he called Karim this morning, when he came to the theater looking for him," Holly added disgustedly.

One of the knots began to loosen, and Rickhauser tried

to slip the tail of rope through it. "What happened at the theater?"

"Karim and I slept on the couch in the ticket office last night. He was really scared to turn himself in, but he finally agreed I should call my professor. She offered to help us last night. I didn't have her home number with me, but there was a college directory there, so I called her office. I was just leaving a message when I heard someone in the auditorium. I went to check it out, and that's when I ran into Tyler. He was all bent out of shape. I was afraid he'd pick a fight. No way Karim could defend himself, not with his broken foot and Tyler outweighing him by about sixty pounds. I tried to draw Tyler away, but he caught me when I went to slip out the trapdoor on the stage. He dragged me out through the tunnel and across the field to Bethany Hill, and then—I couldn't believe it! He tied me up and threw me down here! But at least," she added angrily, "he didn't get Karim."

Rickhauser sighed. He had to tell her. "I'm afraid he did, Holly."

The girl froze. "What do you mean? Karim's all right, isn't he?"

"No, he's not."

"He's hurt?"

"Holly, I'm very sorry. Karim is dead."

"*What?* No! Oh, please—no! Tyler went back? But Karim was helpless! It was all we could do to make our way to the Lizzie last night, with his crutches and the snowfall and everything. It's all my fault!" she cried. "Tyler pretended to be his friend, but I should have seen how jealous he was! And then I had to go and give Karim those stupid skates! Oh, God, I'm sorry! I'm so sorry...."

Rocking as she cried, the girl kept thudding against Rickhauser's back. Her grief seemed genuine, he thought, and his instinct was to comfort her. But there was something about this whole affair that still didn't gel, and it nagged at him—not to mention the fact that every brush of her body sent bolts of searing pain through his head.

"Holly? Listen to me, please! I'm real sorry about Karim, but you have to keep still. I'm going to pass out if you don't quit banging into me."

She stopped at once. "No, don't do that! I've been alone for hours down here!"

"I'm going to try real hard not to, but if I do—"

"Don't, please!"

"If I *do*," Rickhauser repeated, "there's a cell phone in the left pocket of my overcoat."

"I heard it ring a while ago."

"There you go. I'll try to free your hands so you can get it out, but if I lose consciousness again, you're going to have to get the phone some other way—with your teeth, if you have to—and press 911."

"I can press it with my nose."

"Good girl. Tell them where we are." He paused. "Do you *know* where we are, exactly?"

"At Bethany Hill, under the barn. There's a trapdoor in the floor." Her voice broke, and she began to cry softly again.

"We'll get out of here, Holly, and we'll get Tyler Newman, I promise, but I need you to stay calm. Now, hold still," Rickhauser said sternly. He continued to struggle with the stubborn knots in her ropes. It was damned difficult, with so little range of movement, and his left hand getting more numb by the minute, his head pounding, and his arms and legs cramping up. Suddenly, another rivet of pain spiked his brain, and Rickhauser's body went rigid once more. The room began to spin. He heaved and would have been sick, except there was nothing left in his stomach to throw up.

"Are you okay?" Holly cried out behind him. "Please, don't die on me!"

He couldn't seem to find his vocal cords, much less the will to reply. Holding himself as still as he could, Rickhauser dredged up everything he had left, but knew he was in worse shape that he'd originally thought and was sinking fast. Holly's panicky voice sounded again, but indistinctly, echoing down a long tunnel. "I'm sorry," he whispered.

"It's *okay*," he heard her say. "I'll get the phone. You just rest, okay, Len? Please?"

Gratefully, Rickhauser relaxed, letting himself sink into the earth as his barrel chest rose and fell like a Pacific tide. He felt a warm glow envelop him. He saw his kids running on a beach—but they were small again, he noted curiously, the girls about seven and five, long pigtails streaming. His son wore tiny bathing trunks that swelled over a fat diaper as his pudgy legs toddled across the sand. Summer vacation, Rickhauser remembered. San Diego. He and Wendy were home from Maryland to visit the family. They'd taken the kids down to the beach at La Jolla to watch the seals, black and slick and playful, basking on the rocks.

Suddenly, he was out on the shoals himself, lying with the seals. Wendy waved and smiled at him from the shore. His father-in-law stood next to her, wearing that big, old straw hat of his, his heavily accented English ringing clear across the water, *"Time to get berries loaded! Time to go market!"* A truck rolled down the beach, a storm of dust clouds swirling behind it. But as it pulled alongside his family and the dust settled, Rickhauser saw that it wasn't Hiroshi Nakamura's old farm pickup. It was a U.S. Army transport. Soldiers jumped off the back and beckoned to

Hiroshi and Wendy and the kids. As each member of his family scrambled into the transport, the soldiers slapped red paper suns on their backs. Rickhauser bellowed in protest, but his voice was drowned out in the crashing of the waves and the barking of the seals around him. The transport pulled away. As it climbed the bluffs, Rickhauser saw his kids' tiny fingers and dark eyes over the rear gate. Wendy gazed back at him sadly, her beautiful, silky black hair blowing in the wind. Then they were gone. Rickhauser's throat constricted, and tears welled in his eyes.

One of the seals nudged him comfortingly, but it irritated him, tickling his nose. Hairy little devil, he thought, opening his eyes to blond curls.

"Hey, Len?" the seal asked. "Are you okay?" It was the girl. She'd worked her way around him once more. "Are you still with me?"

"My wife," Rickhauser wheezed. "Camp—during the war—took her back."

"It was a dream," Holly said gently.

He felt the panic inside him, a demon seed gone wild. "No! My kids, too! I saw—"

"You were hallucinating. They're *okay*, I promise! But Len? You've rolled forward. I can't budge you, and I can't get at the phone. Do you think you can try to move yourself back?"

He exhaled wearily. "—tired—".

"Try. You have to try!"

He lay still for a moment. "—tell Wendy—love her—?"

"That's your wife?"

"Yeah."

The girl's pale eyes filled with tears, and she shook her head. "You just hold on, and when we get out of here, you can tell her yourself, okay?"

32

"What's going on here, Leya?" John Merriman asked. "Who the hell *is* that guy?"

"The bane of my existence," she replied, sighing with frustration as vanAken's car disappeared down the road. She closed the front door and turned to Merriman's worried face. "We'd better talk, John. I haven't been fair with you, and you deserve some explanation."

His head gave a quick shake. "It can wait. You look awful, sweetheart."

"Why, thank you."

"You should be in bed, recuperating. You go lie down, and I'll fix you some tea. How about something to eat?"

"I'm fine," Leya said, unbuttoning her coat. "I couldn't eat."

Merriman rushed to help her out of it, then withdrew a wooden hanger from the hall closet. After he'd slipped it through the coat sleeves, he fastened the top button and slapped the fabric, brushing off dust she'd picked up from the stage at the Lizzie. The hall light glinted off his tortoiseshell glasses as he gave the coat a shake, cleared a space in the closet, hung it up, and smoothed it down one more time before finally shutting the door. Massaging her tender neck, Leya watched his precise movements with irritation and guilt.

Turning at last, he fingered the sleeve of the blue hospital gown stuffed into her skirt. "What happened to your own clothes?"

"Lost them to the emergency-room scissors."

His knees suddenly dipped, and his eyes went wide. "Your neck is all scraped and covered with bruises!"

"They didn't tell you what happened?"

"Just that you were attacked inside the theater."

She hedged—loath to give details, knowing it would just set off another round of horrified exclamations. "Someone tried to strangle me. The emergency-room staff cut me out of my clothes to avoid too much movement, in case I had a neck injury—routine precaution."

"Oh, Leya!" he fretted, reaching out for her.

She stepped back. "I'm *fine!*" It was the umpteenth time she'd said it that day, and she was sick to death of the refrain and of her own voice, repeating it ad nauseam. "Look, how about if you put on the kettle while I change, and then we'll talk, okay?"

Merriman hesitated, then nodded and strode up the hall, coattails flapping like impeccable Burberry sails. Leya shook her head wearily and cut through the living room toward her makeshift bedroom. Passing the fireplace, she sensed something out of place—no small feat, given the room's general state of disorder. She stepped closer and found a picture frame, facedown on the brick hearth, surrounded by tiny shards of glass. Once glance at her photo collection on the mantel, and she knew which one was missing. She also had a reasonably good idea how it had come to be where it was. She crouched and turned over the shot of her father, taken years earlier during his East African posting. He was leaning back in a heavy, scrolled mahogany chair, one hand gripping the old ebony-and-ivory walking stick propped between his knees, his expression austere and ironic, like some powerful chief dispensing tribal justice. Broken glass had scored a deep, diagonal gash across his face. The picture was ruined.

Hand trembling from emotions she could scarcely identify, much less deal with, Leya laid the picture back on the hearth, facedown, then rose and went to the dining room. She rifled through boxes until she found socks, underthings, a sweatshirt, and a faded pair of jeans. Her skirt and the hospital gown slipped to the floor, as she went numbly through the motions of changing.

From the kitchen came the hollow sound of water running into the kettle. On reconsideration, Leya thought, the prospect of bed held some appeal—although for none of the right reasons. She could tell John she was exhausted, send him away, then crawl under the duvet and pull it over her head to block out the world. A tremor ran through her as she saw the scheme's fatal flaw. The scent of Peter and the memory of his touch lay in ambush under that quilt. Anyway, hiding from the mess of her life might be tempting, but it was gutless. There was no avoiding the painful choices forced on her—choices she'd already made, Leya realized, although they brought neither comfort nor resolution, only more problems.

Running a hand distractedly through her hair, she steeled herself for the next ordeal, which was to face the music with John. A high-pitched whistle interrupted her thoughts. It started, stopped, then started again.

"Leya?" he called from the kitchen. "What is that?"

"It sounds like an alarm of some sort, or—no! I know what it is."

As it sounded again, Leya spun around, eyes searching for Peter's cellular phone. She tore the duvet off the bed.

Nothing. She was halfway to the living room when it sounded once more. Upstairs. Flying into the hall, taking the steps two at a time, she rounded the top of the stairs as it rang again. *Hold on!* she prayed. She charged across the floor and dove for the pile of bedding in the turret. Fabric flew as she tossed the blankets aside—and found it. Flipping open the compact phone, she scanned the face for an answer key. Her finger stabbed a button, and she put it to her ear. The phone rang again. She tried another one. "Hello?" she said breathlessly.

Silence. Then a peevish voice asked, *"Who is this?"*

"Leya Nash. Who's calling, please?"

"Special Agent in Charge Curtis Pullen, FBI Boston field office. I was trying to reach one of my agents, but I must have the wrong number."

"Not if you want Peter vanAken. This is his phone."

"Oh—good. Let me speak with him."

"He's not here. He left the phone behind by accident—but I can get a message to him," Leya added hurriedly.

"What did you say your name was?" She repeated it. "Aren't you the professor who was attacked this morning at Mount Abbey College?"

"Yes. I just got back from the hospital. Agent vanAken was here, but he left a few minutes ago to meet Assistant Deputy Rickhauser."

"I've been trying to reach the assistant deputy myself. I have urgent information for him."

"I can take a message," she offered again.

"No, thank you. I need to fax him some information. If you could ask one of them to call me as soon as poss—"

"I have a PC and modem. Why don't you send the fax here, to my house?"

"I'm afraid not. This is confidential."

"I'm security cleared, and no one but the assistant deputy or Agent vanAken will see it, I promise."

"You're security cleared? How's that?"

"My father's a retired CIA station chief named Carter Nash. Believe me, Mr. Pullen, my background's been checked from here till doomsday. I also know Len Rickhauser," Leya added, going for broke. "He and my father are associates from way back." No need to mention that they despised one another. "So if this information is urgent…"

"It is, but I don't—"

"I'll turn on my system right now, and take it to them immediately. They've gone to a farm just outside town." When Pullen hesitated, then sighed, Leya knew she'd won. She walked back toward the staircase, phone at her ear, and gave the FBI man her fax number as she made her way down to turn on the computer and set it up for receiving.

She had hung up the cellular phone and was in her dining room, rolling out the computer table and booting up the PC, when she felt John behind her. "What's going on?"

"That was Agent vanAken's cell phone. He dropped it upstairs last night. Someone from the Bureau was trying to reach him or his boss with an urgent message."

"What are you doing now?"

"Setting up to receive a fax." Leya winced as she bent down to the baseboard phone jack, checking the modem connection. "I promised to deliver it to them."

"Deliver it? Leya, you can't be running around all over town! You just got out of the hospital."

Rising as the PC monitor came to life, Leya opened the communications software, then leaned back in her chair. "The man on the phone said this is urgent, John. Holly

Stroud is still missing. The fellow she was with yesterday has been murdered. If she's still alive and there's anything I can do to help her, I intend to do it."

He sighed. "You're right, of course. But when this fax comes, I'll go and deliver it."

"You can't. The only reason they're sending it here is because I assured this guy I'd been security-cleared up the wazoo, because of my dad. I promised to hand the fax directly to Peter or Rickhauser. He's the FBI assistant deputy who's out here with him," she added.

Her phone rang, then stopped mid-jangle. The PC hummed as it kicked into "receive" mode. Merriman shuffled restlessly while Leya watched the screen—ostensibly tracking the transmission's progress, but mostly avoiding the questions she sensed hung in the air.

"Who exactly is this Peter vanAken, Leya? It seems to me he's more than just some FBI agent looking for one of your students."

She took a deep breath and nodded. Now or never. "Why don't you have a seat?" Merriman perched himself on the bed, and she swiveled to face him, hating that he was on the very spot where Peter had been lying next to her, only hours earlier. Watching his anxious face, Leya debated how to tell him gently, then decided on simple, brutal truth.

"Peter's someone I met years ago in Beirut, John, when my father was posted there. We fell in love, but it was during the Lebanese civil war. He was kidnapped and held hostage for four years. Afterward—well, that's a very long story, but the bottom line is that the experience ripped us apart. It wasn't Peter's fault, or mine, and it certainly wasn't what either of us wanted."

"When did you start seeing him again?" Merriman asked darkly.

"Last night was the first time I'd seen him in a decade. I didn't even know he was with the FBI until he showed up here, looking for Holly Stroud. But now..." Her voice drifted off.

"You've fallen for him all over again, haven't you?"

She shook her head. "Not 'all over again.' I never stopped loving him, even when I gave up hope of ever seeing him again. It's always weighed on me, like a stone in my heart. I think that's why I've never fully connected with any other person since. Although," she added gently, taking his hand, "I came closer with you than with anyone else, John. You're a fine man. Any woman would be a fool not to grab you with both hands and hold on tight."

"So what does that make you?"

"A fool," she said. "Guilty as charged."

He fell silent for a moment. "What happens now?"

"I honestly don't know."

"I hate to point out the obvious, Leya, but that guy seemed real reluctant to stick around here, and I don't think it's just because I said I was your fiancé."

"You noticed that, did you?" The PC whistled, signaling that the fax transmission was complete. Leya swung back toward the equipment. After switching on the printer, she punched in a few strokes on the keyboard, transferring the file. When the paper feeder began to churn, she faced Merriman once more. "You're right. I've carried around hurt for a long time, but that was nothing compared to what happened to Peter—physical torture was almost the least of it. His way of coping was to shut down emotionally. At this point, I'm not sure that's going to change."

"If that's the case, what kind of future can you possibly hope for with him?"

She was lifting the sheets out of the printer tray as they came through. "Maybe none. I'm trying not to kid myself about that.'' The first page, she noted, was a case summary of some sort. The second was a brief, two-line report from the FBI's national fingerprint-identification center, and the third was a grainy copy of a photograph that seemed to have been culled from some ancient surveillance file. Shutting off the machines, Leya rose from her oak chair, scanning the photo curiously as she headed for the front hall. ''I'd better go drop these off.''

''I'll drive you,'' Merriman offered.

''No, it's—'' Leya gasped and stopped in her tracks.

''What? What is it?''

Stunned, she stared at the grainy faxed photo, then back at the other sheets in her hand. *''No,''* she breathed. ''Oh, Christ—!''

''What?'' he repeated.

Leya folded and jammed the sheets into the pockets of her jeans, then tore open the hall closet and rammed her feet into the first pair of shoes she found there. When she ripped her coat off the hanger, its top button bounced across the foyer and tumbled into a corner, pinging with the dull sound of plastic on hardwood. ''I have to go. Lock up when you leave, please?'' She headed for the door.

''Leya, wait!'' Merriman protested.

Braking, doubling back to grab her car keys off the hall table, she finally noticed his stricken expression. Leya paused, closed her eyes briefly, and squeezed his arm. ''I'm so sorry, John. This is a lousy way to say goodbye, I know, but—'' She gave a resigned shrug. ''I wish you nothing but happiness. I hope you find the person you deserve. But right now, I really, *really* have to go. I'm sorry,'' she repeated lamely.

Then she left him.

Newton, Massachusetts: 7:09 p.m.

After the fax had gone off to Winslow, Curtis Pullen slumped in the FBI surveillance van, palms pressed into his eyes as he tried to decide whether he dared sneak home to grab a few hours' sleep. The phone rang, but he let the tech take it. "For you," Leung said. "It's the SAC. I mean, Arch McCreary, the *regular*—"

Pullen extended his arm. "Let me have it." His eyes stayed closed and his forehead rested in his free hand as he held the receiver to his ear. "Hi, Arch."

"Hey, Curtis! Been watching you guys on the news all day. Thought I'd call in, see how things are going out there."

"Oh, just peachy," Pullen replied wearily. "I got nine corpses here, one more in the boonies, two crimes that may or may not be related, a bunch of fanatic Arabs with iron-clad alibis, another suspect who's disappeared off the face of the earth, an irate ambassador who wants my little pink ass nailed to his wall, an insubordinate agent who's incommunicado, an ADIC who's gone AWOL, and a mess of contradictory and mutually exclusive shit for evidence— but other than that, Arch, everything's swell, thanks. How's it with you?"

McCreary chuckled. "Not too bad, except I'm getting antsy, sittin' around the house all day. Had about all I can take of Geraldo, and the wife won't let me watch the soaps—says they're too risqué, might give me ideas."

"How's the treatment going?"

"Got that polyp removed. They use local anesthetic, you know, burn 'er off with a laser. Zap! Real slick, except for the smell of your own flesh fryin'. Kind of like goin' to a barbecue, and come to find out *you're* the main course!"

"They got you doing chemo?"

"Yeah, couple more rounds to go. Knocks me for a loop for a day or two, but the doc says if I feel like it, no reason

I can't go into the office in between times. Thought I might work on some of the old files, maybe take some of the admin workload off your hands."

"That's great. Be good to have your ugly mug back around the place."

"You sure about that, Curtis? I mean, I don't want to cramp your style, now you got your chance to shine."

Pullen exhaled deeply. "You know what, Arch? I'm not feelin' real shiny right about now. I'm beginning to think this job of yours is a hell of a lot more trouble than it's worth. So how 'bout you get yourself better fast, and take the goddam thing back?"

Winslow, Massachusetts: 7:13 p.m.

Turning up Hancock Drive, bordering the western edge of the Mount Abbey campus, vanAken spotted a pair of headlights approaching from the opposite direction. He slowed and pulled the Taurus to one side of the narrow road, peering at the other car as it squeezed past. It was a Winslow-based Checker cab. The cabbie, who seemed to be alone, gave him a nod.

After he'd passed, vanAken continued until he came to a wooden mailbox. Built in the shape of an old-fashioned tugboat, it was mounted on a wooden fence post. Artificial geraniums sprouted from its pseudo-smokestack, and the hand-painted name on the prow, spot-lit from below, said Bethany Hill. He parked the Taurus next to it and got out. Across the road, through a copse of trees, he made out the flood-lit, classical profile of the Elizabeth Wilkins Theater, the rear view of the idyllic scene he'd observed the previous night.

VanAken turned and walked up the drive, scanning for Rickhauser's car. Lights were on in the downstairs of the house, but the ADIC's ride was nowhere to be seen. The only vehicle in the yard was an old Chevy van parked between the house and the barn, which stood behind and to one side of it.

As vanAken approached the house, someone passed at a window. The place was an old, Colonial-style clapboard with a steeply pitched, dormered roofline, painted white with black trim. Shuttered casement windows flanked the front door, and through tieback curtains, vanAken saw the kitchen on one side of the front door and, on the other, a sitting room furnished with pine furniture upholstered in gingham and calico. Mounting the stoop, he reached for the bell, but his hand paused when a shadow fell from the kitchen window across the wooden planks of the stoop. Voices murmured through the glass.

Holding himself near the wall, vanAken sidled up to the window and peered in. A small woman with the round, settled body of middle age was walking toward a wooden trestle table set near the center of the room. The sleeves of her embroidered blue shirt were rolled back above the cuffs of a white turtleneck, and she wore the shirt loose and open over a long flowered skirt. VanAken inched forward, then froze, startled. Carter Nash sat at one end of the table, coatless, in a blue plaid shirt and dark pants, one of those bloody walking sticks he always toted lying next to him. VanAken watched, mesmerized and repulsed, as the woman's silver blond mop of hair bent toward him. She lifted the old man's weathered face, cupped it between her hands, and kissed him full on the lips. Nash's liver-spotted hands slipped over her hips and across her backside, pulling her close. The woman straightened, and she nestled his head against her ribs as she caressed his snowy hair.

Pulling back, pressing himself into the cold wooden

clapboard siding, vanAken felt his heart take up a furious rhythm. What right did that man have to comfort? he fumed. His scarred fingers reached for the hard butt of his gun, as lost years and waylaid justice tangled in his brain. Now, he thought. It could all end, here and now.

VanAken forced his hand down. Rickhauser. *Remember what you came for.*

That must be Newman's mother, he thought. Leya had said her name was Joanna, but hadn't mentioned that Nash was involved with her. Another private compartment? *Thank you very much for that, Leya.* Although, vanAken conceded, it wasn't like he'd encouraged her to talk about the old goat's retirement pastimes. It was even possible she didn't know about these two. Keeping a casual mistress or two on the side was typical Nash behavior. Leya had always seemed to regard her father as some noble, tragically lonely figure. VanAken hadn't tried to disabuse her of the notion when they were together in Beirut, but he'd been aware even then that the reality was a little less saintly.

Lost in his dark thoughts, it was only when the wooden porch vibrated under his feet that vanAken realized he'd been spotted.

"What do you think you're doing?"

A tall, fair-haired young man in jeans and a red down ski jacket mounted the top step. It was the waiter vanAken had seen the previous evening, attending to Leya and her father at their corner table—Tyler Newman, himself, apparently. The strapping guy dipped slightly to one side, glancing through the window—bigger than himself, van-Aken registered warily. Not as big as Rickhauser, maybe, but damn solid. Plus, he had youth on his side.

Newman pulled back from the window and scowled.

"Who the hell are you? And what are you doing, spying on my mother?"

"You're Tyler Newman?"

"That's right."

VanAken reached into his pocket and withdrew his badge. "Special Agent vanAken, FBI. I'd like a few words with you."

Newman's eyes narrowed as he studied the badge, then shifted to vanAken's left, where the front door was opening. "Tyler? What's going on out here?" a voice called.

"I found an FBI agent out here, Ma, spying on you."

VanAken turned to face an anxious Joanna Newman. Another shadow fell on the open door, and Carter Nash's scowling face appeared behind her. "VanAken!"

"Do you know this man, Carter?"

"He's the one—the one who turned my daughter against me!"

"Oh, dear!" The woman's expression hardened. "What do you want?"

"I'm looking for a colleague of mine," vanAken said evenly. "He left word he was coming here. His name is Rickhauser, an assistant deputy with the FBI."

Nash's scowl deepened.

"Has he been here?" vanAken asked.

"Not to my knowledge," Mrs. Newman said.

"How about you, Tyler? Have you seen him? He's a real big man, hard to miss."

Newman glanced at the older couple in the doorway and he shook his head. "No."

"Well, maybe he got called elsewhere. But as long as I'm here, I wonder if I could ask you a few questions."

"You've no business being here!" Nash snapped.

"As a matter of fact, I do. But if Tyler doesn't want to

cooperate, no problem. I'll just arrest him and take him in for questioning. Is that what you'd prefer?''

"No, of course not!" Joanna Newman said hurriedly. She patted Nash's arm. "It's all right, Carter. We'll let him ask his questions, and that'll be that. All right?''

"I still don't like it."

"Tyler? You don't have any problem with answering this man's questions in the kitchen, do you, son?''

The burly jock peered nervously behind him, as if he expected to see enemy Mongol hordes come galloping up the drive, but the night was still and cold as death. "I guess not.''

"Good. Let's get this over with." Mrs. Newman was a mother grizzly defending her den. She opened the door wide to let vanAken and her son pass into the house. His old nemesis, vanAken noted, looked inclined to finish the job crazy Ali had botched in Beirut. The old man's finger jabbed the air. "I'm watching you!''

VanAken returned his glower. "Nash—don't push your luck with me.''

Leya peered through the windows of the black Taurus. "Damn!'' she muttered.

She made her way up the drive to the old farmhouse and immediately spotted Peter's back at a window to the right of the front door. Hovering by the trunk of an old oak tree, Leya watched him, trying to decide what to do. He seemed, by the movements of his head and hands, to be talking to someone else in the room. She shifted position and caught a glimpse of Tyler Newman's strawberry-blond head.

When Leya finally approached the door, it was Tyler's mother who opened to her knock. Joanna's bright blue eyes went wide. "Leya! What are *you* doing here?''

"I need to speak to Agent vanAken, Joanna. I know he's here."

"Yes, he is. But I should warn you, dear, so is your father."

"My—! Oh, great!"

"He's very upset. Maybe this isn't a good time—"

Leya shook her head. "I have an urgent message for the agent."

"Well, I guess you'd better come in then, hadn't you?"

"After you," Leya said. The older woman led the way, and as they entered the kitchen, Leya spotted her father off to the left, leaning heavily on his cane, his eyes on Tyler near the head of an old wooden trestle table. Joanna put a hand on his shoulder, and Nash glanced down at her. Leya realized she was outside the range of his limited peripheral vision, and he hadn't spotted her.

VanAken had, however, and he posed the same question as Joanna, although his tone was more irritated than surprised. "What are you *doing* here?"

"I need to talk to you."

Carter Nash spun around. "Leya! What the—!"

"I told you there's nothing to talk about," vanAken said, ignoring him. "And even if there were, this is hardly the time or the—"

"Oh, lighten up, Peter! This isn't about you and me. I have a message for you—from someone named Pullen? He called your cell phone not long after you left. I found it upstairs and answered it."

"Fine. I'll call him back later. Now go home, would you?"

Nash harrumphed. "For once, we agree."

"Stay out of this, Dad! Peter, it can't wait."

"Why? What did he want?"

Leya glanced at the others, then cocked her head toward

the doorway. "Outside. I promised him I'd deliver the message in private."

VanAken sighed, then pointed a finger at Tyler. "I'll be back in half a minute. Stay put." He crossed the floor and gave Leya an exasperated look. "Let's go."

She turned, but before they'd gone two steps, Leya heard a click, and felt the rush of air behind her as Peter spun around. Following suit, she saw a gun in Tyler's hand, trained on them. He shook his reddish blond head. "I don't think so," he said suspiciously. "You two better just sit yourselves down."

Leya sighed. Glancing at vanAken, she held up her thumb and forefinger. "We were that close. If you were just a tad less pigheaded—"

"What's going on here?" he demanded.

"What's going on," Tyler Newman replied, "is I don't have time for this shit. Now, sit down and shut up!"

"You hold, mister!" Nash snapped. "That's my daughter you're addressing!"

"You shut up, too, old man!"

"Tyler!" his mother protested. "Don't speak to Carter like that!"

"Listen, Ma—if this G-man and that big old coot I caught snooping around the barn have already shown up, how long do you figure it'll be before the whole goddam army rolls in here?"

"Rickhauser *did* show up," vanAken said. "Where is he?"

"Tied up with other business."

"What about Holly?" Leya asked.

"She's the other business," Tyler said, grinning at his own cleverness. His smile vanished as quickly as it had appeared, and he pulled two chairs out from under the trestle table. "Now, siddown!"

When they still hesitated, the gun shifted, and Leya found herself peering along the wrong end of its sights, straight into Tyler's clear, blue eyes. She felt Peter bristle beside her, like an animal tensing to spring.

"You may think you can drop me, fibbie-boy," Tyler warned, never taking his eyes off her, "but she'll be dead before you do."

"For God's sake, vanAken, sit!" Nash ordered. Van-Aken dropped into the chair, and as Leya settled beside him, her father turned to Joanna. "What's going on here? What's that boy of yours been up to?"

"Tyler's a fine young man, Carter, you know that."

"Sure," vanAken said. "A swell guy who assaulted and murdered a young engineering student. Right, Tyler? Now that you've shown your hand, I'm guessing you also planted that bomb Holly Stroud's car dropped yesterday. Oh, by the way," he added, turning to Nash, "your girl-friend's terrific kid also lynched your daughter this morning."

"He what?"

"I never touched her!" Tyler protested.

"No, he didn't," Leya agreed.

Peter frowned at her. "What do you mean?"

She shook her head, exasperated. "That's what I wanted to tell you. They found a fingerprint on a bomb fragment recovered at the Data-Trax site. Pullen faxed the ID results for me to give to you or Rickhauser. As I was driving over here, the penny dropped. I realized the bomber was the same person who attacked me at the Lizzie."

"Who?" Peter asked.

Leya reached into her jeans pocket and pulled out the folded, crumpled fax sheets. "It was that smell like Ivory Snow that clinched it," she said, looking up at Joanna Newman as she smoothed them on the table before her.

"I couldn't put my finger on what scent I'd picked up at the theater, until I saw this picture of you that came with the fingerprint information. And then, I remembered I'd noticed the same scent when you sat with my Dad and me at Tyler's."

Nash was incredulous. "They found *Joanna's* fingerprint on the bomb? Impossible!"

"No, Dad. Her name isn't Joanna Newman. It's Annabelle Deaver, and she's an old sixties radical that everybody thought had been dead for twenty-five years." Leya slid the fax sheets across the table toward her father and the older woman.

"Rickhauser was right all along," vanAken said. "He just had the suspect wrong. He kept saying the MO in the Data-Trax incident fit a serial bomber case he'd been following for years. He suspected a member of the Weather Underground, some guy named Michael Gore, who'd been involved in a Greenwich Village blast that ostensibly killed Annabelle Deaver and three others."

"The government didn't believe it, but Michael did die that day," Joanna said sadly. She studied the photo with Nash, whose stunned gaze alternated between it and her. "Look how young I was, Carter! Pretty, too, don't you think? I could sit on my hair back then. Michael loved it. Of course, he was beautiful himself. Tyler looks a lot like his father," she added.

His gun still trained on Leya, the object of her adoring smile was busy opening and closing kitchen drawers. Finally he seemed to find what he wanted—a roll of black electrical tape. Leya watched as he passed his gun to his mother, then walked behind the chairs. Joanna put a little distance between herself and the others, while her son patted down vanAken's jacket and relieved him of his weapon. Tucking it into the waistband of his jeans, Tyler went to work binding Peter's hands to the spindle-backed chair.

Peter, meantime, was studying Joanna. "Tyler wasn't Michael Gore's only son, was he? There was another child in Michigan."

The older woman's face contorted. "Ellen Fraser's little abomination! You know, they used to say that the only position for women in the left was prone, and Ellen was living proof of that. She was weak and unworthy of our trust. Then, five years after she defected, she had the nerve to give an interview to *Time* magazine—one of those 'Where are they now?' pieces on the radical left. Like *she'd* ever been a leader of the movement," Joanna said contemptuously. "There was Ellen, in her fat-cat Grosse Pointe mansion with that pig of a doctor she'd married, lying about Michael, saying how she was raising their son to see the error of his father's ways. And the little monster—staring at the camera with Michael's beautiful eyes! But *he* wasn't Michael Gore's heir. *My* son was! And I raised Tyler to be a visionary and a leader, just like his father."

"So you killed Ellen Fraser and her five-year-old child."

"Well, of course. I had to, didn't I?"

"And the Columbia prof you mailed a bomb to?"

"Lionel Monk, another traitor. He'd had links to the Black Panthers. They were supposed to be allies of the Weather Underground, but we always suspected that Lionel was an FBI informer. After Michael and Kyle and the others died in that FBI raid, I was convinced of it. I couldn't believe the bastard escaped."

"And the others?" Peter asked. "Obviously, they were marking anniversaries of the explosion, but the targets—?"

She shrugged. "An army recruiting center, obviously, because they were always the enemy. And the FBI, for what they did to Michael—except that device never reached its destination. The stupid mail was so slow, the thing went off while it was still in a post office." Joanna brightened. "But what a stroke of luck we had today! When we saw that federal man on TV this morning, I just *knew* from his big, ugly mug he was the same one who'd destroyed our headquarters and murdered my comrades. And then, I come home this afternoon and Tyler tells me he's got the awful man trussed up under the barn. Your father would be *so* proud of you, son!" She beamed.

The revolutionary heir, however, was too busy strapping Leya to her chair to bask in his mother's praise. Leya winced as he bound her wrists tightly.

"Joanna—or do you prefer Annabelle?" vanAken ventured.

"Oh, call me Joanna, I'm used to it. I haven't been Annabelle for a long time. Of course, by tomorrow, I'll be someone else again. We've got our new identities all ready, don't we, Tyler? It's not like I haven't done this before, you know."

"Joanna," Peter continued steadily, "they had trouble identifying those victims in the Greenwich Village blast, but apparently they knew from bone fragments that one was female. Who was that?"

She waved a hand airily. "Some flower child Michael had picked up in Central Park. Michael was like Tyler, you see—charismatic. People used to follow him like puppies. Although you both could stand to be a little more discriminating," she chided her son. "A revolutionary movement is the vanguard of the people—the natural leaders. We'll take over when rotten government finally crumbles, but people like Duncan and his friends—well, they have their uses, I suppose, helping to disrupt the system. But they're not leadership material, are they?'' She waved a hand at Peter. ''See what a nuisance Duncan's lack of discipline created for us?''

''Sorry, Ma,'' her son muttered from behind Leya's back.

Joanna slapped her hands together—as if she were shaking off pastry flour Leya thought, ''No matter. In—'' she glanced at the sunflower clock on the wall ''—fourteen minutes, all this will be erased, and the movement will move on.''

Leya looked over at her father. His color had risen, and he leaned heavily on his cane. Finally, he seemed to find his voice. ''What do you mean? What happens in fourteen minutes?''

''At 8:00 p.m. precisely, Bethany Hill will be no more. I've had explosives laid out around the perimeter of the buildings for months now, as a precaution, while I prepared for this anniversary—although, to be honest, I *had* hoped we might be able to stay on this time. I've done a lot of moving in the last twenty-five years, but I'd gotten attached to the place. If Holly and Karim had died at Data-Trax like they were supposed to, the authorities would have been so fixated on the Arab connection that we might have been able to ride this one out. I didn't care who got credit, as long as our objective was achieved.'' She shook her head fretfully. ''I just don't understand what happened! Karim said his appointment was for four-thirty. I set the timer for four fifty-five, just in case they ran late. But they said on the news it went off after five.'' She tapped her cheek thoughtfully. ''The watch must have been running slow. It was a cheap one I'd picked up over at Haddad's. I needed the plastic crystal, but they don't always keep the best time. Still, I don't understand how those two got away.''

VanAken sighed. "The hubcap fell off her car after Holly hit the parking curb.''

"Oh, she *would,* wouldn't she?" Joanna said, irritated. "That girl is just the worst driver! And what do her parents give her? A Mercedes, and she—!''

"Am I to understand,'' Nash interrupted, "that the rest of us are to die, while you and this son of yours make off for parts unknown, assuming new identities?''

Joanna looked up at him, eyes wide. "Oh, Carter, not *you!* Is that what you've been thinking? Of course not! You've been really helpful.''

"I beg your pardon?''

"Well, you *would* have been, if we'd needed an alibi after Karim was found. You'd have been a terrific witness. You're *so* authoritative. We were awake when Tyler came in from work last night, weren't we? And I made sure you saw him again this morning, before we left. I knew he'd gone out again in between, of course, but you slept like a baby through that, sweet thing. Anyway, we want you to join us, don't we, Tyler?''

Her son nodded—although, Leya thought, he seemed a little underenthused about the idea.

"You know what the really funny thing is, Carter?'' Joanna asked. "Originally, you were to be the target for this anniversary!''

"*I* was?''

"Yes, after you told me about your background. I'd been scouting for a target for months, and there you were, right in front of me—a former top CIA official! But they treated you shabbily, didn't they? I realized you'd be a brilliant addition to the movement, with your insider information—help us pick out weak spots in the enemy's defenses. As an alternative, of course, we did have Ambassador Stroud's daughter—what a pompous ass *he* is, don't you think? Originally, we'd planned to recruit her—"

"Until the fucking raghead came along," Tyler muttered.

"Holly simply wasn't good enough, son, for you or the movement," Joanna said, shaking her head. "And that poor, naive Karim, with his reluctant radical connections and his big interview at Data-Trax. He thought they built medical equipment. We know differently, don't we, Carter? *We* know all about how their satellites spy on us."

"Us?" Leya's eyebrows went up. "Americans, you mean?"

The older woman gave her a pitying look, as if she were mentally deficient. "Well, of course. Except those of us who take precautions."

"What kind of precautions?"

Joanna pushed up her sleeves, revealing deep scars on her inner arms. They looked as if a piranha had been nibbling on them. "I was in hospital twice, for an appendectomy, and to give birth to Tyler. That's when they do it. They like to get you when you're at your weakest, you see. They'll tell you they're drawing blood, or putting in intravenous tubes, but what they're really doing is implanting tiny microtransmitters, smaller than the human eye can see. That's how the satellites keep track of us. You can be sure I cut *mine* out just as soon as I got home," she added smugly, dropping her sleeves.

Nash shook his head in disbelief. "You're a raving lunatic."

"Don't say that, Carter! I'm going to save you."

"Save me? *Save me?*" he bellowed. "You tried to murder my daughter! What makes you think I'd want anything to do with you?''

"I didn't plan to kill her! At breakfast this morning, she didn't seem to have a clue. But then Tyler called in a panic just after you left, said Holly was claiming she'd left a message at Leya's office saying *he'd* bombed Data-Trax. I couldn't have Leya blabbing something like that, could I? I went by Mount Abbey to check up on her, and when I saw her running to the theater, I knew Holly hadn't been bluffing.''

"Actually, she *was* bluffing," Leya said. "She never mentioned Tyler's name on that message.''

"Really? What a duplicitous little liar she is!" Joanna's face softened once more, and she gave Leya a bland smile. "No matter. I knew you'd find Karim, and I had to slow things down, didn't I? We weren't ready to leave. I needed time to dig up our identity papers, contact some sources, pack.''

"So you followed me to the theater—where I, helpfully, even left the doors open for you.''

"Joanna, how *could* you?" Nash cried.

"She betrayed you, Carter! She went over to the enemy's side. But not to worry. You'll come with Tyler and me. We'll be your family now, and we'll work together, until the whole, rotten superstructure collapses.''

Leya's father fell silent. His color was dangerously high, she noted. She recalled the medication she'd picked up for him that morning. Had he taken it or had he forgotten, with all the day's disruptions? How many skipped doses and how much stress did it take for his blood pressure to go critical?

"You won't get away this time, Joanna," Peter said. "Forensics have come a long way in twenty-five years— DNA typing, just for starters. Even if you blow this place up, they're going to know how many bodies are here, and whose they are. And, who's missing.''

"We'll be long gone by the time they figure it out. People go underground in this country every day. You people aren't half as clever as you think," she said contemptuously. She turned back to Nash. "Eleven minutes, Carter. We really have to be going. What do you say? Are you game?''

His hands trembled on his stick, and his voice, when he spoke, was almost feeble. "You're on my side, Joanna? You want me with you?''

"That's what I'm trying to tell you, sweet man! I'll prove it," she said brightly, turning the gun on Peter. "I'll execute this one for you. You can watch him die before we go. Would you like that?'' It was as if she were asking him if he wanted dessert, Leya thought.

"Dad, tell her no! She's nuts, can't you see that?''

Her father's gaze shifted listlessly from her to Peter.

"Please, Dad—I love him!''

Nash's breathing came slow and labored. Suddenly, his neck seemed to go limp, and his head lolled to one side. His legs buckled, and he keeled over, facedown on the planked pine floor. Leya and Joanna screamed in unison. Leya tried to pull out of her constraints, but Tyler clamped a firm hand on her shoulder.

His mother fell to her knees beside the old man. *"Carter!''* Laying the gun aside, she turned him over onto his back, frantically patting his face.

"Dad!" Leya cried softly, watching them. His eyes were closed, and although she tracked his chest closely, she saw no sign of movement.

Joanna bent close to him. "Oh, no, Carter!'' she groaned, collapsing, grief-stricken, across his prostrate form, her tears running into his collar.

For a long moment, the others watched the old couple on the floor, waiting for Joanna to accept that he was gone. Leya was too horrified to speak. Finally Tyler said, "Ma? Come on, Ma, get up. We've got to go. He's done for."

Nash's blue eyes popped open. "Not quite," he said, shoving the woman's prostrate form aside. As Joanna rolled onto the floor, eyes closed, Leya saw a broad red patch in the center of her embroidered shirt.

Tyler let out a roar, but his cry was halted in mid-breath by a deafening crack. Leya gasped as he slumped across her shoulder, then slid to the floor between the two chairs—quite dead, she realized, looking at his strawberry-blond hair, awash in red. Stunned, she and Peter both looked back at her father. Joanna's gun was in his right hand, a thin wisp of smoke rising from the barrel. His left hand gripped the headless ebony shaft of his cane. Leya's eyes moved once more to the woman beside him. The red patch on Joanna's shirt had spread. The carved ivory handle of her father's walking stick rose above it, like statuary in a fast-blooming garden of roses. It took a second for Leya's confused mind to understand that he'd had the thing retrofit to hold a blade, and that probably every damn cane in his collection had been similarly modified. No wonder he'd always been so possessive about them.

Her father, meantime, lumbered slowly to his feet, his blue plaid shirt smeared with blood. From a butcher block on the kitchen counter, he withdrew a carving knife, then walked over and loomed behind vanAken.

"Planning to put that in my back?"

"Don't push your luck with *me*, buster," Nash grunted. He bent and sliced through the electrical tape binding van-Aken's hands and arms, then moved to his daughter and cut her free, as well. "Come on. We'd better find those other two before the place blows."

"The barn," Leya said, rubbing her wrists as she got to her feet. She glanced at her watch. "Nine minutes."

"Unless the timer's running fast this time," vanAken noted.

They ran for the front door, but as they stepped onto the porch, they were blinded by spotlights that suddenly kerchunked to life around the perimeter of the farmyard. "FBI! Hands up!" a voice shouted through a bullhorn.

"*I'm* FBI!" vanAken shouted back, although he lifted his arms as a precaution. Leya and her father followed suit. She squinted, but couldn't make out a soul behind the glaring lights.

"It's Agent vanAken!" someone yelled. "It's okay, let 'em pass."

The three ran down the steps and toward the barn, where they were intercepted by half-a-dozen people in FBI windbreakers and police uniforms. "Collins? Berger? That you?" vanAken asked, shading his eyes. "What are you doing here?"

"We got a call about five minutes ago from Holly Stroud. She said she and the ADIC were being held hostage here. We were just scrambling into position. We've called for SWAT backup, but—"

"No need," vanAken said. "The suspects are inside the house, dead. Rickhauser and the girl are under this barn somewhere. What we *do* need is the bomb squad, stat!"

A cop in a Winslow PD uniform and Kevlar vest shook his head. "Haven't got a local bomb squad. We'll call in the county boys, but it'll take at least twenty minutes for 'em to get here."

VanAken pulled open the barn door. "No time. The entire place is primed to blow at eight o'clock, but I wouldn't count on accuracy. Collins, Berger, you better get everybody back, now! And I mean *way* back!" Van-

Aken glanced at Leya and her father. "You two—go! I'll find them, and we'll follow."

Leya gave him a scathing glance. "Get serious!" she said, pushing past him and running into the barn.

"Get out of there, Leya!" her father yelled from the open doorway. Glancing back, she saw him being grappled and held by a couple of the burly guys in windbreakers.

"I intend to, just as soon as we find them!" She whirled around once more. The barn was lit by a line of bare bulbs running down the center. Although there was enough hay strewn about for a small herd of animals, the place appeared empty. "Holly!" Leya shouted. "Where are you?"

"VanAken! Make her leave!"

VanAken had already followed Leya inside and was whipping open stall doors. "She's been badly raised, Nash," he yelled over his shoulder. "Doesn't listen worth a damn, and I don't have time to argue with her right now. Berger! Collins! Get the old guy out of here, and hold everyone else back. We'll be right out." He turned to Leya. "The woman said *under* the barn. Look for a trapdoor of some kind."

Leya scrambled from stall to stall, calling as she went. She dropped to her knees in each stall, hands raking through straw, fingers scraping against rough wooden flooring as she searched frantically for any sign of a hinge, trying not to think about the ticking clock. VanAken was doing the same down the center aisle and along the opposite side. Nothing.

At the far end of her row, near the barn's back entrance, Leya came to a room with a padlocked door. This time, when she called Holly's name, a faint answer came back. Leya tugged at the hasp. "Peter, here! Help me get this off!"

He ran across the aisle and yanked at it, trying to wrench

it loose. Spinning, Leya spotted a pitchfork propped against the back door. She grabbed it. "Here! Use this!"

He wedged the pitchfork under the hasp. After a couple of shoves, wood splintered, the hasp fell off, and they opened the door to what must once have been a tack room. Only now the room, about ten by twelve, was lined from floor to ceiling with gun racks, loaded with a veritable arsenal of pistols, shotguns and automatic assault rifles. A dozen or more empty slots hinted at missing weapons, which Leya guessed were in the Chevy van outside, the vehicle the Newmans had apparently been planning to use to make their getaway.

Peter nudged her arm. "Look up there." Leya followed the direction of his finger and spotted something even more disconcerting, packed tight into the beams just under the rafters some eighteen feet overhead. "Plastic explosives and blasting caps," he said, following a line of fuse wire that ran the full length of the barn, connected at intervals, like beads on a deadly chain, to more molded lumps of detonator-studded plastique. Running down the wall in one corner of the tack room, the fuse disappeared behind a gun rack. Leya fell to her knees and peered underneath. She saw the fuse reappear for a few inches, then disappear into the hay-strewn floor.

"Holly?" she cried once more, brushing at the hay. This time, she clearly heard the girl's voice. "I hear you! We're coming!" Leya cried, raking faster.

VanAken was beside her, his ravaged hands tamping and digging frantically. "I found an edge!" He crouched low, blowing on the crack in the floor. A clump of straw shifted, and a recessed pull revealed itself. "Bingo! Stand back!"

Leya scrambled against the doorway, glancing at her watch as he heaved the trapdoor up and propped it against the gun rack. Four minutes. Peter peered into the hole, then gripped the sides and jumped in. Looking down after him, Leya saw Holly's frizzled head about ten feet below. She was sitting on the ground, leaning against an earthen wall, her hands behind her back. Rickhauser's head lay in her lap, the smiling red face of Elmo standing guard over him. The phone lay open on the ground beside them, and Leya heard it crackle. VanAken picked it up. "We've got 'em. Get an ambulance and stand by," he said. He lay the phone down and put a finger to the assistant deputy's neck.

"He's hurt real bad," Holly said. "He had seizures. He's been unconscious for a while, but he managed to get my feet loose before he passed out. I had a lot of trouble getting to his phone."

"You did real good, Holly. We're going to get you out now, but we don't have time to untie those ropes. We'll cut 'em off outside, okay?" The girl nodded. VanAken looked up at Leya, his gray eyes worried. "Do you see a ladder up there anywhere?"

She looked around desperately, then peered over the edge of the hole once more. "No."

"Okay. I'm going to pass Holly up to you. I want you to grab her and get the hell out of here, understand?"

"Send her up." Leya lay on her stomach, watching as he gently slid Rickhauser aside, then helped Holly to her feet. The girl seemed shaky and stiff, and Peter caught her just before she fell. He lifted her at the knees, hiking her up to the opening. Leya took hold of Holly's shirt and began to pull. "Higher!" she gasped. VanAken shifted positions, moving down Holly's legs and lifting her higher. Leya had the girl's arms now, but her grip was precarious. Peter crouched once more, hiking the girl's feet onto his shoulders. Leya scrambled to her knees, pulling, until Holly's torso was finally over the lip of the opening. At that point, Holly's legs kicked into action, and Leya helped her draw them up over the edge, then pulled her to a kneeling position.

"Okay, run!" vanAken yelled from below. Leya glanced at her watch. Two minutes. Maybe.

She lifted Holly to her feet and pushed her forward to the door. "*Run,* Holly, as fast as you can!"

Holly started, then her legs buckled. Leya grabbed her as she began to tumble. "My legs are numb from sitting," the girl cried.

"Holly, listen to me! There's a bomb. You've *got* to run. We'll meet you outside."

"Leya!" vanAken yelled. "You, too! Go!"

"No! What about you?" she asked, looking down.

He was crouched beside Rickhauser. "I can't get him up without a ladder. He's too big."

"I'll get help! We can—"

"There's no time! You can't let anyone else in here. The place is going to blow!"

As Holly whimpered, Leya looked at her, then back at the pit, torn between them. Holly was shaking with fear and fatigue, and Leya knew she'd never make it to the road without stumbling. If she fell with her hands tied— "Peter, please, I'll help you get him out and then we—"

"He's too big! Just run, dammit!"

Leya stared at the fallen giant, and she knew Peter was right. It had been hard enough to get Holly up and out, but Rickhauser would be dead weight. But that was no reason why Peter had to remain behind, too. "Peter," she said quietly, "you can't save him. You have to come out."

"No! I'm not leaving him all alone down here!"

"Come out!" Holly screamed. "Please! I don't want that man to die, but *I* don't want to die, either!"

Leya dropped to her knees at the hole. Holly fell beside her, but Leya saw only the pit and the man. "Peter, please, get out of here! I can't lose you again! I can't!"

"I can't leave him like this," he insisted. "Not after everything he did for me."

"I love you, dammit! I want us to have a life together."

He shook his head sadly and looked up at her. "I'm really sorry. I wanted that, too, once. I wish things had been different. But it wouldn't work anymore. There isn't enough of me left to build a life on."

"I don't believe that! You're still young. We could—"

"Listen to me, Leya. The people I loved most in this world are all gone. Except you, and you're doing what I *should* have done with my life." He glanced at Holly. "You help kids learn to think and grow into responsible, caring adults. That's the only way this world is ever going to get any better. I'm begging you, if you love me at all, keep doing that for me—please?"

He really wasn't coming, Leya realized, horrified. Holly was on her knees, crying softly beside her. She had a choice. Stay with Peter or save Holly. A sudden gust of wind whistled down the length of the barn, and for a split second, they all froze, wondering if that was the last sound they'd hear before Armageddon.

"Professor Nash?" Holly pleaded.

"Leya? Do it for me?" Peter repeated. She nodded blindly. "Thank you," he murmured. "Now, run!"

Leya stumbled to her feet and helped Holly back up. When she glanced at Peter one last time, he was kneeling, his gnarled hand resting on his friend's shoulder. He looked up at her, and suddenly he smiled—the same, dazzling Peter smile that had captured her heart so long ago. Somehow, Leya mustered one up in return.

Then, putting an arm around Holly's waist, steadying

her with the other, she began to run. They flew down the aisle, out of the barn and across the yard. At the rutted driveway, Holly stumbled. Leya caught her, and they ran on toward the road and a long line of cars. A young man broke from the crowd and ran forward. When he reached them, Leya was astonished, through panic and dread, to see him actually tug his forelock.

"Special Agent Wilf Berger, ma'am. Let me help you." He scooped Holly into his arms. "Okay, let's go!" he said, running back to the road, Leya right behind.

The next moment, dawn arrived with a deafening roar. Blown to the ground, Leya covered her head, as burning shingles fell on the yard. When the fusillade died down, Leya peered back under her arm. The house was gone, scattered from one end of the farmyard to the other, only a few burning bits of frame still clinging to what was left of the large, glowing brick chimney. The oak tree in the center of the yard was on fire.

Lifting herself to her elbows, still stunned by the force of the blast that echoed in her ears, Leya caught sight of something sparkling on the ground nearby. She scooped up what turned out to be a small, stained-glass sun-catcher, and she held it up against the light of the burning tree. The glass representation of a bird glowed against the backdrop of the fire, appearing to rise from the flames. A phoenix, Leya thought.

Then she dropped the bauble and leaped to her feet. The barn was still standing. "It didn't blow!" she cried. "We can get them out!" She took a step forward, but someone grabbed her and pulled her back.

"Hold it!" It was the agent Peter had called Collins. "Did you see any explosives in there?"

"Yes, but—"

"Then it could still go. No one goes in until the bomb squad gets here."

"But there are two men still in there! Len Rickhauser and Peter vanAken! You can't leave them." Leya glanced at her watch—two minutes after eight.

"There could be multiple detonators," Collins said. "We can't put any more lives at risk when we don't know what we're dealing with."

"We have to do something!"

"The bomb squad's on the way. Meantime, I suggest you pray, ma'am."

"Listen!" Holly cried. "More sirens. Maybe that's them!"

Young Berger put a hand on Leya's arm. "Hold tight, Miss Nash. Agent vanAken knows what he's doing. He'll be okay."

A hubbub arose behind them, and a flurry of hushed conversation. Collins turned back to Leya. "You know that old man who came out of the house with you?"

"He's my father." Leya glanced around. "Where is he?"

"He said he wasn't feeling well. The paramedics put him in the ambulance, only now—"

"What happened to him? Has he had a—"

"He's disappeared."

"*What?* Where's the bloody ambulance?"

"Over there," Collins said, pointing to an opening in the woods on the Mount Abbey side of the road, "only it seems your father's not in it anymore."

"How could he disappear? Wasn't anybody watching him?"

He shrugged. "Apparently they just—"

Another thundering roar stole his words. A rush of air knocked Leya flat on her back. She lay there, stunned, for a few seconds, then rolled onto her side and looked up the drive.

"*No!*" she screamed.

The fire in the skeletal remains of the house had been snuffed out. Only now, the barn, too, was gone.

Friday, August 4, 1995

More Than Kin, Less Than Kind

_____ Epilogue _____

Kneeling by the flower bed below her veranda, Leya settled back and wiped a gloved hand across her sweaty forehead. Shading her eyes from the hazy August sun, she scanned the yard and surveyed her work. Since noon, she'd cut the grass, front and back, with her garage-sale push mower, edged it with the bright orange weed-whacker Kerry Nyland had bequeathed to her on the day he'd left for Arizona, and tamed into submission four sprawling, overgrown beds of fern, peony, lily-of-the-valley and ivy.

Margaret Harmer herself must have planted these beds forty or more years ago, she decided. No recent owner would have cared enough to take the trouble. Leya was beginning to feel a real kinship for old Maggie, as she'd come, affectionately, to think of the lady who'd stayed on alone in the house after her husband had died. On windy nights, when sighs echoed through the attic rafters, she could swear it was Maggie's voice she heard, whispering words of solace and encouragement. Encouraged or not, Leya knew she would carry on. Survival skills, after all, had been bred in her bones. It was what she did best.

Holly Stroud had stayed with her during the last few weeks of spring term, avoiding the media and curious stares on campus. And although she'd dropped out of *Hamlet,* she'd somehow managed, between crying spells, to tough her way through term finals. She was spending the summer with her older brother in Houston, but Leya had received a letter from Holly that morning, and she'd written that she was registered for the fall term at Mount Abbey and wanted to rejoin the theater troupe.

"I found out I can't run away," Holly wrote. *"No matter where I go, people know who I am and what happened, so I might as well be back with my friends, who care about me. What really hurts, though, Professor Nash, is that nobody really cares about Karim. Nobody knows who he was, or what he had to offer. Except me."*

Poor Holly, Leya thought. She, too, was a survivor. She'd pull through this—but at what cost?

Gradually, Leya herself was becoming resigned to the notion of a solitary life. Caught up with planning for fall classes and new theater productions, she sometimes got through entire hours without thinking about what might have been. And when the thought of wasted possibilities refused to leave her in peace, she could always count on her old house—where something always needed fixing, painting or cleaning—to channel her angry energy.

She laid a hand on the top of her head. It felt hot. She really should get a hat, Leya mused, one of those floppy-brimmed numbers that tied under the chin, the kind old ladies wore. She had a sudden mental image of herself in thirty years—an eccentric, crotchety battle-ax, clomping across the Mount Abbey campus in sensible shoes, nubby tweed skirts, and those surgical stockings that gave you rhino-skin legs. Maybe she'd dye her hair red. Maybe she'd get a cat.

The sound of children's laughter bubbled up from the street behind her. Glancing across the lawn, Leya saw a mother loading three children into a minivan parked at the curb, their chubby arms laden with books covered in shiny, clear library binding. After the kids had bounced into their seats, the woman shut the door and shot Leya a harried smile. She smiled back, and as the van's engine kicked to life, Leya began loading trowels and pruning shears into her garden basket. The crunch of tires on the driveway drew her around once more, but where she expected to see the minivan making a quick reverse, there was a sand-colored Land Cruiser, instead, pulling to a stop behind her blue Civic. When the driver's door opened, Leya froze, motionless, her mind reeling with memories of fire and ice.

It had taken only the blink of an eye for the Newman barn to be transformed into glowing bits of kindling, but in that instant, Leya's hopes and dreams had also turned to ash. Again and again, the memory returned, her mind replaying it in slow motion. She saw herself fall on the snow-crusted ground, shielding her head from firebrands falling from the sky, thudding and crackling all around her. She felt the scream of horror and denial that built in her throat. Heard it pour out in a torrent as she looked up and saw the empty space where the barn had stood, only a split second before.

Suddenly another shout had gone up from somewhere down the line. Silhouetted figures had begun running toward a pile of dark shapes on the ground, halfway between the barn and the road. Agent Berger had had to repeat it several times before Leya had grasped that the prostrate figures—pummeled and flattened by the blast, but very much alive—were Peter vanAken and her father, as well as the unconscious Assistant Deputy Rickhauser.

Ambulances had rolled in rapidly to transport them to Winslow Memorial, so it was only in dribs and drabs that the story had trickled out from the two reluctant allies.

How Leya's father had slipped away from the police line and entered the barn from the back door, just as she and Holly were running out the front. How, working together in the pit, he and Peter had dragged fertilizer sacks from the shelves and stacked them to make a riser, then wrestled the ADIC's massive frame up and out of the hole, half carrying, half dragging him clear of the building in the last seconds before the explosion. All three would have been dead, Leya thought, if Joanna Newman—that thrifty, tradition-bound artisan—had only sprung for better-quality, higher-tech timing devices for her carefully crafted bombs.

Rising now from the lawn, Leya studied Peter as he walked slowly toward her. His expression was cautious— still wearing that getting-ready-to-bolt look, she thought grimly. His hair was a little shorter and looked as if he'd allowed a professional to cut it. The jacket of his light gray suit was slung over his shoulder. In addition to the suit, Leya noticed something else she'd never before seen on him—a tie. He was tanned. His hands were out of his pockets. And his blue oxford-cloth shirt actually fit.

"Hi," he said.

"Hi," she replied, for lack of anything better to say. What was she supposed to do? Welcome him with open arms?

"How've you been?"

"Do you care?"

He sighed. "I know you're probably angry—"

"Damn right, I am!"

"I *had* to leave."

"You took off in the middle of the night!"

"It was 6:00 a.m., and it wasn't my fault. They decided on short notice to medevac Rickhauser to D.C., and I wanted to be there with him."

"That accounts for twenty-four hours—not five months."

"He was in a coma for seventeen days."

"That's completely beside the point—but I know," she added soberly. "He and his wife were in town last week."

"I talked to him yesterday," Peter said, nodding. "He mentioned he'd seen you. He's still trying to piece together what happened that day."

"He vaguely remembered talking to me in the hospital, but that's about it. I took them over to the theater and what's left of the farm, and showed him pictures of Holly Stroud, but—" Leya shook her head. "Wendy Rickhauser said the doctors warned him those memories might never come back. I guess he finds it really frustrating."

"They removed a fist-size blood clot from his brain. It's a miracle he survived at all. Tyler Newman damn near killed him."

"I think he's indestructible, like my father."

Peter hesitated. "How is your father?" he asked finally. Leya scrutinized his tone and his expression for sarcasm, but it wasn't there.

"Fine, I suppose. I haven't seen him lately. He's staying with my sister in upstate New York." Leya rubbed the tail of her T-shirt, working out a patch of mud. "It's just as well. He has three children. It's long past time he mended fences with the other two."

"You're still angry with *him,* too, aren't you?"

She looked up sharply. "And you're not?"

"It hardly seems worthwhile. That man is so full of self-hatred that anything I have to offer is just overkill."

"Self-hatred? *My* father? Please!"

Peter's feet shuffled—real shoes, she noted, and polished, too. "He told me, Leya," he said quietly, "when he and I were in the emergency ward, waiting to be patched up. He told me you came home pregnant from Beirut—and about what happened afterward. I'm sorry you had to go through that alone."

She felt the tears spring to her eyes. They infuriated her. "Does he think that justifies what he did? He raised me to take responsibility for my actions! But could he let me do that? No! What he did—"

Peter sighed. "Don't you get it, Leya? He looks at you, and he sees your mother. He looked at *me,* and he saw himself—the person he most despises in this world, because he feels he lured her away from home and led her to her death. When you and I got together, he thought history was about to repeat itself. No way could he let that happen."

"Well, isn't that just typically arrogant of him? For all he knows, she might have been hit by a bus if she'd stayed home! Maybe it was just her time to go. Besides," Leya added angrily, "she loved him. You only have to see those pictures of her in India to know my mother *wanted* to be there with him. Why can't he accept that she made her own choices, like I made mine?"

"Don't hate him," Peter said quietly.

Leya threw up her arms in exasperation. "How can I hate him? But I'm so angry with him, I don't know where to put myself!" She paused, frowning. "Don't tell me you've decided to forgive him?"

"I have to."

"Why? Because he went back into that barn?"

"Partly. But mostly, because if I don't, he'll always own a piece of me. Don't get me wrong. It's not that I'm being noble. I don't think your father and I will ever be the best of ls, but I can't live with him under my skin any- ybe I understand him better now. All I know is,

I hate what he did, but forgiving him is the only way I know to move on. Otherwise—'' He shrugged.

Leya slumped onto the bottom step of the veranda, shading her eyes as she looked up at him. "Len Rickhauser told me you resigned from the FBI. He said you went back to Beirut. Have you been there all this time?''

He nodded. "I taught a summer course at the American University.''

"How are things over there now?''

"A little tense, but better. The neighbors are still making trouble, but Beirut itself is rebuilding.''

"The phoenix, rising again from the ashes." Leya studied him. "Did the AUB ask you to stay on?'' He nodded again. "And?''

"I haven't given them an answer. My father's old department also has an opening.''

"In Chicago?'' Exactly how far away was Chicago? Leya wondered, rapidly calculating travel times by car and by train. Then she pulled herself up sharp. What difference did it make whether it was Chicago, Beirut or Timbuktu? Clearly, his plan was to go somewhere—anywhere— where she wasn't.

But then, she had another thought, and it made her almost as mad. "Hold on one minute—you didn't put that tie on for *my* benefit, did you?'' Damn, he was presumptuous!

"What makes you say that?''

"Because I happen to know the Mount Abbey history department is interviewing for someone to replace Kerry Nyland.''

"Nyland—is he the guy who lit out for the west on a Harley-Davidson hog?''

At the thought of Nyland's ponytail and his silly bike, Leya felt a smile rise on her lips, in spite of herself. "The same. You applied for his job, didn't you?'' Peter nodded. ''And? Have they offered it to you?''

''The board said they'd be in touch.'' He leaned against the railing. ''But as I was leaving just now, the chairman caught up to me in the parking lot. He said the job's mine, if I want it.''

''What did you tell him?''

''That the decision's not mine to make.'' Peter settled across from her on the step. ''I saw where your office is, Leya. We'd see each other every day.''

''That'd be awful.''

He seemed taken aback. ''Well, yes—so—anyway—if you'd rather I didn't—''

Shifting to face him, she leaned against the wooden rail. ''What am I supposed to say?'' she demanded. ''You have a lot of nerve, you know that? You keep popping into my life, wreaking total havoc, then popping out again. You disappear for five months—not one word! You think I've been sitting here, holding my breath, waiting for you to deign to grace my life once more?''

''No, of course not. I just—''

''That's exactly what I've been doing! And I *hate* it! What if I say yes? How soon before you disappear again?''

''Never—I swear. You don't know how close I was to giving up. It was only when I watched you walk out of that barn with Holly that I knew how much I wanted to live.'' He paused, examining his scarred hands. ''You pulled me off a precipice, Leya, but I had to get the rest of the way back myself. I had a lot of issues to resolve. There was your father, of course, but in the end, that one was fairly easy. Whatever he did wrong, Carter Nash did one thing incredibly right. Whatever we disagree on, there was one thing on which we're in total agreement.'' Peter reached out, running a finger across her cheek. Then he drew back once more.

"But there was also Beirut and everything it represented," he said. "If I didn't face up to it, I knew I'd never be free."

"And now?"

"I haven't had a nightmare in months. I want my life back, and I want it to include you. Do you think that's possible?"

Leya shook her head slowly. "I don't know. It depends."

"On what?"

"On what you think of my house."

"Your *hou*—?" He looked up at it, puzzled. Then, slowly, the old Peter grin finessed its way across his features. "Well, you know me," he said. "I've always been a sucker for an ancient ruin."

"Does that extend to ruined women? I sure hope so, because God knows, I'm ruined for anyone else."

Peter took her by the arms and slid her across the step. "I don't know about women in general, but you are definitely getting better with age."

As the space between them narrowed, Leya's hand interceded between his soft silk tie and her mud-spattered T-shirt. "Careful," she warned. "I'm all sweaty and full of dirt. I need a shower, desperately."

Peter glanced up at the front door. "You actually *have* a shower these days?"

"Yep."

"Big enough for two?"

Leya smiled and got to her feet. "I don't know," she said, tugging at his tie. "What do you say we go research the topic?"

Available in August from
New York Times bestselling author

PENNY JORDAN

THEY WERE A LOVING FAMILY—
LIVING IN A HOUSE OF LIES....

Devastated by a painful miscarriage, there was nothing
Claudia or Garth wouldn't have done to make a
family—or so Claudia thought. Then she found out
just what Garth *had* done to give her the baby she
craved. She couldn't forgive him for lying to her, even
though she'd lied herself. The only truth left was how
much they both loved the daughter they shared—and
how at risk she was as long as they kept their secrets
to themselves....

TO LOVE, HONOR AND BETRAY

On sale mid-August 1998
where paperbacks are sold!

MIRA